DRONE CATCH

Book 2 of the *Fearless* Trilogy

T R Schumer

Drone Catch, Book 2 of the *Fearless* Trilogy
Copyright © 2016 by T. R. Schumer
All Rights Reserved Worldwide

Published by T. R. Schumer
ISBN-13: 978-976-95924-4-5
Printed Edition v1.0 - September 2016

Cover Design by Damonza
Editing by Scribendi

This is a work of fiction. Names, characters, places, and incidents either are the product of the author's imagination or are used fictitiously, and any resemblance to actual persons, living or dead, business establishments, events, or locales is entirely coincidental.

DRONE CATCH

T.R. Schumer is a writer and adventurer, an instrument rated pilot who once copiloted a single-engine aircraft around the world, an avid scuba diver, and sailor. The author is currently sailing around the world, and as of 2016, after departing from Palma de Majorca in the Balearic Islands, has passed the halfway mark of New Zealand. The author's first novel Death Catch was published in New Zealand, while book two of the Fearless Trilogy, Drone Catch, was written there. As of June, 2016, T. R. Schumer has reached the islands of Fiji and is currently writing the third book of the trilogy- SEAL Catch.

Thank you New Zealand!

Epigraph

The conditions of small wars are so diversified, the enemy's mode of fighting is often so peculiar, and the theaters of operations present such singular features, that irregular warfare must generally be carried out on a method totally different from the stereotyped system (for regular war). The art of war, as generally understood, must be modified to suit the circumstances of each particular case. The conduct of small wars is in certain respects an art by itself, diverging widely from what is adapted to the conditions of regular warfare, but not so widely that there are not in all its branches points which permit comparison to be established.

— Charles E. Callwell, 1906 Small Wars: A Tactical Textbook for Imperial Soldiers

Chapter 1

Alex Moss squints against the midday sky above him, a view distorted by the blurred silhouettes of chopper blades that whip through the bright sunlight. He glances across the helipad at his best friend, Malcolm Rafferty, and then back up at the approaching chopper just as a movement grabs his attention. Moss hardly has time to focus on the massive object, to fully process that it is, in fact, a huge tiger shark, before it hits Razz. Once it registers, Moss instantly realizes this shark is nothing like the rotting, reanimated horde he and his crew fought off five years ago. This one is a perfect specimen.

The shark is airborne, its jaws fully open when it rips into Malcolm Rafferty's torso. The attack is shockingly precise, a perfectly placed bite that tears mercilessly into human flesh. Moss instantly lunges for his friend with all he's got. He leaps forward and reaches for Razz. He has to get to him before Razz is pulled overboard, but it all happens too quickly. He's too far away, and he can only watch in horror as Razz disappears into the sea.

Moss rockets upright in bed. His pulse races as his eyes dart around the room. He's disoriented, he can't recognize where he is. Then, a delicate voice draws him back to reality. "Hey? Are you okay?" Moss looks down at the beautiful woman lying next to him and settles comfortably on her pale blue eyes. She gazes up at him and smiles sympathetically. "You had that dream again, didn't you?"

"Yeah," Moss replies. "It was the same one… the same as always…"

"It's just a dream, babe." She sits up and slips her arms around him, and his pulse drops back to normal. Moss can feel her warm breasts against his back as she begins gently kissing his skin. It's an invitation he would like to accept, but he's on a schedule. He's due back on board, and as always, there's work to do. "I gotta go…"

She stops kissing him, gives him a brief squeeze, and then draws her arms back. "Yeah, sure, I understand…"

Moss turns to look at her. "Hey, Trish, I'm sorry… I have to get back to the ship. They're expecting me."

"No worries. No seriously, Alex, there's no issue here…" Trish pauses as she bites her lip. "I'm flying back to Sydney." She waits a moment to judge his reaction. "My dad called again. He wants me to come back home and join his firm. He's offered me a junior partnership."

Her words aren't a surprise, but they still hurt. Moss reaches for her hand and squeezes it gently. "I really wish I could stay…"

"I know…" She smiles back at him. "Look, it's been great, and working here in L.A.'s been great, but dad's right. He's not getting any younger. He wants me to take over his law practice eventually, and if I'm not there, it will never happen, so I have to go home."

She leans over and kisses Moss on the cheek. "I'll make you some toast and coffee while you shower."

Moss watches as this beautiful, bubbly, intelligent woman hops from her bed and then grabs a robe from the back of a chair on her way to the kitchen. As she disappears from view, his mind battles his heart with each step... *Don't let her go like this... don't end this great time on a low note...*

A life of duty, responsibility, and sacrifice has defined Alex Moss's existence to the point that it's become automatic—a groove cut so deep that it's as if he has no choice but to follow it. After the Philippines, however, he's made a conscious effort to change... to take more time for himself... *to lighten up.* The groove always comes back, though, and in this case, Moss really does have a shadow of responsibility looming over him, and he can feel its guilty pull dragging him back into his old self.

For Moss and the rest of his crew who survived the horrific battle aboard *Fearless,* the struggle to cope has manifested itself in various ways, but one stands out above all the others: nobody talks about it on board—*not ever.* With each year that passes, the silence remains. It's hard to believe that five years have gone by; it all feels much closer in Moss's memory. He may not speak of it, but it is always with him.

In the aftermath of the attack on *Fearless,* and her subsequent grounding, the salvage operation got underway immediately. The foundation flew in an international team of specialists from Dubai. So Moss sent his own crew home to recover and reconnect with their families... including Razz. Rafferty protested bitterly, of course, but Moss wouldn't hear it. So Razz booked a flight out of Manila and flew back to California to see his son. Mark was only six at the time. He was living with his mother on her family's ranch in Marin County.

When Malcolm Rafferty stepped out of his rental car, his ex-wife, Robyn, took one look at him and burst into tears. The last time she'd seen him in that kind of condition, he had just returned from fighting the war in Iraq.

What was planned as a weekend visit evolved into a six-week recovery not just physically but emotionally. Six months later, Alex Moss stood once more as Razz's best man at his second wedding to the same woman. A year and a half after the wedding, Robyn gave birth to their daughter, Alexa. Moss laughed when he heard they'd named her after him, but as Razz explains it, if Moss hadn't forced him to go home, his daughter would never have been born.

As for Moss, he considered his own recovery to be the privilege of overseeing the rebuilding of *Fearless*. The project had the full backing of the foundation after a thorough review conducted by the foundation's senior directors. Ultimately, his command decisions were not questioned—even down to his decision to toss a live grenade onto the deck of the ship. This shocked Moss more than he even realized. He hadn't held anything back during his deposition to the foundation's lawyers.

At the onset of the investigation, Moss fully expected to be asked to resign, so he decided to be brutally honest. Moss looked at his inquisitors directly as he spoke: "It reached a point where we all realized we would not be surviving this attack. We were up against an overwhelming force, and we knew it. *I threw that grenade as a last act of desperation... I knew it was literally a hail-Mary pass, with little if any odds of succeeding, but I had to do it. At that moment, I was willing to do anything to save my crew.*"

Moss directed the initial cleanup, then after the salvage team from Dubai wrapped up their job, Moss took over once more. He had *Fearless* towed to a commercial shipyard in Kaohsiung City, Taiwan, where she would spend the next six months undergoing repairs and refit. Moss also took the opportunity to harden on-board security and refine his crew's defensive capabilities.

Pete, the ship's engineer, finally got the diesel–electric hybrid propulsion system he had wanted to install during the initial build in Germany. At the time, the foundation had taken his highly detailed, written proposal seriously; however, they eventually deemed the cutting-edge technology to be still too experimental. This time around, however, Pete wasn't backing down, and in Moss's opinion, his engineer's argument was rock solid: *how can we call ourselves a science vessel if we don't take our own environmental impact into account?*

Sharks… There's been a hell of a lot of shark study being conducted on board, and it's often left the crew feeling uncomfortable. Some even quit because of it. During the four years since the relaunch of *Fearless,* Moss and his crew have suffered through every mundane detail in what feels like an endless cycle of shark biologists studying everything from shark reproduction and genetics to tracking their speed, how far they migrate, and even down to which species has evolved the most efficient bite.

The science teams have often included the same PhD ichthyologist, Alistair Fairchild. Moss considered Alistair to be both capable and highly intelligent when he was first on board as one of Dr. Peter Marsh's student assistants. These days, however, Dr. Fairchild is often the lead scientist, and despite his youth, Moss can see that the man is highly dedicated.

Under Dr. Fairchild's direction, Moss and his crew have sailed *Fearless* from the California coast to Hawaii, and then across the Polynesian archipelago, on to Australia, and then Cape Town. They've crossed the Atlantic and combed the Caribbean chain end to end. Along the way, they've collected countless specimens—mostly tiger sharks but also other aggressive species, including the great white. Moss is convinced that all of this activity is the source of his reoccurring nightmare. But knowing where it comes from doesn't seem to make it go away. The crew tends to deal with their personal anxieties in different ways, mostly by employing a lot of dark humor. At last count, nearly all the guys now sport a shark-themed tattoo, a ritual Moss and Rafferty have avoided.

Moss, with assistance from Rafferty, decided early on to deal with his anxiety by employing a more pragmatic approach: he heightened security protocols. He and Razz have made it a policy to personally interview each member of every team. They ask a mixed bag of questions about the team member's personal hobbies, family history, spiritual beliefs, and social activism. If they fail the interview, they are promptly sent home. If they pass but leave Moss feeling suspicious, they're kept track of much more closely.

In the past five years, Moss and Rafferty have managed to uncover a pair of bush-league drug smugglers, one very sneaky thief, and one prominent team member's past association with the radical environmental group Earth First. Under questioning, the guy admitted to sabotaging logging trucks. He even recounted, in harrowing detail, how he and his girlfriend had spent ten weeks camped at the top of a tree to prevent it from being cut down by loggers. All of this stuff has been pretty small potatoes in Moss's opinion. Fortunately, in four and a half years of interviews, no one else has turned out to be the descendant of a long line of Vodun shamans, who happens to be carrying a cursed talisman capable of reanimating the dead.

. . .

Sitting on the edge of Trish's bed, Alex Moss stares at his sea-worn face in the mirror. The old Alex would already be out of the shower by now and preparing to walk out of this woman's life once again while carrying a torch, not as much for her, as for his relentless dedication to duty. Alex Moss looks himself in the eye: *not this time...* He gets up and follows Trish into the kitchen. She's just putting a fresh filter in the coffee machine when Moss walks into the room. Trish turns to see Alex enter the kitchen, and her quiet face suddenly lights up with a bright smile. "I see you changed your mind..."

"No," he answers... "You did..." Trish giggles wildly as Alex pulls the robe off her shoulders, and then grabs her playfully and tosses her, now shrieking with laughter, over his shoulder. Trish is still giggling when he carries her back into the bedroom.

Chapter 2

On the day of his release, after five years spent in the New Bilibid Prison, a sprawling, patchwork complex located on the rough outer edge of the Philippine capital city of Manila, Dr. Thomas Falcon is now many things: a convict, a gang member, a student of martial arts, a teacher to drug lords, a novice shaman, and an amputee, but what he isn't is free. His mind remains imprisoned by his past deeds, shackled permanently with guilt for those who lost their lives because of his ignorance.

Falcon walks out of the tattered front gates of the Philippine's largest prison and immediately takes notice of a young man leaning against the fence. Falcon's instincts tell him that this kid is waiting for him. He has no idea who the young man is, but the most obvious thought flashes through Falcon's mind... *is he a relative of someone who died in the beach resort attack five years ago?* Falcon's connections assured him that his release would not be made public.

As far as the Philippine Justice Department is concerned, Thomas Falcon has served his time, and, therefore, the matter is closed. Yet, here stands this kid staring at him. Falcon sees no reason to avoid the inevitable, so he decides to walk right up and

8

face him. If he's looking for a fight, so be it. Falcon studies the young man's soft features. He looks to be in his late teens and has still not quite grown into his lanky frame, but he's muscled and fit—*definitely a fighter*—and he looks to be a true native, most likely from one of the mountain tribes.

At the time of his arrest, Dr. Thomas Falcon was first suspended and then formally dismissed from his university position upon his conviction under the charge of *Inciting hooliganism that resulted in death and property damage*. The authorities initially found it difficult to charge him with any sort of crime: "How does one command an army of sharks to attack?" Falcon's court-appointed lawyer had argued. But the judge overseeing the case knew he couldn't allow Falcon to simply leave the Philippines; the public was demanding retribution, hence, the charge of hooliganism.

With the sole exception of his sister, Marcella, Thomas Falcon has lost contact with everyone he thought he was close to. He has lost his home, his savings, and his retirement pension, but the most painful of all has been the loss of his work: all of his professional correspondence, research papers, computer files, and lab specimens have been remanded to the university. Dr. Thomas Falcon is no longer a respected academic and internationally renowned shark biologist. He is fully disgraced.

Locked inside the Philippine's most notorious prison, Falcon fully expected and accepted the worst. He was certain he wouldn't survive, and yet he did, and he adapted. Step by step, he made connections. Over time, he used his skill as an educator to build valuable status amongst the cadre of gang leaders and drug lords who control the prison's population. Bahala Na philosophy is simple and clear: *Come what may...* Falcon embraced the infamous gang's fatalistic anthem the moment he first learned of it, and at this very moment, as he walks toward the young man leaning against the fence, it oddly gives him comfort.

Falcon continues on a straight path toward the young stranger. Moving with quiet confidence, he looks at the young man directly. His assured gaze does not waver; yet, all the while, the expression on Falcon's face says nothing. Falcon's body language is ambiguous and without emotion. As far as Thomas Falcon is concerned, this very moment is as good a time as any; he might as well face up to whatever is coming. If he gets arrested again, so be it. If he's put right back into the prison he has just been released from, then so be it. And if he dies, so be it.

Falcon is only a few feet away when the young man speaks, "Dr. Falcon, hello. My name is Bayani." Bayani steps forward and offers Falcon his left hand.

Falcon doesn't miss a beat and accepts the gesture. "So, does this mean you are not here to kill me?"

"No, sir, I was not sent here to kill you. I'm here to bring you back to my village. My grandfather sent me. He says we have much work to do."

"Is that some Falcon looks the kid over once more. There's something familiar about him, but Falcon can't place it. The young man's accent is clearly American. "Your English is excellent. Where did you learn it?"

"Mormons, Dr. Falcon. They are very good teachers of English. Now, if you don't mind…"

"Yes, of course." Falcon smiles cordially. "We have much work to do. Please, do lead the way, Bayani. I'm all yours."

The pair sets off together, and before long, they are steadily threading their way north through a labyrinth of noisy, congested streets. Manila at midday is sweltering, but neither man complains.

Falcon treks on beside Bayani and says nothing. After the two of them have walked in silence for nearly four hours, Bayani suddenly stops. He turns to look at Falcon. "You are an interesting man, Dr. Falcon."

"Why is that, Bayani?"

"Your silence speaks to me. It says many things about you. My grandfather was right."

"Perhaps, but you will have to wait and see, just as I will."

Bayani smiles. "Come on, it's not too much farther to my aunt and uncle's house. They live in Las Piñas. They are expecting us."

As the two men continue to walk, the streets gradually become narrower and greener. Falcon is reminded of his native Jamaica as the pair enter into residential neighborhoods lined with a jumble of palm, banana, and tropical fruit trees. Eventually, Bayani leads Falcon down a small side street paved with cement block and lined with small homes packed closely together.

Falcon follows until Bayani stops in front of one of the houses. The home is painted in pastel green, with a tiny flower garden behind a chain-link fence. Bayani unlatches the small gate and enters just as the front door of the house opens. His aunt and uncle emerge smiling. Bayani turns to Falcon. "Dr. Falcon, I would like to introduce you to my aunt Angelica and my uncle Joshua."

Bayani turns back to his family. He steps forward, gently takes the hand of his aunt, and then draws her hand to his forehead as a sign of respect. The round woman hugs and kisses Bayani warmly, and then she turns to look at Falcon.

Falcon smiles and greets Angelica politely in Tagalog, "Magandang hapon"... *good afternoon.* He then continues to speak in the Filipino language: "It is a pleasure to make your acquaintance, madam. My name is Thomas."

Bayani flashes a surprised glance at Falcon. "Ah, I see you speak Tagalog very well."

"Prison," Falcon replies with a wink. "I took the five-year total immersion course."

Bayani smiles. "Are you always so funny, Dr. Falcon?"

"It's a nervous reflex. I don't intend to be impolite."

"Relax, Dr. Falcon. You are amongst friends here."

Bayani's uncle Joshua steps forward to greet Falcon, and as Joshua grips Falcon's hand, Falcon can't help but notice the severe scars that cover the man's hands and upper arms. Joshua smiles warmly and then points down at a basket filled with an assortment of house slippers. Bayani and Falcon each trade their street shoes for a pair of rubber flip-flops and follow the couple inside.

The simple home is well furnished and extremely clean, with walls covered in family photos and mementos. A large television rests in one corner across from an arrangement of overstuffed sofas that sit clustered on the opposite side of the room beneath a small crucifix. Falcon can see through the rear windows that the home opens to a larger garden, and outside, under a wood frame and sheet-metal porch, a table has been set for dinner. The aromas filling the house tell Falcon he is about to eat well, a pleasure he has not experienced in a very long time.

Bayani's aunt Angelica excitedly ushers everyone through the house and then out onto the tile-covered patio, where she points to the head of the table and invites Falcon to sit down. Falcon hesitates, glancing once more at Bayani.

"Please, Dr. Falcon. My aunt is merely being polite. You are here at the request of her father, who is a respected shaman in our home village. She sees you as an important man."

Falcon feels a pang of guilt at the suggestion that he is anything other than a recently released convict, but he obediently takes his seat at the head of the table. Meanwhile, Bayani's uncle Joshua sits down at the opposite end, with Bayani taking his seat in the middle. The elder man then begins speaking to Falcon in Tagalog: "So, Thomas, I see you and I have some things in common…"

"We do? How is that, sir?" Falcon answers politely.

"This is a very special day, Thomas, I know. I, too, was once in the New Bilibid Prison, but it was many years ago. It's why I now have these scars that you see on my hands and arms. Did you lose your hand in the prison?"

"No, sir. I was in the sea when this happened." Falcon holds up the scarred and calloused stump where his right hand once was and looks at it. "The hand was taken by a shark."

Bayani's uncle is shocked by Falcon's response. He glances nervously at Bayani, who assures him that the story is true and then goes on to explain how Falcon's right hand was indeed bitten off by a shark and that it happened during a fierce battle.

Falcon is amazed and yet also suspicious. *How can this kid possibly know all of this?*

The conversation ends abruptly when Bayani's aunt Angelica arrives carrying elaborate plates of food. The woman smiles proudly as she lays them out on the table. The sight of the festive dishes leaves Falcon speechless.

Bayani excitedly explains the cuisine to Falcon's delight: "Yes, well this is *lumpiang sariwa*, which are vegetable spring rolls wrapped in soft rice paper, along with *achara*, which is a pickled salad made of sliced green papaya, carrot, and white radish. And this one is very special," Bayani points toward a steaming noodle dish. "This is *pancit*, which are thin noodles mixed with vegetables and sliced boiled eggs." He glances back at Falcon. "This dish represents longevity and good health."

"Oh my!" Falcon suddenly feels as if he is about to eat for the first time. "I can't wait to try them all."

"Be careful, Dr. Falcon." Bayani chuckles. "I know my aunt. This is only the beginning."

After the starter plates have been scraped clean, Angelica brings out a large bowl of steamed rice to accompany the main dishes, the first being *kaldereta*. This version is made with chunks of braised goat meat and sweet potatoes stewed in tomato sauce. And there is *kare-kare*, oxtail, and vegetables slow cooked in peanut sauce. Angelica drinks red wine while the men polish off several bottles of San Miguel. The meal and the conversation drift on into the night. The celebratory feast is topped off by a special dessert called *bibingka*, a cake made with rice flour and coconut and topped with butter and sugar.

"This one is my favorite." Bayani's eyes glow as his aunt places the cake on the table.

Falcon holds up his hand. "Wait, please, before we cut this lovely cake." Falcon pushes his chair from the table and then stands. "I feel I must make a toast to my generous hosts on this beautiful evening…" Falcon pauses to compose himself. "I walked out of prison this morning not knowing where I would go or what would become of me, and to be honest, I didn't care."

He turns to look at Bayani. "This young man was waiting for me. I didn't know why or how. I don't even think we've met before…" At that moment, Falcon freezes. A flash of recognition bolts through his brain, and Falcon realizes that they have, in fact, met before. He focuses again on Bayani's eyes as they suddenly revive a memory—a memory so powerful that it goes off like a bomb in Falcon's head. It is a memory so painful that it causes Falcon to momentarily grip the table to keep from losing his balance. *My God… of course… the beach resort… the shaman. This is the young boy who was with him that day. Bayani is the boy who translated for the old man. He is the shaman's grandson.* In that moment, Falcon sees Bayani's knowing gaze shift to satisfaction; Falcon has finally figured it out.

Falcon turns to his hosts. "Angelica, Joshua, thank you so very much for this incredible meal." Falcon sits back down, and as he does, his perspective has completely changed as he realizes that there is only one reason why Bayani would be bringing him to see his grandfather: *We do have much work to do, and most certainly, it will be difficult… and dangerous.*

Chapter 3

At fifteen minutes past 02:00, Dr. Alistair Fairchild stands quietly in a far corner of the darkened combat information center of the *USS Storm*. The small, cyclone-class naval vessel is currently positioned at a full stop twenty-two miles off the coast of Libya in the Mediterranean Sea. She is on high alert. Every station in the CIC is manned, every radar screen and weapons system fully operational.

Of all the officers and enlisted men on duty in the CIC, only one is familiar to the young PhD shark biologist. He is Lieutenant Commander Joseph Parnell, a scientific, technical, and intelligence liaison officer. Alistair knows the naval intelligence officer well. Parnell has been his project's STILO for the past eight months, ever since his drones came fully on line and of great interest to the United States Navy. Tonight will be the moment of truth—the first live combat test of the MS41-T—and both men are confident of its success.

The Office of Naval Intelligence chose the target carefully—a recently discovered jihadist training camp set up by remnants of what was once known as the Jabhat al-Nusra. The terrorist group was one of several that was dispersed and expelled from post-civil war Syria, but this particular terrorist organization has since regrouped and has only recently resurfaced in Libya. In the wake of the Syrian conflict, cleaning up the mess left behind has proven to be an extraordinary challenge. And ever since the official end of hostilities, United States and NATO forces have been on a relentless mission to chase down the numerous jihadists that remain, shattering the diaspora of militant groups into pieces, only to watch them converge, regroup, and form new organizations.

The targeted jihadi training camp is located nine kilometers inland from the coast and up a steep valley in the northeastern district of Darnah. Unlike the vast deserts that dominate Libya's landscape, this area is lush by comparison—a semi-mountainous region that rises sharply from the Mediterranean coastline. The area consists mostly of fertile farmland and thick forests. Darnah is the district that also happens to share a border with Egypt. If the intelligence reports are to be believed, a major gathering of the jihadi group's leadership is currently taking place at the camp. But even with his limited exposure to top-secret special operations, Alistair has already learned that most of these reports turn out to be completely bogus. Nonetheless, after five years of nonstop work, the opportunity to test his MS41-T biological assault drone in combat is too good to pass up.

Alistair briefly scans the data displayed on the small tablet computer he holds in his hands. The illuminated screen relays a constant stream of real-time telemetry sent to it from the drones themselves. At the moment, Dr. Fairchild is monitoring his drone's temperature, which is currently reading at a uniform minus five degrees Celsius for all ten units. In other words, they are absolutely perfect. Over the past two years, he and his team have conducted numerous successful tests, including participation in three war games operations. Dr. Alistair Fairchild is highly confident that his biological combat assault drones will perform exactly as they have been designed.

Alistair looks up from his tablet to see Lieutenant Commander Parnell heading his way. "Dr. Fairchild," Parnell says quietly, "we just received the green light to proceed with the operation from the tactical action officer. The ship is in position. Are we ready to deploy?"

"Yes, sir," Alistair answers softly and without hesitation. "We are ready to deploy."

Under the darkness of a moonless night, Alistair works with his technicians to prepare the drones for deployment. All ten units are now lined up side by side across the aft deck of the ship. The drones are enveloped in a continuously seeping, ethereal fog that flows from their solidly frozen bodies as they lay fully exposed to the Mediterranean summer air. The handful of seamen and officers present are certainly curious, and more than a little skeptical, as they observe what appear to be ten very large, and obviously dead, tiger sharks laid out like fishing trophies on the deck of their ship.

Meanwhile, three senior naval intelligence officers are also watching with keen interest. All three have been fully briefed on the MS41-T, and all are eager to see it in action. Alistair checks the data coming from his tablet one last time and then catches the attention of Lieutenant Commander Parnell: "We have all ten units remote targeting systems up and running, Commander. Guidance and control are online via secure satellite link. The drone control center is standing by; just give the word."

The corner of Parnell's mouth turns up slightly as he glances down at the row of frozen sharks and then back at Alistair. "okay, kid, show these guys what you got. Turn those puppies loose."

From the opposite side of the deck, two enlisted seamen survey the frozen shark spectacle with bemused speculation. "This is such a total FRED, you know?" one of the two men grumbles quietly. "I mean, honestly? This has to be the lamest shit I've ever seen."

"Yeah… fucking ridiculous economic disaster… you nailed it," the other whispers sarcastically. "What the hell are these things anyway? The deadly fish-sicle?"

At that moment, a low audible hum silences the two seamen. Their mouths unconsciously drop open as they gape in stunned amazement. Incredibly, in an instant, all ten sharks are suddenly no longer frozen as the energy field that powers them engages, ignites, and reanimates their corpses. To the pair of observing seamen, the sharks appear to be inexplicably no longer dead. The seamen's amazement quickly shifts to fear, however, when the ten huge tiger sharks laying a mere eight feet away from them subtly begin to move.

Alistair and his team signal for everyone on deck to stand clear. Dr. Fairchild quickly relays to the drones' remote operators in Long Beach, California that the drones are ready to deploy, and with this final stroke against his touchscreen, the ten MS41-T drones vanish from the deck of the ship, leaving nothing behind but a dull splash as they slip effortlessly into the Mediterranean Sea.

After witnessing the successful deployment, the ship's captain approaches Alistair. "I'm impressed, son. So will these things be coming back?"

"Only after they have completed their mission, sir," Alistair answers confidently. He scans the complex telemetry streaming across his tablet, "which will be in just under three hours." He looks back at the ship's captain. "The drones' onboard cameras will allow us to directly monitor and record their activities."

"I'd certainly like to see that video feed, Dr. Fairchild," the ship's commander answers.

Alistair swivels back toward Parnell, who nods approvingly. "Captain Sutton holds the appropriate clearance. That's why we're here aboard his ship, Dr. Fairchild. You could say this sort of thing is the *USS Storm*'s specialty." Parnell turns to the ship's captain. "The feed will be visible in the CIC sir."

Infrared satellite imaging displayed on one of the monitors inside the CIC reconfirms the camp's activity as multiple heat signatures register what look to be approximately forty individuals. Alistair's technicians have their own computers up and running in the CIC—laptops that are directly linked to the tiny cameras mounted inside the dorsal fins of the ten sharks currently racing toward shore.

The captain, Parnell, and three naval intelligence officers study the technicians' laptop screens with interest and anticipation. "Of course, at the moment, sir," Alistair explains, "there's not much to see, as they are currently in transit." The officers all silently agree; nonetheless, they can't take their eyes off the near-black displays.

"How fast are they traveling?" Captain Sutton asks.

"Fifty knots, sir."

"Fifty?" Sutton blurts. "How is that possible? No shark in the world can swim that fast."

"They aren't actually sharks, sir. They're biological assault drones engineered to resemble a tiger shark. They're weapons, sir, and highly effective, as we will demonstrate."

Captain Sutton nods with approval. "That is very interesting, Dr. Fairchild. How soon before they reach shore?"

Alistair exhales calmly. "From the time of launch, the drones will reach shore in 26.4 minutes." Alistair eyes his watch. "Calculating from the team's current position, we will see them emerge onto the beach in 9.6 minutes—"

"Did you just say *emerge* onto the beach?" Captain Sutton interrupts. "These things are amphibious?"

"Not just amphibious, sir," Parnell interjects. "The MS41-T is a fully weaponized, sea, air and land combat assault drone."

"Are you telling me these things are SEALs?" As the words leave his mouth, Captain Sutton realizes he may be witnessing naval history. He turns to look at the three navy intelligence officers standing behind Alistair. They're all smiling, which means he most likely *is* seeing history in the making and, with it, possibly the end for manned special operations forces. It's at this point that Captain Sutton decides to keep his mouth shut. He lets his previous question go because he already knows the answer.

At precisely the moment Alistair calculated, ten biologically engineered and remotely reanimated tiger sharks emerge from the sea and onto the beach. Each one is a perfect specimen—an artificially enhanced representation of the beauty, power, and grace of a fully mature tiger shark. They are all exactly identical—clones developed and grown from the tissue of a single female captured during one of Fairchild's scientific expeditions aboard the research vessel *Fearless*.

The point of landfall, route to the target, and location of the target have been preprogrammed into the GPS guidance and control modules implanted inside the body of each drone. The navy officers look on with amazement as the camera feed shows the drones advancing rapidly across a narrow patch of beach and then up a dry riverbed.

A sudden flash of intense light momentarily overwhelms the drones' onboard infrared cameras and causes the laptop screens to flare completely white. "No worries, gentlemen," Alistair interjects, his native Kiwi accent slipping out. "That's just a car passing over that small bridge in front of them. There's a road that runs along shore here. The team is unaffected."

Alistair is enjoying his captivated audience, so he continues. "It's interesting to point out that a shark's skin is non-reflective, making it naturally camouflaged, and at the rate our team is moving, they'll be almost impossible to see."

"How is this accomplished, Dr. Fairchild?" Captain Sutton inquires. "It looks impossible, but I must admit, I am seeing it with my own eyes. I mean, what's driving them?"

"It's the remote energy field that drives the units, sir. The field generates an extremely powerful surge that surrounds each drone and allows them to travel over ground as if they were still in the water." Alistair pauses. "They literally float slightly above the ground, sir—a bit like the magnetic monorails at Disneyland."

"Well, I'd say this ride looks a hell of a lot more exciting, Dr. Fairchild," one of the ONI officers interjects.

The small group of career navy officers find themselves riveted to the video feed flowing across the laptop screens in front of them. Despite originating from fish, these drones move with the same speed and agility on land that they demonstrate in the sea. The ten drones rapidly and effortlessly advance up steep, rocky terrain that would have taken a human SEAL team hours to cover. From the vantage point of the cameras mounted in the drones' dorsal fins, it indeed appears as if they aren't even touching the ground but are instead floating slightly above it.

. . .

Inside the militants' camp, the jihadists' clandestine meeting with a pair of covert, far-right French operatives is underway. Once the final negotiations are concluded, the militants will be resupplied with the latest in NATO weaponry, along with the funding they so desperately need, the ultimate goal being to use the jihadis as a proxy force to overthrow the existing, and struggling, Libyan government.

Once the operation is concluded, this low-budget, hybrid war will establish a strict Sunni theocracy with direct ties to the French government post elections. This *small war* will provide the newly elected right-wing French nationalists with hefty profits. They'll have exclusive control over Libya's vast oil fields and lock in lucrative contracts for French corporations, along with the icing on the cake: the adoption of the old colonial franc—the *Communauté Financière d'Afrique*, known as the CFA—as the nation's currency.

The guard standing watch along the camp's northern perimeter stops to light his cigarette. He draws in a long, deep drag and then exhales slowly as he stares down the rocky canyon that leads to the sea. The sparse scenery is starkly muted by the moonless night. The man gazes across the empty expanse as the Mediterranean Sea spreads out from the coast beneath him—a pale gray plain flowing to infinity and framed by the darker walls of the canyon. With his vintage AK47 slung loosely from his shoulder, the guard takes another long pull from his hand-rolled cigarette just as something catches his attention—a movement, perhaps an animal...

The drones are completely silent. The first to reach the guard slashes viciously across the man's torso. The second, only a split second behind the first, takes the man's head from his shoulders. The only audible sounds are the muffled crush of bone and soft tearing of flesh as the guard's body is shredded by ten fresh, perfectly engineered and reanimated tiger sharks. The team's first combat kill is over in under three seconds. The drones advance quickly into the camp, leaving behind the guard's severed arm where it fell on a nearby rock, still holding the smoldering cigarette between its fingers.

The drones fan out as their scientifically enhanced electroreceptors—what in a natural shark are known as *ampullae of Lorenzini*—rapidly detect multiple new targets. As the team advances deeper into the camp, the jihadists' meeting with the two French operatives has been steadily progressing inside a small stucco house. A sudden disruption outside interrupts them. The brief burst of automatic weapons fire abruptly halts the meeting, and the shots are followed closely by a man's scream.

The two veteran French commandos immediately leap to their feet and draw their weapons while the Jihadis shout at each other as one wall of the small house collapses. The mercenaries have guns in hand when the long, heavy wooden table they were sitting around is upended. The men freeze in complete disbelief when suddenly confronted by the completely impossible sight of two very large sharks on the rough tile floor in front of them. The highly trained Frenchmen recover quickly enough to fire their SIG SP 9mm pistols at point-blank range, but the drones are unaffected. The cloned female tiger sharks whip outward in opposite directions, instantly killing two of the jihadists standing next to the Frenchmen.

Drone Catch

The panicked French operatives continue to fire their pistols as a shower of human blood explodes around them. In the ensuing mayhem, each manages to escape through the opening in the side of the building. Outside in the pine-scented night air, the two Frenchmen sprint through the darkened forest while sporadic automatic weapons fire and the cries of the men they left behind echo around them.

One of the operatives pulls out his phone as he continues to run and tries to signal the third member of their team, who is waiting in a nearby coastal village. He is about to send an automated text when he trips over a rock and falls to the forest floor. His partner briefly looks back, only to see his colleague viciously torn to shreds by two huge tiger sharks. The victim's attempt to cry out is choked off by his own blood.

Gunfire and dying screams from the camp fade into the distance as the lone Frenchman sprints through the forest. His breathing is heavy as he runs for the road he knows leads down to the coast, but the drones are rapidly closing in on their final target. The natural electromagnetic life force emanating from the Frenchman's body is the only one still active. His is the only remaining signal drawing all ten drones toward him.

The Frenchman glances over his shoulder; *he can see them.* He's running flat out through the trees, but he can sense the sharks all around him. They're on either side of him and closing in like a pack of rabid wolves. Fear-fueled adrenalin surges through the Frenchman's body and propels him to run harder, faster in a desperate attempt to escape and to survive.

Streaks of light sift through the trees in front of him. He can see the headlights of an approaching car; it's the road. He pushes on, filled with the sudden realization that escape is, in fact, within his reach, when something hits him like a truck from behind. His body slams hard to the ground as he skids face-first across the pine-needle carpet of the forest floor. The veteran French commando turns toward his attackers and fires the last three rounds from his 9mm with no effect. He attempts to shout for help just as the car traveling along the road twenty meters away passes him by and ten perfectly engineered drones savagely tear him apart.

Chapter 4

Exiting the Seaside Freeway, Alex Moss weaves his Arkonik customized Land Rover Defender 110 through late-morning Long Beach traffic. The sprawling Port of Long Beach commercial docks lay in front of him as he winds the matte-black Land Rover onto Navy Way and then crosses over to Nimitz Road. As he drives parallel to the shipping container rail lines, Moss catches a distant glimpse of the bright-white super structure of *Fearless* through a gap in the container stacks. She's a reassuring sight. The only woman he's managed to commit himself to fully—a relationship that has lasted for nine years.

His role as the research vessel's chief of operations is not just his job; *Fearless* is home, and her crew are his family. The only thing Alex Moss actually owns at the moment is the Defender. As he drives, he takes in the morning sun and the industrial view across the port's west basin. Moss drops down to approach speed as he slowly guides the Land Rover out along the thin finger of concrete that once housed the navy refueling depot. The proximity to the Pacific excites him. He's nearly there. Soon, he'll be back on board and at sea once again.

Moss drives to the end of the pier, and his ship comes into full view. Her ninety-seven-meter-long, gleaming, gunmetal gray hull reflects the sunlight bouncing off the water like a rippling jewel. He can see his crew has been hard at work while he's been on vacation. Moss parks the Land Rover and then suddenly hears someone knocking on the side of the vehicle. He lowers his window to see Murray's giant grinning face. "Chief! Great to have you back!" Murray leans inside the window. "Hey, you smell girly… Mmm, is that strawberry?"

Moss smiles back at Murray. "Nice to see you too, mate. How is everybody?" Murray steps back as Moss opens the door. "How's the provisioning going?" Moss gets out of the Defender and then walks to the back of the vehicle to open up the rear as Murray follows.

"Well, Chief, everything's just peachy. We've got it all sorted, the guys and I… Well, we were just offloading the last two delivery trucks when we spotted you pulling in." Murray quickly goes for the open rear door and grabs the duffle bag sitting inside before Moss has a chance to reach for it. Murray swings the bag up onto his shoulder and then starts walking toward the ship when Moss stops in his tracks and places his hands on his hips. "Okay, what's going on? Where's Razz?"

Murray stops briefly and turns back toward Moss. "Oh everybody's on board. They're all waitin' for you, Chief. We're on a schedule, right?"

"Yeah, right…" Moss locks up the Land Rover and then turns to follow Murray, who is already several meters ahead and walking briskly toward *Fearless*. As Moss strides across the pavement, he clicks off a quick SMS to a private car storage company: *Ready for pickup, usual spot…* The response is nearly instantaneous: *Message received, flatbed dispatched. Have a nice trip…*

Two large vans are backed up to the gangway that leads on board *Fearless*. One belongs to a wholesale beverage company, and the other is a local organic pork and chicken purveyor. As the remaining crates come off the back of the two vans, Moss catches sight of several large boxes labeled "All Natural Free-Range Bacon."

I gotta get these guys on a better diet, Moss muses as he walks by the crates. *None of us are getting any younger…*

On board, Moss is immediately hit by *the wave*—a euphemism that comes to mind whenever he returns to the ship after being absent. It consists of a chaotic cacophony of cheerfulness as crewmen and civilian staff welcome him back. After a few dozen responses of "thanks, guys," "yeah, it was great," and "it's good to be back", Moss finally weaves his way up to the bridge.

He walks in to his command center to find that the place is deserted. Moss pauses, then looks around suspiciously. He spots the charts for Catalina Island spread out on the mahogany table in the center of the room. The nav station is lit up and ready for departure; instruments have been set to course, but nobody's here. He walks to the broad spread of windows in front of him and looks out at the expanse of the forward deck and the helipad below. The ship's helicopter, a Bell 429 GlobalRanger, is securely tied down and fully covered for the passage, but no crewmen are in sight. Moss turns and walks back out into the passageway, only to find it deserted as well. The ship's gone totally silent; Moss no longer hears or sees any of his crew. Something is definitely up.

He decides to head back down stairs. Moss reaches the ship's central corridor, only to find no sign of anyone. The ship is completely quiet; even the lights are off. A subtle coldness washes over him as his well-honed survival instincts kick in. Cautiously, he begins making his way toward the galley. If nobody's in there, he reckons, then something's seriously wrong. Moss reaches the door to the crew mess. He sees no light coming through its window; the room beyond is totally dark. He decides to enter and check the galley. Moss slowly opens the door to the crew mess. He reaches over and flips on the lights as an explosion of sound hits him head-on: "SURPRISE, MOTHERFUCKER!"

"Ah shit…" Moss grins as the room fills with cheers and applause. "OK, you guys got me. You seriously got me."

Razz walks over. "You didn't think we'd let you off that easy, did you?"

Moss hugs his friend. "I was hoping I could slip by. My birthday was last week, guys. I thought I planned it perfectly." Moss turns toward the table as the crew steps back to reveal a large cake perfectly modeled to look like *Fearless* herself. Moss is ecstatic. "Wow! Guys, thanks so much, I don't know what to say. This looks amazing! I better have a piece now. This won't last long around here."

The room fills with laughter as Alex grabs a large knife from the table and approaches the masterfully detailed cake. Then, he notices two large number candles atop the cake that read "48." The sudden confirmation of his age jolts through Moss unexpectedly. He hadn't given it much thought, but then again, given his previous line of work as a navy SEAL, with two tours of duty in Afghanistan, one in Iraq, and countless other missions around the world, he never thought he would see forty. Now here he was at forty-eight.

The party, if one could call it that, is a brief affair, certainly minus alcohol, and a bit rushed due to the research vessel's departure schedule. Moss doesn't care, though. In his opinion, it is the best birthday surprise the guys have ever pulled off.

With his bridge crew now in place and two weeks of vacation time behind him, Alex Moss reverts effortlessly to his role as the ship's chief of operations. Radio in hand, Moss directs calmly as he looks out through the large windows of his bridge. He's filled with deep satisfaction as he watches his forward deck crew slip the bowlines. First mate, Malcolm Rafferty, is outside with the deck crew. A cluster of digital monitors allows Moss to observe the activity aft as his helmsman begins guiding the 318-foot, state-of-the-art science vessel away from her home berth.

Computer-controlled hydro-jet thrusters gently ease *Fearless* laterally out from her pier as Moss signals the engine room to increase power to the ship's diesel–electric hybrid propulsion. Once free of her mooring, Moss receives a radio call from the port's command center giving him further clearance to proceed. As she slowly moves into the west basin, *Fearless* is running solely on her electric lithium power cells. The ship quietly glides out of the west basin. She runs so smoothly and silently that the only way someone would know the ship was underway is the scenery moving past the windows.

As *Fearless* makes her way through the narrow slip leading to the Long Beach Channel, she passes in front of the harbor control tower. The bridge of the gleaming science vessel is nearly at eye level with the harbormaster. He watches from the harbor's radio control center as *Fearless* goes by, and then he reaches for his comm. "Ax, you guys have a good trip. Stay safe out there." Moss hears the transmission and responds, "Will do, thanks Jim."

The ship clears the channel and heads out into open sea. Moss radios down for Pete to bring her twin diesel engines on line and then increase speed to twelve knots. Moss glances over at the digital chart plotter and checks the course that's been programmed into the ship's navigation system: 29.3 nautical miles to Catalina

Island. Their destination is the Wriggly Marine Science Center, where they will rendezvous with the new science team coming on board.

Moss turns the bridge over to the first watch crew, scoops up an overstuffed file folder he left on the chart table, and then heads below to his first mate's office. Moss finds Rafferty's door open but knocks anyway.

"Razz, hey. I finally got the file on the new team we're picking up."

Rafferty looks up from his duty roster. "Well, it took them long enough, and let me guess, it's another pile of paper. What's wrong with these guys? The foundation can't even give us a PDF on a memory stick? We gotta read a damn paper file?"

"Seems to be the case," Moss grumbles sympathetically. "But, Razz, I'm just the guy who runs the ship. I don't ask questions."

"I heard that. I like my job, too."

Moss leans in toward Rafferty's desk. "Security's been pretty tight lately… more than usual… I don't know why." He holds the heavy file up in front of Razz. "This showed up at Trish's place yesterday. It was delivered by private courier. It's our new mission for the next four months." Moss drops the thick file on Rafferty's desk. "And get this. Razz, the guy had a portable scanner. I had to sign for this thing with my own eyeball."

"What the hell is this?" Rafferty spins the file around in front of him and opens it.

Moss points a finger down onto the center of the first page, "This? This is no more goddamn sharks."

Rafferty smiles. "I like the sound of that. So what kind of fish doctor are we getting this time?"

"A biomedical marine research specialist from the UK. Her name is—"

"Whoa! Did you just say her? The new pointy head's a woman?"

"Relax, Razz. The file says her field of study is bio-marine molecular chemistry. She has both a PhD and a medical degree." Moss straightens, he folds his arms in front of him as he speaks. "This woman is an incredible genius, she was a child prodigy. It says here she earned her undergraduate degree at age fourteen, Razz. Then, she graduated with a medical degree from Harvard at age twenty."

"I am impressed…" Razz flips through the pages.

"Me too," Moss adds. "I've been going over the file, and it's remarkable what this team is doing. They previously worked on extracting chemical compounds from marine life that they synthesized into pharmaceutical therapies. According to this, their efforts led to the creation of new drugs that are now on the market as treatments for diseases like multiple sclerosis and Parkinson's. For this expedition, however, they'll be continuing their research into rapid growth and cell regeneration."

Razz scans down the page to the photo of Dr. Samantha Randal. In the sparse image, she wears a lab coat, and her dark hair is tightly pulled back while her brown eyes seem to stare out at the world with indifference. "So tell me what all this means in English please…"

"Dr. Randal and her team will be looking for compounds in sea life that they can synthesize into chemicals that heal damaged human organs and tissue. According to this file, Razz, this woman's team has already managed to extract chemicals from sea creatures and then used the compound to get a rat to grow a whole new leg."

"Wow, that's pretty cool. But I still don't understand all the cloak and dagger. I mean, this should be big news, right?"

"Like I said, Razz. It's not my job to ask. I just run the ship."

Chapter 5

In his dreams, he still has two hands, and the most disturbing one is always the same. He is working in his old lab at the university, and he's just found the answer he has been searching for, when his department head walks in and informs him apologetically that his funding has just been discontinued and the chancellor has asked for his resignation.

Falcon awakens in a cold sweat. It's not the dream itself that he finds so disturbing; it's the fact that when he has the dream, he's whole, and when he wakes up, he's not. Falcon is disoriented as he looks around the tiny bedroom he now finds himself in. Early predawn light is just beginning to filter through the window.

He sits up, swings his feet to the tile floor, and quietly collects his thoughts. *This is not a dream… I really am out of prison…* He wasn't certain he was ready to be released… or wanted to be. Falcon had established himself in Bilibid. He had connections, influence, and powerful allies. He was respected. As his release date drew closer, however, Falcon's anxiety over what would become of him on the outside grew more intense. He had even contemplated committing a crime so that his sentence would be extended. His life seemed meaningless, but then he had the vision.

Falcon hadn't experienced a vision in over two years and had considered the possibility that perhaps he would not have one ever again. Then, one day, as he stood under a tree in the prison recreation area, a bird landed on a low branch in front of him. The bird was beautiful and colorful, and it sang to him. Falcon couldn't take his eyes off it. Then suddenly it was gone. Falcon looked down and realized he was no longer inside the prison yard. Instead, he was wearing his white lab coat, and he was walking down the corridor that led to his old lab at the university.

Falcon walks into the lab, and there, sitting at his desk, is his longtime friend and colleague, Dr. Peter Marsh. Marsh looks up from his computer screen and smiles. "Did you finish up those cryosections, Tom? Do you have the samples prepared? There's nothing better than a day spent completing matrix-assisted laser desorption/ionization mass spectrometry to get the old gray cells pumping, right? You'll be needing those plates, Tom. Do you have them?"

Falcon looks down at his right hand. He is holding a box of laser-sliced cryogenic tissue samples cut to the diameter of a single cell and mounted on glass slides. On the top of the box is a hand-written label: MS41-T. "Yes, Peter," Falcon answers. "I have them right here."

"Good work, Tom," Peter responds cheerfully. "I knew you'd pull through, old friend. You were always good at finding the solution no matter how difficult the problem."

"So what are we working on this time?" Falcon asks,

"What's gotten into you, Tom? Don't you know?" Dr. Marsh briskly rolls his chair away from the computer and stands up. Then, the ghost from Falcon's past walks right up to him. "Tom, this is the toughest thing you'll ever do. It's the most difficult problem any of us have ever encountered." The look on Peter

Marsh's face is sincere and honest, just as he had always been in life. "But if anyone can find a way to solve it, it's you, Tom. You'll find a solution; you have no choice."

At that moment, Falcon found himself back in the prison yard, standing in the oppressive tropical heat of a summer day on the outskirts of Manila, but knowing that he did have something to do once he was released. The only thing was, he had no idea what it would be until he met Bayani and found himself in this tiny house, enjoying the best meal he'd eaten in over five years.

As Falcon sits on the edge of the bed, he rethinks the vision and as he does, all of the pieces begin to pull together: *Fearless,* the sharks, the talisman, and Bayani's grandfather on the beach; the images link together in his mind, and the picture they form isn't looking good.

After breakfast, Falcon and Bayani prepare to leave. Falcon kisses Bayani's aunt Angelica on the cheek and thanks her warmly for her lovely meal and wonderful hospitality. She smiles as she hands him a large shopping bag full of food for their trip. "Have a safe journey, Thomas, and may God be with you."

Bayani is already outside with his uncle Joshua when Falcon walks to the doorstep. He hands the shopping bag to Bayani and then stoops to remove his house slippers and place them back inside the basket. The simple act causes Falcon to suddenly realize how much he'd forgotten during his prison term, reminding him of how wonderful simple courtesy is and the sublime pleasure of a warm family home. As Falcon sits down on the step to put on his street shoes, he smiles, and, for a moment, he is happy.

The feeling had long ago become foreign to him, but in that moment, he feels like the man he once was. Falcon quickly slips on his dilapidated Nike runners—the only shoes he owns—given to him by a Catholic prison charity.

It's just before seven in the morning, Joshua's old Toyota pickup is waiting, and they have a long drive ahead. The three men climb inside: the oldest will be driving, the youngest will sit in the middle, while Thomas Falcon will sit by the window and gaze out at a country he has been living in for the past five years yet has never seen.

"Getting out of the city will be the most difficult part," Bayani comments as his uncle Joshua maneuvers the old truck out from under its sheet-metal shed.

"Yes, but it's still early," his uncle adds with a chuckle, "so maybe the traffic will only be terrible instead of impossible." Two hours later, the faded blue Toyota pickup passes through the toll plaza leading to the Pan-Philippine highway. The elevated freeway reveals the seemingly endless reaches of Metro Manila, a super-city of twelve million. The concrete urban sea still surrounds them as the tiny truck folds slowly into a thick mass of vehicles traveling north. Falcon has been watching the spectacle of the city pass by with great interest. The streets are a labyrinth of ceaseless activity, bursting with the energy of millions of industrious inhabitants.

Four hours later, the moist, tropical countryside opens up in front of Falcon with the distant pale outlines of the central Luzon Mountains rising above a layer of haze. The air flowing across Falcon's face from the partially open window has shifted from the hot, acrid smog of the city to the pungent odor of wet earth and fresh rain. He turns to Bayani, who is rummaging inside the shopping bag of food his aunt packed for them. Bayani smiles as he pulls out a bundle of Filipino beef empanadas wrapped in foil.

"Are those the beef?" Bayani's uncle Joshua asks eagerly.

"Yes, Uncle," Bayani answers. "But there are also some made with vegetables."

"No vegetables," Joshua answers sternly. "What about the banana fritters? Did she pack those?"

"Yes, Uncle. Would you like one of those first?" As Bayani speaks, he turns and winks at Falcon, who is watching and listening to the family banter with delight. Bayani carefully unwraps the bundle of delicate fried banana fritters covered in sugar and hands one to his uncle. Falcon looks on as the man eats the entire fritter in one mouthful. The sight and smell of the food reminds Falcon of how hungry he is. Bayani turns to Falcon and hands him one of the beef empanadas. Falcon looks at it briefly before he bites into its delicate pastry shell. Its seasoned meaty center fills his mouth, and for a moment, he is lost in the experience.

An hour later, Joshua exits the highway and pulls into a petrol station. He pushes his door open while Falcon leaps out to assist. "Please, allow me, sir." Falcon grabs the pump handle while Bayani goes inside to pay for the fuel. As Falcon begins filling the truck with gas, Joshua observes with interest, his attention suddenly drawn to the small tattoo on the side of Falcon's left hand: a stylized question mark located just above the knuckle of his thumb. The figure has the initials "B L N" etched into his flesh above it. "That is a powerful gang tattoo you have there, Thomas. Did you join the Bahala Na in prison?"

"Yes," Falcon answers flatly. "I have several more tattoos. Would you like to see them?" Falcon is suddenly overcome with embarrassment by his sarcastic quip. "Joshua, I apologize."

"There is no need for that, Thomas," Joshua answers thoughtfully. "Inside the Bilibid, the first rule is survival. The gangs offer protection. I understand this. I was there myself, remember?"

"Yes, of course," Falcon answers. "What happened to you? I mean…"

"Oh, you mean this?" Joshua briefly holds up his arms, which are covered in vicious scars. "I was a foolish young man at the time this happened. I was only seventeen years old. I should have been thinking of my own life and my family. But I joined a protest group. It was forty years ago, and we were under the rule of Marcos then. My cousin and I were arrested and taken to Bilibid. We were both tortured. I never saw my cousin again. I don't know how I survived, but here I am, and Marcos, well, he is dead."

Joshua moves closer to Falcon. "This is how the world works, my friend. It is easy to become caught up in the moment, and for that moment, it can seem as if the entire world is at stake. Then, the moment passes, and if you're lucky, if you survive, then you realize it was never that important to begin with."

After nine and a half hours on the road, the Toyota comes to a stop at a high-altitude clearing on the edge of a broad valley. The air is fresh and cool as Falcon steps out of the truck. He takes in a deep breath and then looks out at the jagged ridge-line of jungle-covered mountains that stretches in all directions. Falcon looks back at Bayani. "So where do we go from here?"

"From here, we continue by foot," Bayani answers. "There is no other way into the village."

"Well, then," Falcon answers cheerfully, "it will be good to stretch my legs after the long drive. Which way do we go?"

Bayani laughs. "Well, we can't go to my grandfather's house empty-handed. My uncle has some things in the back of the truck for us to carry down to the village." Falcon walks over to the truck and looks into the bed as Joshua removes a tarp. Underneath are four cases of San Miguel beer. He then watches in astonishment as Bayani deftly lifts two of the shrink-wrapped boxes containing twenty-four cans of beer each to the top of his head. Joshua then takes one of the cases and places it on top of his own head. He then looks at Falcon. "The last one's for you, Thomas. Let's get going. It will be dark soon."

The slender stone trail leading down the mountain in front of him forms a meandering silver thread through the tropical forest canopy. A light rain has begun to fall as the three men hike down the ancient walking path. The stone steps are slick and uneven, but Falcon feels invigorated as he steadies the beer case on top of his head with his left hand while using his right arm for balance. Then, the jungle opens, and for the first time, Falcon can see the entire valley spread out beneath him. The scene's incredible beauty stops him in his tracks.

"It is amazing, isn't it, Dr. Falcon?" Bayani comments as he, too, stops walking. "You are looking at the land of my people, the Ifugao."

Beneath the two men lies an endless vivid green sea of gently cascading waves that descend the walls of the valley by the hundreds; waves that are clearly man-made. The late afternoon light bathes the valley in shafts of gold that seem to reach out like the delicate fingers of angels.

"What is it?" Falcon gasps. "I've never seen anything like it."

"They are rice terraces, Dr. Falcon. My people began constructing them thousands of years ago, and now there are too many to count. We still farm them today. The terraces take constant care to maintain, but it keeps us connected to the land and to what is truly important."

"I can tell you what's important," Bayani's uncle loudly complains, "getting down to the village before dark! You can sightsee later. Let's get going!"

Chapter 6

Captain Sutton finds it difficult to keep his eyes on the live video feed streaming over the laptops. He is unprepared for the raw, brutal violence flashing in front of him. At several moments during the operation, he feels forced to look away. Alistair, too, is shocked by the brutal reality his creations are currently manifesting. His own eyes reflexively close when one of the cameras catches the expression on a man's face as his head is ripped from his body. The indelible image of the disembodied head now hangs frozen in Alistair's mind. *But the mission is a success,* Alistair reassures himself. His achievement is a scientific first—an extraordinary accomplishment. But, of course, the project is above top secret and will never be publicly recognized.

As with all weapons of war, the goal is to take life so swiftly, efficiently, and horrifically that no challenger will dare rise against you. The atomic bomb is the most publicly prominent example, but smaller, more covert weapons can have an equally chilling effect. What the human mind can imagine is often far worse than reality, but this reality, the one now playing out in front of Captain Sutton and the small group of naval intelligence officers, is truly terrifying.

As Alistair studies the video feed, he assures himself that the MS41-T will ultimately save lives, that the men dying violently in front of his eyes are terrorists with the potential to kill thousands of innocent people. He has now stopped them. Years of effort have proven that a biological combat drone can indeed replace a man, sparing his life, and at a fraction of the cost to train and maintain him as a navy SEAL. With the risk of soldiers' lives removed from the equation, another moral argument against the expensive, ongoing war against extremists can be eliminated; only the logistics remain.

At two hours and forty-seven minutes post deployment, the ten drones return to the aft deck of the *USS Storm*. Captain Sutton and his deck crew are now changed men. They keep their distance as the ten tiger sharks leap from the water and land silently in front of them. Sutton turns to Alistair.

"That was highly impressive, son. Scary as hell, but impressive. So, what do we do now? What do you do with these things?"

"We deactivate them, sir," Alistair answers coldly. "These units have served their purpose."

"So now you kill them?" Sutton asks,

"Actually, sir," Alistair turns to look the captain in the eye, "they were never alive to begin with. Now, if you will excuse me, sir, we need to wrap this up."

"Of course," Captain Sutton replies. "You did a fine job, young man."

"Thank you, sir."

Alistair turns away from the ship's captain and types a series of commands into his small tablet computer. The crew on deck are startled as a sudden muffled series of low-impact explosions rifles through each of the shark's bodies. The sound is only slightly louder than a pistol mounted with a silencer. They are, in fact, micro-blasts—tiny detonations triggered inside the sharks' internal control units. The purpose is, of course, to destroy the evidence.

As their bond with the energy field that once gave them false life is severed, the ten cloned tiger sharks now lay motionless on the deck of the ship. Alistair and his team of technicians carefully inspect the row of carcasses and note the damage each unit took during the operation. Most of the drones show signs of small-arms fire, and one has a laceration that looks to be caused by a blunt object, but overall, the damage is minimal. After recording the condition of each drone, Alistair and his technicians quickly wheel in a compact, specially designed, hydraulic lift. Then, the ten dead sharks are unceremoniously dumped into the sea. The three naval intelligence officers view the activity nervously from a distance. One turns to Lieutenant Commander Parnell. "Is this a good idea?" he asks hurriedly. "We could be risking discovery here. These units are above top secret."

"It's the best way to dispose of them, sir," Parnell responds. "These are single-use biological drones, and they will decay at a very rapid rate. The carcasses will sink to the bottom... eventually..." At this point, Parnell displays a sly smile.

"So, what exactly do you mean by *eventually*, Lieutenant Commander?" his superior inquires in a somewhat irritated tone.

"Sir, at our current position, the bottom of the Mediterranean is 2,450 meters down," Parnell answers. "That's over 8,000 feet, sir." Parnell's tone is respectful and measured. "It's my opinion that—"

"Yeah, yeah, I get it already," the officer interrupts, his voice still showing irritation. "I'm sorry I asked."

Drone Catch

The top-secret mission of the *USS Storm* is now complete, and the details will be carefully recorded and protected for decades to come. Captain Sutton's personal file, and those of his crew, will not mention this event. No commendations will be issued, no medals awarded. With all physical evidence of the drones now destroyed, the cyclone-class vessel quietly departs the area. Over the next two days, the *USS Storm* will sail five hundred miles on a direct course for the US naval air station at Sigonella, located on the Italian island of Sicily. Known as *the Hub of the Med,* the military facility is also used by NATO, as well as the Italian Air Force.

As the *USS Storm* motors across the Med, Alistair spends the time working with his scientific and technical team to process the data they collected. He is extremely satisfied with the performance of his MS41-T. It's been a long, hard road getting to this point, and the depth of his accomplishment hasn't quite sunk in.

Just over an hour after their late-day arrival at Sigonella, Dr. Alistair Fairchild, his four technicians, the three naval intelligence officers, and Lieutenant Commander Joseph Parnell are on board a private Gulfstream 650ER, one of three in the foundation's fleet. The jet is currently en route to the US state of Maryland, where a high-level briefing at the Office of Naval Intelligence has been scheduled. Deep into the flight, an evening twilight sky casts a dim glow over the frigid North Atlantic south of Greenland. Alistair takes a rare moment to relax as he sips a beer and looks out as the jet races toward the northern coast of Canada at Mach 0.85. He can't help but contemplate the logistics of deploying his drones in a polar environment: *yes*, he reasons, *we could operate here… we could do it…*

Chapter 7

As Brian stands quietly backstage, he breathes in deeply, exhales, and then shakes out his arms and legs as if he were an athlete preparing to take the field. He feels surprisingly calm, given the circumstances. This will be the largest audience he has ever addressed. A young woman carrying a clipboard approaches him. "Dr. Mathews?" she questions softly. "How are you feeling? You're on in thirty seconds. How is your headset? Are you ready?"

Brian looks at her calmly and whispers, "The headset fits okay. I'm fine, thank you… I'm ready… Um, do they have a count yet? I mean, how many people will be watching online? Do they know?"

The young woman grips her clipboard a bit more tightly and smiles. "Don't worry about the online viewers, Dr. Mathews. Just put them out of your mind and focus on the people out there." As she speaks quietly, she gestures toward the open stage.

Brian contemplates her expression. He's not nervous as much as curious. "It's okay, I won't freak out on you. How many?"

The woman purses her lips, glances back over her shoulder briefly, and then leans in closer to Brian and whispers, "They say it will be close to a million."

Brian is stunned, yet also strangely energized. A sly grin crosses his face as he winks at the young woman. She smiles and then gives him an encouraging thumbs-up; "Go get'em, Dr. Mathews."

A few seconds later, he hears his introduction: "May I present our keynote speaker for this year's International Conference for Truth… Dr. Brian Mathews."

Brian exhales once more and then turns and strides out confidently to loud applause from an audience of nearly three thousand attendees and invited VIP guests. He walks to the center of the stage enveloped inside the roar. He gazes out across a sea of faces focused solely on him, waits for the applause to die down, and then he begins. "Thank you, ladies and gentleman, and I would also like to thank the organizers for giving myself and my esteemed colleagues this opportunity to present our research at such a receptive and professional forum. By joining forces, we've become stronger and even more resolute in our collective quest for truth."

Brian gestures to his audience as he moves slowly from one side of the stage to the other. "In only a few short years, we've experienced surprising success with increased media coverage, new whistle-blowers coming forward, and investigations reopened due to public demand. I would like to urge everyone to attend as many of the formal presentations and spot briefings as you can. I know it can be difficult, even overwhelming, to be confronted by such a vast array of suspected government-sponsored criminal conspiracies and officially declassified cover-ups. But learn as much as you can, and spread the truth. Because a world where seeking truth and speaking the truth are ridiculed is not the world any of us here want to raise our children in."

A surge of energy hits Brian as the audience in front of him once more erupts into loud applause. He pauses until the applause tapers off, takes in another deep breath, and then Brian starts his keynote.

"I would like to begin by presenting you all with two questions. The first is *what do we believe?* And the second is *what do we know?* These are both important questions to think about, and each is different. As a scientist, what I believe is pretty much meaningless. Yet, what I know takes a very long time to achieve. Science is difficult. Science can take years... decades... even whole lifetimes to separate the facts from mere ideas. We must first develop a sound hypothesis. Then, we must discover the evidence to support the hypothesis. Then, we test it, and then lots of other scientists must be able to repeat these tests over and over until your kids can perform the experiments at home and achieve the same result... the same success. It's only then that we can claim to know something."

"But enough about science," Brian begins pacing the stage. "Let's talk about crime." Murmurs of laughter ripple through the audience as Brian comically rubs his hands together and smiles. Then, he stops, lets his hands drop to his sides, and looks out at the audience. "And, of course, this is a whole other thing. If there is an antithesis to science, crime would not be a bad choice."

Brian paces the stage as he speaks. "Crime is arbitrary." Brian stops briefly and then continues. "And... although crimes are often similar, each one is unique in its own way. So, to repeat a crime absolutely down to the letter is pretty unlikely. Crimes have perpetrators, and they have victims. Evidence is often left behind at the scene, and there are usually witnesses."

"Yet, we often find that what the witnesses think they saw is in conflict. Most of this conflicting information is due to each person's own unique point of view: Where were the witnesses standing at the time the crime took place? Were they on the street? In the doorway of a building? Or near the grassy knoll?" Brian hears nervous laughter rise from the audience…

"Indeed," he continues, "some crimes are very famous. So famous in fact, that I don't even need to mention them by name to bring them up in your minds." Brian pauses briefly, peers into the faces of the front row, and then picks up where he left off. "But in order to solve a crime, it often takes science. And then, of course, we find ourselves back at square one. What do we believe? And what do we know?"

He picks up his pace. "But there is a third question, and this is a really dangerous one. A question with the power to obliterate everything else we've just talked about. That question is *what do we want to know?*"

Brian pauses to allow his statement to sink in. Then he starts walking again. "In crime, the perpetrator wants the cops to think it was someone else, whilst the cops may think they know who the real criminal is, but they don't have the evidence they need to prove it. So the police may fudge a bit; they may even lie. It's not legal, of course, but if the guy who actually did commit the crime gets nabbed, then who's going to complain, right?

"It gets worse, though, because, whether it is the police, our elected officials, or agencies of the federal government, once people realize they can abuse the power they have been entrusted with, they tend to keep abusing it, even going as far as to legislate their illegal activity in order to shield themselves from public scrutiny and prosecution."

At that moment, a member of the audience stands up and shouts, "You got that right!"

A few people whistle in agreement as chuckles rise from the crowd. Brian gives them a few seconds to settle back down. Then, he walks back to center stage as the image projected behind him switches to that of a large great white shark leaping out of the water with its massive gaping jaws only inches from the camera.

"So what does all this have to do with a series of mysterious mass shark attacks that took place five years ago? To find out, we need to go back to the beginning." He stops to briefly look up at the giant shark projected behind him. Then, he turns back to his audience. "So what do we know? And what do we believe?"

The next image flashes up to the screen behind him, and the sight of it sends gasps through the audience.

"This is a digital image I took with my camera phone just as we were being evacuated by helicopter from the research vessel *Fearless*. This was taken during the attack, and as far as I know, the photos I am sharing with you now are the only documentary evidence in existence."

As the next image appears, it triggers more gasps from the audience, "In this photo, we are a bit higher, and you can see hundreds of what look, at first glance, to be sharks. Those men you see in the circle on the helipad are firing hundreds of rounds of ammunition, desperately trying to kill sharks that were, in fact, already dead. What I am trying to get across here is that the media story that these shark attacks were somehow natural is completely false." The murmurs rippling through the audience suddenly cease, and the crowd goes completely quiet.

"So here is where we get into murky territory." Brian knows he is about to step off a ledge here, but he feels confident that his audience is ready go with him. "How does a PhD ichthyologist like myself apply legitimate shark science to the phenomenon captured in these photos? That of zombie sharks." Murmurs rise again, but so far, everyone is still seated, so Brian continues. "Yes, I agree. Just saying the words does feel odd, doesn't it?"

The next photo flashes on the screen, and once more, it's followed by big gasps from the riveted crowd. Brian looks at the image and then back at the audience. "I am a shark biologist by profession, and I can tell you I saw sharks attacking people that had been dead for at least a week. Their bodies showed extreme signs of mortification, and they had all clearly been mutilated by finning operations. This was the subject of our work aboard *Fearless*. We had been studying and tracking the fin boats for months prior to this event. And as you can see in this photo, all of these sharks have had their fins cut off."

Brian gestures to his audience. "The photo evidence is compelling." He continues to slowly walk the stage. "But decades of hard scientific research have taught us many things about sharks. For example, we know that no shark can survive after its fins have been removed. This is a well-established fact. They can't swim, and they certainly can't leap onto the deck of a huge ship and attack people. But as you can see in this photo, these sharks are doing just that."

Brian finishes his talk by showing video clips and images that he shot while researching natural shark behavior. He then makes detailed comparisons between these images and the ones he took during the attack. After fielding questions from the audience, Brian pauses a moment. "One of the most common questions I get from people is, how can I possibly go back into the water with sharks after what I experienced." Brian stops, he stares out at the people in front of him. "And my answer is always this: what I experienced is exactly the reason why I have to get back into the water with sharks."

Brian walks once more to the center of the stage. "So what do we believe? And what do we know? Well, if I've just done my job, then you all know things now that you didn't before I began. And with a bit of persistence, perhaps we can share our knowledge so that others who merely believe can also know. Thank you."

As Brian walks off stage, the roar of applause still fills the auditorium. One of the lead organizers meets Brian as he exits back stage. "Brian, great job, and nice touch. Thanks for mentioning the other movements."

"Thank you, Jake," Brian answers politely. "I really felt I was getting my message across this time."

As the two men exit the main auditorium and walk out onto the sprawling convention floor, the atmosphere is subdued, professional, and, above all, respectful. There are no individual booths; instead, the modern, elegantly furnished seating areas are divided by subject, the main feature being the volunteer briefing staff, each of them experts in their chosen subject. They roam the convention floor, offering spot briefings to anyone who is interested.

Brian and Jake are walking across the main hall when they catch sight of an American news crew. The camera operator is leaning against a wall along with his lighting and sound technicians. All three are looking bored as they stare at their phones while their lead reporter stands off to one side. She is clearly in the midst of a highly animated phone conversation and seems frustrated.

"Where are the kooks?" she complains angrily. "Why did you even send me down here? I could be in Brussels right now covering real issues, but no, you had to send me to Dusseldorf... Yeah... right... Well, you can tell me I have to have footage or it's my ass, but I'm telling you there's nothing here. These people are too fucking normal! I was expecting costumes and crazies; instead, I get people who just look like a bunch of lawyers."

Brian and Jake listen silently to the reporter's rant, and then Jake leans in. "We're making waves, Brian," he whispers. "I'm actually encouraged by this woman's conversation. But, of course, the mainstream media is having its usual field day calling us the 'tinfoil hat convention.' But, so far, all they can do is make unfounded claims. We aren't giving them any visual fuel for their fire. By the way, attendance is through the roof this year."

"Really?" answers Dr. Mathews as he glances around. "The crowd seems about the same as last year."

"Oh, I'm not talking about standard attendance. I'm talking about government spooks." Jake glances around as he speaks, and then his voice drops another level. "The place is crawling with them. We were forced to double our security this year due to more reprisal rumors."

"Why do you think that is? I mean, what's different this year?"

"In past years, we had government-sponsored criminal conspiracies divided into two halls: one for the historical, fully exposed cases that are now a matter of public record, such as *Operation Gladio, The Bay of Pigs Invasion, MK Ultra, Project Merlin, COINTELPRO, Operation Olympic Games,* and *Operation Condor...* Then, a second hall for open cases that are still ongoing, such as 911, Bali, Boston, Paris, Brussels, Mumbai, and the London 7/7 bombings."

Jake scans the convention floor once more and then looks back at Brian. "What we did this year was combine these two sections and mix the subjects together. What we've found is by doing this, people can make a direct comparison between the open and closed cases. It makes it much easier for visitors to recognize the familiar patterns during their briefings. As people move from one session to the next and listen to a variety of cases, they can more easily connect the motive to the crime. Once people are shown the patterns, they are able to recognize government fingerprints all over other events through side-by-side comparison."

"Dr. Mathews," Jake continues, "we're pushing buttons we didn't know existed. We've seriously stirred the pot. It's exciting, but I admit it can be damned scary too. All of us on the organizer's committee are under surveillance. We are getting pulled aside and hassled when we travel. It's a standard intimidation tactic. We all know it comes with the territory, but I was worried we'd lose people. Surprisingly, it's drawn us closer together. If what we are doing here is truly meaningless and crazy, as the media loves to hammer into the public, then the various government agencies involved would ignore us completely. But they are obviously threatened by our activities, which frankly makes them look even more guilty."

At that moment, a middle-aged man wearing an austere gray suit approaches the two men. The official credentials of a conference briefer with expertise in the 911 attacks hang from a lanyard around his neck. "Dr. Brian Mathews?"

"Yes?" Brian answers cordially, "What can I do for you?"

"I'm sorry to interrupt, but I missed your keynote. I was working the floor at the time. May I ask you a few quick questions privately? I am very interested in your work."

Brian turns to Jake. "Do you mind? I'm sure it won't take long. I'll meet you at the cafe, okay, Jake?"

"Sure, Brian," Jake answers, "see you in a few." Jake watches as Brian walks over to a secluded seating area with the briefer. Jake doesn't recognize this volunteer, but he was observing him carefully as the man spoke with Brian, and his credential tags are legitimate, so Jake turns and heads off to find a cup of coffee.

As the two men settle into a set of couches, Brian can't help but notice that the man sitting in front of him seems nervous. "Are you okay?" Brian asks innocently.

The man ignores the question as he quickly glances around to be certain they are alone, and then he looks Brian in the eye. "Dr. Mathews," he says quietly, "is your phone on?"

"No," Brian answers. "Actually, I don't carry it when I speak publicly. What is this about?"

"Dr. Mathews," the man continues, "I only have time to say this once, so please listen carefully."

Brian is now fully focused on the stranger sitting across from him. "Yes, I'm listening."

"There was an incident a few days ago. It took place in the Mediterranean Sea off the coast of Libya. It involved a small Navy coastal patrol ship, the *USS Storm*, and someone you know—Dr. Alistair Fairchild. Word is they took out a jihadi training camp with a new type of drone—an amphibious, biologically engineered combat assault drone that looks exactly like a tiger shark. The mission was highly successful."

Brian is stunned. He had been hearing rumors and fragmented chatter about this project from other sources for more than a year, but nothing concrete. "What do you want me to do with this information?" he asks.

"I don't need to tell you how many laws I just broke, Dr. Mathews." The man looks extremely tense. "But I am under orders. My superiors have been watching this development for some time. They feel it is time to act and that you should be brought on board."

Brian's back stiffens. "How do I proceed from here?"

"Very carefully, Dr. Mathews. I strongly advise that you keep this information to yourself. We will be in contact." At that moment, the man in the gray suit gets up and walks off without looking back.

Brian sits alone for a few more minutes, processing what he's just heard. The one thing he does know absolutely is that even if the initial operation was a success, Alistair is playing with fire, and it's only a matter of time before he gets burnt.

Chapter 8

The clattering sound of anchor chains rapidly spooling off her bow catches the attention of tourists on shore as *Fearless* arrives at Catalina Island. Above the small, rocky inlet, *Fearless* has dropped anchor inside looms the ultra-modern Wriggly Marine Science Institute. The arrival of the research vessel has not gone unnoticed within the walls of the facility, as members of Dr. Samantha Randal's team hurriedly ready bags of gear and organize crates of equipment.

"Your ship has come in, Dr. Randal," one of her lab technicians jokingly announces.

Dr. Randal eyes the young woman slyly, her head cocked to one side. "Oh you've been just waiting to launch that line, haven't you, darling?"

"Ouch! Aren't we the clever one?" the young technician quips sarcastically. She turns toward the window. "Dr. Randal, just look at her." The two women marvel at the impressive profile of the three-hundred-and-eighteen-foot-long ship. "She's magnificent, and she's here for us."

"She is beautiful." Samantha then turns away and looks nervously around the room. "Does everyone have their gear ready? If you've left anything behind, we won't be coming back for it. You know the whole ship is run by former military; they'll have no tolerance for disorder."

Twenty minutes later, Dr. Randal stands on the dock with her six-member science team and a mountain of gear. She's filled with anticipation but also a twinge of anxiety. The foundation will be expecting significant results from their investment, and she knows she must deliver.

From his vantage point on the bridge, Alex Moss focuses his binoculars. "Looks like we'll need a second RIB just for their gear. These ladies didn't pack light." He lowers the binoculars and then turns toward Murray. "Better take a couple extra guys with you to help load their equipment."

"Will do, Chief," Murray responds. "And might I suggest we split the load and make two trips? You know how these boffins are always leaving something behind."

"Good call. I'll radio down to Razz and let him know. You better get going."

"On my way, Chief. We're on a schedule, right?" The Australian swiftly heads out the door as Moss turns back toward the window.

"Yeah," Moss mutters. "Feels like my entire life has been on a schedule."

As the two black, six-meter-long rugged inflatable boats arrive at the dock, Malcolm Rafferty hops out and quickly searches the group for Dr. Randal. He recognizes her from her photo, but just barely. The woman standing amongst her all-female science team doesn't look anything like the coldly professional researcher wearing a boxy lab coat pictured in her file.

This Dr. Randal is wearing a form-fitting T-shirt and shorts while her long dark hair falls loosely past her shoulders. *Not bad for a genius scientist,* Rafferty observes.

"Dr. Randal?" Rafferty inquires politely. "My name is Malcolm Rafferty. I'm the first mate aboard *Fearless*. On behalf of the crew, it's a pleasure to meet you."

Dr. Randal smiles as she grasps Rafferty's hand firmly. "It's a pleasure to make your acquaintance, Mr. Rafferty. My team and I are anxious to get going, as I'm sure you are as well."

Alex Moss waits on deck by the gangway alongside his crisply uniformed crew: white polo shirts emblazoned with the *Fearless Research Foundation* logo, navy blue Bermuda shorts, and matching deck shoes. Moss evaluates the passengers and gear inside the two fully loaded RIBs that slowly motor toward his ship. The conditions are excellent for the transfer from shore; the sea is nearly flat calm.

A rough arrival aboard ship is never a good start to an expedition, and the worst by far was that of Dr. Thomas Falcon five years ago. Moss still blames himself for Dr. Falcon's treacherous arrival via a rescue basket lowered from a mammoth navy transport helicopter—admittedly not one of his best ideas.

If the initial transfer had been more benign, Moss has reasoned, Dr. Falcon would have been better prepared, more emotionally stable, and far less likely to unwittingly unleash a zombie shark apocalypse. It's taken Moss years to accept that the most efficient way to complete a task is not always the best when there are civilians involved.

Crewmen eagerly assist the arriving group of attractive female researchers. Dr. Samantha Randal is the first to step from a RIB. She smiles as she looks up at the massive ship. She's been excitedly looking forward to working aboard *Fearless* from the moment she was awarded the grant. It's a dream come true for any marine scientist—an opportunity she can't wait to take advantage of.

Moss extends his hand as Samantha reaches the top of the gangway and then steps aboard for the first time. "Dr. Randal, it's a pleasure to meet you. I'm Alex Moss, ship's Chief of Operations, and on behalf of my crew, we would like to welcome you and your team aboard *Fearless*."

"Thank you, Mr. Moss." Samantha grips his hand firmly as she smiles up at the six-foot-four-inch former Navy SEAL. "It's a pleasure to meet you as well. It is an extraordinary privilege to be here. My team and I are eager to begin work."

With the new science team settled on board, Moss once again has his crew in place as they prepare their ship for departure. Meanwhile, Dr. Samantha Randal's personal luggage sits untouched in her cabin. Instead, she's already working in the ship's main lab and directing her team as they carefully lift delicate scientific equipment from an array of large Pelican cases scattered across the floor.

"Mind those liquid nitrogen containers," Dr. Randal firmly directs as her lab assistants lift the stainless steel containers from their foam cradles. "I think we should set up the cryogenic equipment over on that table over there and the laser over here." Samantha walks over to inspect the workspaces more closely. "This is amazing," she observes. "All of these tables have been designed to hold everything firmly in place." She places her hand on the pristine stainless steel work surface. "What a delight." She turns to see one of her grad students opening up another crate of equipment. "Make sure all of those specimen containers have been sterilized before you store them please."

The young woman pauses and looks up. "Yes, Dr. Randal."

At that moment, the team in the lab hear the rumbling clatter of anchor chains as *Fearless* prepares to depart. Samantha pauses a moment as she senses the ship moving. Her six lab assistants all stop what they are doing and look at each other with a knowing smile; it's their turn this time, and they are ready.

Alex Moss directs from the bridge as *Fearless* maneuvers away from Catalina Island to begin her voyage south. As her engines come up to speed and the first watch crew takes over, Moss turns toward the mahogany chart table at the center of the room. Spread across the beautifully varnished table is a large oceanic chart for the Eastern Pacific, along with more detailed charts covering the Baja peninsula and the Sea of Cortez. They have a four-day passage ahead of them. It's nearly eight hundred miles to the southern tip of the Baja Peninsula and the mouth of the Gulf of California.

• • •

Two days at sea and *Fearless* is back in her element as her crew comfortably slip into their daily routines. Moss and Rafferty have each taken note of how efficient and on task the new team appears to be. Their round of security interviews went off smoothly—zero flags.

Over the past nine years, Moss and Rafferty have witnessed dozens of marine science specialists come and go, and although all of them were highly professional, only a few stood out as exceptional. Based on what they've observed so far, Dr. Samantha Randal appears to be the latter.

• • •

It is after eight in the evening, and Moss is in his office with his laptop open as he reads Dr. Brian Mathew's *Shark Truth* website. He scans through the latest posts, lets out a sigh, and drops his head in disgust at the sight of another article with his name in it.

A knock on his door is a welcome interruption. Moss clicks away from the webpage, gets up, and opens the door.

"Dr. Randal, how can I help you?"

"Mr. Moss, I hope I'm not disturbing you."

"Not at all. It's my job to assist the science teams in every way possible," Moss answers flatly.

"I want to ask about positioning the ship farther north once we arrive in the Sea of Cortez. Two years ago, we were able to collect a number of excellent specimens inside el Alto Golfo de Califórnia, but we ran out of time before we could complete our work there. I've been anxious to return to this area ever since."

"Absolutely. Show me exactly where you need to go, and I will make the necessary arrangements."

"Thank you, Mr. Moss. That would be excellent."

As Samantha speaks, she glances down at Moss's desk and spots a copy of Dr. Peter Marsh's posthumously published book, *The Boy from Opua: A Marine Scientist's Journey.*

"A friend gave me a copy of this." Samantha lifts the book and then opens it. "It's wonderful. Have you finished it?"

"Not yet." Moss glances at the book's cover and then focuses on Samantha. "I start reading, and I see what a dedicated man he was... a gifted scientist... and I wish I had taken the time to know him better." Moss's eyes shift back to his desk. "I can see how much more he had to contribute, and I get angry over what happened." Moss looks back at her. "He was a good man. He deserved better."

"Oh dear." Samantha self-consciously lays the book down and then steps back. "I'm so terribly sorry. I'm being insensitive. Please forgive me."

"For what? You're not insensitive. You're just being polite. Besides, it was five years ago. We've all moved on. It's just that sometimes, old wounds still hurt."

"It must be incredibly difficult. I can't imagine how painful it must be for you and your crew after what happened aboard this ship."

Moss looks down, smiles, and then chuckles softly to himself.

"What is it?" Samantha's face becomes flushed with embarrassment. "Did I just say something stupid?"

He glances back. "No, ma'am." Moss's voice is firm but sincere. "Not at all. It's just that... at some point during each expedition, I get the same thing from almost every member of every team that's been on board for the past four years, and the next thing, of course, is that they want to ask all kinds of questions about the attack. They all want to find out what really happened. And I can't talk about it. It's not that I don't want to sometimes, but all of us are under strict confidentiality. We've all signed nondisclosure agreements. All the research that goes on here is proprietary, as you well know."

Dr. Randal's posture straightens. "Of course, you are absolutely right, Mr. Moss. I must admit I do feel a bit silly right now."

"Look, it's my problem, not yours, and I do appreciate your thoughtfulness."

"I understand completely," Samantha assures. "I'll inform my team not to bring up the subject."

"Thank you, I appreciate that."

As Dr. Randal leaves his office, Moss makes a note to position the ship farther north once they reach the Sea of Cortez. Then he refreshes his laptop and retrieves Dr. Brian Mathew's website. His jaw tightens as he reads the post that mentions him personally and wonders why the foundation hasn't taken stronger action to shut this kid up.

Chapter 9

A rooster's crow jolts Falcon from a sound sleep. The bird is just outside his window, and it is persistent and loud. Falcon tries to ignore the rooster and let sleep return. The previous evening had been spent listening to hours of animated conversion. Falcon was exhausted when he was finally shown a bed. Unlike the celebratory dinner at Joshua and Angelica's home, Falcon was not the center of attention this time. As a matter of fact, he was hardly spoken to. Instead, it was Bayani to whom everyone seemed to be drawn. The entire village was waiting for him when the three men arrived.

The rooster crows again. Falcon gives up on sleep and gets dressed. He walks quietly through the darkened home of Bayani's mother and finds the doorway leading outside. He reaches for the handle, opens it, and there, facing him, is Bayani's grandfather.

The old man stands like a weathered and gnarled stick that has been planted into the ground. His slight, boney frame is regally adorned in the same brightly colored native dress he wore the day Falcon first encountered him on the beach five years ago. Falcon says nothing as the old man stares at him. Then, the shaman begins to speak in Tagalog, and this time, Falcon understands him perfectly.

"Now that the two of us share a common language," the shaman says calmly, "we can get to work. Come with me, Falcon. We have much to do." The old man then turns and walks off.

Falcon quickly puts on his shoes and follows the shaman into the jungle.

The morning air is cool, pungent, and laced in mist as Falcon keeps pace behind the shaman. The old man veers off the main track and then heads up a narrow jungle path. Despite his advanced age, the shaman is nimble as he effortlessly navigates the steep, winding trail.

The early morning calls of rainforest birds and strange animals enchants the scientist in Falcon as he hikes along behind the old man. Heavy dew drips from the broad leaves of tropical plants that wet Falcon's arms as he passes. The two men walk for more than an hour, and then Falcon begins to pick up the sound of a waterfall.

They reach a clearing in the jungle that reveals a dark, clear pool of water shrouded in a shower of spray. The waterfall's thunderous roar drowns out all other sounds. The old shaman continues to climb. He steps lightly over the large volcanic rocks scattered around the pool. Falcon tries to follow. The whole time they have been walking, the shaman has said nothing. He hasn't even turned back to see if Falcon is still behind him. Falcon looks up briefly at the beautiful plunging wall of water cascading off the mountain into the volcanic rock pool, and then he glances around and realizes he has lost sight of Bayani's grandfather.

Falcon nervously searches the edge of the pool until he spots him. The shaman is standing on a rock near the waterfall and is obscured by thick clouds of spray. Falcon can barely see him. The shaman gestures to Falcon, beckoning him to follow, and then he disappears. Falcon climbs to where the shaman had been standing, but he has no idea where the old man went. The spray from the waterfall soaks Falcon's clothes, and the roar of the falling water is deafening. He finds it hard to think. Falcon becomes confused, he doesn't know where to go, and then suddenly, everything is silent.

The sun is high when Falcon regains his sense of awareness. He is sitting cross-legged on a large boulder. It's hot. Intense rays of sunlight filter down through the broken shade of the jungle that surrounds him. Falcon is disoriented. He has no idea where he is. He no longer hears the waterfall. He looks down and sees that somehow, his clothes are now completely dry. Falcon looks up to see that the shaman is sitting a few meters away from him on the same huge rock. The shaman's face has no expression, and his eyes do not blink; he is simply staring at Falcon. The shaman then nods in approval as he looks at Falcon. Then, he points off into the jungle.

"Your path is there," the shaman directs. "Follow the path, and see where it takes you."

Falcon struggles to stand. His arms and legs are stiff, and his body is sore. He reckons he must have been sitting there a long time, but he doesn't know how long or even how he got there in the first place. Falcon says nothing as he rises to his feet and obediently walks off in the direction the shaman pointed.

It is now late in the day. Falcon feels the pain of hunger in his gut, and he is dehydrated, but he keeps walking. He doesn't know where he's going, but he continues on through the jungle as the shaman instructed. He walks for hours—or at least, it feels as if he does—and then he pushes through the large leaves of a taro plant and suddenly finds himself standing on a beach.

Falcon stops and looks around. He is no longer in the jungles of the Philippines; he is somewhere else... somewhere very far away. He can see surfers riding large breakers in the distance and a crowded beach bar with a thatched roof. People nearby don't seem to notice him, but he can hear them speaking Spanish. Falcon turns to see the shaman standing next to him.

"So, Falcon," the shaman begins, "this is where your path leads."

"I don't understand," Falcon answers. "Where are we? How did we get here?"

"I wouldn't know," the shaman replies quizzically. "This is not my path. I am only the guide." Then, the shaman turns and walks off down the beach.

Falcon puts his left hand on his hip and studies his surroundings more closely. The sandy beach is broad and flat in both directions. There's a small tourist town nearby and a narrow beach road with traffic. He doesn't recognize any distinctive landmarks. Then Falcon overhears lively conversation in English. Falcon turns to see that it's coming from a pair of Americans behind him. Falcon watches as they walk by. Each is carrying a surfboard, and they are dressed in surfing wetsuits. Falcon observes them carefully, then he notices something on one of the surfboards; a large stylized logo: *BAJA*.

In that instant, Falcon finds himself once again sitting on top of the same boulder as if he had never moved from it. He looks into the face of the shaman sitting across from him.

"So, Falcon," the shaman inquires, "do you know where your path leads?"

"Yes," Falcon answers, "but it is a very long way from here, and I have no idea how I will get there."

"The spirits will show you," the shaman replies. "Just listen to them. They will take you where you need to go."

Falcon is exhausted, severely dehydrated, and overcome with hunger when he and the old shaman finally reach the village.

Bayani is waiting for them. "Dr. Falcon," Bayani hands him a large bottle of water, "here, take this, but don't drink it too quickly."

Falcon grabs the bottle and begins desperately chugging it down, and then he doubles over, chokes, and spits most of it out onto the ground in front of him.

"Dr. Falcon, please," Bayani pleads. He puts his hand on Falcon's shoulder. "You've been on a long journey. It will take time to recover. You must drink slowly."

Falcon nods silently in agreement as he struggles to compose himself. He sets the bottle down, steadies himself, and breathes. Then, he takes the bottle, straightens up again, and forces himself to sip the water slowly. Just then, he catches sight of Bayani's uncle Joshua coming out of his sister-in-law's house. He carries a basket and busily picks fruit from a nearby tree. Joshua notices Falcon and smiles.

"Ah, Thomas, you have returned!" Joshua stops picking fruit and walks over to where Falcon and Bayani are standing. "How are you feeling?"

"I'm not sure what happened to me," Falcon replies as he continues to drink from the bottle. We only left this morning."

Joshua chuckles with bemusement. "Thomas, my friend, you didn't leave this morning. You've been gone for nearly four days! My father-in-law may be old, but he is incredibly tough. He will most likely outlive all of us. It's no wonder you are nearly dead!"

Falcon looks at Bayani in bewilderment. "What is he talking about? Have I really been gone that long?"

Bayani flashes a somewhat irritated glance at his uncle and then looks at Falcon. "What my uncle says is true. You followed my grandfather into the jungle more than three days ago. I myself have been on many spirit quests with my grandfather. I know how difficult it can be, but it is also a powerful awakening experience."

Falcon's bewilderment rapidly shifts to recognition and then understanding. He looks over at the old shaman, and Bayani's grandfather nods approvingly. "You two now have much to discuss. I must rest. I am going to go have a beer."

Falcon takes another drink from the water bottle and then looks at Bayani. "I did have a vision, Bayani. It showed me a place very far from here. I have no money and no passport, but somehow I have to get there."

"I believe we have both seen this place, Dr. Falcon," Bayani confides. "I have also experienced a vision, and in my vision we were both standing on a beach in Mexico."

Falcon is stunned. "Baja," he answers softly, "I was in Baja."

"Yes, this is true." Bayani assures him. "I have spoken about this with my uncle, and he has arranged for us to take passage on a freighter bound for Panama, but we must both work. Do you think you can handle it? Are you ready, Dr. Falcon?"

"Yes," Falcon answers confidently, "I'm ready"

Chapter 10

The Gulfstream 650ER lands smoothly at Washington Executive Airport then taxis in to park inside a private corporate hangar after a nonstop flight from Sicily. The engines are still winding down as the plane's passengers gather their belongings. Alistair glances at his watch while the flight crew open the main hatch, and the plane's hydraulic stairway extends smoothly down to the hangar's spotlessly polished floor.

It is nearly midnight on the east coast, but Alistair is still running on European time, so it already feels like the next morning to him. He zips shut his computer bag and stands with the rest of the plane's passengers. They quickly file off and into a group of waiting black SUVs. Alistair nods to his team as the four technicians pile into one of the waiting cars. He's a bit jealous; they're all heading off to a comfortable hotel with a well-stocked bar, while his work is just beginning.

Twenty minutes later, Dr. Alistair Fairchild is handing over his credentials and identification to a heavily armed guard who is standing outside a high-security entrance to the headquarters of the National Maritime Intelligence Center, which is located on the grounds of the Suitland Federal Center in Suitland, Maryland. The

NMIC houses the headquarters for the intelligence offices of the marines, navy, as well as the United States Coastguard. The two-hundred-and-twenty-six-acre complex also hosts the Census Bureau, Washington National Records Center, and the Atmospheric Administration, but it is the six-hundred-thousand-square-foot NMIC building that dominates.

The three naval intelligence officers lead the way as Lieutenant Commander Joseph Parnell and Dr. Alistair Fairchild trail them into the massive security complex. The building is eerily quiet as the five men pass through another security checkpoint, into an elevator, and then down a series of hallways until they reach a large conference room. It has a tall ceiling and a number of large flat-screen displays.

Alistair walks into the room to find a mob of very serious-looking navy brass staring him in the face. He is not intimidated in the slightest, however; he knows he has what they want. Why else would they all be here waiting for him in the middle of the night? At the center sits the commander of naval intelligence himself, Rear Admiral Johnston Allen O'Sullivan. The admiral and his respective cluster of aids remain seated as Lieutenant Commander Parnell introduces them to Dr. Fairchild.

The admiral has been briefed, but he is keenly interested in hearing directly from this wonder kid who just pulled off one of the most impressive *and cheapest* covert counter-insurgency operations in decades.

Alistair quickly takes his laptop out from his backpack, powers it up, and then relays it over to one of the large flat-screen monitors mounted on the wall. The first thing he wants his audience to see is the video feed his team took off the drones themselves.

"Sir," Alistair begins, "what you are about to see is a condensed video recording of the operation itself. The images are graphic. Once you have viewed the video, I will explain the technology behind the operation. Shall I proceed?"

At that moment, the admiral gives a nod to Parnell, who then looks over at Alistair. "You may proceed, Dr. Fairchild."

Alistair doesn't watch the drone video; instead, he stands at a distance and carefully studies the expressions and reactions coming from the cadre of career ONI officers sitting in front of the display. He is fascinated by their individual reactions as he observes a palpable, gut-churning mashup of emotional turmoil cross each of their faces. Conventional weapons deployments against surgically selected targets are much easier to watch, Alistair has surmised. What these men are looking at now is no fireworks show; this is raw death taking place in front of their eyes. These men may be battle hardened, but the battles they've witnessed took place in the twenty-first century, not the twelfth.

The video is without sound, yet even seen under the ethereal glow of night-vision cameras, the images are highly disturbing. The final sequence of the lone man running desperately through the forest is perhaps the most difficult for the officers to watch. To the trained eyes of the ONI officers, his clothing, his weapon, and his appearance point to the fact that this man is not a jihadi extremist but a member of NATO Special Forces and most likely French. What he was doing there is a matter for speculation, but the senior naval officers watching him die violently know that whatever the reason, his presence in the camp will need to be investigated.

"We are calling this product the MS41-T," Alistair begins. "Its code name is Multi-Striker." Alistair pauses. It's obvious that he does not yet have the men's attention. He can see from the officers' faces that they are still recovering from what they've just witnessed. He looks over at Parnell, who waves his hand slightly, signaling Alistair to give them a minute. Then, Rear Admiral O'Sullivan takes a deep breath, straightens himself, adjusts his uniform, and looks directly at Alistair.

"Dr. Fairchild, this is one hell of a monster you've created. What the hell is this thing?"

Alistair coughs nervously. No one as yet has ever referred to his drones as *monsters*. To Alistair, they are sophisticated, efficient, biological weapons—and revolutionary ones at that. He clears his throat and quickly regains his composure. "What my team and I have engineered, sirs, is the first fully biological combat assault drone, and as you can see, it looks exactly like a tiger shark. That's because this technology employs a cloned tiger shark as its platform—"

"I read this in the brief," one of the officers interrupts, "but please explain this, Dr. Fairchild. Are you really telling us you cloned a shark?"

"Yes, sir," Alistair answers. "We have cloned hundreds, as a matter of fact. But they aren't just cloned sharks; they're much more sophisticated than that. We biologically engineered them to function as drones. We have many more units stored at our main Baja facility, and we can deploy at a moment's notice."

The officers glance at each other and then back at Alistair, "… and we can clone more, sirs," Alistair adds. "As many as we need. Scale is not an issue. With our advancements in rapid growth technology and cell generation, we have the entire process down to three months from start to finish. The advantages of the Multi-Striker are truly significant."

Alistair can see that he now has the room's full attention, so he moves in closer. "First of all, because these drones are grown, rather than built, labor and materials are a fraction of the cost of conventional drone technology. This concept alone is revolutionary."

"So these things are purely biological?" one of the officers asks. "Dr. Fairchild, do they have some kind of reinforcement? I mean, how are they armored?"

"The Multi-Striker is indeed purely biological. It is not armored in a conventional sense, however, because it doesn't need to be." Alistair pauses. "And, I might add, this drone is also environmentally green... it's one hundred percent biodegradable." The comment draws light chuckles, which breaks the tension. Alistair relaxes. "What is truly ground-breaking is that the Multi-Striker is the ultimate in drone stealth. These units don't contain enough metal parts to be detectable by standard methods. They are invisible to conventional radar. They emit no sound, and there is no heat signature, which makes the Multi-Striker immune to infrared detection."

Alistair stares directly into the eyes of the men in front of him. "Sirs, we can send these drones right up the Moskva River to the Kremlin if we so desire, and nobody would ever know we were there."

"What powers it?" Admiral O'Sullivan questions. "I mean, are you using fuel? Nuclear propulsion? Batteries? How long can it operate? Is this thing alive? Did you train it?"

"No, we don't train them, sir." Alistair smiles. "No disrespect, sir, but these are sharks, not dolphins."

Another wave of brief laughter ripples through the room.

"None taken, Dr. Fairchild," the admiral replies. "Please continue."

"Once the drone is deployed, it is no longer alive. The units are not self-powered; instead, they run off of a remote centralized power source that we control. They will operate until we decide to shut them down. We preprogram each unit's onboard computer and then direct them remotely using satellite GPS tracking and navigation, just as you would a conventional drone—"

One of the officers cuts in: "It appears to me as if they have the ability to track multiple targets independently. How is this achieved?"

"That is an excellent question, sir," Alistair responds. "The Multi-Striker has an additional internal electromagnetic tracking sensor. We achieved this by taking advantage of the natural anatomy of the shark itself. Sharks are the most electromagnetically sensitive creatures known to man. They can detect prey that is actually miles away. What the shark is actually doing is tracking potential prey's life force, if you will—the electromagnetic field every living thing generates. We have enhanced this natural trait and tuned it to target the energy each living human naturally emits. Once the drones are deployed, they are impossible for the enemy to evade. The Multi-Striker won't stop until every target in the planned attack zone has been neutralized. And we can send them anywhere sir: sea, air, and land."

Admiral O'Sullivan clears his throat. "Judging by what we've just seen, and what you've just described, Dr. Fairchild, what you have created here is a Navy SEAL in the form of a drone. Is this a correct assessment?"

This is a moment that Alistair and Lieutenant Commander Parnell have discussed at great length. Alistair glances at Parnell and then back at the admiral. "Sir, at this moment, I would like to defer to my project's STILO."

"Lieutenant Commander Parnell?" the admiral inquires. "You have something to contribute?"

"Yes, sir," Parnell replies as he takes a step forward. "I will personally back up everything Dr. Fairchild has been telling you, as will the technical data inside your briefing packets. We can deploy the Multi-Striker wherever a conventional SEAL team would be deployed, sir. The drones will perform exactly as they are programmed. They are not alive in a conventional sense: they cannot think, and they have no fear and no sense of self-preservation. Once their mission is complete, we simply switch them off. The remains can be retrieved, or they can be left to decompose naturally as any dead fish carcass will."

Parnell can see by their expressions that his superiors are intrigued. "Please continue, Lieutenant Commander," the admiral orders.

Parnell glances over at Alistair and then picks up where he left off. "What Dr. Fairchild and his team are doing here, gentlemen, is presenting you with a tool that will save American lives in the field and change the face of modern asymmetrical warfare. As you know, a single special operations forces soldier costs the navy millions to train, arm, maintain, and deploy. A soldier has a family, he requires medical care, he has to overcome his own fear to be effective, and regardless of how well he performs in training, there is always the question of performance in the field: some will perform better than others."

"The alternative we are presenting is a fully armed, strategically uniform fighting force; a fully operational substitute for the special operations forces soldier at a fraction of the cost. We took out an entire training camp from the deck of a coastal patrol boat, and we did it without firing a single shot, without the need for air support, without a single missile or explosive, and the entire op went completely undetected by the enemy; they still have no idea what happened. Our post-deployment assessment is that the negative psychological effect this weapon has manifested is severe. Where the risks are too high, where the need for total secrecy is paramount, Dr. Fairchild and his team have developed the ultimate covert combat weapon."

$$\bullet \; \bullet \; \bullet$$

With the meeting concluded, the officers get to their feet and begin filing out of the room. Admiral O'Sullivan pulls Parnell aside.

"I want a tight lid on this, Lieutenant Commander. I want your personal guarantee that there will be no leaks."

"You have my guarantee, sir," Parnell answers.

"We need this thing," the admiral continues, "and I don't want any of the other branches getting so much as a whiff. The last thing we want is to have this thing go public. Look what happened to the Air Force once the Reaper was exposed: they lost control of it to the damned CIA. The ONI is the oldest intelligence organization in US history. We were here first, and with this new drone, we can gain back the upper hand. I don't want to risk losing that upper hand. Do you understand me, Lieutenant Commander?"

"Aye aye, sir," Parnell responds.

Chapter 11

Alex Moss stoops to peer inside a saltwater specimen tank mounted on a table in the ship's main lab. His natural curiosity draws him in close to observe the small, colorful creatures nestled inside. Along with the rest of the crew aboard *Fearless*, he has thoroughly enjoyed the past five weeks they've spent working in the most northern region of the Sea of Cortez. The science team has kept the crew busy, and Moss is intrigued; he wants to learn more. "So, Dr. Randal, are these the invertebrate filter feeders you were hoping you would find here?"

"Yes, Mr. Moss," Samantha replies enthusiastically as she looks through the tank's glass from the opposite side. "They aren't very exciting, I'm afraid, but they are the current focus of my research. This particular species is quite rare. Locating them took a bit more time than I had anticipated. I feel fortunate, and I have you and your crew to thank for it." She straightens and looks across the tank at Moss. "Hold on," she pauses. "You just called them *invertebrate filter feeders*, didn't you? Most laypeople would simply say *sea squirts.*"

"Dr. Randal, I've spent the past nine years working with all sorts of marine scientists," Moss replies. "I guess some of it's rubbed off. What's the story on these little guys, anyway? I mean, why are they so important?"

"Well, Mr. Moss," Samantha folds her arms in front of her, glances briefly at the tank, and then looks back at Moss, "believe it or not, we humans share seventy percent of our genome with the tunicates you see in this tank. Scientists have been studying these creatures for a long time, in fact. There was once a Russian embryologist named Alexander Kovalevsky, and in 1866, he and Charles Darwin corresponded about the morphological similarities between ascidian larvae and vertebrates." Samantha pauses. "Of course, ascidian larvae are—"

"Tadpoles," Moss answers. He smiles at Samantha. "Please continue, Dr. Randal."

She flashes a smile at Moss. "I must admit, I am impressed, sir… Anyway… um… Kovalevsky's work helped Darwin to postulate about the origin of the vertebrate phylum. And now we know Darwin was right. The creatures you see in this tank are some of the closest extant relatives of vertebrates, which makes them an excellent study subject. They're ancient, Mr. Moss. There is a massive amount of information locked inside of them, and my job is to find the keys."

At that moment, Malcolm Rafferty enters the lab. "Chief, sorry to interrupt, but can I speak to you a minute?"

Moss can see by the look on Razz's face that something is up. "I'm on my way." He turns to Samantha. "If you'll excuse me, Dr. Randal, I better get back to work."

"Absolutely, Mr. Moss. I appreciate your interest in tunicates."

Moss grins. "Well, to be honest, Dr. Randal, I just like the fact that they don't have fins and sharp teeth."

Moss leaves the ship's main lab and finds Rafferty waiting for him in the corridor. "Razz, what's happening?"

"It's probably nothing, but a couple of the guys went out on an exploratory dive this morning. They were looking for more of those sea squirts the science team is so excited about. Anyway, they went inside an undersea cave, and they found something kinda strange."

"Look," Moss sighs, "if it's some leftover cartel contraband, just tell them to leave it be. We don't need to get involved."

"They didn't find drugs, Ax. They found this cave stuffed full of dead sharks."

Moss sighs. "Well, in that case, definitely leave it be, Razz. I don't want anything to do with it."

"I feel the same as you about sharks, Ax, believe me. But after listening to the guys' descriptions, my gut tells me we should check this out. If it's okay with you, I'd like to take Murray and go have a look for myself."

Moss is getting a bad feeling, but anything involving sharks gives him a bad feeling. That said, he's learned to respect Razz's intuition. "If you feel it's important, Razz, then sure, go check it out."

The hydraulic dive deck of *Fearless* smoothly lowers to the sea with a soft purr. Murray gives Razz a thumbs-up as he steps off the edge of the platform and splashes into the water below. Rafferty follows, performing the same giant stride maneuver. Beneath the surface, the two divers immediately turn to each other. Murray flashes a quick OK to his dive buddy while Rafferty signals back that both he and his equipment are also functioning perfectly. So the two divers descend in search of the cave.

Rafferty has the coordinates of the cave programmed into the dive computer strapped to his left arm. The computer's readout tells him it is approximately one hundred meters away, but the visibility is low due to the high plankton count. He and Murray can only see clearly for about ten meters; beyond that distance, the view quickly fades into a milky blue haze.

A long, low extended moan suddenly grabs the two divers' attention. The sound sends a subtle vibration resonating through their bodies. Murray turns to Razz and forms the shape of a whale's tale with his hands. Razz nods, and by the intensity of the sound level, he reasons, the mammal is close by. Then, they hear it again, but this time, the sound is louder, and now it's clear that what they are hearing is actually coming from multiple individuals.

Razz and Murray steadily descend latterly in the direction of the cave until they reach their planned depth of twenty meters or approximately sixty feet. Then, Murray shakes his rattle, a closed metal tube filled with small ball bearings attached to his buoyancy compensator. The distinct sound alerts Rafferty. He turns to see Murray pointing up, and as Rafferty looks up toward the bright, sunlit surface, he can just make out the defused, dark outlines of two humpback whales—a mother and her calf—passing slowly overhead. The sight is mesmerizing. The whales momentarily captivate the two war veterans. The incredible sight reminds them of how lucky they both are, and how magnificent the natural world can be.

They continue on until they spot a large, muted dark outline in the side of a mountainous rock wall; they've found the cave. The opening is wide enough that the two divers can easily swim through it side by side. The cave's entrance is encrusted with soft corals and peppered with sea life. Once inside, the two men switch on their dive lights and head deeper into the overhead environment. The interior of the cave opens into a much larger space. Scanning the walls, Rafferty's light paints a colorful swath of bright orange sponges and delicate purple gorgonians. Murray searches the cave's floor, passing his light over a tumble of large boulders carpeted in growth.

They penetrate deeper into the cave and search more than thirty meters of it. Rafferty is about to give up and turn back, when, once again, he hears Murray's rattle. He looks down to see Murray's light illuminating dozens of large shark carcasses lying in a pile amongst the boulders. Both Murray and Rafferty recognize the species immediately; all tiger sharks. By the looks of it, the corpses are fairly decomposed, but there's no mistaking the dark striped pattern that still lingers across the sharks' decaying sides. Rafferty makes careful observations and then signals to Murray that it's time to return to the ship.

Moss is waiting for them when the two divers climb back onto the dive deck. He stands by quietly as Rafferty and Murray pull off their masks and their neoprene dive hoods and shed their heavy dive gear as two crewmen assist them with their tanks. Then, Rafferty looks sternly at Moss. "There's a lot of them, Ax—thirty, maybe forty—and they're all exactly the same size and type."

"Razz, please don't tell me they're tiger sharks—*anything but tiger sharks.*"

Rafferty's expression goes cold. "Sorry, Ax, but yeah, they're all tiger sharks."

Samantha is preparing to extract genetic samples from one of the specimens in the tank when Moss walks in. "I apologize for my intrusion, Dr. Randal, but something's come up, and I'd like to ask for your help."

Samantha immediately shifts her focus. She pulls her safety goggles down around her neck. "Mr. Moss, of course. What can I do for you?"

"Three of my guys were out looking for specimens this morning, and they came across a cave packed full of dead adult tiger sharks. It seemed strange, so I sent two more divers down who confirmed the find. I know this is out of your field, Dr. Randal, and I hate to ask you to divert from your work, but if you could take a look at this, I'm certain you can give us a plausible scientific explanation as to why they're there and—"

"Ease your mind, Mr. Moss?" Samantha interrupts.

Moss looks her in the eye. "Yeah… something like that."

A sudden look of concern flashes across her face. "Yes, absolutely. I'm happy to help in any way I can."

"I really appreciate this."

"I know you do, Mr. Moss." Samantha smiles sympathetically. "We'll get to the bottom of this straight away, but I'll need an intact specimen to examine, and a decomposed adult tiger shark is bit more difficult to retrieve than my tiny tunicates. Can your men manage it?"

Four hours later, Moss is improvising once again. Although the crew of *Fearless* has retrieved more large shark specimens in the past than any of them could accurately count, those were all fresh kills and much easier to handle than the delicate, decomposed corpse they are currently working to get on board in one piece. Moss is standing on the aft deck and operating the mini-sub's hydraulic lift. Meanwhile, Rafferty, Murray, and Dan are down in the water in scuba gear, attaching a large net to the sub's lifting cable. Their aim is to form a sling that will gently hoist the eight-hundred-pound carcass up from the sea and onto the deck of *Fearless*.

Extricating the five-meter-long corpse from the cave's depths was a major undertaking in itself. It took two alternate teams of divers nearly three hours of dive time just to dislodge an intact specimen from the tangled pile of carcasses and then gently remove it from the cave. Once clear of the boulder-strewn opening, getting the shark to the surface was relatively easy—just a matter of attaching lift bags and filling them with air from the diver's own tanks. But getting the massive dead fish on deck in one piece is another matter entirely.

Moss focuses on Rafferty, watching for hand signals as he slowly takes up the slack in the lift cable. Murray and Cal are positioned on opposite sides of the shark carcass. The three men are working hard to hold the net in place while they try to stabilize the specimen in the swell.

Dr. Randal and two of her lab technicians stand by and observe the retrieval spectacle with interest. They have testing equipment ready to deploy as they anxiously peer down at the divers bobbing in the rolling swell and struggling with their unruly specimen.

"All go, Razz?" Moss shouts. Rafferty glances back up at Moss as he is tossed precariously in the waves. Then, he raises his arm above the swell and twirls his index finger up in the air, signaling for Moss to begin lifting the shark out of the water. Moss engages the lift and then monitors the operation carefully as the net tightens around the corpse. Once the three divers in the water see that the shark is rising above them, they swim clear, just in case something goes wrong; nobody wants to be under this thing if it decides to come crashing back down into the sea.

Dr. Randal looks on anxiously; she can sense the danger, and in this swell, any number of things could go badly. She studies the dead shark's corpse as it is slowly lifted from the sea. It is a significant specimen—enormous, actually—and it is fully intact. She knows Moss wouldn't be taking this risk if it wasn't important. She is already formulating the battery of tests she wants to perform, but first they've got to get this thing safely onboard.

Chapter 12

Bayani steadies himself atop a shipping container positioned forty feet up from the deck of the *Cell Star*. The seven-hundred-foot-long cargo ship is carrying nearly one thousand five hundred containers, and she's been his home for the past forty-three days. It's almost eleven in the morning, and the Pacific Ocean is glassy smooth. Bayani searches the horizon; there's still no land in sight, but the isthmus of Central America is now so close he can smell it.

Bayani gazes across the container's already sizzling roof at Falcon. He, too, stands balanced on top of the heavy steel box—one of hundreds that form a vast, multicolored patchwork that surrounds the two men.

"OK, Dr. Falcon, are you ready? I won't be taking it easy on you this time," Bayani announces cheerfully. "You may be my elder, but in this situation, you are now my opponent. I wouldn't want there to be any bad feelings between us."

Falcon takes on a defensive pose and smiles broadly back at Bayani. "No bad feelings at all, my young friend. You didn't defeat me last time, and now I know how you fight, so this time, I am even more prepared."

The sentence has hardly left Falcon's mouth when he is suddenly hit hard from behind. Falcon coughs uncontrollably and staggers as he tries to regain his footing. He saw Bayani move, but his defensive tactic wasn't nearly quick enough. *The kid is good...*

Falcon recovers and counters Bayani's next attack by rapidly shifting laterally. He then smoothly dodges a third strike from Bayani, changes his angle again, and then moves out of Bayani's range of attack before the teenager has another chance to strike.

Falcon steps back, grins with satisfaction, and then swiftly deflects Bayani's attacking hand with his right arm. Falcon's sharp-angled movements evade Bayani's attempts to hit back, but then the teenager nimbly drops down, avoids a strike from Falcon, and moves in to hit Falcon once more across his back.

On the bridge, the ship's captain, himself a student of Filipino martial arts, has his binoculars out and watches intently as the two men fight. "Well, there they go again," he mutters to his first officer.

"Do you want me to break it up?" the first officer responds anxiously.

"Let them have their fun," the captain chuckles. "They are practicing *kali*, and they're both pretty good by the looks of it. Neither one of them has a knife in his hand. They are only using empty-hand technique. Besides, we arrive in the Canal Zone tonight. I expect we will be seeing the last of them soon. It's a shame, though; they have both been good deck workers."

* * *

Minding the stow is a never-ending job aboard a container ship at sea. It's hard work that Falcon has discovered he takes particular pleasure in. During the passage, his first watch typically began at midnight and ran until 0600. Falcon's second watch started at midday and continued until 1800. Sometimes, he shared his watch with Bayani, but mostly he was paired with more experienced crew—tough, able seamen, or *ABs*, as they are known, and all of them men he would come to respect.

The hundreds of containers stacked in tight rows need constant maintenance. Each one is held in place by a complex system of interlocking galvanized steel lashing rods and twist locks that are attached to the ship's own fittings. All of it must be constantly monitored and adjusted as conditions change. As the huge commercial ship navigates over the waves, she, too, is constantly moving, bending, and twisting with six degrees of motion: surge, sway, heave, roll, pitch, and yaw. As the hull of the ship moves, so does her stow, and the only thing holding it all in place are the lashings.

. . .

Falcon is still smiling as he gets to his feet and attempts to recover from Bayani's latest attack. Even though his forty-seven-year-old body is currently in pain, he hasn't been this physically fit in years.

"Have you had enough yet, Dr. Falcon?" Bayani taunts.

Falcon answers with a fast angled leap and then doubles back to knock Bayani's knees out from under him. Bayani lands flat on his back. The nineteen-year-old lets out a brief groan but is instantly back on his feet and coming at Falcon again when he suddenly stops in his tracks.

Falcon is about to strike when he realizes Bayani is no longer in the fight. "What's wrong?" Falcon asks, "Are you okay?"

"Nothing is wrong, Dr. Falcon," Bayani answers excitedly. "Look!"

Falcon turns toward the bow of the ship and catches his first glimpse of land in more than a month. They are merely small, pale specs—distant rocky islands shrouded in thick haze. The coast of Panama is still some seventy miles away, but the sight still thrills him. "Those must be the Pearl Islands," Falcon observes. "We're nearly there."

"Nearly there," Bayani answers, "and you are nearly defeated!" He lunges again and knocks Falcon to the ground.

Falcon lies across the container's hot, hard surface and coughs uncontrollably. His spine painfully protests the abuse as he breathes heavily and looks up at the nimble teenager standing over him.

"*Kali* is all about taking advantage of opportunity," Bayani instructs as he reaches for Falcon's hand and then helps him back to his feet.

Falcon grimaces. "I did leave the door open, didn't I? So I guess this makes us even… for now."

At that moment, the two men pick up the unmistakable sound of a helicopter. Falcon pauses to listen and then spins around and searches the sky for the aircraft until he sees it. He studies the chopper's flight path for a few moments and then smiles broadly as he rests his arm across Bayani's shoulders. "You see that?" The helicopter is still over a half mile away, but closing fast, and on a direct course for the container ship.

"It's a helicopter," Bayani answers. "What is it doing so far from shore?"

"That, my young friend," Falcon answers quizzically, "that apparently is our ride." Falcon pats Bayani on the back. "I'm certainly ready to get off this ship. How about you?"

"Are you serious?" Bayani suspects the fall may have had more of an effect on Falcon than he's letting on. "How can that helicopter be coming for us?" he questions. "Nobody even knows we left the Philippines. How can they possibly know we would be out here?"

"Believe me, my young friend... they know," Falcon answers coldly. "We need to clear a landing spot. We have to be ready. We won't get a second chance."

"But my passport," Bayani answers nervously. "My passport is in the safe with the rest of the crew's identification. I shouldn't leave it behind."

"You won't have to." Falcon pats one of the cargo pockets of his faded shorts. "I have it right here."

Bayani is shocked. "How did you get that?"

"Actually, I had some help... The captain of this ship is a piece of the puzzle. That part was quite fortuitous; he had some gambling debts he needed to clear up."

"Dr. Falcon, I don't understand. What is going on?"

Falcon flashes a sympathetic eye at Bayani, "I apologize for keeping you in the dark, Bayani, but it was for your own safety. Once your uncle so kindly arranged our passage out of the Philippines, there were certain people I had to inform. I made a commitment, you see, which included a promise that if I ever left the islands, I would let them know of my plans beforehand. This little arrangement has been in the works since before we left, but it's not for free. I have something the people who sent that helicopter want... something extremely valuable."

As the rhythmic beats of the helicopter grow louder, Bayani grins. "I am impressed, Dr. Falcon. You must be an important man."

"I have some important friends, Bayani, but I certainly wasn't expecting this. Frankly, I thought they would be sending out some old fishing boat."

Falcon and Bayani ready themselves for the helicopter's arrival while the ship's captain is still observing their activities through his binoculars from the bridge. His first officer watches silently as the chopper approaches. "So this is what you were talking about? Who are these guys?"

"It is best not to ask too many questions, my friend," the captain answers as he adjusts the focus of the binoculars. "This will be a good day for both of us. Let's just leave it at that."

The gleaming white Airbus AS365's arrival forces a rush of prop wash across the tops of the shipping containers as it descends. The powerful gust hammers into Falcon and Bayani as they crouch nearby, ready to climb on board as soon as the sleek, bullet-shaped corporate helicopter touches down. Falcon shields his eyes as he watches the chopper land. He knows they must be quick.

"Now!" Falcon shouts, "let's go!" The two men run toward the helicopter as its passenger door slides open. Falcon pushes Bayani inside first and is climbing inside himself when he feels the chopper lift off. He grasps a seatbelt and briefly looks back just as someone roughly yanks him further inside the passenger cabin. Falcon catches a brief glimpse of the container ship rapidly disappearing beneath him, before he is shoved out of the way as someone quickly slides the door shut.

The two men say nothing as Falcon straightens himself, buckles in, and then sees to it that Bayani does the same. They each feel the helicopter quickly gaining altitude as a well-built, smartly dressed Latino man with dark hair, mirrored aviator sunglasses, and a neatly trimmed moustache takes his seat across from them.

Falcon studies his surroundings. The sudden and dramatic change in environment has left him dazed. He silently takes in the pleasures of the passenger compartment's air-conditioning, fine leather, plush carpeting and the elegantly polished details of the aircraft's luxuriously appointed interior. He glances over at Bayani, who also seems to be genuinely fascinated. The stern-faced man sitting across from them must be security, Falcon surmises. *He's muscle... an order taker... nothing more...*

The faint green outline of the Central American Pacific coast is just visible out of the helicopter's starboard-side windows, which tells Falcon they are flying north. It is also clear that they are not, as yet, flying toward land.

Falcon wasn't given any details back in Manila; there wasn't time. Plans were organized hastily. His friend Chia's instructions were sparse but precise: take the job on the freighter, work hard, blend in with the crew, and once you reach Panama, you will be picked up along with *the package*.

The helicopter's occupants fly on for nearly two hours in total silence. Then, Falcon feels the chopper begin its descent. He can see that the two pilots seem to be speaking over their radio headsets. He can't hear them very well over the engine noise, but they are definitely speaking in Spanish. Then, he feels Bayani grab his arm. Falcon can see that he's excited about something, but from his vantage point, Falcon is unable to see what it is.

The helicopter makes a sharp banking turn as it continues to descend rapidly. Falcon knows they must be about to land somewhere, but they are still over open ocean; there's not a speck of land in sight. The helicopter gracefully spirals downward. Then, Falcon finally spots what Bayani was so excited about. She is incredible and enormous. Falcon gazes with wonder at the magnificent mega-yacht gliding gracefully over the sea beneath them.

The ocean-going motor yacht is pure white, and by Falcon's estimate, she must be close to three hundred feet long—a sparkling, floating palace. The chopper lands effortlessly on the yacht's forward helipad. The man in the mirrored sunglasses leans over, slides open the door, steps out, and then stands off to one side.

Bayani and Falcon climb out of the helicopter and stand on the yacht's helipad. Both men are instantly captivated by the strikingly beautiful blond standing in front of them. She is flanked by uniformed staff and is wearing a tight-fitting Hawaiian print dress as she smiles sweetly.

"Dr. Falcon, it is a pleasure to meet you. My name is Kimberly. Welcome aboard *Mysterious.*" The stunning woman steps toward Falcon and extends her hand in a businesslike fashion.

Falcon returns the gesture. "It is a pleasure, madam. And may I present my associate Bayani," Falcon adds as he gently releases the woman's perfectly manicured hand.

"I am certain you two gentlemen must be tired after your long journey," the lovely Kimberly continues. "May I offer you a refreshment?"

At that moment, a young woman approaches Falcon and Bayani. She is holding an elegant silver tray containing two beautifully prepared exotic fruit drinks along with a pair of scented, chilled hand towels.

Falcon glances at the tray; the beverages are amazingly inviting, but instinctively, he knows he must first produce *the package*. Falcon smiles at Kimberly. He then bends down slowly and carefully unzips one of the cargo pockets of his tattered shorts. He watches her expression as he pulls out a slim, wallet-sized aluminum case. Her eyes brighten when she sees it. Falcon places the case on the tray and picks up one of the towels. He wipes his face and hands, places the towel back on the tray, and then takes one of the drinks. Bayani, observes carefully and then does the same.

"Thank you, Dr. Falcon," Kimberly continues. She then signals to another young woman who is standing nearby. "Maria will show you to your cabins. You both will want to freshen up and rest. We will be serving drinks on the aft deck at six and dinner at seven. We will be delighted to have you join us."

Fifteen minutes later, Falcon is standing under a rain forest showerhead as the water gushes over his body. He ponders once again the joys of simple pleasures, such as the ability to take a long, hot shower. The marble bathroom is fully stocked with an array of French soaps and shampoos. Falcon takes full advantage and leaves the bath smelling of lavender.

He wraps a thick Egyptian cotton towel around his waist and walks out into his Italian-designed suite. His toes sink into the carpet as he ponders the sumptuous king-sized bed. He is exhausted, but then he suddenly realizes that he has nothing to wear to dinner. On a hunch, Falcon walks over to the closet, slides open the inlaid exotic wood door, and finds a selection of shirts, trousers, and a dark blue dinner jacket. "Extraordinary..." Falcon then turns back toward the beautiful bed, which is now calling to him like a naked tart, and climbs in.

Three hours later, Falcon wakes from his nap. He blinks as he stares up at his reflection in the mirrored ceiling... *It's not a dream... incredible...* He looks over at a clock on the night stand; it's five-thirty. "Hmm... wouldn't want to miss cocktail hour."

Falcon attempts to straighten the collar of his white linen shirt as he walks down the narrow passageway leading from his cabin. The walls are finished in a mix of elaborately crafted wood marquetry and exotic leather paneling. Falcon takes note of the artwork, which is decidedly of an erotic nature. It reminds him of something an old university colleague, a professor of sociology, once said—that whenever he entered a stranger's home, he could discern nearly everything important about them by examining the books on their shelves and the art on their walls.

"Señor Falcon? Un momento, por favor…"

Falcon looks up to see Maria's wide smile as she walks briskly toward him. She balances a hand-woven basket of leather flip-flops off of one hip. Falcon chuckles to himself… the irony—*the lunacy*—of the circumstances that have delivered him to this moment. *The old shaman was right again…*

Maria quickly sets the basket down in front of Falcon. She kneels on the carpeted floor and examines his bare feet. "Ah, diez…" she utters softly. She turns to rummage through the basket for a pair of sandals that match Falcon's size. She then gently slides one of the handmade leather shoes onto each of Falcon's feet and examines the fit. "Bien."

Maria quickly stands and begins fastidiously adjusting Falcon's dinner jacket and shirt. She smiles pleasantly as she straightens his shirt collar and cuffs. Then, she spies the nearly empty right side sleeve of his jacket. "Mm… no no…" Maria reaches into her pocket and pulls out a safety pin. She holds the pin in her teeth as she neatly folds back the empty end of the sleeve and then gently pins it in place. "Ah, sí." She looks up at Falcon, her sweet smile still perfectly in place. "Señor Falcon, I show you to the lounge?"

The expansive aft lounge area of *Mysterious* is decorated in a photo-shoot ready array of modern outdoor furnishings arranged across what seems like a football field's worth of pristine teak decking. Falcon surmises that there must be enough seating to easily accommodate dozens of guests, but he finds only Bayani standing at the sleek, elegant glass bar.

"I certainly approve of your attire," Falcon chuckles as he sees Bayani is dressed exactly the same as he is.

Bayani glances down at what he is wearing, grins, then he looks back at Falcon. "You are truly an amazing man, Dr. Falcon. It is an honor to call you my friend."

"May I offer you a drink, sir?"

Falcon turns toward the pleasantly smiling bartender. "I will have what my young friend here is having please."

"Yes, sir. San Miguel it is then."

Falcon takes his beer and turns back to Bayani. "Cheers, my friend."

"Ah, the famous Dr. Thomas Falcon!"

The bellowing voice catches both men off guard. Falcon and Bayani spin around as a heavy-set man with thick, flowing silver hair and a salty, scrabbled beard strides toward them from the yacht's elevator.

He is dressed head to toe in white linen and is flanked by three beautiful women, one of whom is Kimberly. Falcon notes that the knockout blond has changed her dress to willowy white silk.

The man smiles warmly as he approaches Falcon. "I am Marco... just Marco, nothing more. It is indeed a pleasure to make your acquaintance, sir." He gregariously shakes Falcon's hand. "And this must be your sidekick, Bayani! It's a pleasure, young man." Marco grabs Bayani's hand and shakes it enthusiastically. "I have heard interesting things about you as well." Marco then quickly turns to the women standing around him. "Of course, you have already met my darling Kimberly, and joining us this evening will be Cynthia and Shelly." Marco then gestures toward a set of muted gray sofas accented with bright turquoise pillows. "Let us sit, gentlemen. There is much to discuss."

As Marco takes his seat, Kimberly joins him while the other two women sit on either side of Falcon and Bayani. The bartender arrives bearing an ice bucket with a bottle of champagne rising from its center. Marco grins happily when he sees the ice bucket, then he turns toward Falcon and Bayani. "I see you are each enjoying my favorite beer. But for this occasion, I insist we have champagne." He turns and lifts the chilled bottle from its ice bath and examines the label. "Ah, Dom Perignon 1988—an ideal choice, Francis."

"Thank you, sir." Francis then smoothly spins back toward the bar and signals to a waiting steward, the man promptly arrives carrying a tray of crystal champagne flutes. The barman then deftly opens the bottle and pours a sample for Marco, who simply takes a quick whiff of the wine's fragrance. "Yes, it's perfect as usual, Francis." The man nods briefly and then proceeds to pour a round of glasses.

Meanwhile, Falcon is mesmerized by the spectacle—the unrestrained flamboyance of this man. The steward politely takes the beers from Falcon and Bayani, places them on his tray, and hands them each a glass of champagne.

Marco then holds up his glass. "To our shared success, my friends."

The subtle symphony of citrus, floral, and slightly nutty effervescence passes over Falcon's lips. He finds himself transfixed by the decadent pleasure of the moment—a moment he wishes he could lock inside a box and revisit again and again. As Falcon sips lightly from the slender crystal flute, Marco begins to speak to him directly.

"You fascinate me, sir." The man's grayish-green eyes radiate with intensity. "I am very interested in your story... your life. You must tell us about your adventure with the killer sharks. I want to know every detail."

Falcon pauses awkwardly. He is stunned that this man would know anything about him at all, much less what happened to him five years ago. "I'm not sure what to tell you, sir," Falcon stammers. "To be honest, I haven't spoken about it much. It's a difficult subject."

"Yes, I know!" Marco lets loose with a boisterous laugh, but then he catches himself. "Please, Dr. Falcon, forgive me. I am being insensitive, but as you yourself have often said, *levity is a powerful stress reducer...* At that moment, Marco fixes his gaze directly on Falcon as if he has the power to see straight through him, which Falcon now realizes he does.

"Let me first tell you about myself. I am in the information technology business, Dr. Falcon, and it is far more valuable than you realize. Multinational corporations, major governments, they will do almost anything and pay almost any amount to get their hands on certain types of knowledge, as well as to keep it, of course. I provide this information, I manage it, and I decide where it goes and to whom it goes. It is my job to know everything, and I take great pride in my job, sir."

Falcon puts his glass down and clears his throat. "Well, in that case, by all means, ask away, sir. I will gladly tell you anything you want to know. But, first, you must tell me something."

Marco breaks out in laughter again, yet his eyes never once leave Falcon. "I do like you, Dr. Falcon. I like you very much. Perhaps you should come work for me? I know your question before you even ask it, so I will go ahead and answer it. The encrypted security case you gave to my dear Kimberly contained computer chips."

Falcon finds this puzzling. "I don't understand the value of a few computer chips."

Marco briefly tips his head to one side and rolls his eyes. "Of course the world is full of them, my friend, much like the sand they are often made from. However, we are not speaking of ordinary chips, Dr. Falcon." Marco then turns to Kimberly, "I love this part!" at which point Kimberly flashes a sultry smile back at Marco as she squeezes his knee.

Marco's sizzling green eyes return to Falcon. "While you and young Bayani have been safely hidden away at sea, half the planet has been searching for what you had stuffed in your pocket, my friend. Getting them successfully out of Asia was a hat trick of grand proportion, and Chia is a genius to have used you to bring them to me. You missed your calling, Dr. Falcon. You should have worked for MI6."

Bayani's face goes pale. He shifts nervously in his seat and then looks at Falcon, who reaches for his glass and gulps down half of it.

Marco chuckles. "Of course, the best part of all is that they are worth hundreds of millions in the right hands, Dr. Falcon. And mine, I assure you, are those hands. You don't believe me? The world's most powerful Western government once stole an entire Malaysian airliner full of passengers right out of the sky because they thought some of their critically sensitive radar-avoiding computer chips were about to fall into the hands of the Chinese. What you were carrying is even more important, Dr. Falcon. You've just helped to pull off the heist of the decade. So please, now that I have the legendary one-handed shark doctor on board my yacht, you must tell me your incredible story."

Chapter 13

Alistair steadies himself as he navigates the passenger stairway leading down to the tarmac of Van Nuys airport. His body is exhausted, he is a dozen time zones out of synch, he hasn't slept in nearly eighteen hours, and he's strung out on Red Bull, but mentally, he feels oddly energized. He turns to look at Parnell, who is gingerly navigating the steps behind him.

"You look like shit," Alistair says with a grin.

"If I look half as bad as I feel, then it must be buzzard shit."

The remainder of Alistair's team exits the aircraft, their faces equally pallid. The men collect their luggage from the crew of the Gulfstream 650ER and then climb into three waiting black SUVs parked nearby. Parnell will be heading home to his family, while Alistair and his team still have work to do.

It's nine in the morning, and the Los Angeles sky is painted in a pasty yellow haze as the sun's rays stretch out over the city. It's Sunday, so traffic is reasonably light on the 405 as the two matching SUVs carrying Alistair and his team head south toward Long Beach. The catering onboard the flight from Teterboro,

New Jersey, was uncharacteristically sparse, so after a brief exchange by phone between the two vehicles, the drivers make a quick detour off the 405 onto Venice Boulevard.

With their brief stop complete, Alistair and his technicians all greedily tear into steaming-hot breakfast club sandwiches from Sunny Grill as the SUV glides smoothly down the freeway toward the headquarters of the Fearless Research Foundation.

After three hours spent downloading, cataloging, and backing up the scientific data from their latest mission in Yemen onto the foundation's secure servers, what the ONI had labeled *Operation Gamefish* is now history. The latest data is invaluable, and will be referenced again and again as Alistair continues to refine the capabilities of his Multi-Striker biological combat assault drone. During the flight home, Parnell told him that the ONI has been so impressed with their successes in Libya, Indonesia, and now Yemen that they would most likely be giving his drones another mission soon, so he needed to be ready.

Alistair fishes out another Red Bull from the refrigerator in his office. He desperately wants to go home and sleep, but the servers are still running through the final backup cycle. He won't leave until he is certain the data is secure. He stands in front of the windows of his office and looks out toward the Pacific. He misses being at sea; he misses his time aboard *Fearless*.

His desk phone begins beeping methodically. Alistair walks over, lifts the receiver, and hears the polished voice of Marcus Waverley, the foundation's director. After a brief exchange, Alistair hurriedly hangs up the phone, quickly pulls a small mirror from his desk, checks his teeth and hair, and then grabs a mint from a tin and is rapidly chewing when Marcus walks in.

"Alistair, how are you feeling?" The shortish, blond-haired man wears a fixed grin on his golf course tanned face. He is dressed in a pink Izod polo, beige trousers, and Gucci loafers. He walks briskly toward Alistair. "That was quite a trip, and honestly?" He looks Alistair over. "You look like crap. But when I heard you were back, I had to come into the office and congratulate you personally." Marcus shakes Alistair's hand while he pats him on the shoulder with the other.

"Thank you, Mr. Waverley."

"Alistair," the blond-haired man says reassuringly, "in the past six weeks, we've deployed the Multi-Striker successfully inside three combat zones. You've proven yourself. Enough with the *Mr. Waverley* shit. You've just made us the most profitable nonprofit in the country. Call me Marcus."

"Yes, sir… um, Marcus. "

"OK! Great!" Marcus slaps Alistair on the back. "Let's get down to business. I know you need to go home and get some rest, but I wanted to let you know we have another mission in development."

"Oh right. Lieutenant Commander Parnell said there would be another mission soon, sir. We're ready to deploy. Just give the word."

"That's fantastic news, but this mission won't be carried out under the ONI's direction. The boys on the seventh floor at Langley will be taking the lead on this one. This next mission will be run by Special Activities Division."

Alistair is stunned. He's been working closely with the ONI for nearly a year. He had always thought his combat drone had been developed specifically for use by the US navy. "Uh… you mean the CIA will be running this mission? What about the navy?"

Marcus squints at Alistair with bemusement. "You're a good egg, Alistair. Of course the navy will be involved. The CIA will be needing a ship, of course. That's the navy's job, right?"

Six days later, Alistair finds himself once again inside the darkened CIC of yet another cyclone-class vessel.

It is one o'clock in the morning aboard the *USS Chubasco*. This particular coastal patrol boat is attached to the US navy's fourth fleet. She was deployed out of Mayport, Florida and had been on scheduled patrol in the southern Caribbean until US Naval Southern Command unexpectedly ordered her to sail immediately for the navy's installation on the island of Aruba and await further orders from USSOUTHCOM.

Alistair and his seasoned team have grown familiar with the procedures and protocols inside an active combat information center. He calmly directs from within the CIC as his technicians on the ship's aft deck prepare twenty fresh Multi-Striker drones for deployment. The one element that is missing from this mission is the project's former STILO, Lieutenant Commander Parnell. Alistair was dismayed when Parnell was reassigned, but other than his absence, everything feels normal as the mission proceeds on schedule.

Alistair's brow creases as he looks up from his tablet computer to see three senior CIA intelligence officers heading his way... *More questions no doubt...*

"Dr. Fairchild?" one of the men begins. "Are we ready to deploy? We are on a tight schedule here."

"Yes, sir. I understand," Alistair answers flatly. "My team is currently communicating directly with our drone operations center in Long Beach. Once we have confirmation of the satellite link, we will initiate guidance, lock in GPS tracking targeting systems, and deploy. I estimate three minutes before we have all systems online."

. . .

His name is Juan Carlos Azarola, and he is a legend inside the darkest recesses of the CIA. Code named *Lachesis,* the infamous Colombian drug lord has been on and off the CIA's payroll since the Reagan administration.

Azarola was recruited by the CIA in 1982 at age twenty-four and went on to graduate from the notorious *School of the Americas* at Fort Benning, Georgia. The anti-communist, counterinsurgency training center's reputation eventually became so well-known, and despised, that it was eventually rebranded as the *Western Hemisphere Institute for Security Cooperation.* However, globally, it's still known by its colloquial moniker: *the School of Dictators and Assassins.*

For the past forty years, Juan Carlos Azarola has functioned reliably as an informant, successfully carried out covert assassinations, aided the Colombian government in its efforts to battle FARC, and, most notably, facilitated the CIA in funding the agency's more distasteful extrajudicial black ops through highly profitable cocaine shipments into the US.

But as senior CIA Special Activities Division intelligence officer, Jeff Buxton watches Alistair type in the final commands and bring what his superiors are now calling their new *kill team* on line. He nervously ponders the level of blowback that will no doubt occur from the power vacuum created after Lachesis's permanent *retirement.*

They hadn't planned to use drones. What Buxton and his operatives working inside Colombia had meticulously organized was a clean kill—a targeted assassination of Lachesis himself. The plan was classic, old-school CIA black ops; Lachesis was to die in a plane crash.

His private Hawker jet would go down over the eastern Caribbean Sea due to mechanical failure during a routine flight from Cartagena to Cancun, Mexico, but at the last minute, Juan Carlos canceled. He then had his mechanics tear the plane apart. They discovered the carefully hidden sabotage that would have brought the plane down, and that's when he went dark.

He's been off the grid for nearly a year... until tonight. The option to use a Reaper drone armed with hell-fire missiles was quickly dismissed as being too messy, too expensive, and too obvious as to who took down the drug lord. What Buxton's superiors are demanding is the sort of kill that will appear completely disconnected from Washington. Buxton knows that they have only one chance to take Lachesis out; *the Multi-Striker drones have to work.*

Alistair stands on the aft deck of the *USS Chubasco* and supervises his team of technicians as the first ten Multi-Striker drones are run through their final checks. These will be the most challenging conditions his drones have ever been deployed under. The ship is currently positioned a mere three nautical miles off the Colombian coast, but their target is more than two hundred kilometers inland.

The route to the target is lengthy but well within his drones' capabilities. Once deployed, they will head straight for the Magdalena River delta on the Colombian coast near the town of Barranquilla. The river is currently swollen due to recent rains, so the biologically engineered tiger sharks will have excellent cover as they swim upstream through a densely populated region to the target zone located near the mountain village of Tenerife.

Satellite surveillance has revealed that Lachesis's heavily forti-fied compound is currently being guarded by his private army of armed mercenaries. This fact alone is the reason Alistair wants this mission, more than any other he has undertaken so far, to be suc-cessful. To send in a human SEAL team to do the job would likely result in multiple casualties; his drones will spare their lives.

Buxton observes curiously as ten solidly frozen, eight-hun-dred-pound tiger sharks are suddenly activated. Despite being fully briefed on the technology and reading Dr. Fairchild's per-sonal file, Buxton is thoroughly impressed as he watches this ge-nius kid Fairchild punch up a few swift commands on his tablet computer and then casually deploy his designer pack of killer drones.

After the first ten sharks silently disappear into the warm Car-ibbean Sea, the second group is rapidly brought into position. The plan is to hit the compound with two separate teams spaced just minutes apart. The first team will initiate an incursion on the com-pound's most heavily fortified north side, while the second will hit them from the weaker south.

The strategy is to draw the mercenaries' fire away from the compound's weakest point and leave the back door wide open for the second team. Once the drones breach the compound's outer perimeter, there will be no stopping them until the gruesome job is done.

Alistair's technicians scramble to ready the second team of Multi-Striker drones. Ten minutes later, Buxton looks on with a sneer of satisfaction as the second team deploys exactly as planned.

. . .

Jeronimo Jesus Fuentes glances at his watch, it is 0330, and It's been another quiet night. Once more, he is relieved. It has been a stressful week. His employer celebrated his sixty-second birthday three days ago, and the family is still here: his wife, three adult children, their spouses, and nine grandchildren. Tomorrow, they will all leave, and in his opinion, the sooner the better.

Fuentes scans the bank of digital displays spread out in front of him once more as multiple forward-looking infrared (FLIR) ground surveillance radar feeds show no activity. As a seasoned veteran of the Colombian Special Forces, and after ten years as Juan Carlos's chief of security, Fuentes has found that boredom is a rare comfort. He had advised strongly against the family spending the week at the compound. He had pleaded in fact, but thankfully, his fears appear to have been unjustified.

Fuentes takes a sip of coffee just as something on one of the radar screens suddenly catches his attention—a rapid movement that flashed briefly. The shape gave off no heat signature; it was dark... *like a shadow.* Fuentes focuses closely on the displays and searches each of them for anything further but sees nothing. He sighs just as an electronic alarm begins beeping on his security control panel. The alarm was triggered by an old-school motion detector located just beyond the compound's northern perimeter.

Without hesitation, Fuentes instantly grabs a handheld radio and alerts his security team outside, and then hurriedly calls his second in command inside the house.

"I know what time it is!" Fuentes scoffs angrily in Spanish. "Wake up everyone. I want the family moved into the bunker now!"

Only moments after giving the order to evacuate the family to the compound's custom-built, underground bunker, Fuentes hears multiple bursts of automatic weapons fire erupt outside. He spins toward the gun rack behind him and grabs a Kevlar armored vest, an Israeli-made Tavor TAR-21 .45 caliber assault rifle, a 9mm pistol, and an ammo belt stuffed with thirty-round clips. Fuentes then bolts from his security office near the swimming pool and sprints for the main house.

• • •

Buxton finds himself riveted to the live camera feed streaming across the laptop screens in front of him. He and his two CIA colleagues watch the attack unfold in total silence. They've never seen anything even remotely similar these drones in their collectively lengthy careers, and if the MS41-T can perform at this level throughout the entire op, they'll be sold; *and grateful.*

In between glances at the telemetry feed displayed on his tablet computer, Alistair gazes down at the three open laptops with cold indifference as the first ten drones quickly overwhelm the perimeter guards, brutally kill every last man, and advance relentlessly toward the outer wall of the compound itself.

Buxton follows the action closely. He can't believe what he is seeing. He briefly glances over at Alistair. "When will the second team hit the compound?"

"They are just coming out from the river now, sir," Alistair replies without looking up from his tablet. "In two minutes, they reach the pool area, then they will be inside the house."

• • •

Fuentes bursts into the now fully lit main house through a set of French doors that lead from the patio that surrounds the pool. His senses are immediately overwhelmed by the chaotic panic fully combusting inside the house. The now constant, rapid trill of automatic weapons fire coming from outside adds to the turmoil of anguished screaming mothers with crying babies in their arms. Guards rush the family toward the downstairs bunker as Fuentes searches the crowd of terrified family members for Juan Carlos, and then, he sees him.

"Comandante!" he shouts. "You must go into the bunker with your family! Now! Please!"

Juan Carlos is still in his pajamas, but he's already wearing a Kevlar vest, and he has another TAR-21 slung over his shoulder and a 9mm pistol in his right hand.

"It is a commando assault," he announces confidently. "I am certain it is the Americans. Your men are positioned on the roof with artillery? Why do I not hear the fifty-caliber guns?"

The explosive crash of glass, door frames, and smashing furniture sends the two men spinning as they see three massive sharks rapidly coming for them. The absolute disbelief, the complete impossibility of what they are now looking at, costs them the precious few seconds they have to react. Juan Carlos begins firing his pistol at one of the huge tiger sharks while Fuentes opens up with his TAR-21. The bullets have no effect. Three more guards join the fight as they unload full bore and the room's stucco walls vibrate percussively with deafening machine gun fire. But the drones are unfazed; they just keep coming.

. . .

"Whoo-yaah! Yeah!" Whistling applause spontaneously breaks out inside the CIC as Buxton turns and high-fives his two colleagues after the three CIA officers suddenly recognize Juan Carlos himself on the video feed.

"Fuck yeah!" one of the agents shouts as he smacks Alistair across the back, but the young scientist doesn't react. Instead, he continues to silently focus his attention on the operation's mechanics and his mission.

• • •

Juan Carlos desperately pumps bullets into the massive shark that is trying to kill him. He fires his pistol directly into the viciously snapping jaws that are advancing rapidly toward him like a giant buzz saw. He drops the empty 9mm and switches to his TAR-21, but as the .45 caliber rounds rip into the shark's flesh, they do nothing to slow it down as the man's total disbelief quickly gives way to pure terror.

Fuentes knows that their only chance is to get to the bunker. He reaches out with his left hand, grabs the back of the Kevlar vest Juan Carlos is wearing, and yanks him away from the giant shark's snapping jaws, while he fires his own TAR-21 with his right. Fuentes shoves Juan Carlos behind him and extends his right arm out to fire at his target point blank. His trigger finger is locked on, discharging the weapon in a continuous flurry of bullets when the gaping jaws of an eight-hundred-pound tiger shark suddenly close around the gun and his right arm.

Fuentes lets go of Juan Carlos as he's thrown to the floor. His right arm is now trapped along with his weapon inside the shark's gnashing jaws. But his right hand still firmly grips the assault weapon's trigger. Fuentes continues to fire off rounds from the TAR-21. The muffled discharge pounds deep inside the shark's reanimated corps.

The tiger shark's teeth are rapidly slicing into the man's forearm, which is only partially shielded by the assault rifle he still holds. Fuentes cries out in agony as he fires off the last few rounds, when suddenly, the killer shark stops moving. A single bullet discharged from his assault rifle has managed to strike and destroy the drone's five-centimeter-long internal control module. With its connection to the energy field now severed, the lifeless shark suddenly falls limp on the tile floor.

Fuentes pushes the dead shark's jaws apart and pulls his mangled and badly bleeding arm free when the blood-soaked screams of his employer fill the room. He looks on in horror as Juan Carlos is torn to shreds in front of him by the other two sharks. Two remaining guards frantically fire their weapons in vain as the sharks go for them next.

Fuentes gets to his feet. His first thought is to try to save his men, but he can't get near them; the sharks are already on them and tearing them apart. Fuentes runs past the gruesome scene and heads for the stairs leading to the basement bunker. The guards downstairs are still pushing family members through the bunker's narrow, reinforced concrete and steel door when Fuentes reaches them.

"Get them in now!" he bellows. "There is no time! Hurt them if you have to, but get them inside now!"

The children are crying loudly as their parents shout and demand explanations that will never come. Fuentes roughly pushes and shoves the adults and children through the door as they yell angrily for him to stop. He ignores their protests and keeps shoving until he and his guards manage to get them all inside.

Fuentes then turns back to help his men as they rush to pull the thickly reinforced, concrete door shut just as the nose of a massive shark forces its way through the opening. The small concrete bunker's thick walls echo with shrill screams as the family inside see their attacker for the first time. Women and children shriek uncontrollably at the sight of the vicious monster trying to get through the door to kill them. In a desperate move, Fuentes pulls out his 9mm pistol as the snapping jaws of the massive shark flash in front of him. In a bold attempt to save the family he has loyally served for over a decade, Jeronimo Jesus Fuentes lunges forward and shoves what's left of his right arm down the shark's throat while he rapidly fires off 9mm rounds.

The shark's jaws immediately snap shut. The veteran soldier cries out in agony as hundreds of knife-edged teeth slice deep into his already badly wounded arm, but he keeps firing off rounds until he can no longer feel his hand on the gun. The two terrified guards fighting desperately to pull the bunker door shut look on in horror as their commander drops to the floor while the shredded stump that was his right arm sprays blood across the room.

Now covered in his own blood, Fuentes screams for his men to close the door. They turn back to the shark that is still forcing its way through the opening. Each man has both hands on the door's handle while the genetically engineered tiger shark's powerful jaws snap just inches from their faces. Kicking and scraping, they nearly have the door shut when two more sharks appear, and then another. The two men cry out desperately as the family trapped inside the bunker claw at the walls to get out and the mindless killer drones force their way inside.

Chapter 14

Dr. Samantha Randal's gloved hands firmly grip a pair of forceps, yet her face shows no expression as she carefully lowers a framework containing six slender cryovials into a stainless steel cylinder filled with liquid nitrogen. The tissue samples she and her team collected from the tiger shark's corpse—the ones that are currently being snap frozen at minus one hundred and ninety-six degrees Celsius—will eventually be subjected to micro-slicing to the width of a single cell and then analyzed under an electron microscope.

On the other side of the main lab, two of Dr. Randal's lab technicians busily run a separate set of samples through a mass-spectrometer. The lab itself is deathly quiet as the scientists diligently go about their work. Once the two lab techs have completed the matrix-assisted laser desorption/ionization process, the metal plates the results will be mounted on are analyzed and added to the growing body of information the science team is painstakingly building.

Inside the science vessel's secondary lab, the other four members of Dr. Randal's team have divided their efforts between mapping the specimen's DNA and examining internal organs they collected after a full necropsy. Already, what they are finding is disturbing, but no conclusions will be drawn until all of their tests have been completed and only after Dr. Randal herself has evaluated every piece of data the team has collected.

What's left of the tiger shark the crew of *Fearless* retrieved from the undersea cave lies on its side across the aft deck. The rotting corpse gives off a distinctive and decidedly unpleasant aroma—a disgusting stench Moss and his crew are all too familiar with.

Moss stands motionless over the dead shark while its pungent odor assaults his senses and conjures long-dead memories back to life. He fiercely battles them to the back of his mind. He has work to do. Moss is still carefully studying the huge tiger shark when Rafferty joins him.

"I made the rounds through the two labs," Rafferty announces flatly. He takes up a position next to Moss and stares down at the dead shark. The rotting corpse is rapidly ripening under a Mexican sun. "Dr. Randal says she'll be ready to give a briefing on what she and her team have found out in a couple of hours."

"Good," Moss says softly. His arms are folded in front of him while his mind is sharply focused on the signals coming from his own observations.

Razz studies his friend, looks down at the shark carcass once more, and tries to hook into what Moss is seeing, but he's not sure what he is supposed to be looking for. "I know you're getting signal, Ax. You wanna fill me in? I gotta admit, this thing just looks like a dead shark to me."

Moss places his hands on his hips and exhales. "I don't know. It could be nothing, but this shark just doesn't look normal to me, Razz."

"Come again, Ax?"

"The minute I saw this thing come out of the water, it just didn't look right, and seeing it up close, well, what I keep coming back to is that this shark is just too damned perfect."

"Now that you mention it," Rafferty adds as he, too, places his hands on his hips, "for an adult female tiger shark, and a dead one at that, she is a bit of a beauty queen, isn't she? I mean, a shark this size would have to be several years old, and well, you're right, Ax, there's not a mark on her."

"My thoughts exactly," adds Moss. "An animal like this, an apex predator this old, would have killed hundreds... no thousands of times during its life. Tiger sharks are famous for eating almost anything, Razz. They're opportunists... some would even say scavengers. But when they do attack, it's aggressive and brutal. A big shark like this one, she couldn't have lived a life like that without her body becoming a roadmap of battle scars, you know what I mean?"

"All I have to do is see my own body in the mirror, Ax. I know exactly what you mean."

"Yeah," Moss's voice trails off as he moves in closer to the corpse. "And look at her fins, Razz." As he speaks, Moss kneels down beside her and runs his hand over the perfectly smooth contour of the shark's imposing dorsal fin. "How many tiger shark specimens have we retrieved over the past four years?"

"More than I care to count."

"Of all the best ones we found—all the most prime specimens—did you ever see one with fins this perfect? *And this large?*"

"Come to think of it, no I haven't." As Rafferty speaks, his voice drops an octave as the pieces start coming together and the anger inside him begins to grow.

Moss stands. "Yeah, exactly. Me neither."

• • •

The science team has completed its final rounds of tests and compiled its data, and Dr. Randal is ready to present her findings. Moss can see from the look on Samantha's face that the news isn't good. He can also see that she's upset, even though she's doing a good job of hiding that fact. Moss says nothing; however, he needs to know what she knows. She has his full attention.

"I would like to start with the genetic analysis," Dr. Randal begins. She reaches down and taps commands into the keyboard in front of her. The first graphs blink onto the lab's large flat-screen monitor. "What we found are anomalies in the tiger shark's DNA... in the gene sequencing of the specimen. These anomalies clearly indicate artificial manipulation of the specimen's genome."

"We ran two sets of tests," Dr. Randal continues, "and compared the results against preexisting data in the lab computer's own memory. The last team on board left quite a bit of data stored on one of the hard drives. I don't think it was intentional, but it was certainly fortuitous on our part. We were loading our own data into the program when we stumbled across a number of older files from a past genetic mapping expedition. That particular team was focused almost exclusively on tiger sharks, apparently. So we used that raw data as a baseline and compared it to our specimen. The results are conclusive, I'm afraid."

Moss listens carefully as he leans against a table. He allows what Dr. Randal has just said to sink in, and then he straightens and moves closer to the screen. "Dr. Randal," Moss questions,

"How does the genetic analysis correlate with the tissue samples? I mean, is there also physical evidence of this genetic manipulation?"

"Unfortunately, the answer is yes, Mr. Moss." Her voice trembles slightly as she speaks, and then she clears her throat, jams her hands into the pockets of her lab coat, and continues. "The tissue analysis should have been almost useless due to the apparent advanced state of mortification. The mass-spectronomy and cryo-sectioning are most effective on fresh tissue, and based on what we have learned during our analysis, this shark has, in fact, been dead for months. Initially, this makes no sense, of course. Under normal conditions, an animal that has been dead this long would be almost completely decomposed. There shouldn't be enough material left to analyze, much less bring this thing on board in one piece; that should have been impossible, actually."

Moss is starting to get angry himself. He looks over at the stern expression on Razz's face and then back at Dr. Randal. "I could be way off base here, Dr. Randal, but it sounds like this shark was engineered by someone. I'm reaching here, but is it possible somebody somehow raised this thing in captivity, like in some kind of artificial environment?"

"You're not far off at all, Mr. Moss." Dr. Randal turns back to the keyboard and quickly taps a series of commands into the computer. She brings up data from a separate program onto the display. "This is data we retrieved from the mass-spectrometer. We found high traces of silk fibroin and synthetic biopolymers, such as polylactic acid, polycaprolactone, and polyglycolic acid—"

At this point, Rafferty jumps in. "Dr. Randal, please excuse me if I sound disrespectful, but could you translate that last bit into English?"

Samantha smiles. It breaks the tension, and Moss sees her shoulders relax as she sighs… *Good boy, Razz,* Moss thinks, *she needed that…*

"Absolutely, Mr. Rafferty," Samantha continues. "These are natural biomaterials, like collagen, for example. The application in this case is highly advanced. These biomaterials were used as scaffolding for a tissue-engineering application. Think of it very much like building construction, using scaffolding to hold the structure in place as it is being built. In this case, the heavy reliance on these biomaterials, coupled with evidence of genetic manipulation, has apparently slowed decomposition."

"When we compared this data to the cryosections, we discovered evidence of cellular cloning and accelerated cell mitosis… advanced rapid cell division that points to an artificially high growth rate. My conclusion, after examining all the data, is that this shark was precisely engineered and grown in a lab in fact. There is nothing natural about it."

"What do we do next, Dr. Randal?" Moss asks. "What more do you need from us in order to proceed with your investigation?"

"That is a highly perceptive question, Mr. Moss," Dr. Randal answers. "I have formed a hypothesis, but in order to confirm it, I will need to run tests on all the shark carcasses in that cave. Of course, bringing them all on board is impractical, to say the least. So what I propose…" Samantha pauses momentarily, she takes in a deep breath as she looks at Moss. "Well, this is a bloody awful thing to have to ask, but the surest way to collect unique tissue from each individual is to take a piece that each shark has only one of."

Rafferty looks at Moss and then back at Dr. Randal. "You want us to dive down and cut the dorsal fins off all the sharks in that cave? Are you for real?"

Moss steps in. "Look, Razz, there's no getting around the fact that this sucks, but I see what Dr. Randal is getting at here. If you and the guys can handle it, I'd like to proceed, but only if you're okay with it."

Razz places his hands firmly on his hips, shifts his weight, and sighs heavily. He then looks Moss in the eye. "Yeah, it sucks, but I'll do it."

• • •

The newly sharpened blade isn't slicing as cleanly as Murray had expected. He's frustrated as a flush of bubbles flows over the front of his mask and obscures his view of the somewhat gruesome task at hand. He looks across the darkened cave and sees the narrow beam of light coming from Dan's headlamp; he's having the same trouble. Then, Murray glances behind him; Razz is just as frustrated. All three divers are rapidly sucking down their third tank of the day, it's getting late, and they've only collected fins from thirty of the thirty-nine sharks left in the cave.

Even armed with freshly sharpened blades, the job is still a pain in the ass. Murray grasps the leading edge of a dorsal fin with his left hand as he cuts into it with the other from behind. The odd angles at which the dead sharks are resting add to the difficulty; they're piled on top of each other, and several are upside down.

The shark Murray is currently working on is wedged between two huge boulders, and just reaching the damn thing was tough enough. Once the blade cuts into the last thick section of cartilage at the front, Murray shoves the large knife back in its holster, grasps the fin with both hands, and tears off the remainder. As another dorsal fin finally breaks away from the corpse it was attached to, Murray quickly slips it into the net bag tied to his weight belt. He flashes two fingers at Rafferty, who does the same. Then, Dan holds up two fingers. They each have only two more fins to slice off and they'll have them all.

. . .

Three days later, after repeated tests and long hours, the science team's results are finally in, and none of it is encouraging. Everyone aboard *Fearless* is in a darkened mood, but none more than Dr. Randal herself. Moss has made a point of keeping a careful eye on his lead scientist. It's clear to him that she is emotionally traumatized. After what happened five years ago, Moss is now on high alert. He's leaving nothing to chance.

He's decided that the best course of action is to get Dr. Randal and her team back to work on their invertebrate research as quickly as possible. He's repositioned *Fearless* to their next planned collection area, and the team has picked up where they left off. The change in scenery has had a positive effect, but the persistent sadness in her eyes tells Moss that something is still seriously wrong.

It's late in the evening—close to midnight, actually—and Alex Moss isn't sleeping. He can't get the constant noise of creeping anxiety out of his head. He gets up, gets dressed, and walks out on deck.

A fiery orange full moon is rising above the stark, jagged, Sierra Madres that dominate the Gulf of California's eastern horizon. Moss takes in the beautiful view. It's the sort of thing Trish would love... *Trish*... She's already back in Sydney and getting settled into her dad's law firm. From her emails, it's clear she's happy to be back home.

Moss leans against the railing and focuses on the path of flaming moonlight dancing toward him from across the calm sea. Then he picks up a faint sound. He looks in the direction the sound is coming from; it's near the helipad. Moss walks over to the front of the helipad and finds Dr. Randal sitting on the deck near the bow. Her arms are wrapped tightly around her knees, and she is sobbing.

She slowly raises her damp eyes toward Moss. Her face is red and innocent. "They used my science to create killing machines, Mr. Moss." She rubs her eyes, and then her expression chills and the anger comes through. "My past work is all over the test results: the stem cell cloning, the accelerated cell growth... *these were my developments...* and I don't know what to do about it. I am a doctor of medical science. My work is supposed to save lives, not take them."

Moss kneels down beside her. "Are you sure about this? How can this have happened?"

"You and I work for the same people, Mr. Moss." Samantha's angry tone resonates. "We both know exactly who is responsible, so I now pose the question to you, sir. What are we going to do about it?"

Chapter 15

The children. Jeff Buxton is the first to catch sight of their tiny, terrorized faces painted eerily in an infrared green glow. They flash like ghosts across the laptop screens that face him. The toddlers, the ones that remind him of his own kids; innocents taken down brutally over a live camera feed. The veteran Special Activities Division intelligence officer falls silent as his gut churns and his mind goes numb.

Buxton's CIA compatriots are slow on the uptake, but once it registers that their superior officer is no longer cheering, that something is up because their number-one guy is out of the game, they decide to look and find out why; they find out soon enough, and what they see shuts them up, too.

Alistair notices the reactions of the men around him. He can sense what must be happening, but he doesn't want to look for himself. Just like that day five years ago when he couldn't bring himself to raise his head and confront his enemy; to look head-on at the terror. On that day he could only muster the courage to view the reflection of what was happening plastered across the faces of the people around him. This time Alistair manages only a single brief glance at the laptop screens ablaze with the deaths of children, and he instantly turns away.

Five hours and forty-seven minutes after twenty MS41-T drones were released from the deck of the *USS Chubasco*, nineteen return. The loss of a unit comes as a shock to Alistair. After three highly successful missions without a single loss, Alistair has grown so confident in his drones' technology that he had convinced himself that losing a unit was merely a remote possibility. The foundation has a contingency plan in place, of course, and even Lieutenant Commander Parnell had warned Alistair repeatedly that a loss was inevitable and to be prepared for it. But despite all logical reasoning, Dr. Alistair Fairchild takes the loss personally.

They were deep into the op when Alistair's lead engineer contacted him from the drone operations center in Long Beach. He quietly reported over Dr. Fairchild's direct comm-link that an anomaly had just occurred in unit seventeen. The telemetry streaming from unit seventeen had just been interrupted. Then, the engineer confirmed the apparent destruction of the unit's control module, with the caveat that, according to data coming off the surrounding units, it appeared as if only the control module had failed; unit seventeen itself was still fully intact. Alistair was shocked and angered, but he ordered the operations center to continue with the mission as planned.

With the mission completed, the *USS Chubasco* turns away from the Colombian coast and makes way for deeper water out beyond the fifteen-nautical-mile mark. Nineteen de-animated tiger shark carcasses now lay motionless across the aft deck of the ship. Buxton and his two colleagues walk amongst the shark's corpses in the early morning light and carefully evaluate the amount of damage each of the drones took during the operation.

"Look here," one of the CIA officers points out, "this one must have taken some pretty hard direct hits." He points to the fact that not only is this particular shark's dorsal fin missing, but a chunk of its upper body is gone as well.

Buxton surveys the damage. "Looks like this came from a high-caliber automatic weapon. That kind of firepower should have taken this thing out, but it kept going, and it returned." Buxton pauses to look more closely at the deep gash running down the shark's back. "That is impressive."

After detailed examination of the nineteen drones, Alistair's team records all aspects of their condition, and then, unceremoniously, all nineteen sharks are dumped overboard. Their bodies will sink over one thousand meters to the bottom of the eastern Caribbean Sea, where they will naturally decay.

Jeff Buxton watches with curiosity, and more than a hint of satisfaction, as the deactivated, top-secret biological drones vanish forever beneath the waves. Despite the unintended deaths of innocent civilians, Buxton is already a fan of this new technology. It's brutal, effective, and not a single American life was put at risk.

Lachesis is now permanently silenced. He won't be leaking anymore classified intelligence, his information and technology trading days are over, and with some persistence, Buxton reckons, the other members of his network will be next, all the way to the very top of the information-trading food chain.

The collateral damage was indeed unfortunate, but as Buxton reasons, Lachesis knew he was a target; he, of all people, knew the rules of the game. Juan Carlos should never have allowed his family near his hideout. *His family members' deaths are on his hands alone…*

The flight back to Van Nuys is a quiet one. Alistair sips his beer and stares blankly out of the private jet's elegant, oval-shaped window. He gazes down at the seemingly endless lights of vast Central American metropolitan areas from Cartagena to Managua, then San Salvador, Guatemala City, the sprawling behemoth of Mexico City, then San Diego, and, finally, Los Angeles. The cities pass silently beneath him as Alistair ponders the blankets of lights. Their snake-like tendrils spread out in all directions, and they remind him of cancer cells seen under a microscope. Alistair dispassionately evaluates the millions upon millions of people living under those lights and comforts himself... *With so many down there, how can the world miss a few more?*

An hour after landing, Alistair is sitting at his desk nursing a pounding headache and extreme fatigue. He's downing a double-sized latte when Marcus Waverley suddenly breezes in through Alistair's open office door.

"Alistair!" His booming voice shatters Alistair's thoughts. "Well done, son!" Alistair stands just as Waverley grabs his arm and pats him vigorously across his back. "You just did something truly amazing!"

Alistair responds sluggishly as he slowly turns to look at his boss. "Yes... the mission, sir. The mission was a success."

"Damn right it was." Waverley stops and stares at his irreplaceable man. "Are you all right, kid? Well, of course you are! You've been working your ass off these past weeks, but I've got good news!"

"Good news?" Alistair asks in a haze. "Um, I'm sorry about the failure of unit seventeen."

"Oh that? Don't give it another thought. We knew this sort of thing was inevitable, right? It's a minor glitch at this point. Damage control has already taken care of it. Our best spooks are already working on it. We have all of the major media outlets covering for us at this very moment."

Then, Waverley catches himself. He pauses to carefully evaluate his prized wunderkind. "You need some time off, and you're going to get it. First, though, I've got a job for you; an easy job."

"If it's another mission, sir, we're ready."

"No! Fuck, no. After this last mission? Hell, the CIA has determined we are now beyond the prototype phase, Dr. Fairchild. They are fully convinced that the MS41-T is reliable and effective as a covert combat drone. We're ready to move to the next level."

"So, what's the next level?" Alistair's mind is now fully focused. He already knows what Director Waverley is about to announce, but he plays along.

"You're about to be promoted, Dr. Fairchild. Your gruntwork days are over. You're being moved up the ladder."

"Does this mean I will be overseeing the training and implementation in order for the CIA's people to take over operations?"

"You've always been a smart investment, Alistair." Director Waverley smiles broadly as his perfectly capped and glistening white teeth flash in front of Alistair's face. "That is exactly what's going to happen next, and once the CIA takes control of the MS41-T program, it will leave you free to return to work on your next-generation MS1GW."

• • •

The MS1-GW had long been relegated to pet project status. It was an experimental prototype that Alistair had begun to develop but was forced to sideline when the MS41-T became fully operational. Alistair had high hopes for the MS1, but the advanced genetic engineering techniques that worked well with their tiger shark specimens proved to be more challenging when applied to the physiology of a great white shark.

The thought of devoting himself completely to the MS1 is highly appealing. The Multi-Striker drone project had actually begun with the concept of using a great white shark as the platform for development, hence the designation MS1-GW. But the time constraints the project was saddled with demanded faster results, so the focus quickly shifted over to the secondary platform: a tiger shark.

The tiger shark proved to be easier to work with and the project scaled up rapidly. They quickly outgrew their original test facility in California, and so the forty MS1-GW prototypes Alistair and his team had painstakingly created were eventually transferred to a cold storage facility in Long Beach. Even with the success of the tiger shark platform, the drones engineered from the great white shark are Dr. Alistair Fairchild's personal favorites, so much so that he chose the designation "MS41" for his production model in honor of the forty MS1 prototypes.

• • •

Alistair smiles innocently at Director Waverley. "Thank you, Marcus. I look forward to returning to my research. I feel I've been neglecting the team in Baja."

"Ah yes, Baja. That's the other thing I need to talk to you about."

Alistair shrugs. "What's up with Baja?"

"We have to close down the La Paz facility. The CIA wants production moved to a more secure site. They're putting us on San Clemente Island."

"But our facility in Baja has always been secure, sir. What's the issue?"

Waverley cocks his head as he adjusts his tie. "Look, Alistair, this is the CIA. They have their own way of doing things. It's not our job to question their motives. Our job is to deliver the product and then cash the checks, you understand, right? Besides, if we could have had access to San Clemente out of the starting gate, I would have gone for it. I mean, the navy owns the whole damn island. It's basically a barren rock with a runway. They only use it for special ops training and target practice; it's perfect."

Alistair sighs. "Yes, sir. I understand. It makes sense. How long do I have to close down the facility and pack up the units in La Paz? How will we transport them? By ship?"

"No ships. We're arranging to fly them out in one load; it's much more efficient."

"Fly them? All of them?" The concern in Alistair's voice is obvious even to Marcus Waverley. "We have one hundred and fifty units stored in Baja."

"Relax. It won't be an issue, not with the plane the CIA is planning to use." Then Waverley evaluates Alistair again. "Look, kid, why don't you knock off for the day, go home, and get some sleep?" He pats Alistair on the shoulder, and then Waverley turns and walks out. Alistair watches Marcus leave. He's already feeling the knots twisting tightly in his gut. *All of them? At the same time?*

Early the next morning, Dr. Fairchild is thinking about his accomplishments and about the path forward for his drones as he gazes out of the broad windows of his office at the misty-gray Pacific Ocean. Alistair then turns back toward his desk and allows his eyes to settle once more on an expensively framed piece of art hanging on the wall above it.

Mounted at the center of a minimalist mahogany frame and surrounded by thick layers of white museum-grade matting is a small bone carving of West African origin. The tiny statue, barely four inches long, had once belonged to Dr. Peter Marsh's colleague, Dr. Thomas Falcon. Tracking it down had proven to be not nearly as difficult as convincing the foundation's board of directors of the reason why Alistair needed it. Acquiring it had been a somewhat risky operation—and expensive.

The foundation quietly contracted through a third party with a team of specialists out of South Africa—professional art thieves who are typically hired by an artwork's legitimate owners. It is an all too common practice when the insured value of a work of art exceeds its current auction estimates. The professional thieves proceeded to break into the cultural museum in Kingston, Jamaica, where the talisman was on display. The South African team took the talisman along with a few other items of both higher and lesser value in order to mask the theft. They quickly disposed of the extras and delivered the talisman to Marcus Waverley personally.

Once Dr. Alistair Fairchild got his hands on the talisman, he had it thoroughly analyzed. The results revealed what Alistair had suspected. The first being that the small statue was indeed very old; the carved bone dated back over eight centuries, in fact. But the X-rays showed that there was much more to the talisman than a simple bone carving.

Alistair took the talisman into his own lab and carefully removed one end of the hollow bone carving. Inside, he discovered a small amount of heavily decomposed beeswax, and something else—something absolutely amazing. The impossibly precise manufacturing, the exotic metal exterior, and the fact that further testing demonstrated that it was indeed an energy source proved Alistair's hunch.

Further testing confirmed that the mysterious object drew its seemingly inexhaustible and highly scalable power directly from the earth's own electromagnetic field.

All of this pointed to a single conclusion in Alistair's mind. Hidden inside this centuries-old talisman carved by a traditional West African healer was a piece of extremely advanced technology—a technology whose origin Alistair was convinced was not of this world. He dubbed it *the node*, and in the right hands—his hands—Alistair knew he was holding the key to making his drone project truly viable... *and he was right.*

Chapter 16

Dr. Brian Mathews fumbles with his keys as he juggles a sack of groceries and opens the mailbox assigned to his tiny San Diego apartment. He flips open the narrow door to find a package inside—an overstuffed shipping pouch. Brian sighs at the now familiar sight; it's the third such package he has received in the past seven weeks.

His first thought is to ignore it. The idea of simply tossing it unopened in the trash or marking it *return to sender* crosses his mind, but Brian knows that, realistically, those options are long gone; *he's in too deep*. He grabs the package and stuffs it into his grocery bag.

Brian enters his studio apartment, drops the grocery bag on the kitchen counter, and opens his fridge. The interior is sparse—nearly empty—but two beers sit on the center rack nicely chilled. He grabs one, opens it, and then pulls the package out from in between a stack of frozen microwave meals.

Ever since the encounter with the gray-suited stranger in Dusseldorf, the painful headaches and nightmares Brian suffered in the wake of his experience aboard *Fearless* five years ago have returned. Adding to his stress level is the fact that it has been a particularly difficult week. But it's Friday, he's tired, and he's looking forward to some much-needed rest.

Brian takes a sip from his beer and stares at the package sitting on the cheap Formica countertop in front of him. He is afraid to open it. He's afraid of the top-secret and highly illegal information he again could be exposed to, but one haunting thought rises above all others: *What have Alistair's shark drones done this time?* The consequences of opening the package are severe, not only due to its potentially dangerous contents, but also because the true intentions of the dark and powerful forces behind it are still unknown to him.

As of this week, Dr. Brian Mathews' current employment as a professor of undergraduate marine biology is now hanging by a thread. His latest review from his department head at the university was, to put it mildly, less than glowing. To be fair, she's been incredibly accommodating over the past three years that he's been teaching under her supervision. Her final warning, however, was clear as crystal.

"You're a good teacher, Brian," she had said sympathetically, "and a solid researcher, but you've got to give up this conspiracy theory shark crusade. It will take you nowhere."

Brian puts down his beer and rips open the package. Inside is a pair of fashion headphones and a set of instructions. The contents of each package have varied. The first, the one alerting him to the Multi-Striker drone's successful deployment in Indonesia, contained an unusual type of LED flashlight. The second package contained a throwaway phone—*a burner,* as they call it in the spy trade.

Those instructions led to details about the drone's top-secret and, once again, highly successful operation in Yemen. The items have all been different, but they have always been accompanied by a set of simple instructions that would be meaningless to anyone but him. This time was no different in that respect. Brian reaches into the package and pulls out a digitally printed note that reads *Coffee tomorrow at eight?*

The next morning, just before eight o'clock, Brian sits with his laptop open inside a small Internet coffee bar located just two blocks from his apartment. He calmly takes a sip of his latte and then pulls the headphones out from his backpack. He plugs them into his computer, and slips them on. As Brian stares at his computer screen, a digitally altered voice suddenly begins speaking to him through the headphones. Brian doesn't react. He simply continues to look at the random webpage in front of him and listen.

"Thank you for following instructions, Dr. Mathews," the monotone digitized voice begins. "There has been another incident. It took place in Colombia. Innocent people were killed, including nine children. Now is the time to act, Dr. Mathews, because this time, Alistair left something behind. We will be in touch."

The cold, emotionless tone of the digitized voice only adds to Brian's grief as he takes off the headphones... *My God, Alistair... nine kids?* Brian puts the headphones away and searches quietly for recent news items about Colombia. He quickly finds a breaking news report on the gruesome death of infamous Colombian drug lord Juan Carlos Azarola.

"In what local authorities are calling a horrific predawn attack, perhaps launched by a rival cartel, a total of sixty-seven people have reportedly been killed. Their bodies were found brutally dismembered. Among the dead are members of the sixty-two-year-old drug lord's own family, including nine children age two to thirteen."

Brian scans through the article until one line hits him like a bullet: *"a large weapons cache and a safe containing over two million U.S.*

dollars were also recovered, but police at the scene also found several much more unusual items inside the illusive drug lord's secret luxury compound hidden in the Colombian jungle. Perhaps the strangest being the remains of a recently caught tiger shark. Police at the scene are baffled as to how or why a large adult tiger shark would be in the middle of Azarola's living room; however, they add, Azarola had a well-known reputation as a big-game hunter and sport fisherman."

Brian is reading the last few lines of the news report when an alert pops up on his computer screen notifying him of an email message. Brian opens the email to see a confirmation notice of his airline ticket to Cartagena, Colombia.

He downloads the E-ticket pdf file and finds that *his flight* leaves at four that afternoon. Brian squirms nervously in his seat as the true reality of his situation sinks in… *They are watching your every move… they even know what you've just read online…* Brian waits a few more minutes and tries to look calm. He continues to sip his coffee and scan webpages. Then, he methodically closes down his computer and leaves.

Brian returns to his apartment and begins preparing for his afternoon flight. He packs with cautious resignation while he obsesses over his employment situation. *It's not such a big trip down there…* he reasons… *I should be back late Monday night—plenty of time before my first class Tuesday morning…* The income from Brian's *Sharktruth!* website barely covers the costs of operating it, and his speaking engagements haven't earned him a dime. His teaching job is currently the only thing keeping him afloat.

Brian grabs up well-used tropical travel clothing and then stuffs the wrinkled garments into a well-traveled backpack. Then it suddenly dawns on him that even the walls around him are most likely listening and watching. The sensation is creepy, to say the least, but he is now obsessed with the idea of finding Alistair's lost tiger shark, and if possible, convincing him to stop what he's doing before it's too late.

• • •

It's just after dark when Brian's flight touches down at Rafael Núñez International Airport. After he clears customs, immigration, and passport control, Brian grabs a taxi and heads for the backpacker hostel he'd located online while he waited for his flight back in San Diego. As an undergraduate student, Brian had once spent his summer holiday backpacking through South America with four friends. His Spanish was only rudimentary then, but over the past three years that he's lived in San Diego, he's made a point of improving his language skills, and the effort has paid off. For this visit, Brian's second to Colombia, he is now fluent.

His lodging at the hostel turns out to be exactly what he was hoping for: cheap and clean. The next morning, after a light breakfast at a local cafe, Brian heads for the Transportes Rapido Ochoa S.A. terminal located in the historic Spanish colonial center of Cartagena. There, he pays the equivalent of twenty-five US dollars for a seat on a modern, air-conditioned bus traveling north to the coastal city of Barranquilla. The two-hour trip along Colombia's scenic Caribbean coast floods Brian's mind with pleasant memories from his student travels, and for a time, he allows himself to relax and enjoy the fact that he's traveling—something he has always loved.

It's almost lunchtime when the large red and white tour bus pulls into the depot at Barranquilla, but Brian doesn't stop to eat. Instead, he heads straight for the city's main police station. Once inside, Brian shows his university credentials identifying him as a PhD marine biologist. Then, he politely enquires about the shark that was reported in the news.

The police station is nearly empty; only a few junior officers are manning its front desk during the lunch hour. As he casually chats fluently in Spanish, Brian discovers that the tiger shark is now in the possession of the local police chief in Tenerife. The man is keeping it in the back of his police station, but he has plans to have it stuffed as a trophy.

"If you want to see this shark, Professor," the policeman advises, "you should move quickly."

The rumbling bus ride up through the jungle-covered mountains is beautifully scenic but nowhere near as luxurious. The dense, humid air wafting through the open window onto Brian's face carries with it a mix of diesel exhaust and pungent vegetation. It is late in the afternoon by the time Brian finds his way to the police station in Tenerife, but once again, Brian is fortunate; the place is nearly empty.

Brian chats politely with the officer on duty, he once more presents his credentials and answers the officer's questions freely. After about fifteen minutes, the man leads Brian through the back of the police station and then outside into a leafy courtyard shaded by large trees and surrounded by a high security fence.

The policeman walks over to a large shape covered by a blue plastic tarp. He kneels down and lifts one corner of the plastic, revealing the dark pointed nose of a very large tiger shark. The policeman glances at the dead shark as a cloud of flies buzzes around it. He then smiles broadly and looks up at Brian.

"Ah, you see, Professor? It is just a big fish, no?"

The sight of the shark—*Alistair's shark*—is startling; it feels as if someone just shoved an ice-cold rod down his spine. Brian walks a bit closer. "It certainly is," Brian answers in Spanish, "may I see the entire animal, please?"

"Why not?" the officer answers politely as he pulls the plastic tarp away to reveal what Dr. Brian Mathews instantly recognizes as the most magnificent specimen of a tiger shark he has ever seen.

"It certainly is impressive," Brian attempts to subdue his nervous excitement, but this thing is freakishly large: five meters long, by his estimates. He walks slowly around the massive shark carcass. He then bends down through a thick cloud of buzzing flies, rests on one knee, and rapidly begins taking mental notes; it's a female, and aside from a few odd bullet wounds, she is absolutely perfect.

The shark biologist in Brian quickly arrives at the conclusion that the elasmobranch lying in front of him has never spent a single day living in the sea as a natural predator. Her body shows no signs of the normal wear and tear such a life would normally leave behind. Her fins are perfect and totally devoid of age marks, in spite of the fact that reaching this size would take nearly twenty years in the wild. Brian runs his hand across the flawless leading edge of the shark's impressive dorsal fin. *It's too big, Alistair… but you always did favor the comic book aesthetic, didn't you?*

Brian stands and turns back toward the policeman. He thanks him for showing him the shark and then begins asking about the story he heard. "Is it true that the chief of police is planning to have the shark stuffed and mounted? Would it be possible to perform a scientific necropsy before they begin?"

"No, it would not, sir!"

The thundering voice behind him catches Brian off guard. The policeman who was showing him the shark suddenly drops the tarp and claps to attention. Brian spins around to face a rotund man wearing the elaborate uniform of a senior Colombian police officer.

"Who are you? Why are you here?" the man demands angrily in Spanish. "And you!" he shouts at the cringing junior policeman. "Who gave you permission to allow this man here?"

"May I show you my credentials, sir?" Brian asks politely in Spanish. "I am merely a visiting marine biologist. I certainly didn't mean to upset anyone. I only wished to examine this shark for scientific purposes." Brian takes out his identification and hands it to the police chief.

The senior Colombian police officer studiously examines Brian's university identification, his US residency card, his New Zealand passport, and his California driver's license, and then he places them all in his shirt pocket. "Arrest this man immediately."

Chapter 17

Thomas Falcon sits down to breakfast aboard *Mysterious*. He forces a smile as Bayani takes a seat across from him. Maria arrives to serve them both coffee. "You are English, Dr. Falcon?" Maria asks as she pours strong Colombian coffee into a delicate porcelain cup. "We also have tea. I know English men like tea."

"That is very kind of you, Maria, but coffee will do nicely." Falcon lifts the cup to his lips. He is consumed by an odd and uncomfortable sensation; an unease that has been clouding his mind since he first woke up. The feeling isn't coming from inside his own body, however; it's coming from someplace else, but at the moment, Falcon can't put his finger on it.

"But, Dr. Falcon," Maria answers, "this is my duty to serve you. If you wish to have tea, I will bring you tea."

Falcon tries hard to be pleasant. "The coffee is wonderful, Maria, thank you." Then, he puts the cup down and briefly looks around. "Maria, may I ask, will Marco be joining us for breakfast?"

He looks up at the woman's kind features only to see them suddenly wilt into sadness. "I am afraid not, Dr. Falcon. Mr. Marco will not be joining you today. I am very sorry."

Falcon looks over the elegantly prepared breakfast table laden with fruits, freshly baked pastries, hot toast, and jam, but he finds he has lost his appetite. The yacht has been steadily motoring north for the past four days. Marco and his wife, Kimberly, have been delightful hosts. Falcon stares across the table at Bayani and observes with bemusement as the nineteen-year-old fills his plate.

"I have something I need to do, Bayani," Falcon announces. "I'll only be a minute, okay?"

Bayani looks up from his food as he stuffs the last of a croissant into his mouth. "Mmm, sure, Dr. Falcon. I'll be right here."

Falcon stands up from the table, he neatly folds his linen serviette, lays it over the armrest of his chair, and then walks off toward the aft deck in order to think. Something strange is about to happen—*he can feel it.* Falcon steadies himself against the glistening varnished railing of the magnificent motor yacht and looks out at the sea passing beneath him.

He is standing only a few minutes before a sea bird catches his eye. Falcon watches the bird dive into the waves for fish, circle above the boat, and then it lands on the railing beside him. Falcon is amazed. The bird is a blue-footed booby; a native of the Galápagos Islands and an extreme rarity this far north of the equator.

Falcon observes with curiosity as the sea bird calmly preens its feathers with its long bright blue bill, and then it flies off. Falcon's eyes follow the bird as it glides toward the bow of the yacht until he sees Dr. Peter Marsh standing in front of him. Marsh looks back at Falcon with a knowing grin.

In that moment, Falcon suddenly realizes he is no longer aboard the luxurious motor yacht. He is aboard another ship; he is aboard *Fearless.* Thomas Falcon stares into the eyes of his long-lost friend with a mix of joy and grief. He watches as the breeze plays with his sandy hair and his freckled skin crinkles around his sea-green eyes. Marsh looks deep inside Falcon, and as he does, Falcon senses a warmth wash over his body as Peter Marsh smiles at him with understanding.

"They were two of my best students, Tom." Marsh begins, "but as smart as they both are, they're each very different. Brian was always the good kid, you know? Brilliant but often so concerned about helping everyone else he neglected his own well-being. Alistair never had that problem, of course. He was just the opposite, in fact, and he was good at playing Brian. He often used him to his advantage.

"I knew from the start that Alistair would need a tight rein, Tom. He is just so incredibly smart, you know? Truly genius-level IQ, but with the sort of personality that could justify anything in order to achieve a goal. That can be dangerous in the wrong environment… like Unabomber sort of dangerous. Do you know what I mean, Tom?"

Falcon looks at his friend with astonishment. "Yes, I do, Peter. Tell me, what should I do?"

"Alistair is being directed by people that not only condone the worst side of his character, they have cultivated it, nurtured it, and weaponized it. I need you to stop what he's doing, Tom. Can you do that for me?"

"Yes, I can, Peter, and I will. I promise you that. I will stop Alistair from going too far."

"He's already gone too far, Tom. You have to stop this from happening again, do you understand?" Peter's words send an ice-cold jolt through Falcon.

"I understand. I will stop him."

At that moment, Falcon hears Maria's sweet voice. "Dr. Falcon? He turns to see her standing behind him. "Dr. Falcon, may I clear away the breakfast table? Mr. Bayani is finished. Do you wish to have anything else?"

"No... uh, thank you, Maria. I have everything I need."

"Yes, Dr. Falcon." As Maria turns to leave, Falcon's mind is churning through the data: *my old lab, the cryosections, the mass spectrometry, Baja, now Brian, Alistair and* Fearless.

The day passes into evening without a single sighting of Marco or his lovely Kimberly. The last hints of a golden Pacific sunset are quickly fading as Falcon sits at the bar with Bayani. Francis serves them each a San Miguel from the bar's own tap. Then, Falcon takes his beer, thanks Francis, and then he subtly motions for Bayani to follow him.

The two men walk off past the pool, drained and covered for the passage, and then on toward the yacht's aft railing. "I had another vision today, Bayani," Falcon begins. "What lies ahead for me will be extremely dangerous." Then, he looks Bayani in the eye. "And I don't want you anywhere near it, do you understand? You have been an incredible help to me, and a true friend, but I refuse to put your life at risk. I simply won't allow it."

The expression on Bayani's face paints a picture of a young man in possession of wisdom beyond his years. He looks at Falcon with a quizzical mix of sympathy and understanding. "Dr. Falcon, you are not the only shaman on board this vessel. We are both on a spiritual journey. We each have a path that lies before us, and I, too, have had visions."

Falcon suddenly feels embarrassed. "Of course, Bayani. I apologize. It's just that I lost a dear friend due to my ignorance once. I can't let it happen again... I won't." Then, Falcon sees a knowing smile cross Bayani's face. Falcon catches himself. "Right then… spill it. What stupid thing have I just said?"

"In one of my visions, Dr. Falcon, I found myself inside an electronics store with my father. He loved technology, and we were just standing there together. It was something we used to do when I was very small. The new flat-screen TVs were just coming to the Philippines, and we were looking at them. Then, my father pointed to one of the TVs, and he told me to look at it. He said 'Watch the TV, Bayani. This is the future.' So I watched the program that was on. I had never seen this program, and it was only on for a few seconds before someone changed the channel, but I have always remembered what it looked like."

Falcon is puzzled but intrigued. "What sort of program was it? What did you see?"

"I saw this moment, Dr. Falcon. I saw you and me standing here on this beautiful yacht. We were having beers and talking."

"When did you have this vision, Bayani?"

"I was eleven years old, Dr. Falcon. It was the year after my father had died."

The revelation leaves Falcon speechless…

"Ah! I see my two friends are having a San Miguel. I must join you."

The booming voice sends the two men spinning. Falcon smiles broadly at Marco as the robust man walks toward them holding a glass of beer.

"I must apologize for neglecting you." He quickly raises his glass to toast Bayani and Falcon. "Cheers, gentlemen."

After the three men each take a sip from their glasses, Marco continues. "I received some troubling news that required my immediate attention, but you and I also have important business to take care of, Dr. Falcon." Marco turns and motions to a waiting steward and a hostess standing a few meters away. "If you will allow me, Dr. Falcon, I have your compensation prepared."

"My compensation?" Falcon blurts. "I don't understand?"

"Of course you don't, sir," Marco responds with amusement. "That is because you are an honest man. I have been in communication with Chia, who, unfortunately, was just recently denied parole once more. I am sad to report that he is still in Bilibid Prison, but he is now a much wealthier man. I am certain the next lawyers he hires will be more successful!" Marco suddenly lets out a roar of laughter as Falcon and Bayani look on in confused amazement.

"I'm terribly sorry to hear Chia was denied parole," Falcon interrupts. "He is actually a good man, Marco, and a good friend."

At that moment, Marco lets out another roaring round of laughter, and then he catches himself as he reads the distraught look on Falcon's face. Marco reaches up and places his hand on Falcon's shoulder as he looks him in the eye.

"There is much that you do not know, sir, and it is best that you don't."

Then Marco's voice drops to a much more serious tone. "Chia is a ruthless man Dr. Falcon, but he is also an intelligent man and a reliable business partner. However, even though we have known each other for many years, I would never once consider him to be a friend."

Marco doesn't give Falcon the opportunity to counter his statements. "Now," he continues, "this will only take a moment, but I assure you it is well worth your time to accommodate my request."

At that moment, Falcon realizes that his best course of action is to shut up and follow instructions. Marco briefly turns away from Falcon and makes eye contact with the still patiently waiting steward and hostess. The hostess steps forward with a tray containing electronic equipment. Marco briefly inspects the two pieces of advanced wireless technology.

"Ah, perfect. Let's begin, shall we?" The steward approaches a now fully compliant Dr. Thomas Falcon.

"If you would place your beer on the tray, please, sir." Falcon silently submits to the man's request. The steward then raises a retinal scanning device up in front of Falcon's face.

"Please remain perfectly still, Dr. Falcon. This will only take a moment, and it is completely painless."

He takes a scan of each of Falcon's eyes. With the retinal scan complete, the steward places the scanner back on the tray and picks up what looks like a small tablet computer. "And now the hand."

With the technicalities completed, Marco raises his glass of beer once more. "To our continued success, Dr. Falcon."

"Cheers," Falcon says with a nervous waver.

"You English gentlemen are too polite," Marco complains. "I know you won't dare ask… it's far too crass, so I will tell you what you have just earned for your efforts, sir. The scans are for identity purposes, of course. You are now in command of an account at a private bank in Singapore. It won't be fully activated until you visit there personally; however, the management will gladly complete the process upon your arrival. It will be worth the effort. You now have seven hundred thousand British pounds waiting in your name, Dr. Falcon. Jason here will give you a packet containing all of the details. I suggest you memorize the information and then dispose of it."

Falcon gasps uncontrollably. "What? That's ridiculous! I don't understand. Seven hundred thousand pounds? For what? I don't deserve it, sir, I assure you of that."

Marco chuckles. "It is a token sum, Dr. Falcon. In fact, it's less than five percent of the total take on this job. So don't think for a moment that I am being generous. I am not. But I couldn't live with myself if I sent you on your way without a dime to your name. I know your history."

A flash of color suddenly catches the men's attention, and they turn to see a stunningly beautiful Kimberly strolling toward them. She is dressed in a long, form-fitting tangerine chiffon gown that gracefully trails behind her. She smiles cheerfully as she makes her entrance. "Dinner is ready, gentlemen."

The meal is exquisite, the wine superb, the conversation entertaining, and with the final courses completed, Kimberly politely excuses herself. Cynthia and Shelly, who sit on either side of Bayani, each flash the teenager a playful glance.

"So, we will see you later?" Cynthia leans over and gives Bayani a quick peck on the cheek.

"You know where to find us." Shelly adds as she stands with Cynthia. Bayani watches the two beautiful women leave and then looks back at Falcon with a cat-ate-the-mouse grin. Falcon winks at his young friend and wonders if Bayani truly understands who are the cats and who is the mouse in this game.

Falcon can't help but notice, however, that with Kimberly's departure, the atmosphere has suddenly lost its magic.

"My darling Kimberly," Marco comments as a steward pours each of the three men a 1963 Lheraud Petite Champagne Cognac.

"She is a stunning woman," Falcon adds.

"She is my most trusted business partner and my partner in life." Marco raises his glass to his guests as he speaks. He sips the cognac and then continues. "She is brilliant, this woman. She was born in Scotland, can you believe that? And I will wager heavily you never detected an accent, Dr. Falcon. Am I correct?"

"Absolutely, sir. I would never have guessed," answers Falcon.

"She speaks seven languages fluently, including Chinese and Russian. She holds a PhD in economics from Oxford, which I hope you don't take as a fault, sir." Marco smiles. "I know you are a Cambridge man."

Falcon returns the gesture. "None taken, of course."

Marco grins. "What I am telling you is a fact, my friend. I found her working at a private bank in London fifteen years ago. She was wholly unappreciated, of course, but I saw her talent immediately, and of course, being a Latin man, I fell in love immediately as well!"

Marco's bellowing laughter fills the room as Falcon casually sips five-thousand-dollar-a-bottle cognac from Lalique crystal and marvels, once more, at this man, who is both endearing yet the pure embodiment of ghastly excess... a romantic and a modern pirate... a criminal who sails the high seas in ultimate luxury whilst he pillages the electronic universe of high-value tech and information. Falcon is in awe of his own fate as he ponders his predicament... *And I am his accomplice...*

"She was twenty-eight when we first encountered each other," Marco continues. "I decided right then that I wanted her. So I swept her off her feet and stole her away from that dreary place. We've been devoted to each other ever since. We have two beautiful children together; they are off visiting their grandparents. Their mother is truly the love of my life. I don't even keep women on the side anymore, can you imagine that? A man in my position? Kimberly is the only woman I think of. She is the only one I want."

Falcon finds himself vexed as Marco's mood seems to suddenly darken. He glances across the table at Bayani, who says nothing. Then, Falcon looks at his host. "Is there something else you need to tell us, Marco?"

"Yes…" Marco sighs. He puts his glass down, folds his hands in front of him, and stares intently at Falcon. "I hate this sort of thing. It is difficult for me to talk about negative things… but something serious has happened, and I know you are the only man who can help."

"What is it? Just tell me what you need."

"Do you remember a young student named Alistair Fairchild?"

"Why yes, I do, sir," Falcon responds. "He was one of Peter's students aboard *Fearless,* the research vessel I told you about."

"Dr. Falcon, the student you once knew is now known as Dr. Alistair Fairchild, a shark biologist who specializes in a highly advanced and experimental form of shark genetics. He has become extremely dangerous. The people he works for are even more dangerous. Dr. Falcon, I want this man dead. But please, don't be alarmed. I know you don't do that sort of thing. I will have him killed when the time is right. What I need right now is my own specialist in sharks, but not just any sharks, sir. Do you understand what I am asking?"

The shocked look on Bayani's face only intensifies the cold chill running down Falcon's spine as the throbbing pain in the right hand he no longer has increases. "I know what you need, but I've got to get to Baja."

"Yes, you do, sir," Marco's eyebrows arch upward. "I have discovered the location of Dr. Fairchild's main laboratory. It is in La Paz of all places. It's hidden beneath a private hangar at the airport. I need you to find out everything you can about these monsters, Dr. Falcon. A longtime business associate of mine has been brutally murdered. I received word this morning, and not only was he killed, but also his entire family."

"My God, that's awful," Falcon answers sympathetically. "My sincere apologies, sir."

"Dr. Falcon," Marco's voice now resonates with intense and rising anger. "This man and his family were torn to shreds by sharks! Of all things! And the children as well!" The fury burning inside Marco quickly overwhelms the elegant dining room. "Dr. Falcon!" Marco's voice rises to a crescendo as tears begin to stream down the man's face. "This man Fairchild turned his monsters loose on innocent children!"

Chapter 18

Alex Moss stands alone on the bridge of *Fearless* and focuses on the calm sea in an effort to quell the storm raging inside his head. He stares silently out through the windows in front of him—windows that have framed his life for the past nine years. He's angry. He's also conflicted, and the feeling is decidedly foreign to him.

Moss has never questioned whose side he's on— *not for one second of his life*. There was no need because the answer was obvious. He has always known his loyalties were well founded, that the people he took orders from were doing the right thing, and that following those orders without question was *the right thing*. Yet, for the first time in his life, he has questions about his superiors that he can no longer answer. He knows the only place to get the answers he needs—the information that will put him back on track—is to pose them to one man, and that man is Marcus Waverley.

Razz enters the bridge and sees Moss standing alone and staring blankly out of the broad spread of windows in front of him. "What's up?" asks Razz. "I know that look. It generally means trouble's on the horizon. You gonna fill me in?"

Moss sighs as he folds his arms in front of him and then turns around to face his friend. "I'm concerned, Razz. These things we found… I wish I had gone with my gut. I wish we would've just left them alone in that damn cave."

Razz places his hands on his hips and glances down at the floor and then looks directly at Moss. "Ax, look, this one's on me, okay? I'm the one who went all gung-ho on this deal. "

Moss takes a step toward Rafferty. "No…" He pauses, exhales, and then drops his hands to his hips. "Razz, it doesn't work that way, and you know it. I made the call. It was my decision to send you guys back inside that cave, and honestly? Once I saw that shark come out of the water, I knew something wasn't right. I'm the one who pushed for more answers because after what happened before… I had to know."

"So what do we know?" Rafferty folds his arms and leans back against the mahogany chart table. "I mean, let's look at the facts we have so far, right? This is always how we begin to work a problem; it's how we operate. I mean, it doesn't matter if it's a crashed computer running the navigation systems, an equipment failure, an electrical problem, or a crew issue, we track it down and fix it, right? So, we know we found a bunch of Frankenstein sharks. This we know for sure. So what else do we know? But more important, what tack do we take from here? Because Dr. Randal is right: there's only one group of people who would remotely be capable of creating something like this."

"Yeah…" Moss folds his arms again. "That's exactly what I've been thinking too."

An hour later, Alex Moss is sitting in front of his computer inside his personal office as he waits for *Signal* to complete an encrypted connection with the computer on Marcus Waverley's desk. As the video feed comes online, Moss suddenly sees Waverley's perfectly white teeth flash across the screen as his boss sits down in front of the monitor. He's dressed in his standard working attire: expensively tailored midnight-blue Italian suit and a prestigious white dress shirt accented with a tasteful silk tie and matching pocket square. Marcus grins cheerfully when he sees Moss. "Chief! How's the weather down there? What's up? What can I do for my favorite captain?"

Moss looks directly at the tiny camera lens on the lid of his MacBook. "Marcus, something came up down here, and I feel it's important enough to fill you in."

"Sounds serious, Alex. What's going on? Are you guys in any trouble down there?"

"No, sir, the ship's fine. But we found something. Or I should say, we discovered something strange while working with our current team. We had divers down looking for some rare invertebrates the science team needs for their research, and the guys came across a pile of dead tiger sharks. The team ran a bunch of tests, Marcus. These sharks were artificially engineered."

The smile on Waverley's face fades quickly. "Alex, that sounds pretty incredible. Are you sure about this? Who do you have on board? Oh, right, you've got Dr. Randal's team. Did she confirm this, Alex?"

"Yes, sir. I had my crew retrieve a specimen, and then Dr. Randal and her team ran a full battery of tests. I feel it is important to inform you, sir, that proprietary technology Dr. Randal and her team pioneered with the foundation's support was used to create the specimen we tested."

"Alex, this is serious." Waverley leans in closer to the screen as his expression hardens. "I appreciate you calling me directly,

Alex. This means a lot to me. I don't know what's going on, but we will certainly get to the bottom of it, I assure you of that."

"What would you like me to do, sir? Just give the word and we will shift our focus. I can redirect the science team to begin a more in-depth investigation—"

"No... Alex, let's not jump too quickly here. Dr. Randal's work is extremely important. I want her and her team to stay on task. What I need from you right now is a full, detailed report. We will need to assess all the data the team collected on this, and the exact location where you found these things. Once I have your report in hand, I will personally present it to the board members. We have to move on this quickly, Alex. I realize this, so it's vital that we head in the right direction. We need all the facts in front of us. Am I making myself clear, Chief?"

"Yes, sir, loud and clear. I'll get right on it. You will be hearing from me soon."

"That's good to know. I can't tell you how much the foundation appreciates your vigilance, Alex. I anxiously await your report, and as soon as we find out what this is all about, you will be hearing from me... You know I love Baja this time of year. The wife and I have a condo down in Cabo San Lucas. We need to get back down there. Hey, maybe we can hook up for a round of golf. What do you say? When was the last time we played a round together? My gosh, it's been too long! Anyway, you guys keep up the good work down there."

"Certainly, sir. That sounds good." Moss smiles briefly back at a grinning Marcus as he logs off.

Moss shuts down his laptop and heads for the main lab. He finds Dr. Randal working with two of her lab assistants as they process data from a spectral analysis of tissue extracted from the latest tunicate specimens the team have collected. She's sitting in front of the lab's main computer when Moss enters the room, and the look on Moss's face does not bring a smile to Dr. Samantha Randal's.

"You've got something to tell me. " The stress in the scientist's voice is evident. "What have you learned?"

"Yeah… I do." Moss sighs. "Do you mind coming up to the bridge? We should speak more privately."

Rafferty is already waiting as Samantha enters the bridge with Moss in tow. The three of them take up a position on either side of the chart table when Rafferty breaks the silence. "How'd the conference with Waverley go?" Then, Razz sees the expression on Alex Moss's face. "That good, huh?"

"So, you did speak to Marcus?" Samantha asks as she looks at Moss. "Did you tell him everything?"

Moss places his hands on the mahogany table and looks briefly down at its varnished surface and then up at Razz and Dr. Randal. "Yeah, I did, and the conversation we just had told me a lot. I was very honest with Marcus. I told him everything that happened and then watched to see what kind of reaction I would get. I was hoping for an equally honest response, but unfortunately, I didn't get it. He's hiding something, and it involves these tiger sharks, but it's bigger than that."

"You could tell he was lying to you, Mr. Moss?" Samantha is intrigued. "How do you know for sure?"

"I've known this man for nine years, Dr. Randal, and he's a very busy guy. He's never been the type to initiate small talk; it's just not his style."

"I'll second that," adds Rafferty. "I've known him just as long, and the amount of time we've spent engaged in idle conversation wouldn't fill a thimble."

"Yeah, Razz is right…" Moss glances toward Dr. Randal and then the creases on his forehead deepen as he turns toward Rafferty. "Razz, he started rambling on about golf."

Razz coughs uncontrollably and then scoffs. "You've never played a round of golf in your life."

Then, Samantha looks at both men. "He is afraid of you, Mr. Moss. It's the only explanation."

"Sounds like it," adds Razz. "So, what else did he tell you? And, more importantly, what do we do about it?"

"He actually told me a lot, Razz. The first thing he inadvertently confirmed is that the sharks we found were not a surprise. He already knew about them, which means the foundation is directly responsible. He asked that I submit a written report of everything we found, and there was one more thing. He also mentioned a condo in Cabo San Lucas."

"Well, that is interesting," Razz breaks in. "We should do some more digging on this. What do you think?"

"My thoughts exactly. But we have to be careful; they'll be watching the ship's movements."

"May I suggest a smoke screen then?" Samantha interjects. "I will assemble a full report of my findings. If we give Marcus exactly what he has asked for, then he'll assume he's in the clear."

"Sounds like a good place to start," Razz agrees as he walks over to the navigation station and examines the chart plotter. "We'll need to go dark if we want to get back over to that cave, Ax." Razz looks up from the plotter at Moss. "It's sixty miles from here. We could outfit a couple of RIBs and make a night run over there."

"We could, but I think I've got a better idea…"

• • •

It's just after sunset as Murray and a second crewman sit inside a RIB positioned next to *Fearless*. Moss looks over the side and smiles. "You guys gonna be okay down there?"

"Sure thing, Chief," Murray yells up to Moss as the two men inside the rugged, six-meter-long inflatable boat steady themselves in the rolling swell. "We're securely anchored, we've got provisions, the Bimini for shelter, water, radios… We're all sorted."

Moss waves down to his crewmen and then steps back from the railing as Rafferty, his handheld radio at the ready, leans into Murray's view. "OK, Murray, on the count of three, you switch on your AIS unit as we go dark, okay? You ready?"

"Ready!"

It's known as an Automated Identification System, and the foundation requires that it be operational at all times so that the location of *Fearless* can be easily tracked no matter what ocean in the world she may be sailing. It is a reliable system used by both commercial and private vessels. The AIS broadcasts a unique signal identifying each ship, but it's only a signal. The moment Murray flips on his portable AIS unit, now programmed to identify the RIB as *Fearless,* Malcolm Rafferty's brief countdown will also be heard by the bridge crew, who will simultaneously switch off the ship's main AIS unit.

With the handoff completed, Moss waves as he looks down at Murray once more. "Take care of my ship, will ya?"

Murray and the second crewman watch from the bobbing RIB as *Fearless* silently moves off under battery power and with minimal lighting in the direction of the cave. The last crimson glow of the evening's twilight is fading fast as Murray turns to his crewmate.

"Right then, I've got my eye on that barbecue beef and cheese MRE. I'll play you for it. How about a few hands of Texas hold 'em?"

· · ·

Motoring at twelve knots across the Gulf of California, it is eleven o'clock at night by the time *Fearless* reaches the location of the undersea cave. Moss doesn't drop anchor, however; he wants to keep his ship nimble. This means the three-man dive team assembling on the darkened aft deck will be making a *live boat* entry from the raised dive platform. It's a three-meter drop into a pitch-black, rolling sea but for the former Navy SEALs, it's just another day at the office.

Rich and Dan check their gear one last time while Rafferty prepares to give the signal to deploy. Dan briefly bends over, shifts his tank forward, and quickly adjusts the shoulder straps of his Halcyon dive harness. He feels the padded stainless steel backplate his dive tank is mounted on snug up against his wetsuit. He straightens and glances over at Rich, who flags a thumbs-up. Dan does the same as Rafferty signals for the two men to deploy. Dan places both hands over his reg and mask as he takes a giant stride off the platform and then plunges fins first into the darkness.

The visibility is near zero as the team switches on their dive lights and start their descent toward the opening of the undersea cave. The plan is to retrieve a second specimen, but first, they have to locate the cave. Rafferty follows the electronic compass on his dive computer as he descends in the cave's direction, when something large streaks in front of his dive light. *It's a shark.*

Rafferty's pulse instantly jumps to overdrive. He turns toward a wide-eyed Rich just as another shark passes between them... and then another. The three startled divers close ranks but soon realize that what they are surrounded by is merely a school of scalloped hammerheads.

Rafferty's pulse rate quickly drops back to normal as he observes dozens of hammerheads gracefully part around them and harmlessly move on in search of squid. He hears Dan's rattle. Rich and Rafferty look in the direction of the sound and see Dan signaling to cut their lights. With their lights off, the divers easily make out the entrance to the cave; it's only a few meters away, and they're not alone.

At a depth of twenty meters, the three divers reach the tumble of huge boulders that lay outside the cave's entrance and duck down amongst them. Shafts of light flutter nervously inside the cave. A few seconds later, two dive scooters emerge with divers onboard, and they're moving fast. Rafferty watches the two scooters rapidly disappear toward the south. He signals to Dan and Rich to stay put and then swims the last few meters into the mouth of the cave. Once inside the entrance, Razz quickly discovers the cave's inner walls twinkling like a Christmas tree. *Shit...*

Rafferty immediately turns back toward Rich and Dan— *There's no time to surface.*

Rafferty switches his light back on as he searches for cover. He knows the shock wave alone will potentially knock them all unconscious or even kill them, but there are no other options; *they can't get clear fast enough.* They need something big between them and the blast, and they need it now. Rich and Dan follow Razz as he leads them farther away toward a bus-sized boulder that looks stable enough to take shelter behind. Less than two agonizing minutes pass before the explosive charges inside the cave deto-nate.

Chapter 19

A fluorescent security light hums endlessly outside the window of Dr. Brian Mathews' jail cell. The rusted fixture is enveloped in a thick swarm of jungle insects that buzz incessantly and flutter about in a feverish cloud as their broad wings flash in its greenish glow. They pass by the hundreds through the open bars of the cell's tiny window and cling to the bare concrete walls, which smell of damp mold. The elaborate patterns their bodies form remind Brian of the illustrated congestion of fauna in a painting by Botticelli.

The biting ones are the worst, while the others are merely interesting. As Brian ponders the insects' incredibly varied shapes and colors, the thought strikes him that he should have been an entomologist... *a much safer study subject... and with better job security.*

Brian had been allowed to make a single brief call before his phone was confiscated along with his backpack. He decided it would be best to hit two birds with one stone, so he called his department head, Dr. Cecelia Wingate, and got her voice mail.

"Cecelia, it's Brian... okay, you were right. Look, I don't have much time. I'm in Tenerife, Colombia. I've been arrested. Can you call my parents please and let them know? I've seriously fucked up. I'm terribly sorry. I know I've let you down."

The back of Brian's shirt is soaked with sweat as he lays on a foam mat spread over a wireframe cot. He tries to sleep, but mostly Brian tries not to think about who may have been his bed's previous occupant. He probably drifted off for a while, he's not sure. He may have even dreamed the voices that first woke him.

Brian opens his eyes; he is not dreaming. One of the voices is clearly American. Brian looks at his watch: 03:27. He hears the voices growing louder and then the jingle of keys as the outer door leading to the room where his cell is located is opened and the light over his head is suddenly switched on.

"He is over there... in the last cell."

Brian sits up just as the police chief who ordered his arrest comes into view. He has a tall American with long, dark hair close behind him.

"You Brian?" the American asks.

"Yeah."

"Get up. You're coming with me. Let's go."

The police chief opens Brian's cell, and in that instant, as the door swings open and his freedom suddenly lies in front of him, the thought that he has no idea who this man is or what his true intentions could possibly be passes quickly through Brian's mind and then out again. Brian gets up and walks out of the cell.

The stranger is at his heels as Brian walks swiftly behind the police chief through a narrow hallway and out into the main station, which is completely dark except for a single desk lamp. The police chief walks over to the large desk. He says nothing as he unlocks a drawer. His expression is flat; yet, he is clearly irritated. He maintains eye contact with Brian as he first pulls out the young

PhD's passport. He holds it up in front of the two men "Pasaporte..." He slaps it down on the desk in front of Brian. "Driver license..." The man's expression doesn't change as he slaps the plastic card down. Then, he reveals Brian's green card and his university faculty identification: "Profesor..." He slaps the final two cards down on the desk. Then, the police chief says in perfect English, "Now, get the fuck out of my town."

Brian fumbles with his wallet and backpack as the tall stranger ushers him quickly outside.

"Get in the jeep."

They climb into a dilapidated Toyota Land Cruiser, and the stranger starts the engine. Only one of the headlamps comes to life, and when Brian tries to reach for his seatbelt, he finds the nylon web strap was long ago cut away for some other purpose. Seconds later, they are roaring off down a pitch-black mountain road that leads back toward the coast.

Brian is too nervous and too unsure of himself to say anything at first. After a few minutes of driving, however, the stranger begins talking.

"Well, hey! That was some fucking jail break, huh?" He looks briefly at Brian and smiles. "Geeez! Relax dude, will ya? I was fucking joking, man! Just chill. We're fucking cool, okay?"

Brian regains some of his confidence. "Is every other word you say always an expletive?"

"Oh man, you are fucking ballsy, dude!" The stranger grins. He trades glances between Brian and the dimly lit road ahead as he wheels the Land Cruiser at high speed. "Hey, I'm Josh by the way—Josh Kranich." He reaches across with his left hand. "Nice to meet you, Professor."

Brian briefly grasps the man's hand. "Thanks for getting me out. And, if I can ask, how did you get me out? And why?"

"You're welcome." Josh flashes another playful smile. "So, how are you liking the spy business, Dr. Mathews? Exciting enough for ya?"

"The spy business? I don't know what you mean?" Brian says haltingly as he grips the handle above his doorframe while the jolting, jerking Land Cruiser catapults down the rough road.

"Un-fucking-believable!" Josh shouts as he slams his hand on the steering wheel and breaks out in laughter. "Dude! You're a natural!" He looks again at Brian and then quickly back at the road. "Look, Brian... Can I call you Brian?"

"Yeah, sure, Josh."

"Great, that's awesome. OK, Brian, look, dude, you know you've been part of an op for like four months, right?"

Brian says nothing.

"Fuck! Dude!" Josh slaps the wheel again. "Respect, man. That's all I gotta say at this point, okay? Fucking respect... okay, um... Let's see... You did your graduate work under Dr. Peter Marsh, right? Yeah, fucking sucks how he went man, that was ugly..."

"I really don't know what you're trying to tell me, Josh. Can you be more specific?"

"Yeah, okay. Let's just get down to it then." Josh clears his throat as he downshifts around a tight turn. "OK, you were first contacted at the International Conference for Truth. The man who spoke to you was in his forties, balding, and wearing a gray suit. Then, you received a series of packages at your home address in San Diego: a flashlight, a burner phone, and a funky set of headphones. Did you like those, by the way?"

"So, you work for them?"

"Yes, I do, Brian, and yes, we've been tracking you the whole time. Oh and nice job on the voicemail to your boss, Dr. Cecelia Wingate. It was honest and touching. I mean really, it was, but I got news for you, dude... you're still fired, okay?"

A piercing pain jabs through Brian's gut. Josh looks over at him. "Hey, don't sweat it, OK? You're doing the right thing." Josh looks back at the road as he grinds the Toyota's gears into submission.

"Am I, Josh? Am I doing the right thing?"

At that moment, Josh looks directly at Brian. "You're on the right side, Brian." He quickly switches back to the road. "Look, you were brought on board because we needed someone with your expertise. But not just sharks, Brian. You know Dr. Alistair Fairchild... you guys were students together, right?"

"Well, yes, but that was years ago..."

"You know him, Brian, and you know sharks. This is why we chose you and also... well... you're a true believer, man." Josh flashes a brief, charming grin at Brian before refocusing on the winding mountain road. "How many of those are left in the world?" Josh aggressively downshifts the Land Cruiser again, and the gears complain as he mercilessly revs the engine.

"So, what did you think of Alistair's creation? You got to see it up close, right?"

"I was appalled... and impressed. He's clearly a genius, but what he's doing is wrong."

"Wow..." Josh briefly eyes Brian and then returns his gaze to the road. "I like you, man, I really mean it. Look, if you ever get in trouble again, whether they pay me or not, I'm gonna get you out, okay?"

"Are you CIA, Josh? Is that even your name?" Brian asks as he tightly clings to the plastic handle above his head.

Josh stares at the road. "I was CIA, but now I work for an independent contractor." Then, he focuses on Brian. "My first name really is Josh; that's no bullshit." He switches back to the road. "I'm gonna get you through this, okay? You're gonna do just fine. You're a natural."

The first hints of dawn glow softly as the Land Cruiser pulls into the Rafael Núñez International Airport parking lot. Josh swings into the first open spot he finds and then shuts down the Toyota's engine. "End of the line, my friend."

"So I can go home now? Really?" Brian says hopefully.

Josh looks at Brian, and the sympathy in his voice actually sounds sincere. "Sorry, man. Look, Brian, you have an important job now, okay? This is your chance to make a difference. You still have work to do."

Brian purses his lips. His disappointment is obvious. "So where am I going, then? What am I supposed to do next?"

"OK! Back on track…" Josh smiles at Brian, then he turns away and rummages through a worn canvas satchel on the floor between his feet. "Here's your plane ticket…" Josh passes the ticket to Brian without looking as he continues to dig into the bag. "And you'll need some cash…" He hands Brian an envelope stuffed with Mexican peso notes. "And a new phone…"

"Why do I need a new phone?" Brian asks as he thumbs through the high-denomination bank notes, and then looks at the ticket. "La Paz?"

"Hand over your phone, Brian."

Brian lets out a groan of protest, and then reluctantly, he reaches down in front of him, pulls his android out from his backpack, and then hands it to Josh.

"Good boy." Josh takes the phone and places it inside his bag. "OK! Let's go get you on your flight! You're gonna do great, Brian. I'm really serious. I'm not shitting you when I say you're a natural. I'm not worried about you one bit. You'll be fine."

Inside the terminal, the two men walk toward security when Brian sees a row of shops. "You mind if I look for something to read?"

"Sure, go ahead. I'll be right here." Josh turns and orders a cafe con leche from a kiosk just behind him.

Brian enters the newsstand and instantly zeros in on several rows of paperbacks. Parsing the titles, he spots a Spanish language translation of John Steinbeck's 1951 Classic, *The Log from the Sea of Cortez*. Brian pays for the book, turns to leave, and nearly runs into Josh.

"I got you a coffee, dude…" Josh holds up a second to-go cup as he sips from his own. "It's Colombian… best fucking coffee on the planet."

The two men reach the security area, and Brian sees Josh confidently pull out his wallet. He spins back toward Brian.

"Check this out, Brian. I love this part… truly the best fucking part of my job, dude."

Brian pulls out his laptop, slips off his watch, and removes his belt for the security line. He observes Josh nonchalantly leave the queue and walk over to the highest-ranking security officer. They speak quietly for a moment, and then Josh shows him something. Brian is stunned to see the security officer nod in approval and wave Josh right past the baggage X-ray machines and metal detectors.

Brian passes through the security check and finds Josh grinning slyly as he waits for him on the other side.

"So, does this mean you're flying with me to La Paz? What about your jeep?"

"Oh that piece of shit? It's a burner, dude."

"I thought burners were phones?"

"In my line of work, Brian, everything's a burner…"

Chapter 20

Falcon awakens once more to his own face staring back at him from the mirrored ceiling above his bed. The image is growing tiresome not only due to a personal aversion to narcissism but also due to the fact that when he sees the reflection, he is nearly always alone.

His second night aboard *Mysterious* was spent with the lovely Cynthia; however, she is strictly a by-the-rules professional. Falcon found the experience hollow and mutually demeaning. His only regret of the past week has been the inability to share his time on board this remarkable yacht with someone he loved. Falcon thinks of her for a moment and then allows her image to quickly fade... *That was a long time ago... and she's long gone.*

Once Marco's two very lovely, and no doubt very expensive, Russian prostitutes picked up on Falcon's lack of interest, Cynthia and Shelly focused their well-paid attentions on Bayani instead.

Falcon mused as, night after night, Bayani flirted and charmed the two women as if the kid had to actually exercise a competitive effort to bed them both.

"I am Filipino," Bayani explained over breakfast one morning. "We are the Latin lovers of the Asian Pacific, and yeah, sure, these girls are professionals, but for me, it's part of the game, so why not have fun?"

Ah to be nineteen again...

As she steadily motored north, the magnificent, eighty-four-meter-long mega-yacht has transited a distance of two thousand two hundred nautical miles during the past seven days.

Falcon lies in bed and then suddenly realizes that, for the first time, *Mysterious* is no longer moving. He hears what sounds like the ship's helicopter preparing to take off. Falcon sits up and looks out of his cabin window just as the gleaming white Airbus AS365 roars from the forward deck and heads for shore.

Falcon scans the view from his cabin port. *Mysterious* is anchored inside the Bay of Cabo San Lucas, Mexico. She's right on schedule—exactly what he, Bayani, and Marco had worked out together during their late-night discussions—but Falcon still feels a pang of sadness. His remarkable holiday is coming to an end, but it is time to get back to work.

Two hours later, Falcon and Bayani stand once more on the helipad of *Mysterious*. Both are changed men, almost unrecognizable from the pair of disheveled deckhands that had arrived the previous week. Marco approaches Falcon as the crew loads their bags and the helicopter's engines spool up.

"There will be a car waiting for you. The driver's name is Esteban. He will take you to the next stop on your journey." Then, Marco places his hand on Falcon's shoulder and looks him in the eye. "Safe travels, my honest friend..."

Lifting off from the deck of the yacht, Falcon and Bayani take one last look at *Mysterious* before the chopper turns toward shore, and their view shifts to the golden sand beaches and resorts of Cabo.

The chopper lands on the far side of the city in an empty field. A black Mercedes is waiting for them. They didn't clear customs, there was no border check and no passport control. The driver approaches Falcon as a second man loads their bags into the trunk of the car.

"Dr. Falcon, my name is Esteban. Welcome to Mexico."

With Falcon and Bayani comfortably in the back, the Mercedes rumbles from the field and then spins up through the winding foothills above Cabo San Lucas.

"The landscape is very dry," Bayani remarks. "I have never seen a desert before."

After a fifteen-minute drive, the black sedan comes to a stop outside the guarded gates of a modern business park. Uniformed, armed security guards speak with Esteban in Spanish while two more inspect the underside of the car with mirrors.

After a radio exchange, the gate glides open, and the guards wave the sedan through. Once inside, Esteban weaves the Mercedes through a series of palm-lined streets and past numerous commercial buildings until he pulls into the circular driveway of a three-story glass and steel office building.

The car rolls to a stop beneath the building's landscaped portico. Esteban gets out and opens the passenger door. Falcon sees two more armed guards wearing the same security uniforms standing in front of the building. As he and Bayani step from the Mercedes, a young man who looks to be in his thirties walks out through the front doors to greet them.

"Hello, you must be Dr. Falcon," the clean-cut American inquires politely. "How was your trip over? All good, I hope. I'm Brandon. It's a pleasure to finally meet you in person."

The young man is lean and fit with light brown hair and eyes. He reaches out to shake hands with Falcon, and then he turns to greet Bayani.

"Hello, kumusta Bayani. Welcome to Mexico."

Falcon looks up at the modern building. "This is quite a facility you have here."

"Oh this?" Brandon quips dismissively. "Yeah, it's nice, but wait until you see the rest."

"Lead on, sir," Falcon answers as he and Bayani follow Brandon inside.

The building's ground floor reception area is sparsely furnished and dimly lit. Falcon and Bayani follow Brandon to a set of elevators.

"We don't get visitors that often," Brandon eagerly shares, "so it's a real treat when we have a VIP like yourself drop by."

He calls the elevator by placing his palm over a digital scanner. The doors slide open, the three men step inside, and the elevator descends four levels.

"We'll head down to the core of our operation first," Brandon announces. The doors open, and a wave of chilled air washes over the three men.

Brandon steps out of the elevator and then turns to face Falcon and Bayani. "So what you see behind me is the heart of our business here." The men walk from the elevator and into a cavernous room filled with row upon row of tall computer cabinets.

"This is enormous!" Falcon gasps excitedly. He walks closer to one of the sleek black computer cabinets. "We didn't have anything this big even at Cambridge. It's incredible!"

"It's a supercomputer, Dr. Falcon." Bayani's jaw is slightly open as he walks up to one of the cabinets, touches it seductively, and gazes at the myriad of tiny flashing lights behind its tinted glass door.

"I see you are a geek of discerning taste." Brandon walks over to where Bayani is standing. "Any questions?"

Bayani grins giddily. "How many teraFLOPS? And how many processors? Um, does it have a name? All the fastest supercomputers have names…"

Brandon chuckles. "Yeah, well, the boss has a sense of humor, so he named her *Jódete*. She's currently crunching data through seven hundred thousand processors with a capacity of eight thousand teraFLOPS. So with each teraFLOP equal to a trillion floating-point operations per second, *Jódete* is easily one of the top three fastest supercomputers in the world. When we opened this facility four years ago, we ran Cray XC40s, but we've recently upgraded. Now we're even ahead of the NSA."

"What about security?" Bayani questions. "How do you maintain system integrity?"

"Wow, you know your shit!" Brandon reaches over and gently presses his fist into Bayani's. "Yeah, well, we're still using the Linux kernel on the new units, but now we have our own in-house operating system running on top. We've made a few custom modifications to the hardware. As for software, we run either our own shit or open source to eliminate the potential for back doors. Of course, the new chips that just landed in our hot little hands will revolutionize our capabilities, and might I add, what you guys did was awesome. Rest assured, they'll be put to good use."

Falcon walks the length of the room and then back again. "This is incredible, Brandon." He folds his arms. "But it's absolutely freezing in here!"

"Yes, well, we have to keep her chilled. Come on. I'll show you the warmer areas where the humans work."

As they tour the next two floors, Falcon finally stops and looks at the clean-cut Californian. "I have to ask, Brandon, and not to be too personal, but… how did you come into this line of work? What's your story?"

Brandon sighs, runs a hand through his hair, and then looks directly at Falcon.

"Well, Dr. Falcon, I used to come surfing down here a lot. It was back when I worked in Silicon Valley. We were all riding high back then—my wife included. Then, tech-bust 2.0 hit, and it all went to hell just like that. We lost almost everything. About that time, a local guy I surfed with invited me to come down here and have a look at his boss's tech company. So I came down to check it out, they made me an excellent offer, and here I am."

"I have to admit," Brandon adds, "it felt really weird at first, but when you have kids to support, you're willing to look past a lot of things, you know?"

"No judgement, Brandon," Falcon cuts in, "but your story is fascinating."

"I hear you… So, yeah, now I do IT for the cartel and, honestly, it's the most interesting and technically challenging work I've ever done. The best part is we've moved out of drugs. Now that most of it is legal up north, there's no more money in it, and frankly, it's small potatoes compared to what we do now."

"Yes, Marco was telling us," Bayani adds, "that you're in the information business now."

"Information is where it's at, Bayani. The world runs on it more than any other single commodity. You can't stack it in a vault, though. It's constantly changing. To stay on top of this business takes the brightest minds we can get our hands on."

They walk past a line of glass offices filled with the sorts of young professionals one would encounter at any top tech firm.

"When I first came down here, I really had my job cut out for me. All they had then was a couple of warehouses, an above-ground T-one line, and rooms full of sweaty hackers stealing credit card data. I could see the potential, though, and they certainly had the budget requirements in place.

At the time, there were a lot of really smart people out of work in California... some of the best tech minds in the world. And for a lot of these guys, it didn't take any effort to switch to the dark side. I mean, we were all young and really pissed off, you know what I mean?"

"I can see your point, Brandon," Falcon agrees as he marvels at the young tech executives passing up and down the halls.

Bayani watches as two shapely young blonds in tight skirts walk by. "This is really impressive. The information business is doing well."

"It's a gold mine, Bayani." Brandon winks.

"You wouldn't know it by watching the corporate-owned news," Brandon continues, "but we're all being forced to live through a second Cold War. The first Cold War was the original war of information, but this time around, it's all gone private. Governments are just enablers. It's a handful of major corporations that actually call the shots. That said, some of our biggest clients are government agencies. We fill a particular niche the deep state can't source any other way."

"History is filled with illicit partnerships between the criminal world and government," Falcon observes. "Take the secret allied agreements made with the Italian mafia during the final days of World War Two—"

"Yes, exactly," Brandon cuts in. "Average people generally have no clue there's been a long cooperative history between organized crime and government, aside from generic graft, of course. The mafia has a long history of doing wet work for the CIA, for example. But since Mr. Snowden alerted the world to the NSA's mass data collection, those fuzzy lines between black and white have gone totally gray. What's right or wrong? What's legal versus what's illegal? I mean, that's just a fairy tale for the kids. Rule of law? It's all designed to control the little people. Power has always done exactly as it pleases."

"Sounds like you know a lot about conspiracies," Bayani comments.

"We rule the dark web," Brandon confides. "And yeah, we've come across some amazing information, and some of it is seriously freaky. It isn't a profit center; it's more of a by-product of what we do.

"Take extraterrestrials, for example. I can confirm it's a very real thing. I've personally read the top-secret files from several nations. Ask me anything about Area 51, I can tell you exactly what they do out there. And 9/11? That was the darkest deep-state black op of all time, meticulously planned from the start, and not by some has-been CIA asset squatting in a cave.

"So, for a while, a bunch of us made digging this stuff up a hobby. The boss is really interested in conspiracy theories. He used to love it. So he gave us free rein to send out what we used to call our own custom-made *freedom of information requests* ... ha ha...

But what we ended up finding got really dark... too dark.

"When we started this thing, some of the guys had the idea to gather the good stuff—the unredacted files—and go public. They wanted to make a big splash at the International Conference for Truth, but in the end, we pulled the plug on the whole thing because we couldn't find any good in it. The truth is out there, but we found truths that are simply too big and ugly to let loose on the public. People have enough to worry about, and now I know stuff that I wish I didn't... things I wish I could forget..."

Falcon's expression goes cold. "Be careful, Brandon. Truth is the most frightening force anyone will ever face."

"I agree, Dr. Falcon. We opened Pandora's box, and we saw what was really inside. In the end, we all decided to leave it alone... It was just too fucking scary."

"Yes, well, this has all been incredibly fascinating, Brandon," Falcon interrupts. "But I think it's time to get down to business. What can you tell me about this project Dr. Alistair Fairchild has been working on?"

Brandon eyes Falcon soberly. "I can give you anything you want, Dr. Falcon. We have everything on him, the foundation that funds him, and his drones. What would you like to know?"

Falcon stares back at Brandon. "Everything."

Chapter 21

Rafferty, Rich, and Dan actually never hear the explosion, which means they are in serious trouble. An undersea exothermic chemical reaction creates a super-heated, highly compressed gas bubble that initially expands at a rate of twenty-five thousand feet per second. The resulting shockwave, traveling faster than the speed of sound, hammers into the three divers as if a dozen angry heavyweight boxers suddenly punched each man at the same time from all directions.

Moss is standing on the aft deck with Seth and two other crewmen. They diligently watch for any sign of dive lights beneath the moonlit sea when they suddenly hear the unmistakable low rumbling of demolition charges detonating beneath the surface. The resulting cavitation sends a corona of seawater spraying up into the moonlight one hundred and fifty meters off the stern of *Fearless*.

Malcolm Rafferty is briefly knocked unconscious—at least, that's what he's guessing as he fights to quickly regain some semblance of coherence and situational awareness. The loud ringing in his head tells him the blast was powerful. The fact that he still has a functioning regulator in his mouth means he's probably okay. Razz reaches for his dive light; it's not working. He raps it against his tank a few times but gets nothing.

In the cerebral haze of the aftershock, Razz struggles to locate his team and evaluate them for injuries. Rich finds his light, knocks it against his other hand, and it comes back to life. He reaches out and grabs Razz by the arm, pulls him up close to his face mask, and stares into Rafferty's eyes. Then, Cal flashes a thumbs-up. He's alright, and he's satisfied that Razz is, too.

Rich and Razz move quickly to locate Dan, but he's no longer next to them. In the darkness and poor visibility, they've lost him. Razz desperately searches amongst the boulders when he bumps into the unmistakable smooth rubber surface of a dive fin. He lifts the fin, but it's empty. Cal passes his light over the rubble near Razz and finds Dan facedown and unconscious. Razz rushes in and turns Dan over as Rich holds the light on his face. Dan's reg is still in his mouth, but he's not breathing.

"Get a rescue boat with searchlights in the water now!" Moss shouts. He grabs his radio and calls up to his bridge crew. "We have a medical emergency on the aft dive deck. I need Dr. Randal up here ASAP." Moss then locks eyes with his ship's medic, but Seth is already two steps ahead of him.

"I'm on my way, Chief," Seth answers before Moss even speaks. "I'll have the crash kit and oxygen up here in two minutes."

In the murky darkness below, Razz grabs the shoulder straps of Dan's dive harness while Rich cradles his legs, and the divers begin a controlled ascent. As they slowly rise toward the surface, Rich shines his dive light up and around in an attempt to signal their location.

From his position on the aft dive deck, Moss suddenly spots the muted flash of a dive light from beneath the surface. The sight brings an audible sigh of relief that the guys survived and they're on their way up. Moss goes to the railing and looks toward the bow of his ship just as a rugged inflatable boat is being lowered into the sea. He calls to the three men inside using his handheld radio.

"They're just off the stern... a hundred meters out at six o'clock," he informs the men inside the RIB. "I can see their light... they're surfacing."

"Wilco Chief, we see them. We're on our way."

Moss spins back toward the dive deck just as Seth and his assistant, Randy, arrive with their gear. Moss is relieved to see Dr. Samantha Randal is right behind them. "What's happened?" she asks, "I heard an awful sound..."

"We had an explosion take place underwater," Moss informs her. "Our divers are surfacing now. We have a rescue boat heading out to pick them up."

"My God! How could this happen? Was it some sort of accident?"

"We don't know what happened exactly, but I can tell you an explosion like the one we just saw go off was no accident."

Rafferty breaks the surface and then struggles to get Dan's head above the rolling swell as Rich pulls his regulator from his mouth. "Over here!" Rich squints into the beam of a searchlight as he fights to hold on to Dan's unconscious body. The waves on the surface batter the trio of men and threaten to pull them apart.

The crewmen in the RIB motor in close, the driver shoves the engine into neutral, and the three men go to work as fast as they can to rescue their shipmates. The three divers are rapidly hauled from the water and into the RIB. Razz and Rich quickly shed their tanks and assist as crewmen carefully lay Dan out on the bottom of the boat. They strip his unconscious body of dive gear while the RIB's driver guns the engine, spins the boat around, and races back toward *Fearless*.

Seth and Dr. Randal stand at the ready as the RIB motors up alongside the dive platform and Dan is brought onboard. Dr. Randal makes a rapid visual assessment of the man's condition, and then her worst fears are realized when she presses a stethoscope against Dan's chest and hears a pronounced, mechanized mill wheel murmur.

"Quickly, gentlemen!" Dr. Randal commands. "We've got to get him onto his left side."

Seth goes to assess the condition of Rich and Razz. He checks their eyes for pupil dilation, their respiration, and their blood pressure, and then he looks for signs of decompression sickness as Dr. Randal places an oxygen mask over Dan's face.

"Is it barotrauma?" Moss asks as he cradles his crewman in his arms.

"I'm afraid so," Dr. Randal answers hurriedly. "Keep his head down. We've got to get his legs and feet elevated and move him into a Trendelenburg position. He has a left-ventricular air bubble. We've got to keep it from entering the coronary artery whilst we move him to the ship's hyperbaric chamber, and it has to happen right now, Mr. Moss."

On hearing this, Razz pushes Seth away. "We're fine. Go help Dan."

Minutes later, Dan is undergoing treatment inside the ship's hyperbaric chamber under Dr. Randal's supervision while Moss and Razz try to evaluate what just happened.

"These guys were pros, Ax. They knew exactly what they were doing."

"You got a look at the charges?"

"Yeah, I did," Rafferty answers. "They used exactly what the navy likes to use: HBX-1. I saw six time-delayed charges mounted around the cave's entrance. Whoever it was, they wanted to make damn sure they collapsed that cave and buried the evidence."

Moss grimaces at the news, but with two of his crewmen still sitting in a RIB on the other side of the gulf, and a medical emergency still ongoing, he has bigger problems to deal with.

"We have to get back across and pick up the guys waiting in our decoy RIB. Dr. Randal says Dan is stable, but we need to get him to a hospital, and in his condition, we can't use the chopper." Then, Moss sighs as he looks carefully at Razz. "You okay? Are you sure?"

"I'm fine, Chief," Rafferty assures Moss. "Let's go pick up the guys. We have to take care of Dan."

Twelve and a half hours after leaving two crewmen behind, Moss stands on the bridge and checks the decoy AIS position once more on the chart plotter. The five-meter-long RIB masquerading as *Fearless* is still anchored exactly where they left it.

The first hints of dawn glow above the horizon as Murray sits on watch. He scans the golden sea and sights *Fearless* approaching from the east. Murray reaches down and nudges his dozing crewmate. "Hey, mate, wake up. The ship's coming back. I can see her."

With the RIB and her crew back on board and *Fearless* once again sending out a legitimate AIS signal to whomever may be watching, Moss turns the ship south and sails for the closest major city with a hospital; in this case, that city is Cabo San Lucas.

Chapter 22

CIA Special Activities Division officer Jeff Buxton slides his phone back inside his jacket pocket as he turns to his two colleagues. "We're on, gentlemen. I just received the go-ahead. They're issuing us a C-130."

"Fuck yeah..." one of Buxton's men growls coldly.

"When do we leave?" asks the other. "Where's the rendezvous point this time?"

"La Paz," Buxton replies. "The doc and his team will meet us down there."

• • •

"Your sparkling mineral water, Dr. Fairchild." The equally sparkling flight attendant places the bottled water, along with a crystal glass and its linen coaster, on the burled walnut tray table in front of Alistair. Alistair briefly makes eye contact and smiles politely as the kiwi metal band Devilskin pounds through his headphones. He leans back in his seat and turns up the volume a bit more while the Gulfstream 650ER streaks through the sky over the Baja peninsula and on to La Paz.

The Lockheed-Martin C-130-E's four massive Allison turbo-prop engines roar at idle as the plane warms up outside of a hangar at Creech Air Force Base, northeast of Las Vegas, Nevada. This particular Herky Bird has seen a lot of action since she first rolled off the line in 1989. She flew covert missions in South America, attended both shows in Iraq, and then saw duty in Afghanistan, followed by Sudan, but by C-130 Hercules standards, her past missions have been pretty standard stuff.

The Hercules has a sixty-plus-year history of continual service, which is an elite record that few aircraft can match. A time-tested work horse, C-130s are currently being flown in seventy countries around the world. A Hercules has landed and taken off at both poles, the highest altitude airstrips of the Himalayas, and even the deck of an active aircraft carrier, but this will be the first time in history that a C-130 will be used to launch the CIA's new top-secret MS41-T assassination drones.

Late-day desert sunlight paints the scene in fiery colors. The three CIA officers emerge from the hangar and stride confidently across the Tarmac toward the waiting Hercules. The men don headsets as they strap themselves into seats designed to carry paratroopers. The Hercules taxis out to the runway, and the heavy cargo aircraft's 4200shp engines' deafening power lifts the hulking plane into the air.

• • •

After landing at La Paz, Alistair and his team quickly exit the Gulfstream and head for a waiting van. The G650's engines are still active as a crew member closes the plane's main hatch and the jet immediately begins to taxi back out to the airport's runway. Alistair doesn't look back when he hears the jet roar off.

He climbs into the front seat of the van while his five-member team silently piles into the back for the brief transfer over to the far end of the airfield. Their combined stress levels are all pretty high, but they're always at peak just before a mission.

When viewed from the outside, the foundation's above-ground facility appears to be nothing more than a standard corporate hangar—one of a dozen on the field. The van carrying Alistair and his team drives inside while the hangar's motorized doors close slowly behind it. Alistair and his technicians exit the van and head straight to the back of the hangar. The group silently passes one by one through a high-security checkpoint and into a large cargo elevator.

Three floors down, the elevator's heavy doors glide smoothly open, and the group of six men exits into an underground warehouse filled with refrigerated shipping containers. A lab tech hurriedly approaches Alistair.

"We have everything ready, Dr. Fairchild."

"All twenty units?" Alistair questions. "You've run the tests?"

"Yes, Dr. Fairchild. All twenty units have been fully tested. The operations center in Long Beach is standing by. We are ready to deploy."

• • •

Just after 20:00 hours, the CIA's Hercules begins its approach into La Paz.

Inside the hangar, a security guard monitors the aircraft's communications with the airport control tower and alerts Dr. Fairchild below.

"We're up," Alistair quips.

Alistair's team scrambles around him as the young PhD walks over to one of the shipping containers marked for deployment and unlatches its steel door. He swings it open, and a blast of frigid air hits his face.

Every MS41-T is stored under deep freeze until activation. Inside each of the reefer containers are ten unmarked, flat black, five-meter-long coffin-shaped transport cases made of high-strength carbon composite. Each transport case houses one fully militarized, biological assault drone waiting to be activated and then released to destroy its target.

Alistair's crew quickly rolls the twenty prepared units out from their reefer containers and across the floor toward the elevator.

Under the cover of night, the Hercules taxis to a stop in front of the hangar. Her crew keeps the engines running as they lower her rear cargo door, and three CIA officers stroll down the ramp to observe the action.

From inside the hangar, the twenty black cases containing the drones are efficiently rolled outside and then up into the C-130's cargo compartment, where they are secured to the floor. Less than twenty minutes after landing, the C-130 will be taxiing back out to the runway and preparing for takeoff.

With the drones firmly secured, the pilots close the cargo door. Alistair and his five-member team rush to strap into their seats. Nine minutes later, the taxiing C-130 receives clearance from the La Paz tower to enter the runway. Alistair tightens his safety harness and then leans back and closes his eyes as the fuselage of the C-130 begins to vibrate harshly. He allows the deafening sound of the engines to obliterate every complicated thought in his head as the plane lifts off and then climbs in a sweeping arc toward the west.

An hour later, Alistair feels someone shaking him. "Hey, Doc... you awake?" He looks up into the face of Jeff Buxton. "Dr. Fairchild, we are approaching the drop zone."

"Right," Alistair snaps as he squirms in his seat to orient himself. "How much time do we have?"

"About fifteen minutes. The flight crew has initiated the descent."

Alistair starts to unbuckle his harness when Buxton grabs his hand. "Now, hold on, kid," he warns. "Did you forget the briefing already? You don't move from this seat unless you've attached your safety line."

Buxton straightens, takes a step back, and addresses the entire civilian team that sits in front of him.

"Listen up!" he commands in a bellowing tone. "I want everyone to grab their safety lines and clip them on."

The men each reach behind them, detach one of several nylon lines that are affixed to the plane's ceiling, and clip them to the safety harnesses they each wear.

Buxton watches as each man clips in. "Good job, gentlemen..." He nods in approval. "Follow the rules and you'll all do just fine. We're going to take this step by step. Am I clear?" He looks down the line as each man nods, and then he continues, "When we reach the drop zone, you guys will leave your seats and prepare the drones for deployment. Once the drones are made ready, you will return to your seats and buckle in. Am I clear?" Buxton once more looks into the face of each man, including Alistair. "Once that door opens..." Buxton shouts at the men as he points toward the plane's rear cargo door, "nobody—and I mean NOBODY—will leave their seat for ANY reason. AM I CLEAR?" He stares at each man with a menacing grimace that seamlessly shifts to a devilish grin. "Happy hunting, gentlemen. Now let's kick some ass, shall we?"

"We're coming up on the drop zone," one of the CIA officers informs Buxton.

Buxton spins back toward Alistair and his team. "Alright, gentlemen, let's get these things ready to fly."

The technicians immediately unbuckle themselves from their seats and go to work removing the coffin-shaped covers of the carbon composite cases and stacking them behind a cargo net. Then, they busily go about hastily removing the tie-downs that hold each drone to the flat base of its transport case. Buxton watches as a technician bends down next to one of the massive frozen sharks and inspects the camera that's mounted in the drone's dorsal fin.

"No cameras," Buxton orders as he wags his finger at the crouching technician. Then, he shouts to the rest, "No cameras! I don't want any cameras activated on this mission. Am I clear?"

With the covers removed, the temperature difference causes the rigidly frozen drones to emit a light fog that seeps away from their bodies and flows out across the expanse of the C-130's cargo deck. The fog builds and thickens around the feet of the men as they finish unpacking the last of the drones and stow the covers. All twenty of the eight-hundred-pound units now lay fully exposed, with each unit resting on the carbon composite base of its transport container—a base that will now serve as a launch pad.

Alistair moves rapidly amongst his drones and quickly inspects each unit one final time. Then, he looks up at Buxton. "We're ready to deploy."

"Take your seats, gentlemen," Buxton orders. "I want everyone strapped in good and tight."

Alistair straps himself in, pulls out his tablet computer, confirms his secure satellite connection, and logs into the drone's control center in Long Beach. Then, an alarm sounds as the plane's rear cargo door opens to the night sky and the fog that had formed a dense layer around their feet is instantly sucked away by the rush of air now circulating through the C-130's unpressurized cargo compartment.

Alistair finds himself transfixed by the moonlit horizon of the Pacific Ocean as it slowly comes into view. The plane now skims less than two hundred feet above the waves that rush beneath them in a shimmering blur. Alistair looks back at his tablet, he leans forward, makes eye contact with Buxton, and flashes him a thumbs-up. Buxton nods and gives the OK. Alistair leans back, and types the final commands into the tablet. The first ten sharks are instantly reanimated, and in nearly the exact same instant, they're gone.

The ten drones disappear into the sea below. Alistair checks his watch, and then he looks back at Buxton. Buxton tracks the seconds on his own watch, and then he looks at Alistair and holds up his hand: five... four... three... two... Alistair turns back to his tablet and sends the command to activate the last ten drones, and then he types in the command to deploy, and nine are instantly gone.

The tenth fully activated drone, unit thirteen, remains strapped down to its launch platform. The massive tiger shark thrashes and snaps madly as it fights to free itself from the nylon tie strap still holding its tail securely to the bottom of the case that is itself secured to the floor of the cargo plane.

Alistair panics. The shark's snapping jaws come within inches of his legs as it continues to struggle wildly against the restraint holding the drone back from its programmed mission. Alistair jerks reflexively away from the shark's flashing teeth, and in his terrorized haste, he loses his tablet.

"What the fuck do we do?" one of the technicians screams. The madly thrashing shark's huge jaws viciously snap like a motorized guillotine in front of the horrified men. They each sit helplessly buckled into seats that run down the side of the fuselage, and each one of them is now desperately searching for some way to escape, but there is no way out but through the cargo door.

"Don't move!" Buxton shouts. "We're climbing. It'll break free. Nobody move!"

The plane slowly gains altitude while the five-meter-long reanimated tiger shark continues to struggle and then violently crash against the opposite side of the cargo compartment. In a torrent of flying fins and flashing teeth, the massive tiger shark flips over backward and smashes into the net holding the stacked covers to the cases.

The technicians on either side of Alistair begin screaming for him to do something to deactivate the drone, but Alistair's tablet is hopelessly cracked and is lying near the edge of the open cargo door.

The giant shark entangles itself inside the cargo net, its jaws savagely shred through the webbing, and the stacked cases break free and then fly around the cargo compartment. One of the five-meter-long boxes strikes the men sitting closest to the door and knocks one of Buxton's guys out cold. The rest of the boxes are tossed around at odd angles inside a force-five tornado of fighting, thrashing shark flesh until the last of them finally fly out of the open door and into the sea.

For an instant, Alistair becomes fascinated by the scene unfolding in front of him. He is uncontrollably drawn into the spectacle, the motion, the total beauty, and the complete chaos as he finally witnesses his drone in action and up close for the first time.

"Fucking hell!" the technician sitting next to Alistair shouts. "Fucking bloody hell! Do something!"

"Shut up! It'll break free!" Alistair shouts back angrily. "Just look at the tie strap; it's nearly torn through! Stop being such a fucking pussy!"

At that moment, the strap holding the struggling shark's tail finally lets go. The shark whips back and then lunges forward, takes the upper body of the man next to Alistair into her jaws, and rips it from the seat he was buckled into. The reanimated tiger shark lashes back again as her teeth gnash into the mutilated partial corpse now wedged inside her gaping maw.

Raw horror instantly paralyzes the helpless men lined up in front of the vicious monster they devoted years of their lives to create. The cargo compartment fills with the panicked screams of the technicians as they are sprayed with the blood of their former colleague. Then, the fully weaponized zombie tiger shark finally launches herself out of the rear cargo door and into the sea.

Chapter 23

Marco gazes into Kimberly's blue eyes as he gracefully sweeps her around the aft lounge deck of *Mysterious*. The couple smoothly dances to a seductive tango as the moonlight plays across the twinkling Pacific sea that surrounds them. Kimberly's perfectly fitted, pale blue strapless dress complements every element of the beautiful scene as she smiles up at her loving husband. As the song playing over the ship's sound system draws to a close, Marco bows to his wife and then turns toward Francis.

"Is there any more champagne left in the bottle, Francis?"

"I'm afraid not, sir. Shall I retrieve another?"

Marco sees the happiness that shapes Kimberly's face. He looks back at Francis. "Why not? Let us open another one…" He returns his full attention to Kimberly. "We are celebrating tonight…"

On the bridge of *Mysterious*, her captain carefully studies a radar display as a member of his bridge crew looks on. "Exactly where did you say you last saw the plane? Show me please."

"It was here, Captain," the crewman directs. "Twenty-two nautical miles northeast of our current position."

"Where did it come from? Where is it now?"

"I saw it briefly enter our twenty-mile security perimeter. It approached from the coast of Mexico, it circled, and then it turned back toward the Baja Peninsula."

"What type of plane was it? What altitude was it flying at?"

"The radar signature matched that of a large military transport, sir… most likely a C-130. The altitude of the aircraft changed dramatically. This is why I called you up here, Captain. The plane descended until it disappeared from radar, and approximately eight minutes later, it reappeared as it regained altitude. I thought it looked suspicious."

The captain briefly looks at the radar screen once more and then eyes his crewman. "Good work. Keep watching, will you? Alert me if you see anything else."

The captain pats the crewman on the shoulder, and then he walks over to his helmsman. "I want a change in course," he says quietly as the man at the helm nods in acknowledgment. "Due west away from the coast, and increase our speed to eighteen knots. I want as much open water around us as we can get."

The seasoned captain, a Spaniard who spent his youth serving in Spain's naval special warfare force, the elite Unidad de Operaciones Especiales, leaves the bridge and heads downstairs to locate the master of the yacht and inform him of the potential danger.

Marco is just raising another glass to his lovely Kimberly when he catches sight of his captain approaching. He puts the glass down as he speaks softly to his wife. "Something's happened. Excuse me please…"

Marco leaves Kimberly standing at the bar and walks over to meet his captain. "Rafael, what is it? What has happened?"

"I apologize for disturbing you, Master. We picked up a suspicious aircraft on radar... a military aircraft."

Marco furls his brow as he concentrates on his captain's words. "Where did it come from? What was suspicious about it?"

Marco listens carefully as Rafael explains the plane's troubling behavior, and his expression grows more serious the more he hears. Marco collects all the details from Rafael, quickly assesses them, and then mentally processes the information with what he already knows.

"Rafael, I fear we are about to be attacked by the same horrible creatures they sent to kill my dear friend Juan Carlos."

Marco's tone is a mix of sorrow and anger as he focuses intently on his captain's face. "We must take full defensive measures." Marco pauses, and then he stares at Rafael again. "We will need to see them coming. Turn on all the hull lights. Then, Marco briefly places his hand on his captain's shoulder. "My friend, if I am correct in my assessment, we don't have much time."

"Yes, sir," the Spaniard answers. "I will see to it immediately."

The captain quickly leaves to alert the entire ship's crew, while Marco turns back toward Kimberly. Her fearful expression alone is enough to fill the man with vengeful rage. "Don't worry, my darling." He takes her hand and squeezes it gently. "We will take care of the problem." Then, Marco turns to Francis. "I want all the women down below, Francis. Take care of my Kimberly please."

"Right away, sir."

Fifteen minutes later, the fully armed crew rushes to assemble their gear on deck. Marco arrives by elevator. He is dressed in fatigues and carrying an RPG-7V2.

A proven and reliable weapon, the Russian-made, 40mm, shoulder-mounted rocket-propelled grenade launcher has been in steady production since the old Soviet days.

Marco is closely followed by a crewman pushing a catering cart laden with an assortment of rocket-powered grenades.

A few minutes later, Raul, Marco's chief of security, arrives by the same elevator. Marco grins when he sees the muscular, mustachioed Mexican swiftly exit the elevator with his two assistants rushing to keep pace behind him.

"I see you have decided to bring the big gun to the party, my friend," Marco quips with satisfaction as he watches Raul march a large rolling platform across the aft deck. The portable steel stand is mounted with an American-made, M242 25mm, electrically powered chain gun.

Raul nods approvingly toward Marco as he passes in front of his boss. "I like your style, too. It's a good night for fishing!"

Raul rolls the platform over to the farthest starboard corner of the aft deck. Then he and his assistants quickly lock the platform in place, fix the 119 kilo auto-cannon onto its swivel mount, and connect its electric motor to a power supply.

A second crewman arrives behind a rolling container packed with 25mm ammunition. The man then rushes to load the weapon as Raul completes the chain gun's final adjustments.

The crew works feverishly to distribute boxes of grenades and extra clips until the men's actions are interrupted by shots emanating from the deck beneath them.

Raul grabs his radio. "What's going on?" he demands. "Do you see something? Or are you just wasting bullets?"

Frantic shouts and rapid automatic weapons fire rise up from the lower deck. The sound drowns out the rest of Raul's sentence.

The hard-nosed security chief shoves his radio back in its holster and works to complete the firing sequence of the M242.

"I've got one in my sights!" Marco shouts excitedly as he aims his RPG just off the stern of his eighty-four-meter-long luxury mega-yacht.

The churning wake rushing off the rear of the ship is lit up like a gigantic disco-decorated Jacuzzi thanks to hundreds of designer LED lights that line the yacht's hull. No one thought to change the computerized lighting program, however. The LEDs are currently synchronized to rotate through a continuously shifting rainbow of festive color.

Marco has a clear sight set on his target—a dark menacing shape cutting through a frothy, electric turquoise lit sea. He aims and pulls the trigger. The rocket-powered grenade fires off into effervescent glowing water that now shifts from violet to bright fuchsia.

The propellants inside the rocket fuel the grenade at one hundred and fifteen meters per second while it sends a plume of flaming exhaust two meters out of the back of the launcher.

Marco is thrilled to see the thermobaric tank-killer warhead explode into its target. His crew cheers as a blinding pyrotechnic burst sends a mass of vaporized seawater and chunks of the huge shark scattering into the air.

"I see more of them!" another crewman shouts.

"Use the grenades!" Raul commands as he points the chain gun down at four fast-approaching MS41-T drones. He carefully judges their speed and range as they swim rapidly toward the yacht in water now brightly illuminated in festive tangerine LED. Raul smiles devilishly as he opens up the auto-cannon and shreds the four tiger sharks with a continuous raining hail of white-hot 25mm rounds.

On the bridge, Rafael calms his edgy crew as their ship fills with the sounds of explosions and high-volume, large-caliber weapons fire.

"They have their job, and we have ours." The captain checks his rate of fuel consumption once more. "Let's see if she can make twenty knots, shall we?" He lays his hand on the throttle and gently eases it up a bit higher. "If they want to chase us, let's make them work hard."

"Should we continue on this same course, Captain?" the helmsman inquires.

"Yes, hold this heading. Don't change a thing. Our guys are using live munitions back there. A sudden alteration could get somebody killed."

• • •

The operations center in Long Beach, California is on full alert as the drone's controllers struggle for the first time since their program went on full active duty.

"We just lost another one!" a technician shouts in shocked disbelief as the telemetry streaming in front of him reports that another unit's control module has just been destroyed. "Shit! What the hell are they using out there? It's a fucking pleasure yacht for Christ's sake!"

His CIA supervisor walks over and calmly studies the screen. "How many drones do we have left?"

"There's only two left in group one, but we still have eight left in group two."

"What about our late bloomer?" The CIA officer grumbles. "They had some trouble with the drop. Apparently one of the drones was delayed exiting the aircraft."

"Oh that one? It's way behind, sir. It's still miles away. I'm not sure what use it will be."

"Well, keep an eye on her. She may be of some help. Just give her a chance." Then, the man glances at his watch. "Have any units made it on board yet?"

"I think possibly, but I can't confirm."

The CIA officer places his hands on his hips and then calls out to another technician. "Can you bring up the surveillance satellite link? Do we have infrared active? OK then… switch it over to station three, will ya? Yeah, this one in front of me. Thanks."

. . .

Marco boldly laughs with sinister glee as he watches another massive tiger shark explode into a flaming fireball in front of him. "Look how the head flies so high into the air!" Marco takes a moment to look up toward the stars. "Did you see that one, Juan Carlos?" Marco shouts. "That was for you, my friend!" Marco turns to the crewman assisting him. "Hand me another thermobaric warhead please."

"I'm sorry, sir, but that was the last one." The crewman quickly examines the variety of rocket-powered grenades he has left on his catering cart. "I have armor-piercing tank rounds, sir."

Marco sighs. "Well, I guess those will have to do…"

A few minutes and several explosions later, the sea around *Mysterious* has finally returned to the peaceful serenity that existed before the attack. Marco, Raul, and the rest of the crew on the upper aft lounge deck watch and wait silently to see if any more drones are left. Marco takes a radio from a crewman and calls up to the bridge.

"Rafael, we may have done it," he announces excitedly. "Yes, yes, I agree. We should maintain speed for a bit longer. Well done, Captain. Well done, my friend."

Marco hands the radio back to the crewman just as he sees Raul approaching.

"Do you think we got them all?" Marco asks. "Did anybody keep count? You know they can only deploy twenty at one time. That is the maximum number."

"We don't have an accurate count, sir," Raul answers. "I feel we should remain vigilant for a while longer."

At that moment, another crew member approaches, and Raul can see that the man is bleeding. "What happened?" Raul demands in an authoritative tone. "Were you injured by the sharks?"

"No, sir. A bullet grazed my arm; it's nothing," the crewman answers. "But Diego is trapped down on the service deck. We need help."

Raul, Marco, and four crew members arrive on the aft service deck and find an incredible sight. A crewman lies pinned between a rack of scuba equipment and the bullet-ridden corpse of a massive female tiger shark.

"My God..." Marco is stunned by the scene in front of him as he rushes to the injured man's side. "Diego, what happened?"

"I think my leg is broken." the man groans.

Raul rapidly scans across the yacht's service deck. It's packed full of water toys, tenders, motor bikes, and other recreational equipment. "Quickly," Raul orders, "we use the winch on the front of that ATV..."

The men start the all-terrain vehicle's engine and then spool out the steel cable from the winch mounted to its front bumper. They run the cable across the floor and hook it around the dead shark's tail.

As the men work to free the trapped crewman, Marco runs his hand down the bullet-pocked hide of the huge dead shark, and then he looks at Diego. "I'm going to have this shark skinned in your honor, and then I will have my barstools covered with the leather." Diego grins at the thought. "Ah! You like that idea?"

A dark shape suddenly catches Marco's attention. He spins toward the fast moving object just as the last MS41-T, *the late bloomer,* flies past him and crashes into a group of tenders and then smashes into a vintage Italian AquaRiva motor launch. Raul and the men around him instantly take up their weapons once more as Marco reaches for the submachine gun lying near Diego. He checks the clip and then joins the fight against the viciously snapping shark.

The biological assault drone flips over and lands on top of a four-meter-long crew RIB, and for an instant, the huge shark flops about inside the rubber inflatable. The artificially engineered female tiger shark's snapping jaws quickly rip through the rubber tube of the RIB, causing it to collapse explosively.

The late bloomer catapults herself from the collapsed tender and lunges at the men, but as she attempts to attack, she becomes entangled in the extended steel cable attached to the winch on the ATV.

The five-meter-long shark tumbles and fights to free herself. The force jerks the ATV violently onto its side, while at the other end of the cable, Diego can feel the shark's tale suddenly jerk and its body lurch away from the scuba rack and then finally shift off of him.

The four crewmen standing with Raul and Marco fire their weapons continuously at the struggling tiger shark as it snaps and crashes into the equipment around it. Then, an enraged Raul moves in closer to the shark's snapping jaws and fires a rapid volley of rounds point blank into its eyes and head while the men beside him pump dozens of rounds into the madly snapping tiger shark's gills and side until the flurry of bullets finally impacts the drone's control unit.

• • •

"Fuck!" The technician monitoring the telemetry back in Long Beach throws up his arms in disgust. "We lost her! We lost the late bloomer!"

Chapter 24

"Well, what do we do now?" Brian asks Josh as the unlikely pair walks through the La Paz airport terminal side by side. You said Alistair's facility was right here at the airport; shouldn't we go stake it out? Shouldn't we be following someone or something? Isn't that what you guys do?"

Josh stops in his tracks. "Brian, wow, chill man, will you?"

"But we have a plan, right?" Brian continues. "We should definitely have a plan…"

Josh throws his head back in disgust. "Geez… dude…" He lets out a long groan as he looks up at the ceiling, "you seriously make my head hurt." He turns to stare at Brian. "Look, dude, this is the real spy business, okay? It's not like that movie shit. This game is all about information. It's nothing but information, and frankly, most of the time it's pretty boring."

Josh starts walking again. "What we have to do right now is wait. We're in the right place, but it's not the right time, okay? This is the other big part nobody talks about: *the waiting* … fuck… the waiting fucking sucks." Josh tilts his head back again, and then he looks back at Brian. "The waiting just drains your spirit down to a tiny ember of its former flaming self, man. So, we need to keep that from happening, right? We have to keep the flame alive, dude. So, as soon as spooks like me hit a new town, you know what we do? We find the bar, dude. We find the best one, and we get hammered."

Brian follows Josh out to the curb and watches as he flags a cab. "Our chariot has arrived," Josh announces cheerfully. The pair climbs inside, and Josh begins speaking to the driver in fluent Spanish. He then turns back to Brian. "You got that, right? Taxi driver's taking us down to the waterfront… a place called Jungle Bar. It's supposed to be pretty cool. Sound good to you?"

The taxi meanders through the streets of La Paz until it turns onto a boulevard that runs beside the city's esplanade. Brian gazes at the bustling tourist town moving past the window of the cab and tries to imagine what it must have been like back in 1940, when John Steinbeck, his friend, marine biologist Ed Ricketts, and the crew of *The Western Flyer* spent time here during their six-week-long expedition. Brian is lost in thought when the cab arrives at its destination.

"Dude!" Brian feels Josh grab his arm. "Wake up, man, we're here!"

They each choose something from the menu. Josh orders a large, Mexican-inspired burger and chili cheese fries, while Brian orders grilled fish and a green salad with dressing on the side. After they finish their meals, Brian watches in silence as Josh drinks one beer after the other for the rest of the evening until the dark-haired stranger finally looks at his watch.

"OK, hey! That wasn't so bad, huh?"

"What do you mean?" Brian asks. "Are we going to do something?"

"You bet we are."

Josh tips up his beer bottle and allows the last of it to freely drain down his throat, and then he slams the empty bottle down onto the table. "I'll go pay the tab and we're outta here, dude." He gets up and then briefly turns back toward Brian. "Why don't you go outside and get us a cab back to the airport?"

It's nearly midnight as Josh and Brian stand alone in front of the airport's lonely cargo terminal. Brian nervously watches their cab's taillights disappear into the darkness. He feels Josh punch him lightly in the arm, so Brian turns to look at his accomplice.

"Follow me…"

Josh spins away and walks off along the airport's chain-link perimeter fence. After about a hundred meters, he stops.

"This looks like a good spot."

Josh kneels down and begins rummaging through his satchel. He pulls out a pair of wire cutters. Josh holds the rusted tool up in front of Brian and smiles. "Pretty sexy, huh?" He turns back toward the fence and quickly cuts through the crosshatched wire mesh and then pushes apart the opening. "After you, dude."

Once inside, Josh strides over to one of the private hangars clustered at the far end of the field as Brian follows. Josh traces along the back of one of the corrugated metal buildings. He stays close to its rear wall, and then he stops and turns back toward Brian. "OK, so here we are…"

"What do you mean?" Brian asks. "Is this Alistair's hangar?"

"This?" Josh gestures toward the hangar the two men are standing next to. "No way, man. We would never be able to get this close. No, sir. Alistair's hangar is over there." Josh points to a larger hangar about two hundred meters away. "You see that? Perfect angle of view, man, so all we do now is wait."

Brian sighs as he drops his backpack to the ground, sits down in the dry grass, and leans back against the hangar's rusted metal outer wall. About two hours later, Josh nudges Brian. "Hey, dude, you hear that?"

"I hear an airplane," Brian answers, "but this is an airport."

"That's not just any airplane, dude. That's the plane we've been waiting for."

Brian sits up on his knees and looks toward the large hangar when Josh suddenly grabs him and jerks him back to the ground. "Geez, dude, don't you know anything?"

He stares at Brian closely as he whispers. "This is a high-security area, man. If they find us, we're dead. You got that?"

Josh lies on his stomach beneath the dry grass and opens his satchel. He hands Brian a cheap set of binoculars. "Sorry, man, they're not night vision or anything, but you should still be able to see what goes on."

At that moment, the sound of the approaching aircraft's four turboprop engines grows louder and then suddenly builds to a deafening level as the returning C-130 taxis past the hangar that Josh and Brian are hiding behind. The two men observe as the cargo plane guns its engines, turns around, and then comes to a stop in front of the hangar owned and operated by the foundation.

Josh grabs a second pair of binoculars from his bag. "Show's on," he whispers, as Brian lifts his binoculars to his eyes.

The huge cargo plane parks at the edge of the concrete apron in front of the hangar. The hangar's doors are already in the process of opening. Brian watches with nervous fascination as the fluorescent lights from inside the hangar project a bright beam across the silhouette of the C-130. It sits in place with its navigation lights still flashing and its engines still running.

Then, the plane's rear cargo door lowers to the tarmac. Brian and Josh look on as several men slowly emerge. They walk down the ramp as others from inside the hangar rush to roll two gurneys out to the plane and then up inside the cargo hold. Then, Brian sees Alistair for the first time in five years. Brian adjusts the focus as he watches Alistair walk down the ramp. He is being helped by another man. Then Alistair suddenly stops and pulls away from the man who is helping him. He doubles over and vomits onto the tarmac beside the plane.

"OK, we gotta go," Josh whispers. "We gotta get out of here. We need to find a car."

Brian scrambles to keep close behind Josh as he walks swiftly along the fence. Josh retraces his steps until he locates the opening he made and returns to the darkened cargo terminal. Brian keeps watch as Josh maneuvers a slim jim inside the door panel of an old Toyota Hilux. The truck is parked amongst several vehicles in the terminal's back lot. He unlocks the truck's door and then proceeds to get its engine going.

"Come on, dude," Josh beckons. "We got wheels, man. Let's go."

Josh drives back toward La Paz while Brian is still trying to process what he has just seen.

"Brian," Josh reaches over and bumps his fist lightly into Brian's shoulder. "You're too serious, man. You really need to lighten up."

"I don't understand anything about what we are supposed to be doing here, Josh."

"That's okay," Josh answers. "All you need to know is that Alistair is here in La Paz, you're here in La Paz, and it's my job to get you two together so you can convince him to stop what he's doing."

"How am I going to do that? Josh, you saw their operation; it's huge. I know Alistair; he's always had a big ego. How can I possibly convince him of anything?"

Josh looks at Brian, and as he does, the coldness in the man's eyes suddenly frightens him, "Brian…" Josh looks back at the road, "Brian, you are a rare individual."

"What is that supposed to mean?"

"It's a compliment, and you should take it as a compliment, and you should know that handing out compliments to people is not something I normally do."

Josh drives across town and then pulls up in front of the security gates of a luxury apartment complex. "OK, so here we are."

"What do we do now?"

"Fuck, dude…" Josh complains, "you're like a broken record, man. It's like we're married or something."

Josh bends down and rummages through his bag again. He pulls out a keycard and swipes it across the gate's security sensor. He then drives inside and parks the truck in front of a row of modern townhouses. He shuts down the truck's engine and then turns toward Brian.

"Please tell me you know what we have to do next, dude. I know you'll have the answer by now, Brian."

"Umm… We wait?"

"Ding ding ding ding!" Josh smiles as he reaches over and pats Brain on the shoulder. "We'll make a spy out of you yet, dude. But we can't wait inside the truck."

The two men sit on the ground near the parking lot and remain hidden by lush tropical landscaping.

Josh briefs Brian on his mission. "The beauty of the plan, Brian, is that all we need you to do is be yourself."

"So you just want me to talk to Alistair? That's it?"

"Yep, that's it."

Josh holds his focus on Brian, and this time, Brian can see he's being sincere.

"We know that Alistair is unhappy," Josh continues. "We've been keeping track of him. What we need is to get someone in front of him that he knows and trusts... someone he feels he can really talk to... you know what I mean?"

"Yeah, so all you want me to do is put the idea in his head that he can walk away. I think I can do that..."

"Fantastic... Um, okay, Brian, let's run through the details one more time, okay? Who did you just bang in unit twelve?"

"Her name's Victoria. She works for a real estate company. She likes rough sex, and she's a redhead."

"Awesome... excellent..." Josh glances back toward the security gate. "OK, he's coming down the road. You better get into position."

Brian grabs his backpack, walks over to the driver side door of the Hilux, and waits. He's peering through the window when Alistair pulls up behind him driving a silver Porsche Boxster. Brian is still looking into the closed window of the truck when Alistair gets out of the Porsche.

"Hey, mate!" Alistair calls out. "Did you lock your keys inside?"

Brian turns around. "Yeah, unfortunately, I did..."

"Holy shit! Brian? Is that you?" Alistair smiles.

"Wow, Alistair? Seriously? Holy shit!" Brian is genuinely happy to see Alistair. He grabs his old friend, hugs him, and then steps back again. "Shit! Mate! It's been like five years!"

Alistair gazes at Brian and assesses his old lab partner. "So I see you're still out backpacking huh? What are you doing here?"

"Oh yeah, well I met this redhead at a bar..." Brian gestures in the direction of unit twelve.

"Victoria? You fucked her?" Alistair is genuinely impressed. He never figured Brian to be the type to go for S&M... "Wow, cool. Hey, why don't you come in for a beer?"

"Sure thing. That would be great." Brian follows Alistair into his apartment.

"Wow, nice place." Brian walks into Alistair's living room. "You sure are doing well."

"Oh, this place? Yeah thanks." Alistair opens the nearly empty Sub-Zero refrigerator in his gourmet kitchen and pulls out a couple of beers. "This is just my work apartment. I own a house in Los Angeles." Alistair hands Brian a beer. "So what are you doing these days? Teaching?"

At that moment, Alistair falls forward, his head strikes the glass coffee table on the way down as his body crashes to the floor in an uncontrolled heap.

Brian is so shocked that for the first few seconds he can't do anything but stare at Alistair's motionless body in front of him. Then, he feels a hand on his shoulder—

"Brian." Josh looks into the stunned man's eyes. "What the fuck did you do? You were only supposed to talk to him!"

Brian is still dazed, but then Josh's face registers. "Um yeah, that's all I was doing, Josh. And then he just collapsed. I don't know what happened."

"We gotta get out of here right now."

"But he's hurt," Brian pleads. "Look at him. We need to perform CPR. We need to call an ambulance."

"Brian, good grief!" Josh complains angrily. "We're in the middle of a covert operation. We can't call anybody; it's too dangerous. I gotta get you out of here now, man, and I mean right now. This whole mission is fucked, and if we don't leave, we're fucked, too. Do you understand?"

Brian is still in shock as Josh drives the Toyota back to La Paz. "What do you think happened? I mean, it's so unbelievable how he just passed out like that."

"I don't know, Brian. I've seen a lot of crazy shit… I don't know… Maybe it was an aneurism, a heart attack, or something. I mean, he did puke back at the airport, you know?" Josh slows the truck down for a turn and then heads onto a side road.

"So, where are we going now?" Brian asks.

Josh smiles. "We've got one more stop to make, then I'm taking you back to the airport and putting you on the next flight back to San Diego." Josh stops the truck, pulls out a 9mm pistol, and shoots Brian in the temple at point-blank range.

Josh sighs. He briefly studies Brian's lifeless body as it lies slumped against the passenger door. Brian's head rests against the window, it's framed in a halo of splattered blood and brain matter that slowly drips down the glass.

Josh softly touches Brian's shoulder. "Sorry, dude…"

He reaches for Brian's backpack and fishes out the envelope full of cash and the burner phone. Josh then wipes Brian's Android of prints and places it back inside. He stuffs the retrieved items back into the satchel at his feet and then rummages inside and pulls out a Ziploc bag. Josh opens the bag carefully and then uses a pair of tweezers to pull out Brian's suicide note. He pops open the glove box and gently lays the note inside. He wipes the 9mm and places it inside Brian's lifeless hand. Then, Josh quickly wipes away the rest of his prints from the inside of the pickup, grabs his satchel, gets out of the truck, and walks off into the desert.

As Josh hikes down a hill overlooking the lights of La Paz, he pulls out his phone and thumbs off a simple text message: *It's done.* A few minutes go by, and Josh continues to tramp through the brush on his way back to town. Then, he feels his phone vibrate. Josh pulls his phone from his pocket and looks at the message: *Both of them?* Josh shakes his head, groans in disgust, and then sends back a one-word answer: *Yes.*

Chapter 25

Thomas Falcon awakens after a comfortable night's sleep. He rubs his eyes and looks up at a plain white ceiling above his head... *Ah... back to normal...* He hears a phone ring. Falcon leans over and fumbles around the nightstand until he locates the Android Marco gave him.

"Dr. Falcon? Hey, it's Brandon. I'd like to meet you guys for lunch today. Would that be okay with you and Bayani?"

"Sure... sure," Falcon answers as he sits up. "Do you want to just meet here at the hotel?... Oh sure... Absolutely... What time? Right, okay, we'll see you then...

Cheers."

Falcon puts his feet down on the ceramic tile floor and stretches. He stands up, grabs the bathrobe he left lying over the back of a chair, and puts it on as he walks to the sliding glass doors of his suite. Falcon grabs the edge of the curtains in front of the doors and draws them back to reveal bright morning sun and a striking view of the Cabo San Lucas harbor. He unlocks the doors, slides them open, and walks out onto the room's private terrace.

Falcon passes by the lounge furniture and leans against a low stucco wall that is blanketed in blooming fuchsia bougainvillea. Falcon gazes out at the lovely panorama in front of him, and then he sees her... *Bloody hell...*

Falcon immediately spins around and strides back into his room to get dressed. He's just managed to pull a polo over his head when someone knocks on his door. Falcon goes to the door and briefly peers through its security hole as he hurriedly tucks his shirt into his trousers. He spots Bayani and opens the door.

"She's here, Dr. Falcon. Have you seen her?" Bayani rushes through the door. "She's right here in the harbor." Bayani swiftly races out through the suite's open rear doors to the terrace.

Falcon finishes tucking in his shirt and follows Bayani outside. The two men stand and stare across the harbor at the striking research vessel. Her white superstructure towers over the private yachts that surround her.

"Isn't that the ship?" Bayani asks Falcon. "That is *Fearless,* am I right?"

"That is her," Falcon answers flatly.

"What are we waiting for? Let's go down there. We must warn them, Dr. Falcon."

"Just a moment, Bayani," Falcon cautions. "Let's think about this; it won't be easy..."

Bayani looks Falcon directly in the eye. "Dr. Falcon, this is our path. We are exactly where we are supposed to be. No spiritual path is ever easy, Dr. Falcon, but we have no choice; we must follow it."

Falcon walks the long, narrow strand of the marina's docks like a condemned man resolved to his fate. He moves forward on numbing autopilot, knowing full well the negative outcome that lies ahead. Falcon comforts himself by contemplating the complete insignificance of his own life—the smallness of his existence. The only thing that has kept him going over the past five years is the drive to atone for his mistake through personal penitence and sacrifice.

Bayani keeps a close eye on Falcon as the two men approach the ninety-seven-meter-long research vessel. She is moored alongside glamorous super yachts, but the toys of the rich and famous pale in comparison to *Fearless*.

"She is a big ship, Dr. Falcon… much larger than I imagined," Bayani comments as he gazes up at the ship's prow looming high above their heads.

Falcon smiles timidly. "She is the most incredible ship of her kind in the world, Bayani."

The teenager and the middle-aged man take a few more steps.

"Oy!"

Falcon and Bayani look up to see a crewman standing on board *Fearless*. The man leans over the railing and stares down at Falcon menacingly. Bayani stares up at the stranger and then back at Falcon.

"Do you know this man, Dr. Falcon?" Bayani whispers.

"We've met before," Falcon confesses. Falcon walks a bit closer, looks up, and then raises his left hand and shields his eyes from the sun as he calls up to the crewman.

"Your name is Murray, right?"

Murray puts down the rope he is coiling. "That's right." He places his hands on the railing and stares down at the two men, "And you're Dr. Thomas Falcon."

"Yes, you remembered." But as Falcon speaks, Murray immediately turns his back and disappears from view.

"What just happened?" Bayani asks. "Did he recognize you?"

"Unfortunately, Bayani, I am afraid the answer is yes, he did."

"So, this man has gone to alert the captain?"

"Regrettably, yes, he has."

As the words leave Falcon's mouth, he suddenly sees the hulking frame of Alex Moss appear at the top of the gangway that leads down to the dock.

"Don't move, Bayani," Falcon warns as Moss thunders down the aluminum ramp toward the floating pontoon. "Don't speak, don't make eye contact, don't do anything…"

Falcon remains in place; he stands motionless and simply watches the six-foot-four-inch former US navy SEAL steam toward him like a freight train. Falcon's body goes cold as Alex Moss powers forward on a direct course and steadily fills his frame of view until Falcon can see only the man's giant fist flying at his face.

Moss is breathing heavily, his intense anger still pumps through his veins as he stands over the unconscious body of Thomas Falcon. Then, Moss notices Bayani standing nearby.

"Who the hell are you?" Moss huffs.

"I am Bayani."

"You know this man?" Moss hisses. "Do you know what this man did?"

Bayani looks Alex Moss in the eye. "Yes, Mr. Moss, I know Dr. Falcon very well… even better than you do."

Moss scowls at the slim teenager. "I suggest you find better friends, young man."

Moss turns his back on Bayani and stomps back up the gangway.

Bayani looks up toward the ship and carefully studies the scene playing out in front of him. He observes Moss silently pass through the group of muscled crewmen gathered on deck to watch the action, and as Bayani looks into the crowd, he suddenly notices the soft features of a woman's face amongst the thick stand of hardened men.

She draws Bayani's attention as she rapidly glances to either side of her and attempts to question the crewmen that surround her, but Bayani can see the woman is getting no answers as each of the men silently leave and return to their jobs. Bayani can clearly see concern on the woman's face as she looks down at Thomas Falcon lying flat out cold on the concrete pontoon below. Then, she briefly makes eye contact with Bayani and walks down the gangway.

Dr. Samantha Randal is still wearing her lab coat as she kneels down to examine the unconscious man. She had been on her way back to the ship's main lab after delivering a set of samples to her assistants working in lab2 when she noticed everyone onboard suddenly rushing outside. Dr. Randal examines Thomas Falcon's eyes, checks his pulse, and then she carefully slips her hand behind his head and finds blood. She looks up at Bayani.

"Are you his friend?"

"Yes, madam."

"Then help me get this man on his feet. He needs treatment."

Samantha has Falcon on an examining table inside the infirmary of *Fearless* when Moss enters.

"Dr. Randal."

Moss' powerful tone shocks her as she suddenly looks up to see his infuriated face. She quickly gathers her composure, looks away from Moss, and returns to treating her patient.

"Do you have anything to say for yourself, Mr. Moss?" Samantha says without looking, "You've given this man a concussion knocking him down like you did. He's still not fully conscious."

Samantha pauses. She then straightens and turns to look directly at Moss. "You are lucky he is still alive, sir."

The veins on his temples throb as Moss struggles to control his rage. "No, ma'am, I am not." Moss lets out an audible growl, "This man…" He takes a breath as he fights to hold on to the beast trying to get out. "Dr. Randal, this man is responsible for the deaths of four of my crew members and scores of innocent people. Dr. Randal, this is the man who got Peter Marsh killed."

Samantha gazes back at Moss calmly at first. "That may be true, Mr. Moss…" Then her eyes narrow and she stares at him as her voice takes on a commanding tone, "but I am, first and foremost, a medical doctor. I took an oath, sir. Did you honestly expect that I would turn my back on an injured person? Especially one whose injuries were caused by you?"

Moss takes a step back, sighs, and then shoots a scathing glare in Seth's direction. "And you're helping her?"

Seth raises his hands defensively. "Chief, hey… I hate to admit it, but the doc's gotta point."

Moss lets out an irritated huff. He turns to leave but then pauses when he spots Bayani standing quietly off to one side. Moss stares down at the slim Filipino. "You're like a bad penny, kid."

Moss leaves a powerful energy lingering inside the room as he walks out of the infirmary. It is an energy that Samantha can still feel as she returns to her patient.

"All right, Seth, I want a full set of X-rays. Let's get his shirt off."

Seth grabs a pair of medical shears and cuts the front of the polo shirt Falcon wears. As the scissor blades pass through the fabric, Dr. Randal pulls the shirt away, and as she does, the elaborate tattoos that cover Falcon's upper body become visible.

"My God…"

Seth gawks at the body art. "Whoa… that's hard core…"

Samantha gently places her hand on Falcon's heart. "What happened to you?" she whispers softly.

Seth briefly studies the designs and symbols. "These are prison tattoos, ma'am, and by the looks of it, they're high status. You can't get tats like these in some ink shop, Dr. Randal; you have to earn them."

"He is correct, Dr. Randal."

Bayani walks over to the table. "Do you see this one?" He points to the largest of the tattoos, a highly detailed image of an open book with its pages spread like the wings of a falcon. The pages themselves are filled with gothic script written in Tagalog. This tattoo alone covers the width of Falcon's upper chest and shoulders, but it is only one of many.

"The words are Filipino," Bayani explains. "They tell other members of Baha la Na that Dr. Falcon was in Bilibid Prison and that he is the professor… the teacher who brought knowledge and gave it freely." Bayani looks directly at Seth. "It is meant as a sign of respect."

Falcon is recovering in the infirmary as Bayani sits by his bed-side. Dr. Randal enters the room carrying a tray, and on it is a medical sampling kit. She sets the tray down and examines Falcon once more.

"You're a lucky man, Dr. Falcon."

Falcon chuckles as she shines a light into each of his eyes. "Am I really? I think that statement is certainly open for debate."

Samantha cocks her head momentarily and smirks. "Well, you hit the pavement pretty hard out there, but your X-rays are all normal. You'll be sore for a few days, but there doesn't seem to be any serious damage. I'd say you're good to go."

"Well, that is fantastic news, Doctor…"

"Oh, of course," Samantha pauses. "How silly of me. I am Dr. Samantha Randal." Samantha unconsciously reaches across the bed to shake Falcon's missing right hand and then quickly draws it back. "Oh, I'm terribly sorry."

Falcon lifts his stump and smiles. "Yes, well, it is a bit awkward, I admit."

"Actually," Samantha looks at Falcon, "this is what I want to talk to you about. I would like to examine your arm more carefully. Would that be alright with you?"

The scientist in Falcon is intrigued. "By all means."

Samantha walks to the right side of Falcon's bed, lifts his scarred stump of an arm, and palpates the tissue with her fingers. She is shocked by what her hands tell her, but she says nothing as she lays Falcon's arm back onto the bed.

"I'd like to run some tests. Do you mind if I perform a biopsy? I have to be honest: it could be a bit painful. But I think it's well worth it."

Falcon smiles up at Samantha. "Consider me your willing lab rat, Dr. Randal."

• • •

Moss is still fuming as he paces the bridge while Malcolm Rafferty flashes a worried look at his friend. "Look, Ax, I don't blame you at all for clocking the guy," Razz admits. "But I saw the whole thing. He knew you were gonna hit him, and he just stood there and let you lay him out cold."

"But it doesn't make any sense, Razz." Moss stops pacing, leans against the chart table, and forces himself to take a deep breath. With his rage finally subsiding, the investigator in Moss takes over. "Why would Dr. Falcon do that? Why even show up if you know what's coming?"

"Maybe he felt he deserved it? I mean, a guy like that has to be carrying around a lot of guilt. Maybe he was looking to offload some?"

"Maybe," Moss ponders. "But I know how this man thinks, Razz. There's more to it than that." Moss starts walking toward the door.

"Where are you going?" asks Razz.

"I'm going down to the infirmary. I need to interrogate Dr. Thomas Falcon. It's something I should have done five years ago, but at the time, I couldn't handle it."

"And now?" Razz questions. "After what I just saw, Ax, I still don't think you're ready."

Moss looks at his friend. "This time I have to be, Razz. I've got no choice."

Chapter 26

Jeff Buxton gets out of his car and walks over to the silver Porsche Boxster parked nearby. He lays his hand across the roadster's mid-engine and finds it cold. Buxton unconsciously feels for the gun he wears under his suit jacket as he walks over to Alistair's front door and knocks. He gets no response. He walks around to the rear patio of the townhouse and peers inside through a set of French doors. That's when he spots Alistair's body on the floor in the living room.

"Dead?... Are you sure?" Marcus Waverley's tone is elevated and uncharacteristically shrill as he demands details that Jeff Buxton doesn't have. "I want this kept quiet. Do you understand what I'm saying?" Waverley listens some more. "I'm on my way down there," Waverley finally announces in disgust. "This is a fucking disaster."

The G650's engines are still spooling down in front of the foundation's hangar in La Paz when Marcus walks down the jet's extended stairway and over to a waiting contingent of project personnel and CIA company men.

"Inside..." Waverley grumbles angrily as he marches past the group. "We talk inside... and I want to talk to you alone, Jeff."

Waverley barks at Buxton, "Get the rest of these people out of here."

The two men stand alone inside the cavernous hangar. "What the fucking hell happened?" an infuriated Waverley demands. He kneels to more closely examine Alistair's cold corpse, which lies inside a partially opened body bag on the hangar's concrete floor. Waverley stands and turns back toward Jeff Buxton.

"Your job was to keep this man alive, remember?" Waverley complains bitterly. "This is one of the reasons we jumped ship with the ONI and went with you guys. You promised us—and I quote— 'a higher level of security…' remember that? Huh? Do you remember telling me that to my face, Jeff?"

Waverley starts pacing, and then he stops in his tracks and glares angrily at Buxton. "Do you know what caused this, Jeff? Was it a professional hit? Do we have any information at all?"

Waverley opens his double-breasted Italian blazer and places his hands on his hips. He glances down at Alistair's pale, lifeless features, and then his eyes settle back on Buxton. "You know, Jeff…" Waverley sighs, "we all used to be on the same team, Jeff… the Stars and Stripes team. We even used to work together sometimes. Remember that?"

"Yeah, I remember," Buxton replies with a sigh.

The distant sadness in Buxton's tone is evident. "Look, Marcus, I can't tell you anything more than what we already know." Buxton raises his hand to his chin and contemplates the body inside the heavy plastic bag. He then lets his hand drop to his side and looks back at Marcus Waverley.

"We examined the body thoroughly, and all we found was that cut you see on his forehead, which frankly, is too small to be what killed him. It's obvious the head injury occurred when he fell and hit the table, which means it was likely an after-effect of whatever did kill him."

Buxton walks up and faces Waverley head-on. "We didn't find any other injuries on this kid, Marcus. If it was a hit, it was high-level, but we don't have the facilities here to perform an autopsy or even a basic toxicology screen. We should also consider that this could have been just an unfortunate natural death, Marcus."

"Point taken," Marcus concludes. "OK, look, we can't sit around here whining with our thumbs up our butts. We need to move on."

"I agree."

"So, on to the next issue," Marcus growls as Jeff Buxton grimaces. "What happened to the mission, Jeff? It was a total cluster-fuck. Can you explain that one to me, Jeff?"

"Look, Marcus, we talked about this." Buxton's tone deepens. "I was assigned to this project because of my experience overseeing covert weapons development, and if you recall, Marcus, I warned you at the beginning not to get too cocky, remember?"

Marcus purses his lips. "Yes, Jeff… I remember."

"Good." Jeff nods. "So, let's talk about the mission, shall we?"

He steps closer to Marcus. "We have good news and bad news, and the bad news isn't terrible. So as far as I'm concerned, we still have a project with a lot of potential. We had a string of successes—impressive successes, I might add—but we'd been following the same formula for each of those missions. We also chose targets that fit that formula. So, the boys upstairs decided to up the ante on us. They wanted to push the envelope and see what would happen."

"I'm listening…" Waverley grumbles.

"So instead of launching from a stationary ship under ideal conditions, they had us launch from an airborne aircraft flying at night and at less than two hundred feet above the Pacific. That factor alone should have tanked us, but it didn't. It's a testament to the versatility of this drone that we were able to launch successfully—"

"Launch successfully?" Marcus breaks in. "One of my guys was killed, Jeff. He was bitten in half, for Christ's sake. We only got the lower portion of his body back, and I'm the one who will have to inform the kid's family, Jeff. Do you know how hard it'll be to come up with an explanation for something like that?"

"Difficult, I'm sure," Buxton adds. "But it's the sort of thing that's bound to happen when you're dealing with a dangerous weapon like the MS41, and frankly, Marcus, your guys were way too cocky. Alistair was way too cocky, and I warned him about that very thing. They were all treating these things like pets."

"So, let's talk about what we learned from this mission, Marcus, which is the most important result of this mission. First off, we learned that we can indeed deploy from an airborne aircraft, which adds to our known capabilities. We also learned that the MS41can chase down a moving target at sea, and that alone is impressive, Marcus. You should be happy about this, because confirming that possibility is big news."

"This is all very helpful, Jeff," Marcus acknowledges, "but we failed to take out the target."

"Yes, we did," Buxton admits. "So, let's talk about why that happened."

Buxton folds his arms in front of him as he stares intensely at Marcus Waverley. "I know the target, Marcus. I have personally met this man on more than one occasion. We've dealt with him in the past, and he's one of the smartest, most slippery sons of bitches you'll ever see."

"So, what happened?" Waverley asks. "Was he tipped off?"

"No. At least we don't believe so, but stealing and selling information is this man's stock and trade. We suspect he got wind of the operation in Colombia. Juan Carlos was a close personal friend of his. For this reason, I advised Langley to choose a different target, but unfortunately, I was overruled. Anyway, water under the bridge, as they say. In my opinion, the real reason the mission failed was that we lost the element of surprise."

"Really?" Waverley scoffs. "The MS41-T should've obliterated every human being on that yacht, Jeff, and you know it."

"Now you're the one who's being cocky, Marcus." Buxton drops his hands to his hips. "It doesn't matter what armaments you have or how lethal they may be; the element of surprise is the most powerful weapon anyone will bring to a fight... any fight."

"Marco and his gang have some extraordinary weaponry on board that yacht of his. The chatter we've picked up says he's already out shopping for more. The surveillance satellite footage of the op is quite a show. It almost makes me like the guy. They fought hard and kicked ass, if you don't mind me saying."

"I do mind, Jeff." Waverley is surprised. "I mean, whose side are you on here, anyway?"

"I'm merely expressing respect for my opponent, Marcus, nothing more. Anyway, now that we know Marco's capabilities, the next time we go after him, he won't stand a chance. I'm totally confident the man's days are numbered."

"So, what else is there, Jeff?" Waverley questions. "You're holding something back. I can see it on your face."

Buxton sighs. "I'm not that kind of guy, Marcus. I've just been waiting for the right moment."

"So, what is it then?"

"It's that ship of yours, Marcus… the research vessel *Fearless*."

"What about it?"

"At this moment, she's over in Cabo San Lucas."

"Yes I know," Marcus responds. "They had a medical emergency… some sort of dive accident."

"There's more to it than that, Marcus. Your guys have been sniffing around the MS41 project. They stumbled across the test units we lost. Apparently, those drones became trapped in an undersea cave. My point, however, is that these guys are going to get themselves into trouble if you don't do something about it."

"There's no need for concern, Jeff," Waverley answers confidently. "I already know everything about the incident. Alex Moss called and told me they found some sharks in a cave. I've got a handle on it. He even sent me a full report, which I promptly deleted of course. The situation is under control."

"No, it's not, Marcus." Buxton exhales wearily. "Look, Marcus, a guy like Alex Moss is somebody you don't want to let out from under your thumb. The man's a war hero… a decorated Special Ops veteran. He's got a naturally suspicious mind and he's smart… real smart."

"So far, Jeff, you're not telling me anything I don't already know." Waverley's tone is dismissive, bordering on arrogant. "We monitor the location of *Fearless* at all times. I know exactly where she is every moment of every day. I can assure you I have Alex under control, Jeff. He is under my thumb, I guarantee it."

"Really? Is that so?" Buxton is growing irritated. "Well, if that's true, then tell me where she was two days before she arrived in Cabo."

"That's easy. She was at anchor on the western side of the Gulf of California. She was there for nearly a week, Jeff, and she never moved an inch during that entire time."

Buxton snickers sarcastically.

"What?" Waverley huffs, "I monitored the AIS signal myself."

Buxton chuckles some more, but then he catches himself. "Marcus, please, I don't mean any disrespect, and don't take this the wrong way." Buxton looks right at Waverley. "*We are on the same team* ... I can assure you of that. I want this project to succeed. I believe in the MS41. But two days ago, your ship was not where you thought she was. I have infrared satellite images that show *Fearless* traveled clear across the gulf and then returned to the same spot. Those guys pulled the wool over your eyes, Marcus."

"What should I do?" Waverley gasps. "*Fearless* is the foundation's flagship. She maintains our front as a not-for-profit. She's our most valuable asset, Jeff."

"My advice is to move the ship, Marcus. Get her out of the Sea of Cortez, reassign her, or something, but get Alex Moss back under your thumb, and keep him there."

"OK, you win, Jeff," Waverley concedes. "I'll have Alex reposition *Fearless* back to Long Beach. I'll see to it personally."

"OK then, moving on..." Jeff Buxton glances at his watch. "With Alistair gone, we need to select a new project manager, and we don't have much time, Marcus."

"What's the status on the new facility at San Clemente?"

"We have nearly everything in place. It'll be another week at the most. We would like to begin closing down La Paz immediately, so we need to begin preparing the drone inventory for transport."

Waverley glances over at Alistair's body once more. "He was our irreplaceable man, Jeff. I don't know how we can get somebody to fill his shoes."

Buxton looks over at the body bag. "Well, Marcus, you know what they say about irreplaceable men?"

"What's that?"

"The graveyards are full of them."

Chapter 27

"If you plan to punch me again, Mr. Moss, please, go right ahead."

Moss stands in front of Thomas Falcon's bed in the infirmary as the thought of how easy it would be to kill him lingers, and then he lets it go. "Dr. Falcon..." Moss sighs. "Dr. Falcon, what are you doing here? Why did you come back?"

Falcon looks directly at Moss. "Now, we're getting somewhere." He clears his throat as he painfully pushes himself upright. "I came back to warn you about Dr. Alistair Fairchild's tiger sharks, Mr. Moss."

Moss freezes momentarily as Falcon's statement stuns him. "How could you possibly know anything about that?"

"Five years in a Filipino prison," Falcon quips. "I ended up making some interesting connections, and those connections have led me here to you."

The expression on his face sours further as Moss stares down at Falcon. "Five years? After what you did? They only gave you five years?"

"I may have only spent five years in prison, Mr. Moss, but I will be paying for my ignorance for the rest of my life. I can assure you of that, sir."

"After what happened in that country?" Alex scoffs. "It's not enough."

"I agree…" Falcon looks directly into Moss's eyes. "You are absolutely right, sir." Then, he glances over at Bayani, who sits silently nearby. Bayani nods approvingly, and the gesture encourages Falcon to continue. Falcon looks back at Moss. "But we have much more important issues to deal with right now."

Moss grits his jaw. "I've seen one of Alistair's tiger sharks. We were able to retrieve a specimen, and Dr. Randal examined it. So tell me something I don't know. Impress me with your *connections*, Dr. Falcon."

"You allowed Dr. Samantha Randal to examine one of Alistair's drones?" Falcon is surprised and angered. Her file is amongst the trove of data Brandon gave him. "So let me guess: that poor woman discovered that her medical research was leveraged to create the damned thing? That is unfortunate news, Mr. Moss."

"Wait a minute…" Moss is perplexed. "Did you just say *Alistair's drones?*"

"Yes, I did, Alex. Would you like to know more? Because I know nearly every horrid detail of this ludicrous monster the foundation has created. That's why I'm here—to put a stop to it."

Moss exhales. He looks briefly at the floor and then back at Falcon. "Did Dr. Randal find any injuries? What is your condition?"

"She says I'll be fine… just a little banged up is all."

"OK then. Get up and get dressed," Moss orders. "You're coming with me. We need to talk." Then, Moss growls at Bayani, "And you're staying right here, kid."

Ten minutes later, Falcon, Moss, Rafferty, and Dr. Randal are all looking at the lab's main computer, as Falcon, with Samantha's help, downloads the trove of data he has stored on his android phone. The sense of deja vu is palpable as Falcon fights back old demons. He passes the cursor down a list of files and then clicks on the drone's technical schematic. The file opens, and Samantha gasps at the sight of it.

"My God... What have I done?"

At that moment, Moss and Falcon each speak simultaneously as both men attempt to reassure Samantha that what has happened is not her fault. Then, they catch themselves. Moss glares at Falcon, who merely raises an eyebrow at Moss. The two men quickly return to the computer display.

Rafferty meanwhile observes the entire exchange with curiosity.

"OK, let's take a closer look at this beastie, shall we?" Falcon brings up a 3D cad cam rendering. He rotates the schematic and expands it. "So, at first glance, this just looks like a slightly larger-than-average, man-eating elasmobranch. But take a closer look here..." Falcon picks up a pen and points at the drone's control module, "and you see something very interesting."

Moss leans in. "It looks like some sort of computerized power conduit."

"You're not far off, Mr. Moss." Falcon glances at Rafferty. "This is the drone's control module. They all have one. Apparently, this is how the drone's operators back in Long Beach activate the drones, how they program them, and how they deactivate them once they are finished with them."

Dr. Randal moves in for a closer look. "I feel like a complete idiot. I missed this entirely, and we did a full necropsy on our specimen."

"Don't be so hard on yourself, Dr. Randal," Falcon assures her. "It's well hidden, it employs cutting-edge biocircuitry that is nearly impossible to see, and it's only five centimeters long." Falcon looks up at Samantha. "A needle inside an eight-hundred-pound elasmobranch haystack, Doctor."

She studies the image intently. "This is incredibly sophisticated work." She looks up at Moss. "If technology like this were being developed to its fullest potential, Mr. Moss, then every serviceman with a spinal injury would be walking normally again." She turns back to the schematic. "And my guess is that's only the beginning of what it's actually capable of."

"And as it stands, it's only purpose is to reanimate a dead fish," Falcon complains.

Samantha moves in closer to Falcon. "We will need to spend time studying this data, Dr. Falcon." Then, she looks into his eyes. "I would like to personally thank you for what you've done."

Falcon studies her features. "Of course, you are very welcome, Doctor." Falcon draws back, spins away from the computer, and then gets to his feet.

"Where are you going?" Rafferty asks.

"I'm afraid I have another appointment. If you don't mind, I really need to get going."

Moss looks at Falcon. "Make sure you take that kid with you."

Falcon chuckles. "He may seem like a simple teenager to you, Mr. Moss, but he's more important than you'll ever know."

"Is that so?" Moss quips. "I'll walk you two out, Dr. Falcon."

As Falcon and Bayani stand at the top of the gangway that leads down to the marina dock, Falcon turns to Moss. "Mr. Moss…" Falcon's voice is filled with compassion and grief, "we are certainly not friends, sir, and we never will be, but there is no need for us to be enemies either. You and I share this tragedy between us whether we like it or not, so I suggest we work together to resolve it."

"I'll think about it, Dr. Falcon."

Moss turns and walks back inside. Falcon watches him leave, then he and Bayani walk down the gangway on their way back to their hotel and their lunch appointment. Esteban will be picking them up soon.

Falcon and Bayani are walking back when they pass a well-dressed gentleman with blond hair and a pocket square striding in the opposite direction.

"That was a very rich man, Dr. Falcon."

"I agree, Bayani," Falcon answers. "I can still smell his cologne."

Marcus Waverley initially breezes by the two men without a thought, and then something clicks—a sense of familiarity. He stops momentarily and looks back at Falcon. "No way," Marcus mutters. "It couldn't be."

Upon returning to his hotel room, Falcon pulls off the T-shirt Seth gave him to wear, quickly showers, and changes into a fresh linen button-down and trousers. Then, he heads downstairs to meet Bayani at the hotel's entrance. They stand side by side on the curb for only a few minutes when a familiar black Mercedes sedan pulls up in front of them. Falcon recognizes Esteban. "Buenos días, Señor," Falcon says as Esteban holds open the door.

The Mercedes winds its way up into the desert scrub foothills above the coast and then into a gated housing development. Falcon takes note of the fact that there are no armed guards this time—only radio-carrying security. They eventually arrive in front of a classically styled Mediterranean revival villa. A uniformed maid greets Bayani and Falcon politely at the front door.

She then guides them through an inner courtyard garden, past a small koi pond, into the main house, and then out to the pool area and a commanding view of the sea below. Falcon and Bayani walk to the edge of the villa's patio and admire the striking panorama.

"Dr. Falcon!"

Falcon jumps at the booming sound of Marco's voice. He spins around to see the man himself approaching. "Thomas, my friend!" Marco greets Falcon warmly and then he turns to Bayani. "And how are you, young man?" Marco shakes the nineteen-year-old's hand vigorously.

"I thought you sailed south?" Falcon inquires. "Is everything alright?"

"Come sit with me, Thomas," Marco directs. "We have much to discuss."

As Falcon and Bayani sit down, Falcon notices a bandage on Marco's arm. "What happened?"

"Oh this?" Marco turns his arm and glances at the bandage. "It's nothing... a small burn is all." Then, Marco smiles. "A fishing accident." Marco then tilts his head as he evaluates Falcon. "And what about you? It looks as if you have an injury as well, my friend."

"Oh this?" Falcon raises his hand to his bruised left temple. "Ran into an old friend."

"Ah, well, speaking of old friends, I have some news for you, Thomas," Marco's tone is now more serious. "Dr. Alistair Fairchild is dead."

A cold chill jolts down Falcon's spine as the phantom pain in his ghostly right hand suddenly returns. "Dead? When? I mean—"

"It wasn't me, Thomas." Marco puts his hands up briefly. "I had a contract on the man's life, of course, but apparently someone else wanted him dead even more than I."

At that moment, the maid arrives with a tray of fresh lemons, a hand juicer, three glasses, and bottled water.

"Ah, gracias, Marta." Marco picks up one of the lemons and examines it. He then takes a knife from the tray and begins cutting the lemon in half. "Apparently, there was a second death as well, Thomas. The chief of police in La Paz is a very dear friend of mine. He tells me that a man's body was found not far from Dr. Fairchild's home with a gunshot wound to the head."

Marco slices the lemon in two, places one half on the tray, and reaches for the juicer. "This tells me the jackals are congregating." Marco crushes the halved lemon down onto the pointed tip of the juicer. "This situation is becoming very dangerous very quickly, Thomas. You and Bayani must be extremely careful." Marco pours lemon juice into one of the glasses, adds a bit of water, and hands it to Falcon. "Here, drink this. It's very healthy."

Marco reaches for the other half of the lemon and juices it. "I am very sorry to inform you, Thomas, but you knew the second man as well."

Falcon is afraid to ask as his phantom pain increases.

Marco puts the juicer down. "The young man's name was Brian Mathews."

Falcon is shocked. "He was a good kid, Marco."

"A good kid perhaps, Thomas, but he stuck his nose into places he shouldn't have. The police discovered a handwritten suicide note when they searched the stolen vehicle they found the body inside. The note claims that this man Mathews killed Dr. Fairchild out of jealousy because he had lost his university job."

"That's incredible, Marco," Falcon responds. "Brian would never do such a thing. He's simply not capable of something like that. It simply doesn't make sense."

"It makes perfect sense in the world I live in, Thomas. It is surprising how often dead men are capable of extraordinary acts they would never have been able to perform when they were alive. There is an interesting wrinkle to this story, however, because once the police found the body of Brian Mathews, they, of course, went straight over to the home of Dr. Fairchild, but they found nobody there."

Marco pours the juice from the other half of the lemon into a glass, adds water, then drinks it all in one go. Marco sets the empty glass down. "I have experience in these matters, Thomas. I feel that someone went to great lengths in order to bring these two men together. The police suspect that there was indeed a murder in Dr. Fairchild's home. They have found evidence of this. My friend, the police chief, tells me that whomever removed the body was a bit sloppy. Perhaps because they were unaware that there was a second body left so conveniently close by."

Marco squeezes another lemon, mixes the juice with water, and hands the glass to Bayani.

Falcon finishes his juice and then places the empty glass back on the tray. "Well, I am, of course, very appreciative, Marco, but, what should I do with this information?"

"Information is only valuable when it is needed, Thomas, and sometimes the most innocuous bit of data can end up saving your life. I have found that, like money in various forms, it is best to keep lots of it on hand."

Chapter 28

Malcolm Rafferty stands on the bridge of *Fearless*. He is working through an issue in the maintenance schedule when Moss walks in. Rafferty stops what he's doing, takes one look at his friend's face, and grimaces. "It's bad news, isn't it? I can tell just by looking at you."

"This whole thing is beginning to really smell, Razz." Moss walks over to the front windows, gazes out briefly, and then shifts back to Rafferty. "Marcus has just ordered us to sail *Fearless* back to her home port."

"What?" Razz is shocked. "When? Did he say why?"

"Immediately," Moss answers in disgust. He lifts his hands to his hips and exhales as he glances down at the floor. Then, Moss stares at Rafferty. "He didn't give a real reason, Razz. He just kept telling me it was the board's decision. He said it was the other board members who called the meeting and that he'd been over-ruled and outvoted. He did say that he would continue to fight for us and he would try to get us back on task as soon as possible, but apparently, whatever is going on is out of his hands, Razz."

"Do you believe him?"

"I'm not sure." Moss pauses as he lets his hands drop to his sides. "Marcus seemed sincere, Razz. He said he flew down here to tell me personally because he didn't want us to get the news over the phone. I have to admit that I respect that. At least he had the guts to tell me face to face."

"So what do we do? Do you have a plan?"

"We follow orders, Razz. That's all we can do."

"What about that data from Dr. Falcon?"

Moss sighs. "Yeah, that. Well, I've thought about it, and frankly, I'm not sure what good will come of it, Razz."

"Dr. Randal is going over those files as we speak, Ax. Do you want me to ask her to stop?"

"No." Moss folds his arms in front of him. "She deserves to know what's in those files, Razz. It's not my place to tell her otherwise."

"What about Dr. Falcon?"

"I've thought about that, too, and my feelings haven't changed. I don't want that guy anywhere near my ship."

"Aye aye, Chief." Rafferty reaches up and salutes Moss. "So, how about some good news for a change?"

"You heard from the hospital? How's Dan?"

"They're releasing him first thing tomorrow morning. They said it's a miracle we were able to administer treatment like we did. They said under any other circumstances he'd be dead right now."

"We know who we have to thank for that, Razz."

"She's an incredibly capable physician, Ax, and a damned fine woman, if you don't mind me saying."

Moss raises an eyebrow and nods in agreement. "Yes, she is."

• • •

Late that night, Alex Moss is, once again, not sleeping as his mind churns through the dozens of issues he still has on his plate. He gets up, gets dressed, and walks outside on deck. Moss goes forward to the helipad, where he pauses to rest his hand on the Bell 429 GlobalRanger that sits fully covered and securely strapped down to the deck. Memories of the battle he and his crew fought on that very spot flood back into his head. Then, he stops himself. He can't go there; he can't allow himself to start down that road… at least not yet.

Moss walks over to the railing and looks out at the twinkling lights of the Cabo San Lucas harbor. He hears music drifting across the water from the bars and restaurants. He gazes down at the lights of the city reflected in the quiet sea below, and then he sees him.

"What are you doing here, kid?" Moss calls down to Bayani. "Where's your friend Dr. Falcon?"

"I came to speak to you, Mr. Moss."

Moss is puzzled. He puts his hands on the railing, leans forward, and stares down at the slim teenager. "How could you know I would be out here? What are you up to, kid?"

"Mr. Moss, please." Bayani looks up from the pontoon. "It is important that I speak to you."

Moss studies Bayani a few more moments. "Stay where you are, kid. I'm coming down."

Bayani watches as Moss marches back across the deck of the magnificent ship, down the gangway, and then comes to a stop just inches from the young Filipino. Moss towers over Bayani. He folds his muscular arms in front of him and stares down at the slim teenager. "I'm listening."

Bayani looks up at Moss. His expression is calm, confident, and knowing. "Your path and the path of Dr. Thomas Falcon are linked, Mr. Moss. You must understand this, and you must accept it, even though doing so is very painful for you."

Moss frowns. "This is a waste of my time. You've been giving me the creeps since the first time I laid eyes on you, kid." Moss immediately turns to leave.

"Your dream, Mr. Moss!" Bayani calls out. "I know about your dream."

Moss stops in his tracks and spins back. "What the fuck are you talking about, kid?"

"In the dream, you stand on the deck of this ship, Mr. Moss. Right up there, in fact…" Bayani points up to the helipad. "And you see a huge shark—a tiger shark—and this shark attacks your best friend, but you can do nothing to stop it from happening."

The blood drains from Alex Moss's face as he looks at Bayani in total shock. "How… how can you possibly know this? Nobody knows this… I've never told anyone…"

Bayani takes a step closer to Moss and looks straight into the man's eyes with an intensity that startles the veteran special operations soldier. "This dream, Mr. Moss, it is actually a vision, and it is a vision that you and I each share."

Moss regroups and becomes immediately skeptical. "What are you, kid? Some sort of psychic?"

Bayani smiles. "No, Mr. Moss, I am a shaman. We are spiritual healers, but we also act as a guide to help people on their spiritual path. Like everyone else in this world, I am on a path that was chosen for me. I have no choice but to follow it. At this moment, Mr. Moss, your path, Dr. Falcon's path, and mine are crossing each other. This is why I give you *the creeps*, as you call it, Mr. Moss.

It is because of the natural energy that passes between us. You are unfamiliar with this feeling, but I can assure you it is actually a common experience. It is what we traditional healers know as *a spiritual connection.*"

Moss pauses a moment as he stares down at the teenager. He studies the kid's face and his body language, he mentally processes each word he's just heard, and then Moss decides to ask a question. "If what you're saying is true, then what am I supposed to do about it? What can I do about it?"

Bayani sighs in relief. "A vision is only a possibility, Mr. Moss. It is a reality that can happen, and in some cases, it will happen, but not always. Think of it like a street sign, Mr. Moss. You may need to turn at the sign, or you can pass it by, but you can't do this unless you see and understand the sign's importance."

"This vision that you have, Mr. Moss, is a sign, and the fact that you have seen this sign many times means that you have still not grasped its importance. It means you are traveling in circles, Mr. Moss. Until you recognize and understand this sign, you can't continue on your journey, and you won't be able to see the other signs that lie ahead."

Moss looks at the kid suspiciously. "So, you're telling me you are some sort of spiritual guide?"

Bayani smiles briefly. "We are all travelers, Mr. Moss. When you are traveling, you may look at a map before you leave. Maps are not magic, Mr. Moss. We have all seen a roadmap before, but they have the potential to foretell the future. They can even predict the route to your destination. In our spiritual journey, if we know where we need to go, we can look for the signs that will take us there. I help people to see these signs."

Moss is intrigued, but he's not convinced. "So why do you see this same vision, Bayani? How does that work anyway?"

Bayani shrugs. "I wouldn't know, Mr. Moss. I am only the guide."

Moss wants to question Bayani more, but at that moment, the kid simply turns around and walks off. Moss watches him disappear into the darkness. Then, he shakes his head in frustration as he turns back toward the gangway. "This shit's gonna push me off the edge," Moss grumbles as he heads back to bed.

Chapter 29

Thomas Falcon stands on the terrace of his hotel suite and looks out once more at the morning light shining on the marina. He holds a cup of tea in his hand as he stands silently watching.

"She is a very quiet ship, Dr. Falcon."

"Yes, she is, Bayani." Falcon takes a sip of his tea. "She's finally gone green."

Falcon and Bayani observe from a distance as the crew aboard the ninety-seven-meter-long research vessel slips lines and casts off. *Fearless* maneuvers smoothly away from the dock and out into the harbor under hybrid propulsion. Falcon watches the ship depart, and all the while, he is thinking of Dr. Samantha Randal. She is no doubt poring over the data he gave her, and the thought is painful for him. *She deserves better... but at least she will know the truth.*

Bayani watches the ship disappear into the distance. "So she is returning to America?"

"Long Beach, California, actually," Falcon responds. "So, that's where we're off to as well."

"But, Dr. Falcon," Bayani questions, "I don't have a visa to go to the United States, and you don't even have a passport."

"No worries, Bayani," Falcon answers. "We'll get it all sorted."

. . .

As Esteban closes the door of the Mercedes, Falcon politely thanks him once more just as Brandon is walking out to greet them.

"Dr. Falcon, Bayani, good afternoon. Please, follow me." Brandon gestures. "Right this way."

Falcon and Bayani follow Brandon back inside the glass office building, but rather than take the elevator down underneath the building, they go instead to its top floor.

The top floor of the building looks like any other office space. The room is filled with cubicles, computer terminals, and busy people. Brandon spins around as he enters with Bayan and Falcon.

"So, this is the last of our legacy business." He explains matter-of-factly. "I will turn you over to the capable hands of Pepe here."

Brandon turns and shakes hands with a heavy, balding man wearing wire-framed glasses, brown trousers, a short-sleeved dress shirt, and a striped tie. His shirt carries a pocket protector with an assortment of pens, Tronex cutting tools, and a tiny ruler.

As Brandon leaves, Pepe steps forward. "Dr. Falcon, Bayani," Pepe smiles as he first shakes Falcon's hand and then Bayani's, "it is a pleasure to meet you both. Right this way, please."

Falcon and Bayani follow Pepe through a set of doors and into a cavernous studio filled with lighting equipment, graphic design tables covered in computers, digitizing scanners, and printers. Pepe turns to look at the two men.

"So, this is our studio, and I understand that Bayani needs a US visa, and you, Dr. Falcon, would like to have your UK passport reinstated. Am I right?"

"Yes, Pepe, that is correct," Falcon answers cheerfully as he glances around the room. "This place is amazing."

Pepe chuckles. "Well, it's not what it used to be, Dr. Falcon. My department has been greatly downsized over the years, but we can still make the magic happen."

Pepe gestures toward a camera mounted on a tripod. "OK, gentlemen, let's get your photos made, and then we can get to work."

Less than an hour later, Falcon and Bayani find themselves transfixed as they observe Pepe deftly assemble their documents using a customized graphics computer program.

"In the old days, we used to do all this sort of thing by hand," Pepe mentions as he swiftly drags and drops Falcon's photo and then the graphic of his signature onto the electronic facsimile of his passport.

"When the computers came along, it was wonderful; it saves so much time." Pepe then begins creating Bayani's visa using a preset template. "I used to do a hundred green cards a day," the man muses as he puts the finishing touches on Bayani's work visa.

"So, how long would you like to stay, young man? Six months? A year?" He looks over at Bayani. "I think a year. Why not?" Pepe turns back to the computer. "With this, you will be able to enter and leave as much as you like."

Pepe finishes laying out the documents on the computer, and then he sends the files off via the office intranet network.

"OK, we are almost finished…" Pepe leans back in his chair and opens the desk drawer in front of him. Inside is a small plastic storage box. He grabs the box and opens it.

"RFID biometric chips," Pepe says as he holds the box up in front of Falcon. "You're in luck, Dr. Falcon. I happen to have a few UK chips left."

He pulls a pair of tweezers out from his pocket protector, carefully lifts one of the chips from the box, and examines it. "Ah yes, this is the one."

Pepe places the chip inside a small plastic bag. "Well," the rotund gentlemen exclaims, "this has been fun, gentlemen!" Pepe smiles at Falcon and Bayani. "I'll run this chip downstairs so it can be programmed properly, and I will personally see that it is correctly placed inside your new passport. We will add the necessary entry stamps inside for Mexico, and you guys will be right as rain."

"So, how long before they will be ready?" Falcon asks as Pepe walks them out.

"Oh, well, I can have a courier drop them off at your hotel tomorrow morning."

"That would be fantastic." Falcon smiles as he shakes Pepe's hand. "You have my sincere gratitude, sir, and might I add, it has been a privilege to watch you work."

"Oh this?" Pepe laughs. "You should have seen me back in the old days. I was a maestro."

• • •

Two days later, Falcon and Bayani thread their way through the heaving customs and immigration lines at Los Angeles International Airport. As they approach passport control, Bayani looks back at Falcon briefly. Falcon smiles reassuringly.

"You take that terminal over there, and I'll go over here. I will meet you on the other side."

"Next…" an immigration officer calls out flatly as she makes eye contact with Falcon. She then gestures for him to approach.

Falcon walks up to the officer's terminal and hands the woman his passport. She briefly opens it, looks at the photo, and then rapidly swipes the passport through an electronic scanner. She turns back toward Falcon as she flips through the pages. "I see you arrived from Mexico, sir. What is the nature of your visit here?"

"Tourism, ma'am."

"How long will you be staying?"

"Only a couple of weeks."

"Place your thumb on the scanner please, and look into the light."

Falcon has his thumbprint and retina scanned.

As the woman speaks, she eyes the small screen on her right. She waits a moment, and then she reaches over and stamps Falcon's passport. "Welcome to the United States, Dr. Falcon. Enjoy your stay."

Falcon and Bayani make their way outside to a long row of waiting taxis. They walk to the front of the line and climb inside the first waiting cab.

"Where to?" the cabby asks.

Falcon leans forward. "Long Beach, please… the corner of Anaheim Street and Junipero Avenue."

The driver turns and looks at Falcon. "Are sure about that, sir? Do you know where that is?"

"Yes, of course, sir," Falcon responds. "Little Phnom Penh."

The driver shakes his head. "OK, Cambodia Town it is…"

After a slogging taxi ride through LA traffic, the cab finally drops Falcon and Bayani off at their destination.

"Mmmmm." Bayani smiles as he takes in the vibrant shops and restaurants of Cambodia's largest immigrant community. "It smells wonderful, and I am hungry. How about you, Dr. Falcon?"

"Absolutely!" Falcon replies. "Lead the way, my friend."

Fifteen minutes later, Falcon finds himself sitting at a table inside a Cambodian noodle shop, bemused at the site of the ravenous teenager eagerly slurping down the large bowl of kuy teav in front of him.

Bayani suddenly stops eating and looks up at Falcon. "You have to put in the chili sauce, Dr. Falcon… like this." Bayani reaches for a small dish, scrapes the spicy red paste into Falcon's bowl, and then squeezes a lime wedge over the steaming hot noodle soup. "See?" He points. "Like that."

Bayani quickly returns to eating just as Falcon catches sight of four Cambodian youths as they enter the shop. All of them are dressed in black. Falcon continues to eat as he holds the group of young men within his peripheral vision. The youths announce their presence by loudly taking over one of the tables.

A few more minutes go by, and as Falcon savors the soup's rich broth, he notices the four gang members sizing up Bayani. After a short time, they all stand, walk over, and surround the table that Falcon and Bayani are sitting at. Bayani ignores them as he continues to eat, but then one of them speaks.

"You're not on your turf, monkey. What the fuck you doing here?"

A fierce anger suddenly inflames Falcon as he stops eating and looks up at the young men standing over him.

"Excuse me, can we help you with something?"

"Yeah, you can," the young man answers sarcastically. "You can get your fucking pet monkey off our turf."

Falcon starts to push his chair away from the table when Bayani stops him.

"No, Dr. Falcon."

Falcon glares back at Bayani.

"Dr. Falcon, please." Bayani gestures for Falcon to remain calm by lightly resting his open hand on the table.

Falcon sits back down. Bayani returns to eating when one of the young men bends down and spits into his bowl of soup.

Bayani freezes and stares down at the defiled meal in front of him as the restaurant suddenly goes completely silent. Falcon glances over at the restaurant staff behind the counter. He sees fear on their faces. He stares back at Bayani, who slowly shakes his head... *No...*

In that instant, Bayani is out of his chair and striking the man who insulted him. Before Falcon can even get to his feet, Bayani has two more of the Tiny Raskal gang members out of commission and is taking down the fourth when Falcon finally stands, and the young man Bayani is beating sees that Falcon is missing his right hand.

"I'm sorry! I'm sorry! Wait!" the man pleads with Bayani.

Bayani stops beating him, lets the guy go, and steps back as the young man struggles to scramble away and get to his feet. He's breathing heavily as he stares at the question mark tattoo on Falcon's left hand.

"Shit! Shit!" the man shouts while the other three gang members are all still slowly climbing back to their feet. "This is the guy, man!" The street gang members gather around Falcon. They scrutinize his stump of a right arm and his Baha la Na gang tattoo. "This is the guy," the young man repeats.

Then, one of the gang members looks up at Falcon. "Are you...?"

"Yes he is," answers Bayani.

The shift in attitude is instantaneous as the young street gang members suddenly transform into polite, respectful young men. They quickly straighten the table, pick up chairs, and tidy up the mess as Falcon looks on with fascination. Then, the shop door opens, and a man of about Falcon's age, with an irritated look on his face, walks inside.

He wears casual dress, but the younger gang members quickly step aside as he approaches Falcon.

"Please accept my humble apology for the behavior of these boys."

Then, he turns to the four youths and proceeds to chew them out in Khmer. The man walks over to the restaurant's staff, speaks to them softly, and then quietly slips the shop owner some money. Meanwhile, Falcon turns to look at Bayani, and as he does, he no longer sees an innocent teenager on his first trip away from home. He sees someone else entirely... a man he now realizes he has only barely come to know.

The man turns back toward Falcon and Bayani. "May I extend warm greetings to you? My name is Heng."

Falcon and Bayani each shake the man's hand. "Welcome to America," Heng says with a sarcastic grin. "We have much to discuss. Please, my car is waiting."

Falcon and Bayani walk outside to see a man standing on the curb beside a mammoth-sized black Cadillac Escalade. The driver hurries to open the door for Heng and his guests. Once inside the SUV, Heng turns to Falcon.

"So, Chia tells me that I am to take good care of you."

"Yes, this is true," Bayani complains angrily.

Heng gives Bayani a sharp look just as Falcon cuts in. "I am not offended, sir. It was merely an unfortunate mistake."

"Yes, of course," Heng responds hesitantly. "So, Chia tells me you are looking for some sort of artifact? You believe this artifact is located inside one of my buildings?"

Falcon leans forward. "Yes, it's a talisman, actually. It had been in my family for many generations. It was taken from me, and I must have it back."

"Yes, well Chia has spoken of your fascinating and incredible story, Dr. Falcon. It seems good fortune, perhaps, is smiling upon both of us. I happen to be in a unique position to assist, and helping you will place me in a better position to do business with Chia, so one could say that we are each on the same path at the moment, sir. The foundation leases the top six floors of 111 Ocean Boulevard. It's an office building that I currently have under contract. I can get you in there without any problem."

"What do you mean by under contract?" Falcon inquires. "Do you provide security?"

Heng laughs. "No, not security. I run a custodial business. We clean that building."

Chapter 30

Alex Moss walks into the ship's main lab. "Still studying those files, huh?"

The sound of his voice startles Dr. Samantha Randal. She suddenly looks up from behind the computer's monitor at Moss, and with what she now knows, she realizes that the man standing in front of her is actually a complete stranger to her.

"You startled me, Mr. Moss."

"I'm sorry, Dr. Randal. It's just that it's late, and I saw the light on in the lab. "

Samantha rushes to shut down the computer. "Oh... um, yes of course." She looks at her watch. "My goodness, you're absolutely right! It is late..."

Moss walks over. "What's wrong?"

Samantha catches herself. She takes a deep breath, and then she smiles pleasantly up at Moss. "I'm just tired, you're right. It's late. I should call it a night."

Moss folds his arms in front of him. "What's going on?" As the words leave his mouth, Moss suddenly realizes he is frightening her. The expression on Moss's face self-consciously softens as he drops his arms to his sides. "I apologize… Dr. Randal, please, I didn't mean to make you nervous."

Samantha stands up. She's about to leave when she stops and looks Moss in the eye. "But you do make me nervous, Mr. Moss. I'm sorry, I can't lie to you, sir."

Moss is puzzled. "What have you learned from those files? I can understand if you're upset about the drone project but— "

"It's not the drones, Mr. Moss…" Samantha pauses. "Yes, of course they are horrible, but there is quite a bit more information inside these files…"

"Like what?" Moss senses himself growing irritated, and he tries to control it. He steps closer to Samantha and is startled when she steps back.

She looks up at him. "Apparently, the foundation keeps extensive records on everyone that has ever worked aboard this vessel, Mr. Moss. All of our employment records, our personnel files, our research, it's all here. Dr. Peter Marsh, myself, Dr. Falcon, and even you."

A numbness hits Moss as the shock sinks in. "You read my file? My service record?"

"It was wrong, I apologize. I shouldn't have done it…"

"You're damned right you shouldn't have done it."

His voice cuts through Samantha like a knife as she cringes with embarrassment. Then, Samantha finds her strength. "But didn't you read my file, Mr. Moss? You know everything about me, don't you?"

His shoulders drop as he looks at her. "Not everything… especially not what matters. When it comes to what's important, a personnel file doesn't tell you about the person, Dr. Randal; it only lists their actions."

"Yes, that's true, but a person's actions are what they are truly made of, isn't that right?" Samantha's posture straightens. She walks closer to Moss, and she looks him right in the eye. "You killed people, Mr. Moss... a lot of people. You've killed people all over the world, in fact, and you became so expert at it that they even gave you a nickname. They call you *The Ax.*"

Moss glances at the floor and sighs. He then leans back against the table the computer is on and looks at Samantha. "I killed the enemy, Dr. Randal, and the people I killed were trying to kill me. I killed when I was ordered to kill. I was a US navy SEAL. I've served in two wars. I was defending my country."

Samantha's eyes narrow. "Well you were certainly very good at your job, Mr. Moss, and based on what I've read, it seems as if you might have even enjoyed it."

"No." Moss grips the table so hard that the desk creaks in protest. He glares at her. "I didn't enjoy it, Dr. Randal. I just wanted to stay alive more than the guys I killed. We used every weapon available to us and even some we created ourselves in order to keep ahead of the enemy. We needed to make it known that taking us on was taking a major risk. And yes, I encouraged it. I was ready to defend my men at all costs. The more time went by, the more I found my most important weapon in a fight was anger. Anger became my survival tool; it kept me alive and it kept me from thinking too much."

Samantha sees the pain on his face. She drops her head momentarily as she rubs her eyes, and then she looks up. "I feel I owe you an apology, sir. I've obviously opened old wounds, and I am very sorry..." She reaches up and touches Moss's arm as she looks up at him. "Truly I am." She starts to leave, and then she turns back. "Compassion, Mr. Moss. That's what I feel for you at this moment… compassion for a man who is forced to carry a terrible burden."

"Yeah… sure… thanks," Moss grumbles as he stares at the floor. "Being a war hero isn't what it's cracked up to be." He looks back at Samantha. "I don't need or want anyone's sympathy. This is why I don't talk about my past. People either feel sorry for you or they do exactly what you're doing; they make judgements. The only ones who understand are the few who are just like me because they were there."

"And Thomas Falcon?" Samantha asks. "Doesn't he deserve compassion as well? He didn't ask for what happened. It was an accident. If I've learned anything from these files, Mr. Moss, it's that empathy is something all the parties to this tragedy deserve."

"An accident?" Moss stares angrily back at her. "Is that what you call what that man did?" An accident?" Moss stands. "You have no idea how much I wanted to kill that man, Dr. Randal… how much I still have that feeling. When you brought that man on board my ship, that's exactly what I wanted to do. If I didn't have the respect for you that I do, that man would be dead right now."

Samantha looks at Moss as her eyes well up. "What happened to you?" she whispers.

"Like I said before," Moss huffs, "I don't like to talk about it."

The next day, Samantha is in the ship's infirmary with Seth as they follow up on Dan's progress. She's just finishing a blood pressure check when Moss walks in and sees Dan sitting on the examining table.

"How's he doing?"

Samantha looks at Moss and smiles. "I'm happy to report he's doing extremely well."

Moss smiles back. "That's great news."

"It's great news for you, Chief," Dan breaks in, "but, to me, it's amazing!" He hops from the table, grabs Dr. Randal, and hugs her so hard that he briefly lifts her from the floor. He then lets her go and looks at her. "I don't know how to thank you, Doc. You saved my life!"

Samantha blushes. "My goodness, I think you just did." She gazes up politely at the tall, freckled blond. "You are very welcome. I was happy to help."

"So, am I cleared to go back to work?" Dan asks eagerly.

Samantha glances over at Moss and then back at Dan. "I think it's all right, but nothing strenuous, and absolutely no scuba diving."

"Thanks, Doc!" Dan then winks at Moss. "Well, I guess I'm off to work then…"

"Sure," Moss answers. "Go have Razz put you back on the watch schedule."

"Speaking of the watch schedule," Seth adds quickly. "I better get up to the bridge. I'm on duty soon myself."

As the two men leave, Samantha looks quizzically at Moss. "What was all that about?"

Moss scratches his forehead self-consciously. "They think there's something going on between us. They're just being polite."

Samantha blushes again. "That is actually very sweet. They really care about you."

"Yeah, well the real reason I wanted to talk is about last night…"

"It's not necessary." Samantha's voice drops to a serious tone. "I was angry, and I was out of line. I really have nothing more to say for myself, and it's best if we leave the subject be."

"That's just it, Dr. Randal…" Moss pauses awkwardly. "I feel like… well, I think I should talk to you about it."

Samantha puts the sphygmomanometer down on the examining table, folds her arms, and leans back against it. "What do you need to tell me, Mr. Moss?" She cocks her head slightly. "What's happened?"

Moss exhales nervously. "This is really hard for me." He glances at his watch and then back at Samantha. "I am affected by what happened, Dr. Randal. It's with me every day, and I've always managed to push it aside."

The instincts of an expert physician go on full alert as Samantha suddenly begins evaluating Moss in the same manner as she would any other patient. "Have you been experiencing symptoms of post-traumatic stress? Are you having repeated nightmares? Bouts of extreme anxiety? Cold sweats?"

"Yes," Moss answers flatly.

She suddenly focuses on his face. "Are you telling me you are experiencing all three?"

"Yes."

Samantha leans up from the table and takes a step toward Moss. "You once told me that you were able to survive in battle because you very much wanted to stay alive." The sudden seriousness of Samantha's expression catches Moss off guard, "is that still true, Mr. Moss?"

"Yes." Moss folds his arms. "Yes, it is."

"Then, I suggest…" Samantha pauses as she thinks about her words, "only if you are truly open to it, of course, but I feel you should to speak to someone in a clinical setting... a professional setting—"

"No..." Moss interrupts. "No shrinks. I'm not going there." Then, he looks right at her. "I will talk to you, Doctor, but only you."

Samantha gasps. "I am a medical doctor, Mr. Moss, but I'm not a psychiatrist," she cautions. "I'm not qualified."

Moss stares back at her. "You are to me."

• • •

Over the next few days, as *Fearless* steadily motors north toward California, Moss quietly meets with Samantha each evening after his final watch is over. Sometimes, they meet in the lab, while on other nights, they meet in Moss's personal office. His therapy sessions often last for hours as Moss, for the first time in his life, allows someone into the most personal recesses of his past. With Samantha's patient guidance, Moss finds he is able to face down horrors that had long tormented him.

None of this activity has gone unnoticed by the crew, however, as they nod and wink approvingly whenever they see Moss. He only smiles in response, allowing them to make whatever assumptions they wish to make. Samantha meanwhile is fully aware of the ruse but lets it pass, knowing full well the delicate nature of male masculinity. She's trying to help a man rebuild himself, and she can see he's making progress. She won't risk compromising his trust, but she knows there are still places Moss won't take her.

"So what about your family, Dr. Randal?" Moss asks one evening. "What's your history?"

Samantha folds her legs underneath her and leans back on the sofa in Moss's office.

"My mother was born in Karachi," Samantha begins, "back when it was still Pakistan's capital city. The family eventually moved to the new capital, Islamabad. Then, my grandfather, who was a professor of mathematics at the university there, received an invitation from the British to teach at Oxford. So, the family moved to England, and we've been there ever since. My mother eventually became a barrister, and that's how she met my father. They still work together." Samantha draws her cardigan around her slender body more snugly.

"Okay, so now it's your turn," Samantha responds. "Why the navy? What's your story, Mr. Moss?"

"Me?" Moss chuckles at the thought.

"I was always a navy brat, Dr. Randal. My dad was career navy, and his dad. I was born on the base at Coronado in San Diego, where my dad was an instructor. He served in Vietnam; he was an underwater demolitions expert. As a kid, I always considered myself pretty lucky. I mean, kids are always trying to figure out what they want to do with their lives, you know? I never had to think about it, I was navy, and that was it. I signed up at eighteen right out of high school. I served my twenty years, and then this job came along, so here I am."

"Why do I get the feeling there is so much more to your story, Mr. Moss?"

"Well, I guess a lot of stuff happened during that time, but I'm not much of a storyteller, Dr. Randal, and there's just a lot of stuff I don't talk about."

Samantha shifts the subject. "You do have someone special in your life, Mr. Moss, isn't that right?"

"Yeah I do. Well, at least I think I do"

"Her name is Trish, right? And you met in Africa?"

Moss smirks. "Yeah, well, that's one way of putting it."

"Is everything that happens to you an adventure, Mr. Moss?"

"Sometimes it feels that way, ma'am, yeah…"

Samantha then decides to push Moss a bit further. "Tell me about the little girl on the reef."

Moss freezes a moment, and then Samantha sees his shoulders slump as he sits next to her on the sofa in his office. He brings his hands to his face, rubs his eyes, and then takes on a somber tone as the memories rush painfully into his head. He looks at her.

"That was one of the worst days of my life."

Moss turns away, rests his elbows on his knees, folds his hands in front of him, and stares at the wall as he speaks.

"Everything I saw that day connected right back to me. All of it was the result of my decisions and my failure to take appropriate action. If I had handled things differently, if I had handled the situation with Dr. Falcon differently, then that little girl, and all of those people would still be alive today…"

"I disagree, Mr. Moss."

Moss draws back and stares at her.

Samantha straightens, and then she looks Moss in the eye. "You are a powerful alpha male, Alex Moss. There is no denying this fact, but you are not God, sir. You can't control the actions of others, and you had no control over what happened at that beach resort, as much as you may think otherwise. You cannot blame yourself for this; it wasn't your fault."

"Yeah, maybe…" Moss pauses, "but I still want to make things right."

"How do you propose to do that?"

"For starters?" Moss looks into Samantha's large brown eyes. "Kill Thomas Falcon."

Chapter 31

Jeff Buxton finds himself feeling oddly uncomfortable. It's 0200, and he is surrounded by killer tiger sharks. Buxton is currently standing inside the grow room at the foundation's La Paz facility, and unlike his past encounters with the MS41-T, these sharks aren't frozen solid; they are very much alive.

Buxton walks over to one of the five-meter-long fiberglass tanks and peers through its acrylic observation port. The drone growing inside is suspended amidst a customized soup of electrically stimulated, bioengineered embryonic fluid. This particular unit is two thirds of the way through its growth cycle, and although it is nearly full adult size, the embryo is still so physically underdeveloped as to be virtually transparent.

Buxton can clearly make out the tiger shark's beating heart and internal organs as its gills suck in the oxygen and nutrient-rich fluid. He recognizes the drone's small, integrated control unit fixed deep inside the core of its body. Even the outlines of skeletal cartilage are visible, but for the veteran CIA officer, the feature that stands out more than any other is the shark's lethal rows of razor-sharp teeth. The massive fish shifts to one side of its tank as its jaws snap shut. The sudden motion sends Buxton lurching backward.

"They do begin to get a bit frisky at about this stage, sir…"

Buxton spins around to see a young lab tech standing behind him. "Are these things secure in these tanks?" Buxton questions.

"Absolutely," the technician responds assuredly. "We have the lid bolted down. The tank is made of reinforced fiberglass and mounted to the aluminum frame. The whole thing is fixed to the floor, sir. It's not going anywhere."

Buxton sizes up the large room filled with grow tanks. "Looks like you guys have a solid handle on the process."

"We do now," the technician answers glibly, "but you could say it's been a learning experience. We had a few issues at first. Like, we weren't expecting the embryos to become this physically active so quickly. The first tanks we used had an open top, and let's just say, that didn't go so well."

"Is that so?" Buxton winces as he mentally ponders the gruesome outcome of such a scenario. "So, how soon will these last units be ready for transport?"

The technician adjusts his glasses. "Twenty-eight days, sir."

Buxton is not happy with the idea of keeping part of the La Paz facility open for four more weeks. The facility's inventory of fully completed units—all one hundred and fifty of them—is currently being made ready for transport on the storage level one floor up from where he is currently standing.

"Will you guys be able to manage down here until you can get this last group ready to ship out?"

"Oh absolutely, sir," the lab tech answers confidently. "We've got everything under control."

Outside on the tarmac, a Lockheed Martin C-5M Super Galaxy stands ready to receive her load. In service since 1970, the C-5 is the largest American heavy airlift transport that has ever been built, earning it the nickname *Lockheed Hilton*. She has a cargo hold longer than the Wright brothers' first powered flight at Kitty Hawk and is large enough to comfortably swallow six Greyhound buses. Tonight's top-secret airlift will be a first, however, as the huge belly of this particular C-5 will be stuffed full of solidly frozen, artificially engineered, and fully militarized tiger sharks.

As Buxton returns to the hangar level, the CIA's operation *Ice Cream Truck* is just getting underway as the C-5's loadmaster busily calculates his task. The heavy transport aircraft is currently open at both ends as Buxton walks up the aft ramp and into the plane's gaping cathedral-like interior. In the hangar behind him, stacks of black carbon composite containers that house the drones sit waiting to be loaded on board the aircraft when the loadmaster approaches Buxton.

"We got a problem sir..."

The man's words cause Buxton to cringe as he turns toward the senior airman. "Are we over gross?"

"No, sir, we're okay on weight, but these special pallets the boxes are mounted on will eat up a lot of space. You either need to leave them behind or else I can't fit all of your cargo."

"Are you sure?" Buxton asks. "Without those rolling pallets, we'll have to load each one of these damn things by hand."

"Sorry, sir," the airman shrugs. "She's big, but even a C-5 has limits."

Two hours behind schedule, the C-5M Super Galaxy's four General Electric TF39 turbo fan engines rapidly spool up on their way to full throttle as the massive transport begins a short field takeoff procedure from La Paz. She's locked into position at the far end of the runway while her flight crew run the engines up to over forty thousand pounds of thrust each. The twenty-eight wheels of her landing gear assembly strain against the forward inertia until the captain finally releases the brakes and the plane roars down the runway and into the air.

Jeff Buxton breathes a quiet sigh of relief as the deep-throated TF39s smoothly carry the lumbering beast up to altitude. He turns to his fellow Special Activities Division officers, who look equally pleased that they are successfully airborne and the toughest part of their mission is now behind them. The four men are seated in the dignitary's section just behind the six-man flight crew located on the C-5's upper deck. Buxton reaches into his briefcase and pulls out a thermos filled with hot coffee.

He looks across the aisle at his friend and fellow Special Activities Division colleague, Eric Stevens, a man whom Jeff Buxton has worked with many times in the past. "You want a shot?"

"Yeah sure, Jeff, thanks." Buxton hands the thermos to Eric. They share the coffee, and then Buxton settles into his seat and attempts to relax.

An hour and forty-five minutes later, Buxton hears the flight crew announce over his headset that they are beginning their descent into Frederick Sherman Field, KUNC at the north end of San Clemente Island. They are in contact with the tower at the Naval Auxiliary air station when a shudder ripples through the deck plating under Buxton's feet.

"Did you feel that?" Buxton calls up to the crew.

"Feel what?" comes the short reply through his headset. Buxton looks over at Eric, who only shrugs. Then, he senses the rumble again. He looks across at his CIA colleagues, who now seem equally puzzled, but then a much sharper jolt rifles up through the floor.

"What the fuck was that?" the plane's captain calls out over the comm.

A sickening feeling churns through Jeff Buxton's gut as he locks eyes on Eric, who has an equally disturbed look on his face. "You don't think…?"

"It can't be," Eric replies. "We fixed that bug months ago."

"You're right," Buxton responds. "But that was only forty units. We've got one hundred and fifty stacked under our feet."

"They're not active, Jeff," Eric assures him. "There's no fucking way those units can activate on their own. it can't happen again. We fixed that bug, I guarantee it."

At that moment, a loud, three-stroke alarm suddenly fills the cabin as the men inside hear a female electronic voice announce *Missile Detection.* The startling signal is coming from the plane's AN/AAR-47 missile warning system.

Eric glances at Buxton. "It's gotta be a false alarm, right? We're over US waters."

The missile detection alarm goes off a second time, and through his headset, Buxton overhears the flight crew scramble to communicate with the tower in an attempt to find out what's happening. Then, he hears the captain give the order to initiate evasive countermeasures.

"Shit," Buxton mutters as he looks over at the blood rapidly draining from Eric's terrified face.

Outside the C-5, fountains of fiery phosphorous flares flow out from the plane's wings and fuselage, countermeasures designed to confuse a heat-seeking missile and trick its guidance system into tracking the intensely incendiary flares streaming away from the aircraft.

The explosion comes across as almost a dull thud as seven-hundred thousand pounds of aircraft suddenly yaws sharply to starboard. The sharp, jolting movement jerks the men strapped into their seats harshly to port. In the wake of the explosion, Buxton senses that the C-5 is still flying under pilot control, but the rapid exchanges between the flight crew tell him that they've been hit. He looks over at his men.

"Better grab your balls, fellas. If we make it, drinks are on me."

Down on the airfield, emergency vehicles pour out from their hangars and race toward the runway as the critically wounded Super Galaxy limps toward the threshold of Runway 6.

The captain struggles to hold his plane's two-hundred-and-twenty-two-foot wings level as vital hydraulic control systems go into cascade failure. He knows he's lost at least one engine, he has no flaps, and he can't tell if the landing gear actually came down. The veteran pilot is hand flying by the seat of his pants when he sees the running rabbit lights of the field pass beneath his aircraft, followed by the runway's threshold and finally the numbers.

The senior Air Force Captain is landing his plane hot—way too fast for the length of the field and the size of his aircraft. The C-5's captain reverses engines after he feels his aircraft's landing gear firmly touch down. The plane pitches forward harshly then lurches violently to one side as she skids off the runway at midfield in a spinning tumble of dust and flying rocks until the C-5 Super Galaxy finally comes to rest.

Thick, choking dust instantly fills the inside of the plane as Buxton and his men struggle to free themselves from their seats. In the darkness, they feel their way back to the troop seating section located toward the rear of the upper deck and find the drone techs in complete panic as they scream nonsensically at each other.

Buxton yanks two of the shrieking techs from their seats and drags them outside. Through the heavy yellowish dust cloud, Buxton can make out the streaking lights of rapidly approaching emergency vehicles.

"What the fuck just happened?" Buxton hears Eric shout into his ear.

Buxton turns calmly and looks at the guy. "You've never been shot down before, have you, Eric?"

"Fuck no!" Eric screams. "Who the fuck shot us down? Jeff! My God! This can't happen! We're in California!"

Buxton walks back toward the rear of the plane that now leans sharply to one side with her massive wing folded into the ground like a piece of origami. Eric quits yelling and follows Buxton as the rest of the men collect themselves and trail after them.

Buxton stops dead in his tracks when he reaches the truck-sized opening in the side of the cargo compartment. "Shit…"

"Jesus Martha…" Eric mumbles in astonishment as he, too, spots the gaping hole blown into the side of the fuselage. "How the hell did we stay in the air after a hit like that?"

"God bless Lockheed Martin…" Buxton replies. Then, he climbs up through the hole and into the cargo compartment. "Looks like we've got ourselves an even bigger problem, fellas…"

Eric climbs up for a better look as the other two CIA officers peer inside.

"Holy shit, it's empty!"

Eric turns back to catch sight of Buxton walking off across the freshly gouged trenches of desert rubble. Jeff Buxton's stark silhouette is quickly fading into the dust cloud and the mayhem of emergency first responders as the man marches toward the airport's terminal. "Hey, Jeff!" Eric calls out. "Where the hell are you going?"

Buxton stops and looks back. "I'm gonna find a bottle, and I'm gonna drink the whole goddamned thing. You guys coming?"

Chapter 32

Thomas Falcon stands beneath the showerhead in his hotel bath and allows the hot water to flow over his face and down his body. All the while, a stream of constant thought runs through his mind as he ponders the possibility—the remoteness of the odds, in fact—of actually recovering the talisman.

Falcon shuts off the water and steps from the shower stall to grab a towel, when he suddenly realizes he is standing on hot, dry dirt. Dripping wet, and completely naked, Thomas Falcon looks up at an intensely bright midday sun and then gazes out in complete astonishment at the serene living tableau that has suddenly appeared in front of him.

It is a traditional village, and it's filled with people, their activities, and their animals. Falcon recognizes the small mud-brick houses with thatched roofs and realizes he must be somewhere in West Africa.

Nobody seems to notice him as Falcon unknowingly strolls through his own ancestral village. Falcon doesn't know where he is going or why he is here, but he walks on, driven by the need to understand. He passes by clusters of small, circular houses. He sees children playing and women working. He pauses briefly to watch two young boys walk by carrying an impala.

Eventually, Falcon finds himself following a winding path up a parched, grassy hill, where he encounters two girls walking back toward the village. He smiles as they pass, but neither one of them can see him. Falcon reaches the top of the hill and finds a distinctive house covered in elaborately painted designs and patterns. He stops at the front door, and he waits, but then something calls to him—a feeling... like a voice with no sound—so, Falcon goes inside.

Falcon enters the home of the village shaman and marvels at what he finds. The air is thick and ripe with a symphony of pungent odors. The walls are covered in a wide array of charms and talismans, dried bundles of medicinal plants, and animal parts.

He can see the shaman himself sitting on a woven grass mat. The man is working on something—a carving. Falcon approaches the shaman and observes as the man delicately carves designs into a small piece of bone. Then, he sees the shaman reach for a tiny clay pot resting on a flat stone that has been balanced over smoldering coals.

The man carefully pours hot wax from the little pot into the hollow bone carving. Then, the shaman places something shining and gleaming inside of it. Falcon continues to observe as the man continues his work. The shaman pauses. He stops working and sits motionless for a moment, and then he turns and looks directly at Falcon.

Falcon is stunned when the shaman looks right into his eyes, and he realizes that the man can actually see him. Falcon suddenly feels conscious of his nudity. The shaman stands and approaches him. Falcon freezes. He doesn't know what to do. He can't communicate; all he can do is simply stand in one place as the shaman first looks him over, and then the man reaches up and curiously places his hand on the elaborate tattoos that cover Falcon's chest and upper body.

The shaman reaches down and takes Falcon's hand. He lifts it and then opens it and examines his palm carefully. The man first smiles and then grins broadly as he studies Falcon's outstretched hand. The shaman begins to chuckle amusingly at what the lines tell him. He reaches for the talisman and places it in the palm of Falcon's hand. The shaman closes Falcon's hand around the small bone carving and cradles it inside his own hands as he stares at Falcon. Falcon looks into the shaman's face as the man squeezes his hand so tightly that Falcon winces from the pain.

The shaman looks deeply into Falcon's eyes without blinking, without expression, as he grinds the talisman harder into Falcon's flesh. Falcon closes his eyes and tries not to cry out, but the pain becomes so incredibly intense that he can't help himself. *He screams.*

The echo of Falcon's painful scream fills the hotel bathroom. He catches himself. Falcon spins around in confusion until he realizes where he is. He can hear someone pounding on his door. Falcon grabs a towel, wraps it around his waist, and goes to the door of his hotel room. He finds Bayani looking flustered and frustrated on the other side.

"I was knocking a lot, then I heard you scream," Bayani complains. "Where were you?"

"Oh, I just stepped out briefly," Falcon responds glibly.

Bayani covers his nose and grimaces as he walks inside the room. "Well, it is a good thing you are about to take a shower, Dr. Falcon, because you smell really bad."

"Do I?" Falcon sniffs his arm. "Oh my… that truly is incredible."

Bayan closes the door, and then he eyes Falcon more carefully. "You have powerful experiences, Dr. Falcon, but you must be careful. When the spirit travels beyond the body in a vision, it can always return, but when your physical body passes into the spirit world, it doesn't always come back."

Falcon is shocked. "How could you tell?"

Bayani points to Falcon's hand. "You are bleeding, and you smell really bad."

Falcon opens his palm and is astonished by the bloody impression the talisman left behind. "My God…"

"You should wash and get dressed, Dr. Falcon. Heng is taking us to the foundation's offices tonight, and we don't have much time."

• • •

It's after ten when Heng's driver pulls into the basement parking garage of 111 Ocean Boulevard.

Heng turns to Falcon. "I will leave you two gentlemen in the capable hands of Mrs. Oum. She is my best supervisor. She has nearly total access to the building." Heng then hands Falcon a business card. "Call this number when you are ready to leave and my driver will pick you up. I wish you good fortune in your quest."

Falcon takes the card from Heng. "Thank you, sir."

Bayani and Falcon are watching the black Cadillac pull away when they suddenly hear a sharp and powerful voice erupt behind them.

"Hey, you guys!"

The men spin around to find a four-foot-three-inch Cambodian woman in her fifties staring up at them in a rather unpleasant fashion. Mrs. Oum frowns as she sizes up Falcon and Bayani. "Come on," she demands in an irritated tone. "Follow me. I don't have all night. Some people have to work for a living."

Falcon and Bayani find themselves immediately intimidated by the commanding presence of the diminutive Mrs. Oum. They rush to keep pace as she walks swiftly to the elevators, where they encounter a man wrestling with a large floor machine.

The man notices them walking toward him and instantly flinches at the sight of Mrs. Oum. He makes a feeble attempt to look busy as Mrs. Oum speaks to him sharply in Khmer. Falcon and Bayani each step back in order to stay out of the line of fire. The elevator's doors slide open, and the man begins to wheel the heavy machine inside when Mrs. Oum holds up her hand. "No. Take the next one."

Falcon and Bayani follow Mrs. Oum into the elevator. She hits the button for the eighteenth floor and then turns to face them. "Heng explained to me that you are looking for a small carving. He showed me the sketch you made." She folds her arms and stares up at Falcon. "I run a legitimate business here. I won't put up with any monkey business, you get what I'm saying?"

"Yes, ma'am," Falcon answers respectfully. "I assure you I am only seeking an object that was stolen from me and nothing more."

"Yeah, well that better be all it is." She frowns at Falcon again. "I see that tat on your hand. I know what it means. Your type doesn't scare me, you got that?"

The elevator arrives at the eighteenth floor, and the doors glide open. Falcon and Bayani follow Mrs. Oum down a corridor lined with expensively furnished executive offices. She glances back at Bayani. "You look like a worker, kid. What are you doing with this guy? You gotta green card? You want a real job?" She walks a bit further and then stops abruptly at the open door to one of the offices. "I think what you're looking for is in here, and apparently, this guy just died, so they had us pack up his stuff."

"Is that so?" Falcon steps through the door and walks into Alistair's office.

Mrs. Oum waits by the door and watches Falcon's every move. "That box over there. Take a look at that framed statue. Is that it?"

Falcon lifts the frame from the box and turns it around. "My God. I can't believe it…"

Bayani walks over for a closer look. "This is a powerful object, Dr. Falcon."

"Hey… you guys…"

They both look back at Mrs. Oum. "That's it, right? Okay then, get out of my building."

The Escalade drops Falcon and Bayani back at their hotel. Falcon cradles the framed talisman under his left arm as he and Bayani take the elevator back up to Falcon's suite.

"This was way too easy," Falcon observes cautiously as he lays the frame face down on the desk in his room. He begins searching the desk for something sharp when Bayani suddenly flips a fan knife out in front of his face.

"Use this, Dr. Falcon,"

Falcon raises his eyebrows at the sight of the Filipino street-fighting switchblade. "That's a Balisong. Has that been with you the whole time?"

"Of course," Bayani answers wryly. "We Filipinos are a blade culture, Dr. Falcon."

Falcon eyes the deadly weapon. "Quite right…"

Falcon takes the blade from Bayani and carefully slices through the dust cover on the back of the frame. With Bayani's assistance, he lifts out the thickly layered mat board the statue is attached to. They flip it around and lay the board back down. Falcon delicately slices through the strands of clear monofilament that secure the statue to the board.

He hands the knife back to Bayani and picks up the talisman. Instantly, the statuette sears into Falcon's palm like a chunk of burning coal. Falcon's first reaction is to let go, but he resists. He fights against his natural urge to drop the talisman, and instead, Falcon closes his hand tightly around the statue. His agony grows, and a loud, uncontrolled groan escapes from Falcon's mouth, but he continues to tighten his grip until the searing pain finally subsides. Falcon slowly opens his hand and stares down at the talisman resting inside the fresh wound the shaman created… *and suddenly understands…*

Falcon is fascinated by the lingering physical sensation. He studies the small statue for what seems like the first time. The once quaint family heirloom is no more. He now sees the talisman for what it truly is—an incredibly powerful and dangerous object that was created by his ancestor eight centuries ago. Then, Falcon notices something else: the talisman feels much lighter. *Something is missing.*

Chapter 33

Alex Moss sets his coffee down as he adjusts a protractor over the pencil line he has just finished drawing onto a chart of the southern California coast and the Channel Islands.

"We'll be coming up on San Clemente soon," Rafferty points out as he takes a sip from his own steaming mug.

"By my calculations," Moss clarifies, "we're currently seven nautical miles southeast."

Rafferty smirks. "Well…" He glances over at the electronic chart plotter on the bridge Navionics panel, "not bad, Ax. Computer says we're six point eight nautical miles southeast."

Moss studies the image of the rocky desert island. "San Clemente… it's been a lot of years since we were there, Razz…"

"I sure don't miss it," Rafferty comments.

"Yeah, me neither." Moss picks up his coffee mug, walks over to the forward windows, and looks out at the misty golden sunrise reflecting off the mirror-smooth Pacific. He takes a sip and then sets the mug down and reaches for the binoculars.

"Hey, Razz," Moss calls out as he focuses. "What do you make of this?"

Moss hands over the binoculars as Rafferty sets down his coffee mug.

Rafferty peers through the lenses. "Looks like someone lost some cargo." He hands the binoculars back to Moss. "I'll report it to the Coast Guard."

"That's okay, Razz. I'll take care of it." Moss scans the debris field once more as he sighs in disgust. "I get so sick of people dumping shit in the ocean and then just leaving it there."

Moss makes a mental note of the dozens of floating, coffin-shaped black containers scattered some three hundred meters off the bow of *Fearless*. Many appear to be broken, but all of them seem to be empty.

Moss turns to Rich, who has the helm. "Reduce speed and adjust our course thirty degrees starboard," Moss orders. "I don't want these things scratching up the hull."

A little over an hour later, *Fearless* is back on course. Moss is outside on deck with Murray when he spots another distant object floating in the sea ahead, but this one's much larger. Moss radios up to the bridge and then turns to Murray. "Razz is alerting the Coast Guard. Better get a RIB ready. We have to check this out."

Rich guides *Fearless* slowly toward the stricken vessel until Moss radios that the ship is close enough. Rich reverses engines and brings the three-hundred-and-eighteen-foot-long research ship to a full stop about two hundred meters away. Moss and his crew look across with dread at the forty-foot, fly ridge sport fisher; she is adrift and listing badly.

Seth places his medical kit inside the RIB and climbs inside along with Razz and Murray. They cautiously motor across the two-hundred-meter stretch of flat water to the half-sunken fishing boat. As they draw closer, the gruesome scene in front of them comes painfully into sharp focus. Murray looks somberly at Seth.

"This is looking pretty ugly, mate…"

Seth winces at the swaths of blood that paint the aft section of the boat's deckhouse. "It's not how I wanted to start my day, that's for sure."

"Nobody touches anything," Rafferty commands. "None of us goes aboard unless we see evidence of survivors. We have to treat this as a crime scene, and the Coast Guard will be plenty upset with us if we disturb it before they can get out here."

Razz fires off an air horn to alert any survivors who may be inside, and then the men call out to the boat, but they get no response. They maneuver the RIB in close enough to see the full extent of the carnage splattered across the boat's aft deck.

The three war veterans grimace in disgust when confronted by the gruesome partial remains of what look to be two men. Razz feels a wave of nausea wash over him as he gets an unwanted close-up look at the men's shredded and dismembered corpses. "Jesus, not again…" he mutters softly. Razz shoots a worried glance at Murray. "Spin us around. Let's get the hell out of here."

On board *Fearless*, the creases in Moss's forehead deepen as he listens to Razz describe what they found. "We radioed a report to the Coast Guard while you guys were over there. They have the coordinates." Moss sighs as he looks down at the chart plotter. "Let's get moving. We have another sixty-five miles between us and our harbor slip in LBC, and as far as I'm concerned, we can't get there fast enough."

Razz takes over the helm from Rich and reaches for the throttle. "I'm with you a hundred percent, Chief."

Under a cloudless sky, Murray and Dan stand watch on the bow as *Fearless* motors steadily north at fifteen knots. The sun has burned off the last thin layers of morning sea fog. The men have a clear view ahead of them when Murray taps Dan on the shoulder. "What does that look like to you, mate?"

Dan lifts his binoculars and focuses on the dark shape floating atop a glassy smooth sea…"It's more debris. We've been seeing a lot of it this morning." Then, Dan looks again. "Wait… oh no…"

Razz reduces speed as *Fearless* motors slowly past the mutilated body floating face down off their port side. Murray briefly locks eyes with Moss, and then he stares down at the fully clothed corpse bobbing in the ship's wake. "Poor guy was nearly bitten in two, Chief…"

Moss briefly looks down at the grotesque site. "We're not stopping…"

He grabs his radio and calls up to the bridge. "Razz, get us back on course and maintain best speed." Then, he stops to study the concerned faces of the crewmen standing in front of him. Moss clinches his jaw and then snaps the radio from his belt once more.

"Razz."

"Yeah, Chief."

"Tell Flip to get the chopper ready."

"Chief?"

"You heard me."

"I'm on it."

Twenty minutes later, Moss watches from the bridge as Flip and four crewmen remove the tie-downs and pull the last of the protective covers off of the Bell 429 GlobalRanger.

Moss turns back toward Razz. "Alert the science team. I want them ready to evacuate if need be." Moss sees shock flash across Rafferty's face. "Look, Razz, I would much rather be guilty of overreacting than responsible for those women getting injured or killed."

Rafferty nods. "Yeah, sure, I understand, Chief. Consider it done."

• • •

The foundation's Eurocopter EC175 hasn't fully powered down before Jeff Buxton is out and marching across the rooftop helipad of 111 Ocean Boulevard.

"We were fucking shot down, Marcus," Buxton growls as he brushes past Marcus Waverley on his way to the drone operations center.

Marcus chases after him. "How is that possible? I don't understand how this could happen! Jeff!"

Buxton stops and spins back just short of the door. He raises his finger and points it at Marcus Waverley's chest. "I'll tell you what happened, Marcus. They were fucking waiting for us, which means someone leaked our operation."

"That's impossible!"

"Is it, Marcus?" Buxton steps closer, shoves his finger into Marcus Waverley's expensive Italian suit, and leans into his face. "Well, let me fill you in. At this moment, there is a United States Air Force C-5 Galaxy balled up into two-hundred and eighty million dollars' worth of scrap over at the airfield on San Clemente. Someone has just shot down an American military aircraft inside US territory. Do you have any idea how serious this is? The navy jumped on this like flies on shit, and you know what they found?"

Buxton doesn't wait for an answer as he stares down a cringing Marcus Waverley. "They found what was left of a five-meter-long RIB abandoned and floating twenty miles out in the Pacific. The intel tells me that somebody launched a MANPAD surface-to-air missile from a fucking dingy, Marcus. I'll give you one guess as to who has the brass balls to pull off a stunt like that."

A stunned Marcus Waverley catches sight of his bewildered drone techs as they file past Buxton after climbing out of the chopper. He looks back at Buxton. "What about the drones, Jeff? Where are the drones?"

"Well, that is the billion-dollar question, isn't it, Marcus?" Buxton pushes Marcus aside as he follows his team down to the operations center.

"Do you have tracking on these things yet?" Buxton demands as he leans over a drone operator's station.

"We think so, sir," the technician answers nervously.

"You think so?" Buxton scowls. "We've got a live weapons system unaccounted for, son, and innocent people are going to die if we don't get a handle on this situation right now. Do you understand me?"

"Yes, sir," the technician responds as he furiously types commands into his keyboard. "I'm picking up signals now, sir."

"How many?"

The technician studies the telemetry streaming across the screen in front of him. "Guidance is reporting one hundred and forty-three active signals." He quickly types a series of commands into the computer.

"Can you deactivate them?"

"No, sir. I just initiated the command protocol for shutdown, but none of the units are responding." The technician turns to look at Buxton. "There's too many of them, sir. The signal's too strong. It's like they go into overdrive when we have more than twenty units activated."

"Yes, I read the report," Buxton answers. "But these units weren't activated. They were frozen solid. They were in transport mode."

"So were the forty units we lost six months ago, sir. I really thought we had that bug fixed."

"Fixed in computer simulation only," Buxton scoffs angrily. "I could never get Dr. Fairchild to initiate another live test. He knew something, and he was hiding it."

• • •

Alex Moss shields his eyes from the glare as he watches four Boeing AH-64 Apache attack helicopters circle over *Fearless* at low altitude. He glances at Rafferty. "Something's going on."

"That's for damn sure," Rafferty responds as he eyes the formation of fully armed Apaches passing rapidly overhead. "We've seen a Poseidon sub tracker, a couple of Hawkeye AWACS, and a dozen F18 Hornets. The navy's putting on quite a show this morning. Do you think it's a training exercise?"

"No," Moss answers flatly as he studies the Apache formation more carefully. "Those Hydra missile pods aren't training duds; they're fully armed. These guys are on full alert."

"Do you think that fishing boat and the bodies we found are connected somehow?"

"I'm not sure. Maybe," Moss answers indecisively. "This whole situation is giving me a really bad feeling, Razz."

"You and me both, Ax."

Moss follows the formation of fast-moving attack helicopters until they fade into the distance. "The sooner we can get out of this area and back in port, the better."

Chapter 34

"Are you okay?"

Dr. Samantha Randal looks up from the box of samples she is busily packing. "I should be asking you that question, Mr. Moss." She walks over and looks up at a clearly weary Alex Moss. "If you don't mind me saying…" she pauses to briefly study the deepening lines on Moss's pallid face, "you look terrible." She eyes him again. "What's going on?"

"Look, it's just a precaution. It's nothing to worry about."

"Seth told me what happened. He talked to me about what you found this morning. You should have called me."

"You didn't need to see that—"

Samantha cuts Moss off. "I am a doctor. I'm sure I've seen worse."

"Not like this…"

Samantha searches his face again. "There's more… you're holding something back."

Moss exhales as he leans back against a table. "Look, I can't hold back what I don't know." He looks Samantha in the eye. "I purposely didn't read those files from Dr. Falcon. After what happened, I couldn't."

Moss's expression becomes more intense as he speaks. "But as hard as this is for me, I need to know what you found out. I need to know if there's a connection to what we found this morning and those drones."

Samantha thinks for a moment. "It's possible…"

She walks over to the computer and begins searching the database Falcon gave her. "I've spent days poring over these files, and I still haven't read them all, aside from the personnel files. There is over two thousand pages of technical data here."

She glances up at Moss. "To be honest, quite a bit appears to be rather mundane and tedious." Samantha focuses back on the screen and continues to type as she speaks. "The files cover every aspect of the program," she pauses… "But something Seth said this morning struck me. It sounded familiar."

Moss walks over and looks down at the screen. "Familiar in what way?"

"It may be nothing, but first, I have to locate the correct file." She opens a few more pages. "I think I have it." She looks up at Moss. "Have a look at this."

Moss bends down and scans the information displayed on the screen. "This is a standard operations and maintenance schedule," he continues reading until he reaches the section that describes the drone's safe transport procedures, complete with an illustration of the specially designed MS41-T transport containers. "Shit…" Moss bolts upright, and he looks at Samantha. "I'm getting you and your team off this ship right now."

Samantha quickly gets to her feet, "What is it?" she calls out to Moss as he marches swiftly toward the door of the lab. "It's the debris field you saw this morning, isn't it? They are the drones' transport containers, aren't they?"

Moss stops and spins back in her direction. "Yeah, I'm pretty sure they are, and the ones we saw were all empty. Get your team together. I'm evacuating you immediately."

• • •

After a thorough walk around, Flip climbs into the right seat of the Bell's cockpit and grabs the laminated checklist he keeps in a side pocket. The veteran pilot runs through his routine preflight as he systematically powers up avionics and then types his planned route to KLGB Long Beach into one of the navigation displays on the BasiX-Pro™ avionics instrument panel.

Flip focuses on the oil pressure readouts of the helicopter's twin turboshaft engines as the glass cockpit displays come to life. In addition to his instruments, he is actively evaluating one of his passengers. Flip glances across the cockpit at Samantha.

"This your first time in a chopper?"

Dr. Randal nods nervously as she attempts to appear calm.

"No worries." Flip answers cheerfully. "It's a lovely day for a flight. We should get a great view of the city."

He hands her a headset. "Here, why don't you put these on? You can listen to my radio transmissions. Just pretend you're a tourist out for a joy ride." Samantha smiles as she takes the headset from Flip.

"So, why do they call you Flip?"

Flip smirks as he continues his preflight checks. "Oh that. Well, it's kind of a long story. Best to save it for another time," and then he winks at her.

Samantha observes keenly as Flip completes his checklist. She watches his hands move deftly from system to system, and in the process, she spots the small SASR patch tacked under the glare shield. She recognizes it as a Special Forces insignia and decides at that moment not to ask any more questions.

With his passengers loaded, Flip gives a nod to Moss and then begins engine start procedures. Moss and Rafferty clear the helipad as the Bell 429's twin engines spool up to full power. Moss watches the helicopter gently rise from the helipad of *Fearless* and then fly off toward the California coast. He breathes a sigh of relief as the chopper rapidly disappears, and then he turns back toward Rafferty.

"Razz, open up the weapons compartment."

Razz looks back at his friend with concern. "Are you sure you want to do this? We're less than a day out from port, Ax. It's a big risk this close to home."

"It's a bigger risk if we don't." Moss rests his hands on his hips, grimaces at the gravity of his decision, and then refocuses on Rafferty. "Look, Razz, I'm sure about this…"

Razz nods. "Aye aye, Chief."

• • •

"LA Center, November Foxtrot Romeo Niner Seven, I have visual contact, runway three zero in sight."

"Roger Foxtrot Romeo Niner Seven, you are cleared for visual approach runway three zero. Switch to Long Beach tower, one, one, niner point four…"

"Switching to tower frequency, one, one, niner point four, Foxtrot Romeo Niner Seven."

Flip descends from five-hundred feet to below two hundred and flies over the runway threshold. The Long Beach control tower then directs the Bell 429 to divert from the runway and land at Signature JetCenter, a private fixed base operator that the foundation maintains a contract with.

After landing, Flip orders a quick fuel top-up from the ground crew and then goes to help the science team. "It's only an overnight at the hotel," Flip reassures Samantha as he grabs her duffle bag. "No worries, Dr. Randal. Once we arrive in port, you'll be able to collect the rest of your gear. We'll get everything sorted." Flip glances across the tarmac. "Here comes the car now."

"Thank you, John." Samantha shakes the Australian's hand. "You're heading straight back to the ship?"

"Yes, ma'am," Flip responds. "I don't like leaving the guys without their wings."

After only twenty minutes on the ground, Flip is back in his bird and firing up the engines for the flight back to *Fearless*. Samantha watches the helicopter's rotors spin up to full speed and the chopper take off, and then she turns back to her six lab technicians as the women pile into the SUV that will take them to their hotel.

"I'll catch up to you."

Her lead technician gives Samantha a confused look. "What do mean? Dr. Randal? Where are you going?"

"I've got something I need to take care of. I won't be long."

Samantha waves goodbye to her team, and then she walks inside the FBO and orders a cab. "Where would you like to go, madam?" the receptionist asks.

"111 Ocean Boulevard please."

Once inside the building's lobby, Samantha flashes her Foundation Research Fellow identification and is quickly waved through security. She takes the elevator up to the eighteenth floor, where she walks directly to Marcus Waverley's office.

"I'm sorry, Dr. Randal, he's in an important meeting at the moment; he can't be disturbed."

Samantha eyes the secretary sitting in front of her. "Do you mind if I wait? It's very important that I speak to him."

"Not at all, Dr. Randal. I can't tell you when he'll be back, though."

As Samantha waits, she pulls out her phone and sends a text: *Where are you?* A few minutes later, her phone vibrates softly.

Aren't you still on board?

We were evacuated. Flip just flew us in.

Is that so?

Yes, I'm in Long Beach. Where are you?

We're in Long Beach too.

I need to speak to you.

When?

As soon as possible.

Where?

111 Ocean Boulevard.

At that moment, she catches sight of Marcus Waverley as he exits the elevator and walks swiftly toward his office. "No calls, Martha," he barks just as Samantha stands up in front of him. "Oh... it's you..."

"Well, it's a pleasure to see you as well, Marcus,"

"Dr. Randal, you surprised me. We weren't expecting *Fearless* to reach port until later this evening."

Samantha's serious expression goes cold as she stares down Marcus Waverley. "I know about the drones, Marcus."

Waverley's face loses all expression and goes pale. "What? Samantha, what are you talking about?"

"We can talk about it here, Marcus, or we can speak privately in your office."

Waverley closes his office door behind him as Samantha walks over to the room's magnificent ocean view.

"What's this about, Samantha? What's going on?"

Samantha spins back to face Waverley. "It's about the drones, Marcus… the top-secret military drones Dr. Alistair Fairchild created by stealing my work."

"Well, I'm sorry to be the one to inform you, Samantha, but Dr. Fairchild recently passed away. It's a tragedy. The young man's family is devastated. We are all very upset, of course, and frankly, I have no idea what you're talking about."

Samantha holds her phone up in front of Waverley. His face freezes as he recognizes the image of the drone's schematic. "Where… umm," Waverley mumbles, "… what is that?"

Samantha allows her hand to drop back to her side as her eyes narrow. "You can stop playing games, Marcus. I know everything." She drops the phone back into her satchel without taking her eyes off the man standing in front of her. "I know every detail of the MS41-T. I know how it was engineered, I know about the La Paz facility, and I know you've lost them."

"Lost? Dr. Randal, I have no idea where you are getting your information. We haven't lost anything…"

"Marcus."

Waverley spins around at the sound of Jeff Buxton's voice. "What's she doing here?" Buxton demands. "What's going on?"

Samantha looks up at the graying, muscular African American. "I am Dr.—"

"Dr. Samantha Elisabeth Misbah Randal, yes," Buxton replies. "I know who you are. Now answer the question please, ma'am. What are you doing here?"

Samantha looks Buxton directly in the eye. "I am trying to stop a massacre, sir."

Buxton's pauses. "Walk with me."

Chapter 35

Malcolm Rafferty looks down from the bridge as Moss and two crewmen wait near the helipad. Razz can see the Bell 429 approaching from the east; Flip is less than a mile out and closing. Rafferty glances down at the chart plotter and then over at his helmsman.

"Maintain course and speed... nice and easy."

Rafferty watches as the helicopter gradually grows from a dot on the horizon until the chopper fills his frame of view and he can see Flip's face. The rails touch down on the helipad just long enough for Moss to climb inside, and then she's off again.

"I radioed the location of the yacht to the coast guard right after I called you, Chief, but there's not much else we can do."

"There was no sign of survivors?"

"None, Chief."

"Take me over the spot where you saw them. I want a look for myself."

Flip flies back toward the California coastline until he reaches the GPS waypoint he'd marked after he spotted the wreckage of a small sailing yacht. "Looks like they're still here..." Flip observes.

Moss peers down at the churning water below. "They're circling that navigational beacon."

Flip briefly studies the disturbing scene. "The signal from the beacon must be attracting them somehow."

Moss stares at the sinister dark shapes cutting through the water as Flip hovers the helicopter at two hundred feet. Moss tries to ignore his churning gut, but his anxiety only continues to grow as he watches the cloned tiger sharks rapidly circling beneath him.

"There's not that many down there," Moss adds. "I count ten… Oh wait."

"Chief! Did you just see that?"

"Damn, that was quick."

"I've never seen sharks move that fast."

Moss looks over at Flip. "That's because they're not really sharks; they're weapons. Better get us back to the ship."

• • •

"Am I hearing you correctly, Dr. Randal?" Buxton's tone is highly skeptical. "Dr. Falcon is a disgraced ex-con. I don't see how the man could be of any use in this situation."

"Hey, Jeff…"

Buxton turns to see Eric approaching. "We managed to get some movement. You better have a look."

Buxton turns to leave and then quickly glances back at Samantha. "Wait here. I'm not done talking to you."

"What direction are they heading in?" Buxton leans in closer to the drone operator's screen.

"East, sir."

"East?" Buxton flashes a rare look of shock at the technician. "Are you crazy? You're bringing them in toward shore!"

"It wasn't my choice, sir."

"What are you telling me, son? Do you have control, or don't you?" Buxton is growing increasingly irritated. He looks over at Eric Stevens, who shrugs, and then back at the technician. "Do you have control?"

"No, sir, not really."

Buxton raises himself from the terminal and folds his arms in front of him. "I don't understand. We should be able to shut these units down with the flick of a switch." He drops his hands to his hips as he stares down at the screen. "What's the hold up here? Shut them all down!"

"It's not that simple anymore, sir. There's too many active units. We're not sure, but it has something to do with the energy node at the center of the master control system."

"Can you divert them? Can you send them back out to sea at least?"

The technician spins around and stares up at Buxton with bewilderment. "I have to be honest, sir. I don't know how I got them to alter course in the first place, or if it was even my actions that initiated the change.

"Early this morning," the drone tech continues, "when we were first able to track them, they were all over the place. They were scattered in groups of ten and twenty and distributed over a hundred-square-mile area of the Pacific. We couldn't shut them down individually, so we thought if we disrupted the connection with the node and cut all power, it would shut them all down."

"I don't understand. It should have killed them off instantly. Why would it cause them to change direction?"

"The only thing I can figure is that it has something to do with the node itself. Even after we cut the power, it keeps discharging. The energy field appears to be compounding. It's generating a feedback loop. It's still sending a signal to the units, and we can't disrupt it. We currently have one hundred and forty-three fully activated drones heading straight for us, sir. I know it sounds crazy, but it's like the node is calling to them."

. . .

On the corner of San Francisco Avenue and West Cowles Street on the edge of a permanently gray industrial quarter of Long Beach, Rodrigo Sanchez steers his pickup into the parking lot of his cold storage and logistics warehouse.

The forty-six-year-old father of four plucks his keys from the ignition, reaches for his coffee, and gets out of the truck. It's ten minutes before nine, and another hour will pass before the rest of his employees begin filing in for work. Sanchez walks over to his building's loading ramp and then up the stairs to his office door.

He takes a sip of coffee as he fumbles with the stubborn lock, then he opens the door and walks inside. As Sanchez plays back the messages on his answering machine, he hears a sudden but muffled crash. He shuts off the machine and turns to listen when the sound of a second crash emanates from the deep recesses of the building.

Sanchez sets his coffee down and grabs a parka hanging on a nearby wall hook as he quickly heads into the main facility. He walks swiftly through the refrigerated warehouse, past metal shelves stacked to the ceiling with pallets of packaged goods, until he reaches a door at the far end. Sanchez opens the metal door and then flips on the overhead lights. He locates the source of the booming sound he heard immediately. A twenty-foot customized reefer container has somehow managed to crash to the floor.

It's one of ten such specialized containers his company holds in frozen storage under a lucrative contract. Sanchez shakes his head in disgust and bitterly complains as he approaches the expensive container that now lies at a sharp angle with one corner completely crushed. The other end of the container is still resting on the one it was stacked on top of. Sanchez hastily pulls his phone from his pocket when he sees that the door to the container has been ripped open. As he dials 911, the man walks around to have a better look inside and finds the container's interior completely empty.

As he waits for a 911 operator, Sanchez gazes up at the top of the container in front of him. The man is suddenly overcome with extreme panic at the ominous sight of a six-meter-long great white shark. Sanchez dives for the floor just as the artificially engineered killer drone lunges at him.

The great white hits the cement slab floor and whips back. Its crazed, massive, snapping jaws narrowly miss the man as he manages to scramble into a narrow gap between the stacked containers. Sanchez shakily brings the phone back to his ear while the great white's huge jaws bite at him viciously just inches from his face. He desperately kicks at the floor to shove himself deeper into the small gap when the operator comes on the line.

"911… Please state the nature of the emergency…"

"There is a giant shark in my warehouse! It's attacking me!"

"I'm sorry, sir, I can't understand what you're saying. Can you speak more slowly please?"

A storm of flashing, razor-like teeth rages in front of the terrified man. "Please! Please send help! I am being attacked!"

"I show your address at 404 West Cowles Street. Are you reporting a robbery, sir? Are the perpetrators in the building with you now?"

"Yes! Yes they are! Please send help!"

"We have a squad car dispatched and en route. Please stay where you are, sir, and wait for the police to arrive."

Sanchez begins to pray as he hears another one of the containers stacked above him crash to the floor... and then another. Then, the container pressed against his right side begins to shudder violently... and then the one on his left. The devout Catholic cries out for God's mercy just before he loses consciousness.

Outside the building, a police car pulls into the parking lot, and two officers emerge with guns drawn.

One of them speaks into his radio. "We've arrived at the address. It looks quiet out here. We'll go check it out inside."

As one of the officers reaches for the door it suddenly crashes down on top of him. His partner instinctively opens fire on the huge shark now coming straight at him. The officer manages to get off four rounds before the great white seizes the man inside its massive jaws and tears him in half.

With one police officer lying out cold under the door and another's dismembered remains littering the parking lot, Dr. Alistair Fairchild's forty MS1-GW prototypes, the pride of his work, flow rapidly out from the warehouse that had housed their frozen bodies for nearly a year.

A short distance from the warehouse, the perfectly engineered killer drones instantly overwhelm and rip apart two guys loading a truck and then kill a woman riding a bicycle before they race across an empty lot and disappear into the Los Angeles River.

Chapter 36

Flip powers down the Bell 429 while Alex Moss steps from the aircraft and heads straight for the bridge of *Fearless*. Moss can feel his body shaking. He briefly holds his trembling right hand up in front of his face and studies it as he walks, then he closes it into a firm fist and tries to allow his anger to burn away his anxiety.

On the bridge, Moss finds his crew armed and dressed in full tactical gear. It's a sight he hasn't seen in five years and something he hoped he would never see again.

"I've got your gear here, Ax." Rafferty points to a duffle under the chart table.

The knot in his gut tightens when Moss spots the long handles of his kukri blades sticking out from one end of the bag.

"Thanks, Razz. Let's hope this turns out to be just a drill."

"I agree…"

Moss can see the worry on his friend's face. "Razz, what is it?"

"We've been monitoring a number of distress calls, Ax. It's getting ugly out there."

"What's our position?"

"We're nine miles from port."

Moss studies Rafferty's face again. "There's something else?"

Razz looks across at Murray and then back at Moss. "They attacked the Catalina ferry, Ax."

Moss is stunned. "What about the navy? Who's out there?"

"Nobody's putting two and two together," Razz answers. "So far, the Coast Guard is treating these attacks as isolated incidents, and I can see why. They're several hours apart and all over the map. Ax, if the navy knows what's really happening, they're staying quiet about it."

• • •

Thomas Falcon steps from a cab and looks up at the gleaming glass entrance to 111 Ocean Boulevard. He glances back as Bayani exits the car and then stands beside him.

"This is our path, Dr. Falcon."

Falcon raises an eyebrow at the thought. "Well then, let's see where it goes."

The two men head up the marble steps and into the building, but as soon as they pass through the building's revolving front doors, Falcon is suddenly overcome by a wave of intense nausea.

"I can't walk any further... Bayani... I feel..."

Falcon quickly spins around and bolts outside. Bayani follows as Falcon dashes into the lush landscaping to vomit. With his breakfast now decorating the mulch under a thicket of heliconias, Falcon wipes his face with the back of his hand as he looks back up at Bayani.

"This isn't going to work, Bayani. I can't even walk inside."

"You were unprepared, Dr. Falcon. It's okay, let me help you."

"I'm afraid I can't manage. It's too much for me. I'm not ready."

"It's the energy field, Dr. Falcon. It has grown even more powerful since we were first here inside this place. I feel it, too, but for me, it is not as strong."

Bayani places his hand on Falcon's shoulder as he looks into the frightened man's eyes.

"Dr. Falcon, your connection is extremely powerful because it is meant to be yours. You have the ability to control it, but in order to control it, you cannot fight it. You must allow it to enter your body freely. You must welcome it, Dr. Falcon."

Falcon straightens as his painful expression shifts to pointed resolve. "I am nobody, Bayani. I'm a small man who made a huge mistake and nothing more."

"You are a man with a powerful legacy, Dr. Falcon. It is time for you to take control and accept your fate."

• • •

Shafts of bright California sun sift down from above as an eager crowd gathers at the large underground viewing window of Shark Lagoon, a popular premier exhibit at the Aquarium of the Pacific. The centerpiece oceanfront attraction is only a short distance away from the mouth of the Los Angeles River. The crowded marine park is located within the city of Long Beach near the bustling Rainbow Harbor Restaurant and Shopping Development.

Noisy onlookers marvel at the sand tiger sharks, white tips, and zebra sharks slowly circling the enormous tank.

"Hey, Dad, look!" a small boy shouts excitedly. The five-year-old has just spotted a new shark suddenly enter the tank, "it's a great white! Dad! A great white! It's a great white!"

Before the boy's father can respond, the people around him begin frantically shouting in a jumbled cacophony of exclamations ranging from elation to denial and outright fear. The massive, six-meter-long great white shark swiftly circles the tank's outer perimeter and passes right in front of them. The shark's ominous profile fills the large viewing window as it glides by. The sight is a complete impossibility, yet the onlookers inside the room can all clearly see it.

Eager tourists push and shove their way closer to the window as they hold up their phones to capture the event while the deadly drone churns through the tank, sending its panicked inhabitants darting away in all directions.

Almost as quickly as the massive shark appears, it's gone. Loud, agitated conversation fills the void left by the shark's sudden departure. The underground viewing room fills with a rising din until the crowd's excited shouting match is instantly quashed by sudden shrieking screams coming from above.

Several people in the viewing room run outside to see what is happening while others still argue and shout even louder in order for their demands to be heard. The shark tank's onlookers continue to argue over what to do but are suddenly hushed once more by horrific sounds of violent death as hundreds of people outside erupt into simultaneous panic.

The riot now taking place above their heads ignites more people inside the underground viewing area to panic themselves and to run. A large splash on the surface of the tank grabs the attention of the few who remain. Traumatized witnesses gasp and cry out when they recognize a partial human body fall into the water. Still more scream in horror and more run from the room as blood quickly stains the tank and the ravaged upper torso of a young man drifts softly to the bottom of the exhibit.

Faced with the terrible choice of either running outside with the rest or staying behind, the small boy's father has pulled his young son into a corner of the room, where he holds him tightly and tries to prevent him from seeing what is really happening. The now empty concrete room echoes with the horrific thunder of mass death exploding outside as a pack of forty out-of-control MS1-GW drones destroy their targets with extreme prejudice.

The militarized assault drones, drawn by the electromagnetic intensity of the concentrated crowd, launch into a full coordinated attack. They swiftly fan out and rip through the desperately fleeing throngs of tourists as the drones ruthlessly chase down and kill dozens, then hundreds until they sweep through the length of the complex, regroup, then turn and head straight into the city.

• • •

Alex Moss listens with dread as the maritime emergency channel lights up with overlapping calls for assistance as numerous small craft and commercial vessels experience sudden attacks. Moss looks out of the front windows of the bridge at the distant California coast.

"We're getting out of here." He looks back at Rafferty. "Razz, turn the ship around. We don't need to be here."

"I'm with you, Chief," Razz switches off the autopilot, grabs the helm wheel, and turns the ship, when Murray suddenly interrupts.

"Hey, guys, let's think about this. There's a lot of innocent people getting hurt out there. We should be able to do something." He eyes Moss. "Chief, we've got weapons. We can at least try to help."

Moss exhales heavily. "We're equipped for self-defense, not an assault." He studies Murray's pleading expression sympathetically. "My first priority is the safety of this ship and everyone on board. I'm sorry, I won't risk taking *Fearless* back into a dangerous situation."

Murray's eyes narrow with resolve as he folds his arms in front of him. "Right… so what about the chopper then? We can at least fly over and take these bastards out from the air. We've got the firepower for that at least."

Murray looks across the room at Flip, who has been leaning against the chart table and listening intently.

"What do say, Flip? Can we do it?"

Flip eyes Moss and then looks back at Murray. "As long as these things don't shoot back at us, we'll be fine." Then, his focus returns to Moss. "I can do it."

Ten minutes later, Murray is inside the weapons compartment of *Fearless*, sorting through crates of forty-millimeter grenades. "Here they are…" He holds a fully loaded circular six-shot cartridge up in front of Razz. "40x46mm medium-velocity reloads."

"That's some serious fishing gear," Razz quips. He turns and pulls a South African-made Milkor Super-Six multi-round grenade launcher down from a wall rack containing a wide assortment of small arms and exotic weaponry. "It's been a while since I used one of these," Razz comments as he examines the bulky revolver. "But I'm game." He grins at Murray. "Let's go."

Moss stands near the helipad as the Bell 429 lifts off, spins around, and then flies off toward the coast. He watches for a few moments and then lifts his handheld radio. "Stay safe out there…"

"Roger that, Ax…" Flip responds as the helicopter quickly disappears into the haze.

With the side doors open and armed men sitting behind him, the wind buffeting through the helicopter's cockpit sends Flip back to his days flying the UH-60 Black Hawk in Afghanistan. Razz and Murray are positioned on opposite sides of the passenger compartment. Each man holds a loaded MRGL at the ready as he scans the ocean for signs of the deadly drones.

"I have something up ahead," Flip announces through his headset. "It looks like a commercial fishing boat."

The Bell flies closer, and the gruesome scene playing out on the deck of the boat comes into painfully sharp focus.

"Jesus…" Flip mutters. "I'm making a pass. Hey, Razz."

"Yeah, Flip."

"You're up, mate."

Flip descends until he has the GlobalRanger flying one hundred and fifty feet above the waves.

The straps of Rafferty's safety harness jerk tight as the chopper angles sharply over to his side and the ocean opens up beneath him like a giant blue chasm.

Razz adjusts the mic on his headset as he eyes several distinctive dark shapes just below the surface. "I have multiple targets in sight…"

He takes aim and fires off all six rounds in rapid succession. The grenades hit the water and detonate two hundred feet off the stern of the stricken boat. The explosions send a mountain of sea-water billowing up into the air as the pieces of four MS41-T drones scatter in all directions.

"Fuck yeah!" Razz shouts as he watches heaving chunks of tiger shark explode upwards then drop back into the sea. Flip levels the Bell 429 for another pass while Razz reaches back to fist-pump Murray.

"It's your turn, buddy. Show 'em some SAS love."

Chapter 37

"I show four drones deactivated, sir…"

Jeff Buxton abruptly cuts his phone call short and spins back toward the drone operator's station. "Did you do it?"

"I can't confirm." The technician's fingers fly over the keyboard in front of him. "Wait…"

He looks up at Buxton. "Five more drones have just been deactivated, sir."

"Please, you've got to listen to me!"

Buxton pivots toward the sound of a woman's voice to find his CIA colleagues confronting Dr. Samantha Randal. "How did she get in here?" Buxton glares across the room at Samantha. "Get her out of here."

At that moment, Buxton's phone rings again. He grabs the phone from his pocket. "Yeah? Make it quick."

"Yes, sir. There's two gentlemen here in the lobby. They asked for you by name, sir."

Buxton shoots a concerned glance over at Eric. "Go check out the lobby. Somebody's down there asking for me by name."

"I'm on it, Jeff."

Buxton raises the phone back to his ear. "Tell them to wait right there. I'm sending a colleague down to meet them."

• • •

"You are agent Eric Stevens," Falcon announces as he looks the bearded man in the eye.

"And you're Dr. Thomas Falcon," Eric answers in an irritated tone. "Follow me. We need to speak more privately."

As Falcon and Bayani follow agent Stevens into the elevator, Falcon feels his nausea spike again, but this time he relaxes and allows the energy to surge through him.

Bayani makes eye contact when he notices Falcon's discomfort. Then, a thin smile subtly crosses Bayani's face as he watches Falcon painfully adjust and then accept what is happening to him.

The energy coursing through Falcon's body frightens the scientist. It's illogical; it shouldn't exist, and yet he can't deny what is happening to him. For Falcon, it feels like a fiery bomb inside his gut that will go off at any moment.

As he stands inside the same elevator car he rode in with the acidly demure Mrs. Oum, Falcon realizes that he has, in fact, had this feeling many times before, but it wasn't even close to being this powerful.

"Who's the kid?" Buxton demands as he shuts the conference room door behind him.

"I am Bayani."

"Yeah… right…" Buxton eyes Falcon. "I see prison has done a lot for your social life, Dr. Falcon." Buxton steps up close to Falcon—close enough that Falcon can smell his breath.

"Marco is a snake, Dr. Falcon. The man is one of the darkest, deadliest bosses of the underworld. He is extremely dangerous, and should not to be trusted under any circumstances. Whatever he's told you—whatever information he's given you—is designed to serve his purposes, not yours."

Falcon doesn't blink as he stares back at Buxton. "I'm not here to talk about Marco or anyone else, Agent Buxton. I'm here to shut down your drones."

• • •

Moss glances briefly at his trembling right hand and then stares down once more at the helipad from the bridge of *Fearless*.

"As far as we can tell, it's the only one," Seth comments as he carefully evaluates the five-meter-long tiger shark that has now parked itself in the middle of the helipad.

"Nobody goes outside." Moss stares at Seth. "I don't want anyone going out there."

"Chief… uh…" Seth contemplates Moss's emotional state and treads carefully. "Flip needs to refuel. He's on his way back, and the chopper has to land. We have to clear the helipad." Seth watches as Moss's jaw tightens at the thought. "Chief," Seth speaks reassuringly, "we can handle it…"

"OK, but I'm coming with you."

"Are you sure that's a good idea, Chief?"

Moss tightens his right hand back into a fist. "I have to, Seth. I need to do this."

Painful flashes from their shared past rip through their minds as Seth, Rich, Dan, and four more fully armed crewmen walk swiftly down the ship's main passageway alongside Moss. The eight Special Operations veterans hold their weapons at the ready as they advance toward the helipad.

Along with his team, Moss carries an Italian-made Beretta ARX160, a fully automatic assault rifle mounted with a 40mm grenade launcher. Constructed mostly of lightweight, techno-composite materials, it's the latest addition to their arsenal and a fierce weapon Moss has come to respect.

The men pause briefly at the doors that lead to the forward deck. Moss slings his rifle to one side, draws a fully charged Taser, and then nods to his team. They push through the doors and sprint toward their target.

The MS41-T detects a threat moving toward it and launches, jaws snapping wildly, straight for them. Moss aims his Taser and fires. The electrodes strike the drone and harmlessly bounce off its artificially engineered body. "Fuck me…" Moss growls as he tosses the Taser aside, grabs his Beretta, and opens fire.

• • •

From the air, Flip watches the firefight taking place on the helipad and senses his own PTSD trying to take over. He angrily shoves his mental monsters aside and alerts Razz and Murray through his headset.

"We gotta keep clear of live fire," Razz calls back to Flip. "We could get hit."

"I have targets in sight," Murray declares calmly as he loads another cartridge into his MRGL. "Aft starboard quarter and closing."

"Keep 'em in sight. It's your call; you take the shot," answers Razz.

"I got 'em. I can take the shot."

Flip continues his direct course over *Fearless* at midship, arcs wide, and then turns aft down the starboard side as Murray prepares to fire at nine rapidly approaching drones.

Murray can clearly make out the drones' oversized dorsal fins cutting through the waves as he evaluates his targets. Murray feels his harness tighten as Flip angles his bird toward the sharks.

Murray aims and fires.

The six grenades hit the water less than one hundred meters from *Fearless*. The violent percussion sends a shockwave through the ship.

The eight men on deck hear the six, rapid explosions go off behind them. They feel the reverberation that follows as it surges through their ship, but it doesn't interrupt their own battle as they relentlessly pump bullets into the five-meter-long, viciously snapping tiger shark in front of them.

Moss, Seth, and Rich aim directly at the shark's mouth and eyes while Dan and the remaining four crewmen fire into its gills and side. Chunks of the drone's outer flesh fly away as the bullets penetrate deeper into its genetically engineered body until a single bullet finally obliterates the drone's control unit.

Moss squeezes off the last two rounds in his clip and tries to keep firing when Seth reaches for him. "It's okay," Seth says calmly. "We got 'em, Chief."

Moss is breathing heavily as he looks down at the deactivated drone. "Call up the civilian crew. We'll need help moving this thing off the helipad."

"GlobalRanger to *Fearless*."

Moss pulls the handheld radio from his belt. "Yeah, Flip."

"Murray counted nine more sharks heading your way. He thinks he took out four of them, but they're too close for us to make another pass. You better get ready for more of those bastards."

"Thanks, Flip. How's your fuel?"

"We're okay. You guys be careful down there."

. . .

"What makes you think you can shut down the drones, Dr. Falcon?"

Falcon stares confidently at Buxton. "Because I have the power to do so."

Buxton shakes his head in bewilderment. "I told Dr. Randal that talking to you would be a waste of my time— "

"Is she still here?" Falcon asks.

"Hey, Jeff."

Buxton turns back toward the door and sees Eric. "What's up?"

"You're needed in operations."

"I'm on my way," Buxton shifts back briefly in Falcon's direction. "I'll have you and your friend here escorted out."

Falcon watches Buxton leave the conference room, and then he looks at Bayani. "Well, I guess it's time to go then."

Bayani cocks his head. "So, we are not waiting for Agent Buxton's men to return?"

Falcon walks across the conference room and opens the door for Bayani. "No, we are not."

Buxton enters the drone operations center to whistles and cheers. "What's going on?"

His lead technician looks up from his screen. "We just had three more drones go off-line, sir."

The illogical news triggers Buxton's instincts. "Where were they? What is the exact location?" He walks over to the technician's station and looks down at the screen. "Show me."

Buxton watches closely as the technician expands the grid in front of him, then the drone tech looks up at Buxton. "The three drones were exactly nine point four nautical miles southwest of Long Beach, sir."

Buxton scratches his chin, then he places his hands on his hips. "Bring up the current AIS signal for *Fearless*. Let's see where she is."

The technician switches to another computer and quickly brings up the research vessel's location. "Whoa…" the technician looks up at Buxton.

"Let me guess…" Buxton adds before the technician can open his mouth, "she's nine point four miles southwest of Long Beach." Buxton sighs and steps over to look at the AIS signal. "Congratulations, gentlemen, your drones are attacking your own research vessel."

Buxton walks over to another station. "Can we remotely activate the cameras?"

The technician quickly scrambles to access the drone's onboard cameras. "Yes, sir, cameras are now active."

Buxton folds his arms in front of him. "OK, locate the active drones in the five-square-mile area around *Fearless*."

"I show six active drones in that area, sir… No wait, make that five."

"Well done, Alex, well done…" Buxton whispers as he leans in toward the screen. "Switch the cameras to daylight mode, bring up the feeds on the five remaining drones, and relay the feed over to the main screen."

Buxton turns toward the large flat screen on the wall behind him as a grid of five separate live streaming video feeds appears. "Shit..." Buxton mutters as the battle raging on board *Fearless* flashes before his eyes in full color. He walks closer to the screen as the foundation's technicians and Buxton's CIA colleagues gather around him.

"That's hardcore bad ass..." Eric comments.

"Those are our own navy SEAL veterans being attacked out there," Buxton responds angrily. He turns away from the screen as he pulls out his phone and hits a number on his speed dial. "Yes... it's Jeff Buxton... certainly... Admiral Spencer... yes, sir... I realize that, sir, but we have a situation... I would like to make an exception... why? Because we have a scientific research vessel currently under attack that is commanded and crewed by navy SEAL veterans, sir... If I can't rely on your assistance, then who should I contact, sir?... Yes, sir... I understand, sir." Buxton ends the call and shoves the phone back in his pocket as he turns back toward the screen.

"They just knocked out another one, sir!" a technician excitedly reports.

"Keep it up, Alex," Buxton says quietly. "Four more to go. You can do it... just four more..."

Chapter 38

Alex Moss loads a forty-millimeter low-velocity grenade into the launcher mounted under the barrel of his Beretta ARX160. The air around him sizzles with shattering bursts of automatic weapons fire and the acrid odor of smoldering spent munitions casings. He tracks the oversized dorsal fin slicing through the water beneath him, Moss lifts the Beretta, he calculates trajectory, distance, impact, and accuracy all in a single compressed moment. Then, Moss aims and fires the grenade from the railing of *Fearless*.

The 40mm grenade rifles forty meters from the ship and straight into his target. Moss ducks as a shower of seawater gushes over him. He quickly rises above the railing, his ears ringing from the blast, and finds he is surrounded by small shredded fragments of lab-grown shark flesh that now litter the deck of his ship.

Moss spins back to evaluate Seth and his six crewmen still battling two MS41-T drones on the forward deck. He looks up to see Flip circling overhead. The helicopter needs fuel, and Moss knows they don't have much time left. He searches the sea around the ship's port side. It's empty—all clear.

Moss sprints through the aft passageway to the starboard side of *Fearless*. He scans the sea again and finds no sign of the drones.

Cheers suddenly erupt from the forward deck. Moss looks back to see that Seth and the guys have finally nailed the last of the two tiger sharks. Moss grabs his radio.

"GlobalRanger cleared for landing,"

"GlobalRanger to *Fearless*. That's good news. We're running on fumes up here.

• • •

"There are only two men with Dr. Randal," Bayani whispers.

Falcon braces. "You can't be serious." He reaches for Bayani's arm, but Falcon is nowhere near quick enough; Bayani is already gone.

"I don't understand," Samantha argues. "I am a senior foundation research fellow. If you won't allow me to assist, then why won't you allow me to leave?" She is frustrated and angry. She knows the two CIA agents standing on either side of her are lying to her. Samantha is staring straight at one of them when she suddenly senses a strange movement—*almost a blur.*

The armed CIA officer standing in front of Dr. Randal lets out a painful groan as the man drops to the floor. In that moment, Samantha feels the man behind her harshly grab her arm and yank her out of the way. The CIA officer draws a Beretta M9 from the shoulder holster under his blazer just as Bayani knocks it to the carpeted floor.

The young Filipino swiftly angles out of range and avoids a striking blow. The Special Activities Division veteran pulls a fist knife and aggressively slashes at Bayani. Bayani leaps to one side and then moves back in with two Balisong blades drawn. The twin blades make their distinctive scissoring clatter in front of his opponent's face.

T. R. Schumer

The man freezes momentarily at the sight of the fan blades Bayani lightly balances in each hand, and then he lunges again. The teenager drops down with a sweeping motion that knocks the man off his feet. Bayani then deftly flips his blades closed and proceeds to ferociously hammer the CIA agent's face and head with his fists.

"Bayani, no!" Samantha calls to him. "Don't kill him, please!"

Bayani stops beating the unconscious man and looks up at Samantha with eyes that resemble those of an innocent child. "Do not worry, madam. It is not my intention to kill him." He jumps to his feet and returns his blades to their holsters. "We must go, please. Dr. Falcon is waiting."

Buxton, Eric, and the room's technicians are still gathered around the large flat screen and still watching the final active streams coming from the drones that are attacking *Fearless*.

Falcon glances back at Bayani and Samantha and then silently signals for them to follow him. Falcon reaches for Samantha's hand, he then gently guides her forward and in front of him. They pass through an open area and move swiftly toward a corridor on the other side of the room.

Buxton has his back turned toward Bayani, Samantha, and Falcon as they quietly cross behind the men watching the large screen. Falcon glances at the flat screen as he passes. He can see what appears to be two live video feeds streaming onto it. One feed is chaotic, consumed with jerky flashes of what looks to be a fierce battle.

They reach the other side of the room, and Falcon ushers Samantha down a corridor as Bayani follows. Cheers erupt. Falcon ducks back for a second look. The men are all still watching the screen. There looks to be only one feed that remains active, but all it appears to show is water.

Bayani is the first to reach the short flight of stairs that lead to the roof. He opens the door as Samantha passes through it. Falcon steps out onto the roof of 111 Ocean Boulevard and is immediately hit by the chaotic uproar of a city under attack. The energy field coursing through Falcon's body is rapidly growing more painful. Falcon reaches into his pocket and pulls out the small talisman. It feels hot in his hand, and then burns as he raises it above his head.

Falcon focuses his mind on the drones in order to gain control. He closes his eyes, and in that moment, he can see them. He can see each one of them, and also, Falcon now sees what they see. The view terrifies him. The energy field surges, and the talisman suddenly feels as if he is gripping a burning ember. Falcon feels a rushing dizziness overwhelm him. He loses sight of the drones, and with it, control over the raging force driving them.

Bayani is shocked to see Falcon stumble. He thought he was there. *He had control.* Bayani moves in to catch Falcon. To keep him from falling, Bayani pushes against Falcon's shoulders and is instantly sent tumbling backward to the ground by the incredibly powerful force that consumes Falcon's body.

Bayani climbs painfully to his feet and looks Falcon in the eye.

Falcon looks up at Bayani. "I can't do it…" he pleads. Falcon is on his knees, "I'm not strong enough…"

In that moment, Bayani senses a strange, yet familiar sensation. He turns away from Falcon to see his grandfather standing quietly next to him. Bayani glances over at Samantha. She is staring in astonishment at the gnarled old man in brightly colored native dress. Bayani looks back at his grandfather, who smiles at him and nods with encouragement as he points toward Falcon.

Falcon climbs back to his feet and then faces the old shaman. "What do I do?"

"Trust your guide," the shaman replies.

"But you are my guide…"

"No, Thomas." The shaman points toward Bayani. "You have been with your guide all along."

The sounds of sporadic gunfire, human cries, and sirens from an army of emergency vehicles rise to the rooftop as Bayani approaches Falcon. Falcon looks Bayani briefly in the eye and then turns to face the sea.

Bayani lifts his hands. He hesitates a moment, and then he places them on Falcon's shoulders. The sudden surge of energy Bayani feels is painful. Bayani's immediate reflex is to pull away, but he knows he cannot. The intense, searing sensation seems to burn through his hands and then scorch his entire body.

• • •

Alex Moss squints against the midday sky above him, a view distorted by the blurred silhouettes of chopper blades that whip through the bright sunlight. He stands near the helipad as Flip lands the Bell 429. The helicopter's rails lightly touch and then settle onto the surface. Moss smiles broadly as Razz unbuckles his harness and hops out. Murray jumps down from the other side of the chopper and strides over to Moss. Murray is still carrying the MRGL.

"These things are a ripper, Chief." He proudly holds up the multi-round grenade launcher. "Everybody should have one."

"Nice job, guys." Moss looks over at Flip as he climbs out from the cockpit.

"We were dry as a drover's dog up there." Flip looks over at the destroyed remains of three MS41-T tiger shark drones lying on the opposite side of the forward deck. "That's some piece of work. If I didn't hate these things so much, I'd be impressed."

Moss looks back over at Razz as his friend walks across the helipad toward him. "I could sure use a beer. How about you guys?"

In that instant, a motion alters Moss's perception as he catches something moving fast from the corner of his eye, and in that fraction of a second, the tenth MS41-T drone flying across the bow grabs Alex Moss's full attention. Moss looks in Rafferty's direction just as a searing, white hot pain suddenly jolts though his body.

Silence. Moss staggers back from the helipad in complete confusion, the sudden shift scrambling his awareness. He quickly searches his surroundings for answers as he looks rapidly from one side of the helipad to the other. He is alone, and it is night. The Bell 429 sits calm and cold; she's fully wrapped and securely tied down. Moss regains enough coherence to recognize the harbor and the city lights of Cabo San Lucas. He searches the dock beside *Fearless* and sees Bayani staring up at him.

"I don't understand…"

"You don't have to," Bayani responds. "To be honest, Mr. Moss, none of us understand. We can only follow our path and see where it takes us."

"What… What can I do? How can I stop it?" Moss asks hesitantly.

"Trust, Mr. Moss. I am your guide. Trust yourself."

The perfectly engineered eight-hundred-pound tiger shark that has killed his best friend hundreds of times over the past four years flies at Rafferty head-on, and in that moment, Moss suddenly feels his hands grab Razz. *He has him.* Moss shoves Malcolm Rafferty to the deck as the tenth MS41-T drone, the final active unit in the five-square-mile area around *Fearless,* slams into the side of the Bell 429 GlobalRanger. The impact sends the helicopter hurtling from the helipad as Moss pulls Razz to his feet and the two men run.

Murray locks on to the tiger shark fighting to free itself from the helicopter's twisted wreckage. He aims his MRGL. "Grenade!"

Moss, Razz, Flip, Seth, Rich, Dan… the men can only dive for the deck as the Australian SAS veteran fires his last forty-millimeter grenade straight into the chopper. The explosion rips though the drone and the Bell 429. The blast instantly engulfs the aircraft in a ball of flame as a tower of jet-black smoke rises into the air.

Chapter 39

Bayani can see what Dr. Thomas Falcon sees, and it is trying to kill him. The teenager fights to hold on as thousands of horrific images flash in front of his closed eyes: not only the slaughter inflicted by the army of designer killers ravaging the Long Beach waterfront but also the rotting zombie shark horde that preceded them.

Dr. Samantha Randal finds herself surrounded by unbearable chaos: the echoes of human suffering mix with panicked rioting, weapons fire, and police helicopters. From across the city, the wails of emergency sirens rise around her like an audible stench she can't escape. The two men in front of her are clearly in danger. She feels forced to try to help somehow. Instinctively, Samantha looks to the old shaman. Bayani's grandfather gazes back at her and slowly shakes his head... *no...*

Like a rabid wild animal, the energy field Falcon sees in front of him lashes back at him and *then grows stronger...* In that moment, Falcon finally realizes what he must do. He reaches out toward the terrible force again, knowing that this will be his last chance to gain control, and even if he miraculously succeeds, he will still die. Falcon can see a form taking shape in front of him. The agonizing pain is killing him. He is being burned alive, but he reaches for it anyway and touches it. In that moment, Falcon suddenly realizes what he has known all along as he comes in contact with his own face.

Falcon looks into the eyes of his former self and lets him die. Thomas Falcon then reaches out with his right arm and is exhilarated when the raging energy field yields to his will. His pain subsides with each progressive movement as Falcon reaches deeper inside the energy field and draws its outer edges in toward him until the field finally disappears back inside the talisman. Falcon grips the talisman in his left hand, raises it over his head, focuses on the drones, and shuts them all down.

"Dr. Falcon…"

Falcon spins back to see Bayani standing behind him. "It was you…" Falcon utters in astonishment. "Bayani, my God, the entire time… since the moment I walked out of Bilibid in Manila… it was you."

Bayani flashes a knowing smile before his expression shifts to concern. "Dr. Falcon, are you alright?"

"I'm fine, Bayani… never better." Falcon glances around the rooftop. "Your grandfather…"

"Yes, he was here, but he has now returned home."

• • •

"They're all gone!"

Jeff Buxton steps quickly back from the large flat-screen display as his lead technician stands up from his station to face him. "What are you telling me?"

"All of the remaining drones have deactivated, sir… all of them."

Buxton dashes back to examine the technician's control screen. "All of them? Are you certain about this?"

"Yes, sir, absolutely sure. Have a look for yourself."

. . .

Pete jumps back to his feet and then looks down at the carnage on the forward deck from the bridge of *Fearless*. "What the hell?"

The engineer's assistant, Sam, stands up next to him. "I'll activate the DIFFS."

"Yeah, good thinking." Pete is stunned by the scene. He grabs for the comm. "Chief! Chief! Are you guys okay down there?"

"Pete, I think so. Let me get back to you."

The forward deck of *Fearless* suddenly erupts in a shower of fire-suppressing seawater as her crew slowly climb back to their feet. Moss looks first toward the DIFFS. He can see already that the Deck Integrated Fire Fighting System is doing its job, so his attention quickly shifts to his injured crewman.

Seth bends down to examine the wound on Murray's left shoulder. "Don't move. You've got a chunk of aircraft aluminum sticking out of you."

Moss approaches Seth. "How bad is he?"

"It's not as bad as it looks, Chief." Seth turns back to examine the wound again. "I'll have him patched up in no time."

"He's damned lucky it didn't slice open his head." Dan stares down at the bleeding Australian lying flat on his back. "What were you thinking? You could've blown us all up!"

Murray looks up at his soaking wet crew mates gathered around him. "Come on, guys. What was I supposed to do? The chopper was already done for, and I had a clean shot, so I took it."

Moss turns back toward Rafferty, but the crew's attention is quickly drawn toward the destroyed helicopter. "Ax, geez, what a mess..." Rafferty laments. They look on in shock as the fire-suppression system winds down and the full extent of the damage stares starkly back at them.

"She was a good bird, Ax..."

Moss shifts focus to his grieving pilot. "She was, Flip... She sure was."

"And what about you?" Flip studies Moss inquisitively. "That was some stunt you just pulled off. What happened?"

"I don't know what you mean?"

"I saw the whole thing, Ax. One second I was next to you, and the next you're clear across the deck. How'd you do that? I've never seen you move that quick. I've never seen anyone move like that."

Moss shakes his head. "I don't know..."

"And I don't care." Razz grabs Moss and hugs him. "Thanks, buddy." He steps back. "So this makes us two for two then, right?"

Moss smirks. "Two for two? Aren't you forgetting that time in Kabul?"

"Kabul? What about Kenya?"

Moss rolls his eyes. "Don't bring up Kenya, please. Anything but Kenya."

. . .

Thomas Falcon turns his attention toward Dr. Samantha Randal. "Are you okay?"

"No, sir… not really." She stares back at him. "What just happened? What have I just seen, Thomas?"

"Something ridiculously improbable and most likely completely impossible that has, nonetheless, just occurred." Falcon smiles. "Welcome to my life…"

"What the hell are you people doing up here?"

Falcon, Bayani, and Samantha simultaneously spin back toward the roof access door as Jeff Buxton strides angrily toward them. "Two of my men have been assaulted…" Buxton walks up to Bayani, draws his hands to his hips, and stares down at the slim teenager. "You just took down two armed senior CIA officers, kid. Do you have any idea the kind of trouble you're in right now?" Buxton pauses. He takes a moment to size up Bayani with a fresh perspective. "You want a job?"

Chapter 40

Dr. Samantha Randal and her team are back onboard *Fearless* and busily packing up the last of their gear when Moss enters the lab. Samantha looks up from her samples.

"I wasn't sure I would see you again."

"I apologize, Dr. Randal," Moss replies. "I wanted to get here sooner. I've been tied up on shore with meetings and paperwork. I just heard you were back. I didn't want to miss saying goodbye, but also, I wanted to personally thank you."

"I'm not sure what you mean, sir."

Moss smiles. "Do you need any help with your gear? I'll send the guys down to move these crates."

"That would be very helpful, Mr. Moss. Thank you."

Moss looks at her. "Thank you, Dr. Samantha Randal."

• • •

Six weeks later, Thomas Falcon waits nervously at a coffee shop in Knotting Hill, and then he sees her. "Samantha…" Falcon stands as she approaches.

"Thomas, how are you?" She flashes a warm smile.

Falcon kisses Samantha on the cheek. "It's so nice to see you again…"

"How long will you be in town?"

"Not long…"

Samantha sits down across from Falcon. "I'm really glad you're here. I have something for you."

"Really?"

"Yes, but you'll need to drop by the lab. Can you do it?"

"Absolutely."

Two days later, Falcon finds himself siting on an examining table in Dr. Samantha Randal's university research lab. Samantha walks in carrying a tray stacked with loaded syringes. "Don't worry. It looks worse than it actually is."

Falcon chuckles. "After what I've been through? Do you honestly believe a few needles will scare me?"

She puts the tray down. "No…" Samantha walks over, lifts Falcon's right arm, and then examines it carefully. "I must inform you… this may be a complete failure…" She lays his arm back down and searches Falcon's face as he smiles back at her. "You're ready." Samantha winks at Falcon. "Let's give it a go, shall we?" She sweeps away from Falcon and then whisks back holding the first of seventeen genetically customized rapid-regeneration injections. "Let's begin."

· · ·

Bayani stands at the edge of a jungle clearing and gazes with joy at the cascading rice terraces lining the broad valley beneath him.

"So, nephew, do you think you will want to return to the United States someday?"

Bayani turns to look at his uncle Joshua. "I don't know, Uncle, but it is good to be home."

• • •

Alex Moss sips a beer alone at the far end of an empty bar in Marina del Ray while cable news prattles on in the background.

Fallout over the CIA's top-secret assassination drone program, known as the MS41-T, continues. The latest black eye to America's top spy agency stems from yet another huge trove of data leaked online.

The shocking revelations first appeared one month ago today in the wake of the unprecedented and tragic events that took place in Long Beach, California. The files exposed a series of clandestine missions carried out under the code name Multi-Striker. The latest release, leaked by the same anonymous source, includes detailed transcripts of communications, audio recordings, and even video.

The files confirm a direct link between the CIA and an assassination mission that took place in Colombia, in which nine children were brutally killed. That mission targeted infamous drug lord and former CIA asset, Juan Carlos Azarola. CIA watchers and analysts claim the recent rash of assassination missions carried out around the world has been a case of CIA house cleaning—an attempt to cover-up past extrajudicial black operations in light of renewed criticism of the agency's activities…"

Moss sighs. He gets the bartender's attention. "Hey, you mind changing the channel?"

"No. Keep it going." Jeff Buxton sits down next to Alex Moss. "The best part's just coming up."

In a related story, the shadowy nonprofit research arm of multibillion-dollar defense contractor Holton-Bennett Industries has come under fire today with the indictment of the foundation's entire board of directors, including its chairman, multi-millionaire Marcus Waverley. Waverley is seen here being escorted by federal agents following a raid of the foundation's headquarters in

Long Beach. Among the forty-seven charges in the indictment is the first-degree murder of the foundation's lead scientist, Dr. Alistair Fairchild. The indictment claims Fairchild's body was secretly flown from La Paz, Mexico to Van Nuys airport in Los Angeles onboard the foundation's private jet and later shipped back to Fairchild's family in New Zealand.

"That guy's not gonna do well in prison," Buxton comments.

"I don't care. I'm not involved…"

Buxton signals the bartender for a beer and then shifts back to Moss. "No, you're not… you tendered your resignation."

"It was time…"

Buxton thanks the bartender, takes a sip of his beer, and then he turns and looks Moss in the eye. "You're in trouble, Alex…"

"Is that why you asked to meet with me?" Moss stares at Buxton. "To tell me something I already know?"

Buxton grimaces. "It's worse than you think."

"How bad?"

"You need to disappear for a while."

Moss frowns. "I don't understand. I don't know anything."

"Someone thinks you know quite a bit. They're preparing to subpoena you."

"What about my crew?"

"They want you, Alex," Buxton warns flatly. "This isn't just about the foundation. There are other players out there who are extremely concerned over what you may know, so much so that they are prepared to do whatever it takes to prevent you from being put in front of a judge."

"Thanks for letting me know." Moss looks Buxton in the eye. "I heard about what you did… how you made a call on our behalf when we were in trouble out there. Thank you for that. I appreciate it."

"Guys like us should help each other when the opportunity presents itself."

Moss raises an eyebrow. "I looked you up. You were Delta Force before the company recruited you. You did a tour in Iraq."

"That was a long time ago." Buxton stares back at Moss. "Nobody's supposed to know that."

"I pulled some strings. You have a reputation."

"As do you… Ax."

Moss turns back to his beer. "I don't understand the scorched earth on this one."

Buxton flashes a sadistic grin. "Certain parties within the military industrial complex couldn't stomach the idea of a drone that was grown instead of built. American jobs were at risk, but mostly, of course, it threatened their personal profit. The technology itself frightened them. The defense industry thrives on selling Washington complex and often redundant weapons at a ridiculous price. Once appropriations approve a purchase, the manufacturer needs to ensure that their program will keep running decades beyond its usefulness. So, they compartmentalize manufacturing across dozens of congressional districts in multiple states and then finance those congressional campaigns. It's the American way. The MS4-T challenged that entire system, so it had to go."

"So what about you?" Moss asks. "What's next?"

Buxton smiles. "I've got one more year left before retirement, and it looks like I'll be spending it behind a desk."

Moss glances over at Buxton. "I'm sorry to hear that."

"No, don't be." Buxton chuckles. "My wife is thrilled. Besides..." Buxton stands and drops a twenty on the bar, "I was getting too old for the field."

"I know what you mean." Moss stands and extends his hand toward Buxton. "Thanks. I appreciate you coming down here to speak to me."

Buxton grips Alex's hand. "Take care of yourself."

Moss watches Buxton leave, and then he catches the bartender's attention. The man strolls back toward Moss. "You ready for this, Ax?" He lifts a duffle up onto the bar and then cocks his head toward the door. "CIA... I never liked those guys."

"He's okay." Moss takes the duffle. "Thanks, Frank. I appreciate it."

Frank winks at Moss. "No worries, mate. Give my best to Trish."

Moss smiles. "Thanks, Frank, I will."

Moss walks out of the bar and down into the marina. He slings the duffle over his shoulder and threads his way down through the extended network of floating docks until he sees her. The vintage, fifty-three-foot Southern Ocean Gallant has only been in his possession for a month, but already, Alex Moss is in love.

Moss kicks off his shoes, climbs on board the fully restored ketch, and goes below. He stows the duffle and then stops to gaze at the yacht's polished mahogany interior as he runs through his mental checklist. He has everything in place; he is ready. Moss hears his phone. He pulls it from his pocket and spots an SMS.

Are you ready?

Moss Smiles, then quickly thumbs off an answer. *Meet you in a few weeks?*

You bet, babe. Wouldn't miss it.

"Ahoy, Chief!"

Moss puts down his phone and pops his head outside. "Hey!" He climbs up into the cockpit and finds Malcolm Rafferty standing on the dock gripping a baby stroller. Moss smiles, "Wow, look at you, family man..."

Rafferty smirks at the stroller in front of him. "Yep, my new job... it's growing on me."

Moss steps down onto the dock as Rafferty's wife, Robyn, kisses him on the cheek. "We had to come down and see you off, Alex." She looks at Razz's ten-year-old son Mark. "You wanted to say something to Uncle Alex?"

Mark smiles. "Have a great trip, Ax, and if you need a first mate, just let me know."

Moss gives Mark a hug. "You bet, Mark, thanks."

Moss looks down at the tiny girl wriggling inside the stroller. He bends down. "And how is little Alexa doing?" He smiles at the two-year-old.

The toddler stares intently at Moss's face. "Your name is Alex, just like me..."

Moss laughs and then looks up at Razz. "Is she always this smart?"

"Yes, I am very smart. I can read and count and everything..."

Moss smiles at the toddler and then stands. "You're in big trouble with this one, Razz."

"Don't I know it!"

Moss reaches into his pocket. "I almost forgot." He pulls out the keys to his Land Rover Defender. "Razz, you mind looking after the truck for me while I'm gone?"

"Seriously?" Razz takes the keys from Moss. "You bet! Thanks, Ax." He hugs Moss. "So, you're off to Hawaii?"

"Yeah, maybe. But I don't have a real plan... no schedule." Moss smiles at Razz. "Help me cast off?"

"Sure thing, Ax."

Moss grabs his shoes and jumps back on board as Razz walks over to the spring line. He loosens it and then coils the rope on deck. Razz hears the yacht's diesel engine kick over and then rumble to life. He looks back toward the helm as Mark hands Moss the stern line. Moss gives a nod, and Razz coils up the bow line and then places it on deck. Razz steps back as Moss smoothly steers the yacht away from the dock. Malcolm Rafferty smiles at his friend as he sails away. He has no idea when he'll see Alex Moss again, but something tells him he will—*someday.*

· · ·

Marco looks up from his laptop as Kimberly strolls past him wearing seductively flowing fuchsia. "I love that one, my darling. You know how that color sets me on fire..." She flashes a sultry smile back at her husband and then floats over to one of the sofas that decorate the aft lounge deck of *Mysterious.*

Marco returns to his laptop and observes with curiosity as the account he created for Dr. Thomas Falcon is drained down to zero. He continues to study the transactions taking place on the screen in front of him. All seven hundred thousand pounds are then transferred to an account belonging to the medical charity, *Doctors Without Borders.*

"An honest man…" Marco is impressed. "I hope we meet again, Dr. Thomas Falcon…" Marco closes his laptop, lays it on the table, and then stands to join his wife. He glances over at Francis, who nods respectfully from behind the bar. "Why not?" Marco smiles at Kimberly, and then he looks back at Frances. "Champagne!"

###

Books by T. R. Schumer

The Fearless Trilogy

Death Catch

Drone Catch

SEAL Catch (2017)

From the Author

June 12, 2016, I write from Fiji, a remarkably beautiful place. This is especially true after sailing treacherous seas to get here. Our crew and our faithful sailing craft were tested to the limit during the passage from New Zealand, but this part of the world is known for harsh conditions, and when you take up the challenge of sailing oceans, some suffering is to be expected. Prior to our departure from Opua, in Northern New Zealand's Bay of Islands, we carefully studied the region's notoriously changeable weather, we consulted local sailors and watched the winter storm fronts passing and waited for our window, then we set off.

The first twenty-four hours were the toughest and then things got worse. Winds increased to over forty knots and seas rose to five meters during that first moonless night. A deckhand we took on for the passage fell ill and spent the rest of the night hugging the head. Our captain suffered a back injury. Two remaining crew manned the helm for twelve hours straight until dawn. We sailed on in heavy seas and repeated squalls until the winds finally dropped off. At four in the morning, on the third day of our one-thousand-three-hundred nautical mile passage, the decision was made to start the engine, and that's when we discovered our diesel fuel had been contaminated with seawater.

Becalmed with no engine. It is an amazing and sobering experience to float silently in the middle of the Pacific Ocean. We could have easily descended into arguments and anger but instead we used our wits and worked together. Our fuel tanks were contaminated with seawater, our diesel engine was toast, but we still had a working generator. We had taken on extra fuel for the passage, fuel that was strapped to the deck in separate bladders. The challenge was to first clean the small day tank and then replace that bad fuel with the good stuff. It took the rest of the day to complete the task but once we got the generator going and we could again charge batteries, make drinking water and get the fridge and freezer back on line, spirits on board rose considerably.

We waited two days for wind. I sat on deck at two in the morning and looked out across a glassy flat sea lit only by starlight in all directions. The night sky at sea has no equal. Stars by the billions stretch from one seamless, featureless horizon to the other, while bioluminescent sea creatures glow and sparkle beneath the water- line. I peered over the side and discovered we had become a refuge for schooling fish. Thousands were gathered around our keel in a shimmering silver cloud. On the fourth day of the passage the winds returned, only lightly at first, then the trade winds arrived and we were cracking once again.

After a week at sea, the islands of Fiji came into view and we celebrated with hugs and smiles. We sailed through the narrow coral pass then hove to and lowered the RIB into the sea. We used our rugged inflatable boat as a small tug and towed ourselves the rest of the way in until we reached a safe anchorage. We anchored old school, using sail power, and then we popped the champagne.

Exploring the world by sea has changed me. It has shown me parts of myself I never knew were there, revealed a more accurate perspective of the world, and most of all, it has given me the courage to write the book you have just read. I hope you found reading *Drone Catch* an entertaining and enjoyable experience. I wrote it especially for you, thank you, and if real adventure should chance your way, my advice is: go for it.

Reviews and recommendations are the best way for self-published authors to get the word out about a new novel. Competing with the big name publishing houses is challenging, but with your kind support, independent writers like myself can still find an audience. If you enjoyed *Drone Catch*, may I recommend picking up the first book of *The Fearless Trilogy: Death Catch* and if by chance I have truly won you over as a fan my beloved reader, then keep an eye out for the third title of *The Fearless Trilogy: SEAL Catch*.

Also, visit my website (http://www.trschumer.com/), Book-Bub or GoodReads from time to time to check on updates to the book and publication dates for new novels in the series.

With gratitude, T. R. Schumer

www.ingramcontent.com/pod-product-compliance
Lightning Source LLC
Chambersburg PA
CBHW032138190626
46814CB00005BA/1750